DAWN OF THE WATCHERS

DAWN OF THE WATCHERS

Some heroes aren't trying to save the world.

WINN TAYLOR

Winn Taylor

First Printing, August 2022

ISBN: 979-8-9860537-0-7
ISBN: 979-8-9860537-1-4

Cover design by: Winn Taylor
Library of Congress Registration Number: 1-11283494711

Dawn of the Watchers is book two of a Metaphysical Sci-Fantasy series.

The action-packed YA/New Adult series began with ***Rise of the Protector***: Despite Jinx's reckless ways, she managed to free Laris from a simulated Zen world that had trapped thousands of enlightenment-seeking denizens in dangerous lockdown only to discover that there were bigger threats hot on her tail.

It's a futuristic adventure filled with all the things that drive our hero Jinx nuts: geekery, mysticism, and contemplation.

For everyone searching for their place in this world,
and to all the friends who make sure we get there.
In their presence, our skin just fits better.

CHAPTER ONE

"You're absolutely sure *this one* is safe?" Jinx stared at the gluttonous void. Even without the radiant ring of particles swirling around it, the darkness at its core would dominate the blackest pocket of deep space.

"Define 'safe,'" Jacob said, turning from the view beyond the clear quartz shield.

Jinx didn't move to meet his gaze, offering only a furrowed brow in response.

"Yes. For the umpteenth time, yes." Jacob gestured towards the rapidly approaching portal. "The relevant singularity inside colossal, rotating, black holes is technically weak."

Jinx pinched her furrowed brow tighter. "Technically?"

"Yeah. Technically." Jacob shrugged. "Once we exit our galaxy and pop out in the middle of the Milky Way, I'll consider it verifiable. Don't worry. We aren't the first ship to enter this portal."

"Entering isn't the bit I'm worried about."

Jacob laid a hand on Jinx's shoulder. "We'll blast through this black hole without so much as a scratch." Biting back a grin, he added, "Technically."

Jinx scanned the celestial gateway, hoping to find evidence of its benign nature while her nerves ratcheted up their grip. Becoming responsible for the safety of someone other than herself had planted a seed of caution that sprouted a relentless vine.

"If you aren't ready to take the leap, you better let me know," Jacob said as he made adjustments on the ship's control panel. "We're about to move into the portal's field. Once that happens . . ."

Jinx searched her fingers for a patch of cuticle she hadn't gnawed through but quickly abandoned the futile hunt. Crossing her arms, she tucked her hands safely into the fold of her dampening armpits. Shifting her gaze, she met Jacob's effortless expression. His calm assuredness was contagious.

Squaring her shoulders, Jinx stepped up to the windshield. "Let's do this."

"Yes!" Jacob swung his palms together, rubbing them eagerly as he slid into one of two chairs at the base of the control panel. "You might want to settle in."

Jinx narrowed her eyes at the portal before plopping down next to Jacob.

Jacob pulled up a view of the rear. "Time to say farewell." Cameras captured and displayed images of their home galaxy quickly fading in their wake. Little more than a smattering of lights against a raven backdrop filled the screen.

"Farewell to what?" Jinx said as she buckled in. "Everyone I know is either on this ship or headed to the same place we are."

Jacob didn't reply as he stared at the screen. Jinx studied his face, feeling as though she should turn away.

A bottle of bubbling green liquid appeared in Jacob's hand, seemingly out of the ether. Pulling the cork, he lifted it in a silent salute and took a swig before offering it to Jinx. She eyed it sourly.

"It's tradition," he said beseechingly.

"It's litmorian, and it's gross." Jinx pushed the offering away. "Besides, tradition is just another name for rules. I tend to avoid those."

Jacob shrugged and returned his attention to the screen, allowing a private thought to lift the corner of his mouth. "Till we meet again," he said before taking another sip and tapping the cork back in place.

Jinx placed a hand on Jacob's shoulder as the screen shifted from a view of the world they'd known to a flurry of data.

"Everything looks good to go," Jacob confirmed as he scrolled through the information.

"Great," Jinx replied in a tone drained of excitement for the unknown. "How long till we enter the portal?"

"Once I increase our speed, maybe seconds," Jacob said, "but it'll feel instant."

"In that case, how 'bout a countdown before you hurl us forward?"

Jacob flashed a thumbs-up while his fingers danced deftly across his keyboard. A flurry of clicks later, he leaned back and tightened his seatbelt. "Ready?"

Jinx forced a lopsided grin. "Nope. Let's do it anyway."

Jacob waggled his brows and began. "We go in five, four. . ."

Jinx gripped the arms of her chair, locking her attention forward.

"Three, two," Jacob continued, pausing long enough to exchange a nod with Jinx, captured in the reflective surface of the windshield. "One."

In an instant, the darkness of deep space disappeared beyond an eruption of brilliant light. A terrifying emptiness followed, swallowing them in a weighted abyss so dense, it was as if worlds had compressed to the size of a pinhead.

If thought or breath or sound had passed, the memory of it vanished the moment the nothingness burst, giving form to space, stretching it to distortion, and forming luminescent stripes that sped to the edge of eternity.

Suddenly, the portal spit them out amongst a vast expanse of glitter lights that painted the sky in broad strokes. The view was breathtaking, in a gasping-for-air sort of way. The outermost planet in Earth's solar system shifted from a distant spec to a sizable ball in the blink of an eye. Soon, they'd be racing past Pluto and through the asteroid belt before effectively melting into the sun. That is, assuming they managed to make it that far unscathed. At the speed they were clocking, a liquefied death was shaping up to be the only task on today's itinerary.

This was not the celebratory moment Jinx had hoped for. "Slow us down!"

Jacob's brow shot to the ceiling. "What? You mean we weren't headed for the sun? Sorry. Totally misunderstood. I thought this was a suicide mission. Well, that changes things — let me just make a few adjustments." He attempted a smile, but it ended up looking a bit crazed.

"Really. You're gonna joke about this?"

"Would you rather I cry?" Jacob replied. "'Cause that was my second choice."

"No. I'd rather you fix the speed!" Jinx shot back. "You have the power to control technology with your freaking mind. Steering our course *away* from solid objects and floating infernos shouldn't be a problem."

She ran a hand over her tightly shaved head, attempting to regain focus. At the moment, the sun was hardly brighter than a distant star. It didn't seem menacing, but Jinx knew it would turn them to dust before they got anywhere near it. Of course, the asteroid belt might beat the life out of them first. At this pace, it wouldn't take long to meet either gruesome end.

Normally, this would be a noteworthy moment; Jinx had never seen a sun or a planet, for that matter. Life on a ship in deep space didn't come with a view, unless you count pitch black. But she'd experienced the sun's power to embolden — in virtual realities, anyway. This fact did little to anchor the excitement now drifting away with each passing second.

"This isn't the ship's engine propelling us forward. I had our speed down to nearly zero when we entered the portal. It spit us out at a phenomenally high speed, way faster than I ever could have anticipated." Jacob's brow rippled with tension. "I can't just slam on the breaks. It's like asking me to slow down gravity."

"No. It's like asking you to please not melt my face."

Jacob waved a hand across his body, presenting himself while using his free hand to rapidly scroll through data on a display screen. "Mother Nature got all this right, so I'm pretty motivated to avoid annihilation." He pointed to a string of data flashing blue against a white screen. "Maybe if I adjust the quantum accelerator..."

The explanation that followed morphed into an ambient backdrop. Jinx's tuning-out mode automatically triggered when Jacob explained things in high-def geek, a language only his fellow geniuses could ever grasp. Besides, she was busy dodging her own deafening thoughts.

"I got it!" Jacob yelled. "I'm gonna fire up the engine to push past our current speed."

"Great idea." Jinx's voice shot up an octave or two. "Let's die sooner."

"Trust me on this." Jacob stood unblinkingly still.

Jinx latched on to the steadiness of Jacob's resolve. "All right. Let's do it."

Jacob nodded and increased their speed. "Hold tight." A slight tug followed as they pushed past their current clip to regain control and aim far right of Pluto. "Sorry. Dunno what happened," he murmured as he slowed the ship. "My brain froze for a minute. Maybe seeing the origin of human life threw me off." His lips lifted like a shrug, but his shoulders remained on guard.

"No more close calls, genius." Jinx held up her hands, presenting her mangled cuticle beds. "I'm running out of flesh to chew through." She'd picked them clean over the past two days. Being flung into her role as hero, aka Protector, had been a white-knuckle ride that showed no signs of easing up. Sadly, regrowing cuticle flesh at top speed was not one of the powers that came with her illustrious title.

"Promise," Jacob said. "If I slip up, I'll make sure our annihilation is quick and painless."

"How comforting," Jinx said as she watched Jacob's fingers dance across the keyboard with mesmerizing fluidity, punctuating the fact that they both preferred the physicality of life over the powers that allowed them to bypass it. She returned her attention to the sky's undulating lights; her mood rose to meet their shimmer. It was a far cry from the barren view of Redshift 7. Her former space station had picked a lifeless corner of the universe to set up shop. Whether it had been to distance themselves from high levels of electromagnetic waves and high-frequency bands or to exist under the radar or both, it had ceased to be the safe, dark haven they'd flourished in for nearly one thousand years.

Now that their travel itinerary no longer included a one-way trip to the Sun, Jinx scanned the control deck without death looming. The room held little evidence of the war that had erupted there only days ago. A crew had seen to it. The black gouge that had marred the otherwise pristine, white walls had been repaired. And the bloodstain near the control panel was gone, though the memory of delivering a shot to Bayne's knee remained a smile-worthy memory Jinx planned to replay often.

In the center of the room, twelve cryo-tanks remained eerily empty. The spidery arms previously attached to each were retracted, tucked tightly to the ceiling as if waiting for their chance to pounce. Within the circle of twelve neatly arranged cryo-tanks sat a thirteenth as vacant as the others. It had held captive the one thing Jinx would give her life to save: Laris. Not only would she willingly give her life to protect Laris, she was destined to. Jinx would have ripped the contraption into a pile of twisted bits if Jacob hadn't convinced her otherwise, arguing they'd need the parts. He was right, she knew, but the fear and fury they aroused were barely tamable.

Jinx mindlessly lifted a hand to her shoulder. The flesh had been torn, but Owen — lead technician and self-appointed Jinx-wrangler — had sealed it. Two days ago, she could hardly wait to get out from under his watchful eye and rip through the universe on permanent Galactic Release. Today, the thought of him tightened around her heart.

"Hey! How's everything on deck?" The words blasted through an intercom, followed by a series of profanity-infused geekery. "I swear, I nearly soiled myself from excitement when we moved through the continuum."

Jacob's face lit up at the sound of Claire's voice. "Hey, were you able to calculate the..."

Jinx watched Jacob gesture wildly as he and Claire exchanged a mind-dizzying amount of technical terms and elaborate equations. Based on Claire's gasps and squeals, they had gathered some pretty impressive data, all of which entered Jinx's left ear, scrambled her brain, and raced out her right.

While they reveled in their findings, Jinx turned to watch the galaxy unfold at a blissfully non-lethal speed. Soon, they'd be passing Pluto. Even at a distance, she could make out the barren, ice-covered landscape with its chaotic mountain ranges — dark, jagged highlands scarred by deep pits. It was beautiful. It was lonely. A sense of kinship washed over Jinx as she watched Pluto grow in the distance.

Jinx placed a hand on Jacob's shoulder, bringing pause to his arm-flailing. "Hey, brainiacs, can you two put the party on pause for a minute?"

Claire and Jacob replied in unison, "No prob."

The intercom went silent as Claire signed off.

"What's up?" Jacob looked flushed in the afterglow of Claire.

"We should do a fly-by around the other planets and check for anything . . . unexpected."

"What, like unregistered species setting up camp in a supposedly uninhabited and restricted solar system?"

"Yup," Jinx replied. "We aren't registered. Yet here we are, showing up. I want to avoid as many surprises as possible."

Jacob chuckled. "Good luck with that. But sure, I'll check for anything that would suggest lifeforms intelligent enough to pose a threat. Anything with technology will emit a signal. I can also check for significant heat signatures. That's the best we can do unless you want to spend the next few hundred years searching every landscape."

"No," Jinx said, stretching towards the ceiling, feeling her spine loosen one vertebra at a time. "Just a quick scan. The sooner we get to Earth and cloak our presence, the better."

"Looks like Pluto is up first," Jacob said as an image of the planet popped up on screen. "Well, doubtful it's teaming with life. The thermal activity there is practically zero." He pointed to the deep shades of neon blue swirling over the image. "That place looks more dismal than the moon of Kushta."

Jinx furrowed her brow. "The moon of what?"

Jacob cocked his head, offering a baffled glance. "Seeing as how we've been tasked with saving OI, you might wanna do a little homework."

"First of all, it's only been a couple of days since some obscure prophecy hurled us into this madness. I haven't really had time for studying up on my fellow organic intelligences." With a smirk, Jinx added, "Not that I would study anyway."

"Right." Jacob chuckled.

"So ..." Jinx said impatiently. "Give me the run-down. The abbreviated version, please."

Jacob smirked and shook his head. "No. You're being lazy."

"Come on!" Jinx spread her arms wide. "Divide and concur. You take care of all the nerdy stuff you like to do, and I'll focus on my strengths. That is, unless you'd rather spearhead any battles."

"Naw. Blood is really hard to get out of clothes," Jacob said, giving Jinx the once-over.

Jinx rolled her eyes and motioned for Jacob to get on with it. "Info, please."

"Fine," Jacob relented. "According to the information I dug up, Kushta is just one of the many moons where OI is dumped if they can't afford biological shielding devices. Thousands of these desolate outposts, filled with OI suffering from mental or physical disorders, are scattered around the universe." He wiggled as if shaking off an unsettling mental image. "It's pretty grim."

"Who's out there rounding them up?" With a grimace, Jinx added, "And why?"

Jacob shrugged. "Beats me. Maybe they're just being hidden so the rest of the universe won't realize there's a serious problem."

"Or someone is gathering them for another reason. I wouldn't put it past Sartillias to round up OI so he can harvest their pineal glands." Jinx gagged recalling her own encounter with the kingpin's thugs after they tried to remove hers.

"True," Jacob said, "but he wouldn't have any use for their glands. They're probably calcified or worse after being pummeled by EMFs. Doubt he could turn those into decent party drugs."

Jinx raised a hand, feeling for the small, gold tab affixed to her arm.

Jacob noticed and laid a hand on her shoulder. "Don't worry, your EMF radiation blocker is doing its job. You and your pineal gland and the rest of your parts are fine."

"But eventually it won't be enough."

"Then fingers crossed Laris succeeds." Jacob slid his hands into his pockets and sighed.

"Wow. Way to keep things light." Feeling the tension lodged in every muscle crank up a notch, Jinx groaned. "I'll leave you to explore Pluto. I need to check on the rest of the ship."

Jacob laughed. "Sure, the rest of the ship. Tell Laris, I mean the rest of the ship, I said, hi."

Jinx rolled her eyes and turned to go. She considered walking around the circle of cryo-tanks like it was a malefic entity. Instead, she moved through the center, running her hand along the pods, determined to dominate anything that could dismantle her world. The loneliness of Pluto waited in the wings, its isolation never too far away to get a whiff of. The image alone could unendingly fuel the desire.

The door slid open just as Jinx reached for the control panel. On the other side was a pintsize, tween IOI preparing to lunge into the room. Jinx quickly blocked the door with her arm.

"Hold up, Booger! Let me see your hands."

DeeDee — aka Booger, according to Jinx — flashed a sheepish grin. Odd that an inorganic intelligence knew it was being mischievous. These quirks always left Jinx wondering if Owen had programmed DeeDee to be this way or if they were inherited traits from her human donor. Or possibly something far more complex: DeeDee had developed her own unique personality.

When DeeDee didn't willingly comply with a hand inspection, Jinx flipped one over. As suspected, her hand was covered in the usual sticky, ice-cream-coated mess. Jinx shook her head, attempting to bite back a smile. *You can't even eat, you little weirdo.*

"There's sanitizer and wipes by the door," Jacob yelled without bothering to turn around.

"Wow, doing a little housekeeping, I see." Jinx laughed and grabbed a wipe from their appointed place, which, according to Jacob, everything had. Jinx didn't share the same concern for order since she didn't make a point of having crap to find a place for. Handing the wipe to Deedee, she ordered, "Clean."

Deedee simply stared at the wipe, as though baffled by some unfamiliar object Jinx was waving around.

Jinx wiggled the wipe impatiently. "I've got stuff to do, and you need to start wiping your own hands."

"You could wipe her hands for her," Jacob said. "She did save your butt on a few occasions."

"Not the point, Jacob," Jinx replied. "Besides, based on that logic, none of us should ever wipe our own hands."

"I've made a note of your sanitary habits," Jacob said. "You should probably appoint someone to wipe your hands along with doing your laundry. Seriously, you're kind of a slob."

It was sorta true. Jinx wasn't meticulous by any stretch of the imagination. "Hey, I sniff-test everything before I put it on."

"How about just bypass the clothes on your floor and wear something freshly washed?"

"Fine," Jinx said. "I appoint you the official laundry guy."

"You're on. I'll start with your delicates," Jacob said with a laugh.

"You're impossible." Jinx waved the wet wipe again. "Booger. Now. Seriously. I have stuff to do."

Deedee pushed out her bottom lip and attempted to move past Jinx, sans the wipe. She probably would have succeeded if she truly cared. She was, when in fighter-mode, the equivalent of a terminator-ninja packed into a wee warrior. This tween-ified version of Deedee was simply an ice-cream-coated mess with a debilitatingly earnest smile.

Begrudgingly, Jinx took Deedee's hands and wiped them clean. "Go on." She moved to the side to let Deedee through.

Without wasting a moment, Deedee tore into the room as if the invitation had an expiration date of a nano-second.

"Have fun," Jinx called over her shoulder as she headed out the door.

"Oh, I will. And I'll come around to collect your laundry later. If you could just get it ready, that'd be great."

Jinx allowed the door to close behind her without response, though she didn't like relinquishing the last word.

CHAPTER TWO

Jinx stepped into the corridor. Its pristine edges practically vanished in the serene whiteness. She had moved through a hallway identical to this her entire life. It had felt suffocating then. Now, the walls embraced her unwieldiness.

Dragging her hand along their surface, she looked for ways to fortify the space and keep everyone protected. This was her world. She belonged here. More than belonged, life made sense here, in this role. She wasn't fighting her own skin or hoping to discover a purpose in the world that fit. She'd found it. More exactly, it had found her — or summoned.

Stillness permeated the air, but the ship wasn't empty. Everyone had been shaped since birth to observe silence to foster tranquility. Despite being raised alongside them, the design was lost on Jinx. Luckily, Jacob was a recent, prophecy-inspired transplant and not prone to bouts of silence or hours of meditation.

Jinx scrutinized the hall. Nothing looked out of order or displaced since entering and exiting the portal. Apparently, even bursting through the very fabric of space and time to zip between galaxies wasn't powerful enough to disrupt these Zen-baked walls.

As Jinx approached Laris's quarters, she paused outside the door, her finger frozen over a call button. *Maybe I should check on the Attendants first.* It would buy her some time to tame the jumble of nerves wrestling tirelessly in the pit of her stomach. Dropping her hand, her shoulders slumped in response. *Seriously, you've got to get a grip.* Pivoting, she prepared to retreat and move towards a less anxiety-inducing door.

A voice playfully burst from the intercom. "Stop loitering. Come inside."

Too late, Jinx realized and froze in her tracks.

The door slid open, allowing a thick waft of musky-sweet incense to drift into the hallway. Jinx's heart hammered insistently, determined to bully its way out and hide. Taking a steadying breath, she turned back around. The effort to gain composure was lost. Laris stood in the middle of her room wrapped in a towel, hair wet and clinging halfway down her back. Jinx clenched to keep her jaw from flapping open.

Crap. "I'll come back." Her feet rebelled and took root, planting themselves in place as Jinx attempted to flee the doorway.

"Don't be silly," Laris said. "Come inside. Talk to me while I get ready."

"Uh, fine." Stepping through the door, Jinx focused past Laris on an entirely unchallenging spot on the wall. Quickly making her way to the only seat in the room, apart from the bed, she plopped down. Massaging her temples, she tried to dislodge the image of Laris and the droplets of water glistening on her bare shoulders.

"You'd be proud of me. I just worked out for the first time, ever." The sound of Laris's bare feet padding across the room was followed by the bathroom door closing to a narrow gap. Her words continued, now muffled by the barrier. "Well, not counting the times you talked me into playing GetDown3000."

Jinx croaked. "Played? You don't *play* GetDown3000. It's not a game. It's an epic dance battle."

"Sounds like a game to me," Laris replied. "I still don't know how you managed to talk me into it. I'm not coordinated. I'm only built for meditation."

"Hey, you're the one who agreed to the dance-offs. Remember? It was payback for dragging me with you to the library. Sitting in silence while you studied wisdom texts was excruciating." Even the memory left Jinx feeling caged. She shook it off.

"Well, you were supposed to be inspired, not sit and grumble about it. There were so many insights that our fellow denizens discovered while in VR. For instance, there was..."

Jinx shifted her focus towards the floor, watching the bathroom light dim and brighten each time Laris moved past the doorway. The conversation floated in the background like a hypotonic buzz.

Moments later, Laris poked her head out of the bathroom. "Did you hear me?"

The question jarred Jinx from the mesmerizing concoction of dancing light and sandalwood. "Sorry, I spaced out." Pushing to her feet, she headed for the door. "You know what, I can see you're feeling fine, and you didn't disappear in the portal. Let's just check in later. I need to make the rounds."

Laris smiled warmly, but the tone of her voice cooled. "I'll come find you later."

Jinx paused at the open door but gathered what was left of her logic before impulse made a mess of things. Walking out, she felt the stability return to her legs as the door closed behind her. Making her way down the hall, she shook out her limbs, freeing herself from semi-paralysis. She considered jumping into a virtual battle just to get back on her game. It'd have to wait. She needed to finish the status check.

The Attendants all answered their doors completely clothed. Their gender-neutral gowns covered nearly every inch of their body. Not that seeing their skin would have made Jinx look twice. She was imbalanced by only one very specific stretch of flesh. The Attendants all offered few words, but their smiles were penetratingly genuine, unadulterated warmth. She met their unguarded gaze with an unblinkingly fixed stare infused with a promise to protect them.

"Just come find me or Jacob or Claire if you have any questions," Jinx said as she raised her left palm to meet theirs while her right hand lifted to her heart. Peace. Solidarity. Understanding. It was a customary gesture, one that she returned when prompted but rarely initiated.

As she completed her rounds, Jinx checked on Jacob. "How's it going on deck?" she asked, engaging the intercom tucked behind her ear.

"Oh, you mean babysitting? Great. I love kids and cleaning ice cream. Not like I have a solar system to navigate or anything important to occupy my attention."

"Perfect." Jinx inwardly smiled at the thought of Jacob's sterile environment being subjected to DeeDee's indiscriminate hands. "Sounds like you got it under control. I'm gonna jump in a battle."

"Please take your mess-maker with you." Desperation coated Jacob's plea.

"She's *our* mess-maker."

"No," Jacob stated flatly. "Owen programmed her to watch *your* back. She, quite literally, was made for you. So, that makes her *your* mess-maker."

There was always the option to tweak Deedee's programming to remove her obsession with ice cream and the tween tendencies that appeared to be permanent, but Jinx wouldn't do it. No one here would. The dairy addiction was utterly ridiculous, illogical, and pointless. It was also endearing. It was part of who she was, programmed or not.

"Fine." Jinx feigned defeat, releasing the word with an implied sigh. In reality, she was more than happy to charge into a simulated assault with DeeDee by her side. The kid was an elegant beast in battle. "Send her to the cardiovascular unit. I'll meet her there in ten minutes. We can spar Tarxis together."

"Thank you! I'll —" A thunderous crash rang in the background. "Gotta go."

Jinx picked up her pace, winding full-throttle through the silent corridor in the hopes of having a few minutes to warm up before DeeDee pounced, but she was brought to an abrupt halt.

"I'd like a moment of your time." It wasn't a request. The hauntingly majestic voice had the power to still breath.

Jinx stiffened in response. Hadu's indomitable presence always seemed like a precursor to rigor mortis. Slowly, Jinx turned, expecting to be dwarfed by the woman's towering limbs and elongated head, but no one was there. An odd concoction of relief and alarm swirled. She scanned the corridor. It was empty. *Weird*. Hadu's voice had not poured through her earpiece. The words had been delivered without a transmitting device. Jinx hesitantly looked up, as if Hadu had some secret power, like the ability to transform into a bodiless entity. The sound of a door sliding open brought the musing to a halt. Taking a deep breath, Jinx pinned back her shoulders and stepped forward while conjuring excuses to keep the interaction brief.

Resisting the urge to first peek around the door's edge, Jinx stepped boldly into view. Hadu stood across the room with arms folded, as though a lengthy *talking-to* was about to begin.

Jinx guided her hands into her pockets and leaned against the door jam, battling her awkwardness while her heart raced uncomfortably. "Pretty sure that opening the door to my thoughts and letting yourself in is like, ya know, breaking and entering."

"Unfortunately for you, entering your thoughts is far too easy," Hadu said. "I plan to change that."

I'm starting to regret not blinking to spar Tarxis, Jinx silently grumbled.

Hadu spoke as if Jinx had given voice to her annoyance. "Teleporting is always a risk."

It was true, which was one reason Jinx refrained. Teleportation, aka blinking as Jacob coined it, was too new and untested. There was always a chance Jinx could end up some place other than where she had intended on traveling or, worse, end up nowhere. The latter was only a theory, but one Jinx had no interest in verifying. Plus, she lost a little weight with every blink, a side effect that Jacob and Claire were looking into.

"Seriously. You have to stay out of my head. It's unnerving."

Hadu untwined her arms to clasp her hands in a patient weave. "It's my job to find your weaknesses and vulnerabilities and then train you to eliminate them."

Jinx swallowed hard, noticing an acute lack of saliva. "I'll figure it out."

"No," Hadu said. "You'll fall to the level of your training. And *that* is my responsibility."

"I really hope that chipping away at my confidence isn't part of your training program."

Hadu waved a graceful arm as if guiding a whisper through the air, quieting Jinx's defensive rumblings. "When I'm done with you, nothing will shake you from your center." Power reverberated in the timbre of Hadu's words, a promise to shape worlds.

Jinx sagged but caught her shoulders before the plunge gained momentum. "You make it sound like I need to be fixed."

"You are not flawed simply because you are not yet up to the task at hand," Hadu said as she moved through the room. "That's to be expected. Greatness requires training. Failing to address our limitations is what holds us back."

Jinx looked up, raising a brow. "Greatness?" The idea felt comical.

"Were you under the impression the universe had run out of qualified candidates for the role of Protector and simply settled on an obstinate teen?"

Jinx bit back a laugh and pushed off the wall. "You think you're up for the challenge of training me? Ya know, seeing as I'm obstinate and all."

Hadu leveled her gaze, suggesting nothing was outside the scope of her abilities.

"Fine." Jinx shrugged. "But it sounds exhausting."

"For us both, I assure you." Hadu didn't crack a smile, but something bubbled beneath.

"Great. Then I look forward to torturing you during our so-called training." Jinx turned, ready to bolt. DeeDee was likely waiting very impatiently. The little punk was a stickler for timing when it was something *she* wanted. Even a second late sent DeeDee into a tailspin. "Right now, I have plans to go to battle. Pretty sure fighting skills are more important than learning to shield my thoughts or whatever else you have in store for me."

"An understandable assumption," Hadu replied, "but flawed. Laris will deliver challenges far more troubling than physical threats."

Jinx paused. "What are you talking about? Nothing Laris could ever do would be a threat." This wasn't the first time someone had hinted at a dark side to Laris. Bayne had outright said it. Jinx only pushed the idea away. Unfathomable.

Hadu glided airily across the room, but her words had weight. "You'll need to accept the nature of reality and the duality of all things. Where there is light, there is dark."

"Laris isn't in danger of going rogue. There's not an evil or selfish bone in her body."

"Nothing has only one side," Hadu insisted, "and that is where Laris's true power resides. She accepts this about herself and in all others. *This* is why she is able to love unconditionally."

Jinx crossed her arms as her jaw set. "Assuming you're right, which you aren't, what's your point? What exactly should I prepare to do when I come face-to-face with Laris in a tantrum?"

If Hadu was losing patience, she didn't reveal it, which was impressive. Jinx had finely honed the skill of pushing people beyond their limits. "You are to reflect back to her all that she is."

Jinx groaned. "I realize that the New World loves to talk in riddles, but could you please try to be less confusing?"

"When the time comes for Laris to battle her dark side, you will be the anchor for her light. You will guide her back to center."

"Fine." Jinx threw up her arms in an exaggerated swing. "I can't imagine it'll be too difficult. Besides, so what if she has an off day? It's not as if the world will fall apart. Both Jacob and I have loads of crap days, mood swings, and questionable morals. And we're Attendants. The world hasn't fallen apart because of it."

"The power of the universe is prepared to rush in at the first invitation and bring forth that which Laris focuses on. The rest of us have the luxury of time and contemplation."

Jinx stretched skyward, realizing she'd need to warm up while Hadu kept her captive. DeeDee would be ready to pounce. "Great. I can have a crappy thought and the universe ignores it? Good to know."

"If you repeat a thought tirelessly, you will reap the effects of it, for better or worse," Hadu said. "But you are not yet powerful enough to instantly manifest that which you contemplate. Laris is."

Jinx remained decidedly quiet, hoping it would end their little chat. Simply excusing herself wasn't an option. Not with Hadu. She was larger than life, as if the force of a black hole were contained beneath her skin. Yet there seemed to be nothing splitting her in two. Possibly, with five hundred years of life under her belt, Hadu was immune to the emotional challenges of being human. Jinx lifted her arms again, stretching side to side. Intertwining her fingers, she cracked them loudly.

"Thanks for the pep talk, but I gotta go."

Hadu turned away. "Indeed." Her response trailed slowly behind, flowing with the long hem of her robe and merging with the fluidity of her movements. Lifting a piece of paper from her desk, she added, "If you could, please see that this makes its way to Jacob." Extending her hand, Hadu didn't make a move back towards the door. Jinx didn't take a step to fetch it.

The moments slowly ticked by. Hadu wasn't going to back down, not now, not ever. Inwardly groaning, Jinx pressed through the doorway. "Anything else you'd like me to deliver or some other chore I can take care of, you know, during my downtime? I'm sure that keeping the savior of organic life alive won't take every second of the day."

"If I think of any, I'll let you know during our second session," Hadu replied.

Jinx shoved the paper into her pocket and headed swiftly towards the door. "Are we just skipping the first session 'cause I'm *way* ahead of schedule?"

Hadu choked back a laugh — an actual laugh. "No. *This* was your first lesson."

CHAPTER THREE

No way Laris will sink into darkness. Jinx battled the thought as she raced down the hall. Every breath struggled to squeeze through the tension turning her insides to stone. *Hadu just thinks I'll be obedient if I believe Laris could slip off the edge.* She picked up her pace. It did little to drown out the truth. Hadu wouldn't bend the facts. *I can't begin to prepare for Laris turning rogue, but I can sure as drek gear up for someone like Sartillias.* Jinx picked up her pace at the thought of that drug lord hunting down Laris. No telling how many tabs of Euphoria he could process from her pineal gland. Undoubtedly, it would be primo.

Jinx practically slid up to the cardiovascular unit as the door opened. A small hand clutching a headset immediately filled her field of vision.

"You're one hundred and ninety-eight seconds late."

Jinx took the headset and slipped it on, adjusting the nodes to clamp tightly to her temples. "You're timing me in seconds now?"

DeeDee shrugged, then launched into a series of somersaults, scissor kicks, and side punches that spun her tiny frame across the entire length of the bare room. "Ready yet?"

"Let's rumble," Jinx said, moving slowly to the middle of the room, the spongy texture of the floor sinking beneath each step. "Show Tarxis menu." On command, the room dimmed as Tarix-related options were delivered to the nodes clinging tightly to her temples. The end result was a bright, neon directory that seemed to hover in midair. Jinx scrolled through the list. "What's it gonna be, Booger? You wanna battle on a volcanic planet, an abandoned ship in criminal-infested airspace, or jagged terrain covered in a sandstorm?"

"Volcanic planet!" DeeDee declared.

Jinx flashed a thumbs-up and placed the order. "Send sequence 31TXV to nodes one and two."

Instantly, the receivers buzzed, stimulating Jinx's anterior prefrontal cortex and occipital lobe, among other parts of her brain, forcing her view of reality to shift. She braced her footing as the supple floor beneath her rolled, morphing into contours that could match the rocky terrain she would experience. New sounds poured through her headset. The world hissed and popped as heated gas escaped the rivers of glowing red lava that snaked between cone-shaped peaks.

Turning three-sixty, Jinx scoped the rocky terrain, then dropped to a squat, narrowly avoiding a glob of airborne lava as it flew past. She continued to scan her surroundings until spotting DeeDee near a steaming geyser. Its white plumes stood out stark against the harsh, gray backdrop.

"Booger, move away from the geyser," Jinx whispered. "You're too easy to spot."

"I saw you first!" DeeDee's voice erupted in Jinx's headset.

"Lower your voice, Booger."

"It's a game," DeeDee said, twisting her face into a pout. "You're supposed to have fun."

"No. You're supposed to win. Now, go find a less visible place to stand."

Jinx pushed to her feet, moving into a sprint over liquid fire bubbling up from jagged tears. Globs of lava burped free, grazing her ankles between leaps. The pain shot up her legs with every drop that made contact. Real or not, it hurt like hell. Leaping to the top of a rocky peak, she hunted for signs of Tarxis. The sound of gravel trickling down a slope, as if it had been loosened underfoot, pulled Jinx's attention to a nearby summit. If Tarxis was there, he was watching from the shadows where his pewter flesh would blend in with the ashen stone.

"Booger, heads up. I think our target is about fifty feet to the south."

"I'm bored," DeeDee proclaimed as she shot out from behind a billowing cloud of vapor rising from the pitted ground. Bounding from one lava-free spot to another, she came to a stop in a clearing and called out to a shadowy figure in the distance. "Hurry up!"

A roar shook the landscape as Tarxis lunged from the murkiness, sending the dark silhouette of his bulky limbs through the air. The ground rumbled as he landed and continued to reverberate with each weighty step that followed.

"Booger!" Jinx pushed off her peak with enough force to go sailing toward the closest mound, touching down briefly before propelling herself to the next.

DeeDee's pout lifted as she watched Jinx vault from one hardened lava crest to the next in a race against Tarxis.

Adjusting her stance, DeeDee locked her attention on Tarxis, whose inelegant stride barely gained liftoff under the heft of his thick frame. As Jinx closed the gap between them, Tarxis shifted from a two-legged dash to race on all fours. His arms each hinged in three places, acting like a catapult propelling him forward.

Sailing over Tarxis, Jinx prepared to land and spring off the mound to his right, but his fist hammered it first, reducing it to a pile of jagged rubble. Jinx mentally braced herself, but the painful touchdown sent a shockwave surging through her body as razor-sharp points pierced the soles of her shoes. They dug further into her flesh as she pushed off, barely grasping Tarxis's foot as he bolted past.

The ride didn't last long. Tarxis's next step slammed Jinx into the ground, forcing her grip loose. Her breath caught on impact. Peeling her face off the floor, she attempted to suck in a steady breath as she watched DeeDee gracefully welcome the arrival of Tarxis. Spinning her body in a series of effortless pirouettes, DeeDee seamlessly morphed her movements into a precisely planted roundhouse kick. The collision rammed Tarxis's head left, twisting his neck awkwardly. In a fit of rage, he swung blindly, narrowly missing DeeDee as she leapt into a mid-air split. She landed in a low squat and cleared his second fist as it sailed overhead.

"See? This is more fun!" DeeDee squealed.

Jinx pushed to her knees as Tarxis swung around. His lipless mouth curled into a snarl, giving a glimpse of the slender, deadly spikes rooted there. Quickly, she leaned back, avoiding his snapping teeth. His hot breath, thick with the smell of rotting flesh, filled her lungs. Rocking to her feet, she choked down a cry as a relentless, fiery pain emanated from her soles. Jinx pushed to her toes and steadied her focus, watching for the moment to leap. She'd have to latch onto Tarxis to take him down. No way she could fight on her feet. Not for long, anyway.

"Hi, Jinx." DeeDee peeked around Tarxis to wave as he swung full circle to face her.

Jinx didn't return the greeting. Her attention caught on the soft sound of cracking in the distance. She turned to see a fissure slicing across the terrain, splitting it open.

"No, no, no, no, no!"

Ignoring the pain, Jinx planted one foot into the ground and pushed off, launching her firmly onto Tarxis's meaty back. Propelling her body forward, she shot like a bullet towards DeeDee, scooping her up and flying clear of the chasm violently ripping open.

Their bodies crashed onto the unforgiving ground, flinging them apart. DeeDee leapt to her feet as Jinx slowly pushed up, trying to catch her breath between coughs.

"What were you thinking?" Jinx said as they watched Tarxis slide further into the widening chasm and drop below the molten lava.

DeeDee shrugged. "It's just a game."

"Yeah, well, next time, pretend it's real," Jinx said as the virtual reality faded away, taking her pain with it. The room snapped back into focus. "Or, I don't know, find a way to forget it's a game."

CHAPTER FOUR

"We had a deal." Jinx barely snagged DeeDee as she attempted to squeeze past and onto the ship's deck. Pointing at a container prominently displayed on Jacob's meticulously organized sanitation station, Jinx grunted, "Wipe."

DeeDee kicked the empty air as she begrudgingly plucked a sanitary wipe from the box.

"What miracle is this?" Jacob popped his head up from behind the ring of cryo-tanks, nearly busting his skull on one of the mechanical arms that had descended from the ceiling. The metal beast once again looked like a robotic arachnid.

"I saved her from sinking below a river of hot lava with Tarix," Jinx said, eyeballing DeeDee's clumsy attempt at wiping her own hands.

"Wait. *You* saved *her*? Wow. The student has become the master."

Jinx scrunched her face like a foul odor was accosting her senses. "First of all, I was never a student. Claiming this little booger was my teacher is inaccurate."

Jacob shrugged, returning his attention to fiddling with the amplifier. "Hey, you're the one who said you learned your best moves from watching DeeDee take down the Starltonians."

"I instantly memorized her moves," Jinx said. "That's different."

"Whatever you say." Jacob paused his tinkering and studied Jinx for a moment. Furrowing his brow, he added, "What's got your briefs in a wad? Well, more than usual."

"Sorry." Jinx adjusted her posture, resting on her jutting hip while casually watching DeeDee fumble with the wet wipe. "Had a little session with Hadu. Apparently, my training started off with an annoying showdown."

Jacob laughed. "You tried to take charge with Hadu?"

"Not helpful."

"I'm just saying . . . I mean, she's our guide," Jacob said. "I don't think the universe would put someone in charge of training you that wasn't up for the challenge."

"What's that supposed to mean?" Jinx said, locking hands on hips as if gearing up for a tussle.

"You're stubborn, and you don't like to follow direction, rules, instructions—"

Jinx lifted her hands in submission. "I get the point."

DeeDee presented her palms, looking rather pleased with herself, although the sugary evidence that remained left little room for celebration.

"Not bad," Jinx offered, not wanting to burst DeeDee's bubble. "Do one more round to be safe." Handing her a second wipe, she thumbed towards Jacob and added, "You know how he gets."

DeeDee smiled and took the second wipe, seemingly inspired to be more thorough this time. A few moments later, she showcased impressively clean fingers.

"That's perfect, Booger." Releasing her hold, Jinx let DeeDee rip free across the deck, leaving behind an unexpected uneasiness that came with change.

Jacob shot to his feet with hands braced, prepared to spare his toys from a collision with DeeDee. "Hey, you want to help me with something?" The urgency of his question garnered a look of suspicion. "I need you to disconnect all of these cryo-tanks so we can haul them over to Claire's lab." He held up a slender, cylindrical device. "Just push this button." With a click, the top fanned out as metal leaves opened like a bloom. "Then press it into each of the joints," he said as he guided the mandala-esque face of the tool into place. A soft hum, mixed with the clanking of gears, followed. A few seconds later, it flashed blue. "Repeat that on all one hundred and thirty joints."

DeeDee thrust out her hand and eagerly reached for the tool.

Jacob held the device out of reach. "Hold up. That's the easy part. Next, you'll need to..."

DeeDee's gaze fixated on the tool as though nothing else of interest existed.

"Never mind." Jacob's posture melted in defeat as he handed DeeDee the device. "I'll transfer the instructions to your operating system." His expression went flat, apart from shuddering lids, as he drifted into cipher-mode, his very official and occasionally enforced term for mentally moving through machines.

Jinx watched as DeeDee examined the tool, opening and closing the floral tip in quick succession. Within a few rounds, the appeal wore off. She took to twirling it like a baton as Jacob mentally delivered, and likely reviewed, the directions in painfully specific detail. DeeDee, being an IOI, could do countless things at once. Chances were that Jacob's tutorial was only gleaning about two percent of her attention while the other ninety-eight percent was romping around cyberspace.

Jacob snapped back as DeeDee made a beeline for the first of thirteen cryo-tanks she'd be setting free. His features pinched as though he'd been scalded. "Just be careful."

Jinx crossed the room to pull Jacob from the circle of tanks towards the deck's control panel. "How's the approach to Earth going? Find anything remarkable?"

"You mean besides a mind-blowingly awesome tour of human origins?" Jacob said, reluctantly following Jinx with one eye glued to DeeDee. "Naw, nothing noteworthy."

Jinx cocked her head, adding a sour face to her inaudible response.

Jacob smiled innocently. "No, seriously, I'm not getting any sort of signal that would indicate a technologically advanced species has set up camp. But we haven't made it to Earth and her moon yet."

"Oh, great. There's still time for trouble." Jinx mockingly held up crossed fingers.

"Funny," Jacob said.

Jinx glanced at the control panel's display screen. The data looked like gibberish except for one word, Mars. The red planet was quickly filling up the skyscape as they made their approach.

"So far, Mars checks out," Jacob said as they slowed to sail by.

A dust storm was picking up, making it difficult to see much of the landscape. But between gaps in the whirling dust, Jinx caught glimpses of a volcanic-looking terrain marred by craters. Shattered remnants of a civilization peppered the surface. Everything was covered in the same red, chalky dust that blanketed the planet.

Jinx wondered what, if anything, had changed in the last thousand or so years. Chances were, the landscape hadn't. Galactic Overseers had put a quarantine, of sorts, on the entire solar system after an incredibly destructive atomic war waged over the colonization of Mars and mining rights on the gold-laced, mineral-rich asteroids circling Earth.

Only a small sampling of humanity had escaped the catastrophe in time, a ship loaded with DNA and a handful of the brightest minds to ensure survival. It was an effort that had resulted in the creation of the New World station.

Jinx had never thought about it before, but Jacob was clearly human, which meant somewhere in his family tree were two of the very few denizens who'd left the New World station. Maybe grandparents or someone even further back in his lineage had bolted. Unlikely that somebody had swirled some human DNA in a lab and created him, which was how Jinx and everyone on her station had been born. *No*, Jinx thought. Jacob seemed like someone who'd burst into this world from an actual womb.

Jinx made a mental note to ask him sometime. They'd only met a couple of days ago. Apparently, that was enough time for life to turn upside-down, but chit-chats about birth canals didn't tend to come up while breaking into a high-security VR, battling thugs with missile launchers, and getting a handle on newly acquired superpowers. She may not know the details of his life, but Jinx was certain about the nature of who he was.

"Everything checks out here. Let's head to the moon!" Jacob punctuated his statement with a trigger finger rocketing skyward.

With a few adjustments on the control panel, Mars disappeared as they raced towards their final checkpoint — the moon. Jacob slowed as they approached. It looked as lifeless as Mars with signs of doomsday, though it seemed peaceful in the solitude. Warmth percolated from Jinx's core as they circled. Earth hovered in the background like a mother watching over her child. Jinx hadn't expected to feel moved by the sight, but emotion ballooned as she felt Jacob's eyes on her and knew the same awe claimed his face. Most likely, they were the first in a very, very long time to set eyes on their homeland. It wasn't a technology-based vessel floating in deep space. It was a living, breathing mass capable of giving life . . . and taking it.

"Can't imagine she's too happy to see us back," Jinx said, jutting her chin towards Earth.

"Only one way to find out," Jacob replied. "Where did Hadu suggest we land? I'm guessing she's picked a spot since we're heading here by her council."

"Oh, crap." Jinx shoved a hand into her pocket and pulled out a crumpled and slightly sweat-damp wad of paper. "Egypt." She grinned as she handed it to Jacob. "The coordinates are on this."

As expected, Jacob grimaced before taking it. "I don't have enough sanitizer to handle this germ-soaked mess." Unfolding it, he gagged theatrically. "Seriously? I can't believe you guys are still using ink and paper." He studied the note. "She could have just sent me the coordinates."

"Yes." Jinx's brow pinched to a pronounced ripple. "But then she wouldn't have had the satisfaction of schooling me on who's in charge."

"29.9792° North, 31.1342° East." Jacob read out loud as he punched in the new coordinates. "Now we're talking! The Great Pyramid of Giza." He practically squealed. "There's a lot of secrecy around that structure. According to Tesla—"

"Who?"

Jacob's jaw dropped. He started to speak, then paused. "Seriously, I'm gonna hijack your VR games and insert some historical figures for you to battle."

Jinx shrugged. "Fine, but I will not hesitate to flatten them."

"Just remember their names when you do," Jacob teased. "Anyway, according to a famous genius you've never heard of, there are energy lines that cover the Earth's surface like a power grid. The pyramids are built and positioned in a way that allows them to harness and transmit the energy, potentially tapping into torsion fields and scalar waves. These types of structures are all over the Earth's surface."

"So, what, you're planning on firing up the pyramids?"

"Absolutely." Jacob's eyes sparkled with anticipation.

Jinx eyeballed Jacob's eager expression. "No. I'm not going to ask what you're planning to do with the pyramids. Go find Claire. You two can melt each other's brains."

Jacob pushed past Jinx's resistance, pulling up a screen on the deck's main console. "Here's a few tablets filled with fun facts."

"Fun?" Jinx peered over his shoulder and scoffed. "That doesn't look like anything to me, other than a slab of stone with a bunch of lines dug into it."

"It's not stone. It's clay. And those lines are Sumerian text." After seeing Jinx's look, Jacob added, "Sorry. Uh, the short answer: a very ancient civilization on Earth."

"And you can read that?" Jinx asked, staring at the images on the screen as Jacob zoomed in on the detail.

Jacob cocked his head, looking placidly unaware of his impressiveness. "Well, yeah."

Jinx shook her head. "Of course you can."

"This tablet"—Jacob focused on a series of three stones and pointed to one— "talks about the Great Pyramid. Supposedly, it was used to resurrect an Anunnaki god named Enki. In Egyptian mythology, Osiris was resurrected in an adjacent building called Abydos."

Jinx rolled her eyes. "Wow, where to begin?"

"Hey, I'm not vouching for the story, though the Anunnaki were likely just an advanced civilization that came to Earth." Jacob scrolled through a few more images. "I wouldn't mind testing the theory, though."

Jinx raised her hand in protest. "Hey, don't look at me. Not interested in dying so you can test your Anu-blah-blah theory."

"Anunnaki," Jacob said, shaking his head.

"Whatever." Jinx abandoned the cryptic images and turned her attention towards something less complicated: the terra firma ahead. Swirls of brilliant blue and white glowed against the empty, black backdrop of space. It wasn't the barren landscape of the surrounding planets or an ice giant buried beneath a gaseous atmosphere. The view was hypnotic. Peaceful. As though nothing were more powerful than its ability to thrive. A flutter in Jinx's heart revealed itself in a soft quiver around her words. "Are you picking up on any lifeforms?"

Jacob looked up, casting a curious glance towards Jinx.

"What?" Jinx felt her face blush. "It's . . ." Crossing her arms, she struggled to finish her thought. "It's Earth. That's all."

"Yeah. I know." Jacob cracked a smile that could warm a room. "It's emotional."

Jinx whacked his arm again.

Jacob laughed. "I'm serious. I'm not making fun of you. Emotions are good. Feel free to let them slip more often."

"I'll make a note," Jinx said. "Are you picking up on any life down there or not?"

"Not much would have survived," Jacob said, "but it looks like the toxic atmosphere has cleared for the most part. That means sunlight is getting through. We might find some signs of organic life, but it'd have to thrive in high levels of carbon."

"What about IOI?"

"Could be some low-tech bots kicking around, maybe even tapping into Earth's electromagnetic energy for fuel. It looks like there are plenty of satellites still drifting around the atmosphere. Luckily, none of it looks like it'll cause trouble."

Jinx patted Jacob's shoulder. "I'm pretty sure trouble will find us no matter what."

"I'm bringing us in." A broad, goofy grin burst, lighting up Jacob's face. "You ready?"

Jinx noticed her expression shine in response; it beamed in the clear quartz windshield. "I was born ready."

"Truer words have rarely been spoken." Jacob turned back towards his control panel. "Should we go straight for the coordinates or make a fast loop around the surface?"

"Let's go ahead and land," Jinx said. "The sooner we drop out of sight, the better."

"Great. Get ready to have your mind blown," Jacob said as he took the ship rocketing towards the Earth to sail a few hundred feet above the sea.

Jinx threw a wide-eyed glare. "Do you only have two speeds: breakneck and engine off?"

Jacob grinned mischievously. "You're not the only thrill-seeker."

As Jacob punched in a command, the ship slowed to a glide, cruising until the murky blue water became a tide crashing onto the coast. A sprawling desert replaced the rolling waves, marked by an edgeless ramble of tan speckled with twisting funnels of sand. The landscape spun to life with passing spurts of wind. Jinx watched them dance and dash across the surface until they fizzled out.

"Look." Jacob nudged Jinx as he pointed towards three spots breaking up the seamless view. "You'll see the pyramids in a few seconds." As the ship closed the distance, the dots grew into colossal stone structures with edges that radiated the fiery brilliance of the early morning sun.

Jinx began to speak, but sound felt like an intrusion on some sacred ritual swirling between the pyramids, the Earth, and the Sun. She didn't have words to capture the moment anyway.

"The area looks clear," Jacob whispered, breaking the hypnotic grip. "I'm not picking up on anything we should be concerned about. You OK with me taking us down?"

Jinx scanned the barren landscape. "Go for it."

Jacob slowly lowered them down alongside the largest of the three pyramids, which dwarfed their ship. It certainly wasn't the largest structure Jinx had ever seen. The New World space station, when all five hundred and eleven levels were connected, was easily twice the size. And Kepslar 10, the supply station where she'd tracked down Jacob, was phenomenally massive. It could have engulfed hundreds of these pyramids. Yet neither evoked reverence in quite the same way. It was something Jinx couldn't put a name to. The world around it had been dismantled, reduced to dust and sand, it seemed. Whatever power these pyramids contained appeared impervious to external forces, their potential silently waiting for the right moment to rise from hibernation. It was a fitting place to bring Laris.

Jacob engaged his com. "Claire, you there?" After a brief pause, he added, "You getting the camera shots of the exterior?" Another pause. "I know, right? Just keep an eye out for any signs of quartz or gold peeking through the worn-away exterior. There may be a conductive material beneath the stone. In fact, I'm banking on it." Another pause. "We'll wheel the cryo-tanks to the lab once we finish—" Jacob stopped short, searching for DeeDee. "Uh ...." An exasperated groan drowned out the words of frustration that followed.

Jinx followed his line of sight. Twelve of the thirteen cryo-tanks were silently rolling along the deck on their own volition. DeeDee was nowhere in sight. She'd completed the task at phenomenal speed, disengaged the wheel locks, and had begun to cart them to Claire's lab.

Jinx inwardly smiled. *No way that little booger didn't make a pit stop.* The predictability was calming, cushioning the fear of invisible threats. Yet the uneasiness of the unknown lingered. Waving over her shoulder, Jinx turned, moving across the room towards the opening door. "See ya later."

"Where ya going?" Jacob asked, following swiftly in her wake.

"Gotta get my head right," Jinx said. "No telling what's in store."

Jacob's footsteps paused. His voice caught as though snatching back words or searching for the right ones. Instead, he let silence fill the space, landing like an unspoken pact forged over lifetimes long forgotten.

"I'll come find you when I'm done." Jinx's footsteps barely made a sound as she took off through the door and down the corridor. Her heart raced as she sped around an endless curve, pushing faster to cast out the noise of the world around her and the anxious chatter in her head.

The race came to an abrupt halt as she impatiently pressed through an opening door. With the sound of it sliding to a close, she allowed the solitude to wrap her in a familiar embrace. For a moment she stood still, staring at the unadorned room. A pile of laundry, unceremoniously dumped in the corner, was Jinx's version of unpacking. She'd hauled the heap here, wrapped in a bedsheet she'd stripped from her former room, which was currently whizzing through some other part of the universe, along with the rest of the New World space station.

If she didn't know otherwise, this room could pass for the one she'd grown up in and snuck out of on more than a handful of occasions. It was identical, apart from one exception. That single deviation made this space a potential haven, a portal to her version of Zen.

"Engage screen," Jinx said, drawing in a deep, satisfying breath as she moved eagerly towards a large monitor on the far wall.

Popping open a drawer, she rummaged through the only other belongings to her name, most of which were contraband video games she'd had smuggled onto her former ship. One of many defiant acts that had led her to Jacob.

"Run GD3," she said while eagerly pressing a set of earbuds into place.

"Are you ready to GetDown3000?" The words blasted through her buds and raced across the screen in glowing neon before disappearing.

Yeah, I'm ready, Jinx thought, uncomfortably aware of the gripping sensation in her gut. It felt as though it planned to nest there permanently.

While shaking out her limbs, Jinx locked her attention on a silhouette appearing on screen. Music poured through the sound system tucked behind her lobes as the darkened figure came to life, moving in seamless rhythm with the rolling beats. Jinx followed, matching every move as the figure transitioned into increasingly difficult variations.

Soon, the world disappeared beyond a wave of endorphins, allowing Jinx to escape the rumblings beneath her own skin and conjuring a sense peace that nothing else seemed to match.

CHAPTER FIVE

"Stop worrying." Jacob paused to enter a code into the keypad outside Claire's lab. "I'm monitoring our perimeter. If anything comes within visible range of our ship, I'll know."

"*Visible* range?" Jinx choked down a gulp of kæffee as she followed Jacob inside. "Not the fortress I was hoping for."

"Trust me. We're fine for now. Go eat breakfast or, better yet, take a shower." Jacob eyed her and wrinkled his nose. "Or two."

"Hey, this is what ruling GD3000 looks like," Jinx grumbled as she pulled her version of breakfast from her pocket: a half-eaten grub-bar. "Why don't you stop worrying about my hygiene and focus on the security field?"

"Our shield is up," Jacob said emphatically, lifting his hands in surrender.

Jinx responded with a flatline expression.

Jacob shook his head as he wheeled a cryo-tank through the door. The other twelve DeeDee had disconnected from the amplifier sat empty along one wall. Monitors for displaying their activity hung lifeless above them. "Even if something made it near the ship unnoticed, it wouldn't be able to breach the security field."

"How long till—" Jinx was cut short as Claire popped into view from behind a portable stack of electronics. A stream of obscenities rolled off Claire's tongue as seamlessly as the sound of Laris chanting. Jacob's expression burst as if enchanted by some mystical, albeit indelicate, creature. Jinx knew her words would fall on deaf ears now.

"What's the problem?" Jacob abandoned the cryo-tank to practically levitate towards Claire. "Anything I can help with?"

"Something is interfering with the system," Claire said as she wrestled her unruly hair into a barely contained pile. Searching the desktops, she grabbed a random object and skewered her willful mane in place. "I don't know what happened. Maybe moving through the portal shifted something. I may need to recalibrate everything."

Jacob moved to Claire's side as he offered to take a look, which Jinx found comical. He could access every system on this ship mentally, even from a great distance.

Washing down the final bite of her grub-bar with a swig of kaffeine, Jinx freed her hand to take hold of the tank Jacob had abandoned.

"Great," she groaned, touching it as if it were infected. A few days ago, it had practically been a coffin for Laris. It was empty now, but it still evoked unsettling images and the rare urge to scrub her hands.

With a shudder, Jinx wheeled it towards the lineup of other tanks and parked it. Whether it was an aversion to the tank that put her on edge or a visceral response to someone silently moving through the hall, an adrenaline spike lit Jinx's flesh. She whipped around ready to speed across the room towards the door as it opened. Hadu stood on the other side, offering her version of a smile, marked by the ever-so-slight tilt of her lip.

"Happy to see your internal radar is calibrating, but I shouldn't have made it this far before you sensed my presence," Hadu said as she entered. "We'll need to work on honing that during your training." The room and its contents appeared fragile in her presence, as though the power that kept particles spinning in place took notice.

"I've got too much to—"

Hadu gave Jinx the once-over, then raised a brow. "I'm sure you'll find a way to accommodate between virtual battles and dance challenges."

"Hey, that's not all I—" Jinx stifled her protest and groaned. "Fine. I'll add it to my list of hero-tasks."

"I'll expect to see you in my office when the sun reaches the Sphinx and dips below the horizon. For now, we have other things to discuss." Hadu turned to Claire and Jacob, who had halted their meeting-of-the-minds the moment she entered. "What have you two discovered so far?"

"Well, for starters, the pyramid has eight sides, well nine if you include the bottom," Jacob said. "It's very subtle, but the dimensions are far too exact to be a coincidence or some sort of mistake."

Claire nodded. "I was curious about that too and ran the numbers. It shares some important mathematical constants found in nature, but I have no idea why or what the purpose would be for such a complicated design."

Hadu's expression revealed nothing as she moved through the lab, quietly inspecting the space. Jinx guessed this fun fact wasn't news to her. She'd brought them to this spot for a reason. Not to mention she'd prepared for her role as their guide for over three hundred years.

Yeah, she knows all about the pyramid, Jinx decided.

"I picked up on an electromagnetic current running beneath it," Jacob said. "It's possible the pyramid was designed to capture it."

"Maybe it could even harness torsion energy to produce scalar waves," Claire added.

"Or it could be used as a power source for" —Jacob paused to glance at Jinx before flubbing his thought— "for . . . uh . . . something."

Jinx rolled her eyes. "And by something, you mean raising the dead?"

"Hey, I was just relaying information I found, but I'll bet the pyramid functions. No way it's just a mega mound of stone. It does *something*. Maybe not raise the dead, but something cool like opening hyperdimensional fields to access alternate realities."

"Don't tease me with quantum promises," Claire said somewhat breathlessly.

Jinx groaned. "You two are making my head hurt. I just want to know if it has energy we can tap. Is it something we can leverage to expand our security shield farther out from the ship? I really don't like the idea of unwanted guests knocking on our hatch door."

"I've been considering that possibility," Jacob replied. "I have a few ideas, but we should be safe for the moment. I'm not picking up on any life, at least not in range."

"There could be some outdated technology in sleep mode or simply shut down," Claire said. "I mean, if there were any surviving nanites, those little buggers could have self-replicated using Earth's iron deposits."

Hadu lifted a container off one of the desks and rotated it in her palms. Claire didn't flinch, but Jinx knew she was likely boiling beneath her skin. Claire maintained a strict hands-off policy when it came to her toys. Hadu set the container down, moving on to a new point of interest. "Are you able to create something to shield us from any airborne technology so that we can move freely off the ship?"

"Yes, but there are other issues to address," Claire replied. "There could be organic, airborne lifeforms like viruses or insects. We need to shield against those too. Our bodies aren't immune to the same things as our ancestors. Plus, a completely new lifeform could have risen from the disaster." Her voice sparkled with anticipation. "It's a jungle out there. Well, I hope it is, at least. Deadly or not, discovering the first new life to develop would be incredible."

"My primary concern is the pyramids," Hadu said. "Please make certain they are within the security field as soon as possible. I'll need access to begin training with Laris and the other ten Attendants."

Jinx did a mental victory dance for not being included in whatever Hadu had planned. Undoubtedly, it included endless hours of mind-numbing meditation.

Hadu looked at Jinx, allowing her gaze to worm around. "Don't be so quick to dismiss meditation, Protector. You need to master your mind."

"You know what? You need to stop crawling around my skull." Jinx wrapped her palms around her head and moved to the other side of the room, muttering all the way. "I'm gonna build my own security shield."

"You'd have no need for shielding your mind if you mastered it."

Jinx stared back blankly, allowing the silence to stretch.

"Okay." Jacob brought his hands together in a solitary slap as if ready to get moving. "We'll secure the pyramid first," Jacob said. "This will give us our first off-ship area. And there are multiple ley lines running vertically and horizontally across Earth."

"What do mean, 'ley lines?'" Jinx asked.

"They're channels of power that course through the earth," Jacob replied. "Honestly, it looks like some sort of natural power grid or electrical generator. With a little time, I might be able to leverage the lines and run our security shield around the entire planet."

Jinx scrutinized Jacob for a flash. "Seriously?"

"In theory, sure," Jacob said. Furrowing his brow, he added, "I don't know the specifics yet . . . but maybe."

"We just need to figure out a way to harness the energy." Claire raised a brow as she looked towards Jacob. "If you need help, that is."

"Uh, yeah. Of course." Jacob fumbled over his words as he attempted to lean casually against one of the cryo-tanks. His hand missed its mark, tripping him up slightly. Red-faced, he regained footing. "The more brain power, the better."

Jinx bit back a laugh watching Jacob bungle around Claire — the kryptonite to his cool. As Jacob eased the disturbed cryo-tank back into precise alignment with the others, Jinx considered the amplifier it had previously been attached to. Thoughts bubbled to the surface and rolled off her tongue musingly.

"If Jacob and Claire can tap the Earth's energy, can it be used to boost Laris and the Attendants' vibration?" Jinx wasn't really all that concerned about tipping the universe in favor of OI. She just wanted to take some of the burden off Laris. Saving organic life from extinction was a tall order, one she wasn't entirely sold on.

"*That* is what we are here to find out," Hadu said while knitting her fingers into a soft cradle.

Jinx's eyes widened. "It is? I was just digging around." She rubbed the back of her neck in an attempt to ease the muscles tensing around her spine. "Wouldn't it just be easier if you share what you're thinking? I feel like we're wasting time uncovering information that you seem to already know."

"When it's necessary for me to impart knowledge, I will." Hadu paused to regard each of them. "But your evolution depends on your process of discovery. And it would be false to assume that my knowledge is set in stone. Reality shifts in ways we cannot predict. We must look closely and carefully at the results of every action we take and move mindfully without the assumption that we have all the facts or answers."

Jinx snorted. The sound escaped before she had a chance to stifle it. "Great. I love riddles."

Jacob disappeared behind deep contemplation. His eyes jutted around as he dissected some complex equation then shifted as he looked towards the empty cryo-tanks. "I have a pretty solid understanding of what Bayne created. I might be able to replicate it, you know, in a way that *doesn't* involve imprisoning Laris and the Attendants in permanent oblivion."

"What about adding a Möbius coil to the design to produce scalar waves from the frequency Laris produces?" Claire asked. "That way her frequency won't diminish as it moves through space."

Jacob nodded. "Great idea."

Hadu gave a gentle nod as well. "Speak with Bayne if need be."

Jinx's hackles burst at the idea of enlisting Bayne. He'd been in solitary confinement since they'd thwarted his grim plan for saving OI from extinction. Chances were, he was sour about it. His help might come with annoying terms.

As if reading Jinx's facial expression, Jacob blurted, "I don't know how I'll, I mean we" —Jacob motioned to Claire — "will achieve it. But we'll figure it out."

"Heck yes we will," Claire blurted as she flipped a rogue lock of hair from her face.

Jinx fished around her pocket for a second grub-bar but only pulled out a wad of empty wrappers followed by a stream of assorted crumbs.

Ignoring Jacob's cheeky expression, she mulled over the future. "Great, 'cause eventually Owen will arrive along with the rest of the ships —"

"That is not for you to concern yourself with," Hadu interrupted.

When their space station — all five hundred and eleven levels — had separated, each level sped off in different directions of the universe to help protect Laris by concealing her location. Jinx had made a vow at that moment. In her heart, they were all hers to protect, though Laris mattered more to her than the universe combined.

"The safety of Laris and the Attendants are my priority, but—"

"But nothing," Hadu said sharply. "There are great minds on each of those vessels. You must accept that you are not alone in keeping our safety. It's not your job to absorb every blow this battle will deliver or carry the burden of failure or success."

"We need to at least have—"

Hadu raised a hand, silencing the conversation. "They are not expecting to find their new home settled and safe when they arrive. Direct your thoughts solely to mastering your role as Protector. I assure you in that endeavor, you have your hands quite full." Hadu went still. As her eyes closed, she lifted a finger to her forehead. A beat later, her eyes popped open, and she turned to go without explanation. Stopping at the door, she tossed a few final words over her shoulder. "I expect to see you in my office on time."

"Yeah, yeah." Jinx arched her arm overhead theatrically. "When the sun crosses the cat."

"Sphinx," Hadu corrected as the door closed behind her.

Turning back towards Jacob and Claire, Jinx asked, "What can I do to help get our security shield to wrap around the pyramid?"

"We can stretch the field, but it won't be stable without anchors. I need to check our supplies, though I kinda doubt I'll find what I need to anchor silver nanoparticles over multi-walled carbon nanotubes." Jacob chuckled, smiling at Jinx as if she'd totally get the joke.

Jinx rolled her eyes. Claire erupted in laughter. Jacob looked pleased.

Gathering herself, Claire moved to a monitor and typed in a few commands. A list appeared on screen. "So far, this is everything I've found in the lab. There's quite a bit that wasn't recorded in the station's log. Bayne was covering his tracks while he built the amplifier." She cocked her head towards Jacob. "Have you started dismantling his machine yet or just the cryo-tanks?"

"Just the tanks. Why?" Jacob replied.

"Well, there's bound to be materials we can use to create an electrostatic field."

"Deflecting electron beams or capturing them?"

Claire shrugged. "Either could come in handy."

Jacob thrummed his chin. "True. Let's add electromagnetic coils to the..."

Jinx grumbled; geek-speak made her head throb. There was a cap on what she was able to absorb. Electrostatic fields, whatever those were, were not on that list nor likely to ever be.

"You guys just do your genius thing, and if you don't have everything you need, then we'll figure out how to get our hands on it."

"Please tell me you're not considering a blink between galaxies. There's no way to test if you'll make it all the way or what it could do to your body." Claire wrung her hands. "I mean, we haven't even determined what's causing your weight loss after relatively short blinks."

It sounded way riskier outside the privacy of her thoughts, but Jinx tossed up her hands. "Well, there's no way we'll have everything we need here. I'll have to get to the supply station. Besides, the weight loss isn't enough to be concerned about. It's like ounces. I'm just burning extra fuel."

"Hey, I'm all for blinking to the supply station," Jacob said as he scrolled through Claire's list. "All work and no play makes my brain very cranky. But . . . it does sound really risky."

"Hate to break it to you, but there's no avoiding risk," Jinx said. "We are one hundred percent at risk, all the time. Probably forever."

"First of all, I don't plan to be around forever," Jacob replied. "Look what happened to Hadu's skull. After three-hundred-plus years, it's grown taller than my forearm. I can't pull off that look."

Jinx raised a palm to pause Jacob. "Shhh for a second." Her heart kicked up as her body went rigid.

"Why, what's up?" Jacob and Claire whispered in unison.

"I don't know," Jinx said. "I have a weird feeling. Something isn't right."

"Well, our surveillance cameras haven't spotted anything in range." Jacob flashed a wristband. "I've been keeping tabs."

"Maybe I'm just paranoid right now, but something feels . . . off."

"I'll keep a close eye," Jacob said. "If it's technology, I'd sense it even without the cameras."

"And . . . what if the threat isn't IOI?"

"Well, if it's something else, like some sort of organic life, that's another story," Jacob replied. "But it would have to be totally technology-free. Other than the denizens from your station, nearly everyone I've ever run across is augmented. That'd give off a signature I'd pick up on."

Jinx's brows knitted. "You're not augmented."

"I'm an anomaly."

"Let's hope," Jinx said as she headed for the door. "I'm gonna go check the perimeter from the deck."

CHAPTER SIX

Jinx looked out over the sprawling sands of Giza undulating beneath the heat-rippled air. The landscape appeared watery within the distortion. Beyond the pyramids, the horizon sat undisturbed, but her uneasiness wouldn't let up.

The view held an eerie familiarity. Jinx had traversed similar scenes countless times in virtual combat. The memories made the setting seem surreal. What made it different from the virtual deserts she had battled her way through for sport? Maybe nothing.

I wish it was only a game, Jinx mused. Right now, the stakes felt too high.

Putting a finger to her ear, Jinx engaged her com. "Hey, I'm gonna take one of our shuttles out. I wanna double-check the area. Can you make sure the hangar's security field is active? I don't want anything making its way onto the ship when I exit."

Jacob's voice rang through. "You're good to go. Just make sure you take an S.I.S. suit in case you need to get out and walk around. The air has way too much carbon."

"I probably won't," Jinx replied. "There's no way to move around fast in those things. It's like being rolled in foam. I'd love something less crappy."

"If we decide to head to the supply station, we can pick up some. You know, something that wasn't designed four hundred years ago."

It was true. The New World station had kept technology as minimal as possible, which was difficult when you were floating around deep space and training to live in a Zen-inspired VR. But without a need to travel through inhospitable environments, the station hadn't devoted resources to stocking top-of-the-line S.I.S. suits.

Jinx snorted. "Oh, so you're gonna risk your pretty face and let me drag you along on the blink?"

"I trust you to get us there in one piece. If not, just make sure the scars look cool," Jacob said. "But seriously, you won't know what most of the things on this list are. Claire added stuff that even I've never heard of."

"Well, I know what an S.I.S. device looks like," Jinx replied. "Better add them to the list, one for everyone on the ship plus a few extras."

Turning from her view of the Giza, Jinx moved towards the door.

"Expecting guests?" Jacob asked.

Jinx punched in a key code. The door opened, and she stepped out into the silent corridor. "You mean besides the thousands of denizens hopefully making their way to Earth?"

"You want a few *hundred thousand* S.I.S. suits? We'll have to pay extra for the shopping bags to hold all of those."

"Funny. But since most of the denizens heading our way are stuck in cryo-tanks and trapped in the VR, I think we'll be fine with twenty."

"Roger that, Chief. Consider it number two on the growing list."

"What's number one?" Jinx was only mildly curious about Jacob's inventory. It would likely sound like gibberish to her, but it was nice to have his voice in her ear, dissolving the fear that rumbled beneath.

Jacob continued to rattle off items, accompanying Jinx through the hallway. "At least fifty sheets of graphene. Oh, and some litmorian."

"Seriously?" Jinx croaked. "That stuff tastes like bile."

"Well, you're not supposed to eat graphene." Jacob chuckled. "Seriously though, litmorian is an acquired taste. I didn't like it at first, but now that green goodness is my version of meditation. I plan on snagging a bottle."

"Get some seeds. We can grow our own plants and make it." Claire sounded as enthusiastic about gardening as she did about jetting through a portal between galaxies.

The dull hum of a tuning bowl brought Jinx to a pause. "I gotta go, but I'll be at the hangar in ten minutes."

"Roger that. I'll make sure everything is ready to roll. I'd love to go with you, but I have my hands full."

"I know. Thanks," Jinx replied as she approached a door, beyond which the soothing sound rolled.

There wasn't really a reason for her to check on the Attendants, who were likely in deep meditation. She just wanted to see Laris — set eyes on her. It soothed her soul, reminded her what was at stake. Saving organic life wasn't something Jinx could wrap her head around. So what if technology took over? But keeping Laris safe was a no-brainer.

Punching in a code, the door quietly slid open, allowing melodic waves to roll out and across her goose-bumped flesh. Though meditation had always eluded her, sound carried Jinx to another world, a fact she'd only admit in reference to GetDown3000. In the center of the room, Laris sat cross-legged with her Attendants forming a circle around her. Hadu stood at the far end running a padded wand around twelve metal and crystal bowls. No one stirred from the meditation. For a moment, Jinx felt like an invisible spectator.

"I'd ask if you're here to join us," Hadu's voice infiltrated Jinx's mind, "but I'm certain that's not the case."

"Good guess. I'm taking a commuter out to check the area." Jinx didn't utter the words out loud. Seemed pointless since Hadu was already poking around in her thoughts. Reading minds was not a skill Jinx had any interest in developing. Most thoughts were better not heard. Keeping hers to herself, however, was definitely a new priority.

Hadu pulled the wand from the edge of the bowl and set it down, remaining still as the sound slowly drifted away. Ringing a small handheld bell, she brought the room back from beyond. The Attendants opened their eyes at a leisurely pace, shifting their position as they roused. Laris was the last to stir, though a smile emerged as if she'd felt Jinx's presence. Without a word, Laris unfolded her legs and stood. Her Attendants followed suit and turned to face Jinx with bowed heads.

The exchange took Jinx by surprise. She didn't look away, even though she wanted to.

"Just want to make sure everyone knows not to leave the ship until we've secured the area." Jinx didn't think they were planning to. It seemed unlikely they'd eagerly jump into the unknown. But standing there, in silence, made her want to leap out of her skin. "I'll be off-ship for a while checking our surroundings. If you need anything, find Jacob or Claire."

"I'm going with you," Laris said softly, though the words sounded as if forged in steel.

"No, you aren't," Jinx shot back.

"Why?"

Jinx moved towards the door, knowing a battle of wills was brewing. "I don't know what's out there. And I'm not really interested in putting you in the middle of a potentially dangerous and unfamiliar situation that I can't control."

"Sorry, but I overrule your decision," Laris said.

Jinx's shoulders dropped as she clamped her skull. She'd experienced Laris's determination on a few occasions. Turning around, she looked pleadingly towards Hadu. "Can ya help me out here?"

"I'm certain you two can come to an agreement on your own," Hadu replied as she ushered the Attendants through the doorway. The last in line paused to smile brightly with a hint of mischief, then scampered off. The sound of tinkling bells didn't follow, but it seemed as though it should.

"You better hurry if you want to catch up with them," Jinx said, gently nudging Laris towards the Attendants.

"I haven't had *any* time with you in over two years." Laris crossed her arms over her chest.

Jinx braced herself.

"I'm going," Laris announced. "Unless you plan on locking me up, you may as well stop fighting me on this. I want time with you. And what better way to protect me than by keeping me near?" She stepped in close, moving her hand to clasp Jinx's.

Involuntarily, Jinx went catatonic.

Laris sighed heavily. "Please stop being uncomfortable with me."

"I'm not uncomfortable with you, Laris. I'm just . . . it's just that I need to keep my head straight."

"Avoiding me isn't going to help. Just let me in. Or at least let me come with you. Please. I miss you. Whatever I am or am not supposed to be doesn't change that I'm human. I need to be with the people I care for most. This is all new to me too. I need your friendship as much as I need your protection. In fact, I need it more."

I've missed you too, Jinx thought, allowing her shoulders to soften. After studying Laris for an exaggerated moment, she gave in. "Fine. You can come with me on one condition."

Laris's face lit. Turning, she ran out the door before Jinx could list the requirements. Her gown tangled around her legs like a trickster attempting to trip her up.

Jinx shook her head. "If I tell you to do something, you have to listen. I honestly don't know what's out there."

Laris called over her shoulder, "I promise!"

"You don't need to race down the hall," Jinx said, walking at an unhurried pace. "I won't torpedo my decision. Promise. Besides, I don't have the stamina to out-stubborn you."

Laris came to a sloppy stop, arms flopping like a burst of wind had brought her clumsy race to an abrupt end. She turned to face Jinx, smiling as though nothing in the world had changed or ever would. "Yes, you do."

"No. I always cave in." Jinx stepped next to Laris, who flashed an exaggerated eye roll.

Laris nudged Jinx playfully as she locked their arms together. "You never wanted to meditate or study with me. You always refused."

"Yeah, well, it was boring."

Laris laughed. "You think anything that doesn't involve a battle or sneaking into restricted areas is boring."

Jinx allowed the familiar easiness between them to resurface. The simplicity of their friendship always anchored her. "Hey, all those battles helped prepare me for *this*."

"Well, all that studying prepared me," Laris replied. "Sort of."

"Yeah. Sort of." Jinx held Laris's gaze. There was no way to prepare for being key players in a prophecy, for what had happened, for the future they were walking into.

"I'm glad it's you," Laris said, dropping her head to Jinx's shoulder.

It had to be you, Jinx thought as they moved through the hall. *There's no one else I would have fought for.* "Well, I'm glad it's me too. So far, the battles have been epic."

"Whatever." Laris smacked Jinx's arm. "What are we looking for out there, anyway?"

"*I'm* looking for potential threats," Jinx replied, stopping to type in the hangar's security code.

Claire called out from beyond the opening door, "Don't worry. I'll be done in a minute." She didn't bother to turn her attention from the round, compact, two-seater craft she was busily retrofitting.

Jinx untangled from Laris to stride swiftly towards the vessel. Her movements reflected and morphed in the bulbous, clear quartz enclosure of the passenger compartment. "Please tell me you're installing a cloaking device."

"Nope," Claire said while adjusting the small, flat, rectangular device now attached to the rear of the hood. "I'm adding a low-shear-stress microfluidic device to capture biosensitive particles."

Jinx sighed exaggeratedly. "You mean a net?"

Claire glanced up and grinned impishly. "See? You're sharp. I knew you understood more geek-speak than you let on."

"Yeah, I'm a mental giant."

Claire shook her head and returned to tweaking the contraption. "It'll capture samples of whatever is in the air. Then I can analyze the atmosphere and check for any new life that's formed."

"That's it? Nothing I need to do?"

"Nope," Claire said. "We'll monitor your trip from here. If something looks interesting, I can operate it remotely and send sensors into hard-to-reach spaces."

"Don't get your hopes up. The landscape looks like it's flatlined."

"You never know," Claire said. "There might be some tricky li'l invaders out there. The first new life on an otherwise barren planet is bound to be rugged. Hopefully, I can formulate protection against any viruses."

"Great," Jinx said. "I'll handle everything bigger than microscopic and leave any tiny monsters to you."

"The invisible threats are the most cunning." Claire's smile sparkled. "I can't wait to get my hands on organisms I've never encountered before. Might even be some microscopic technology floating around out there."

"I'll try and bring back something truly insidious for you."

Claire flashed a hungry grin as she slid down from the roof of the craft, landing on a portable staircase. "A girl can hope." With the flip of a switch, she was whisked away, riding atop the set of mobile stairs. "She's ready to go."

As the treads came to a halt, Jinx prepared to slide past Claire and take the helm of the ship.

"Not so fast," Claire said, hopping off her chariot to intersect Jinx with a halting arm. "If you're seriously considering a blink to the supply station, I'm going to start tracking your stats."

"What's the hurry?" Jinx said, motioning for Laris to join her. "I'm not blinking anywhere right now."

Reaching into her pocket, Claire pulled out a flat, square tab hardly bigger than the tip of her finger. "I need some sort of baseline to understand what, if anything, is happening when you do." Not bothering to wait for a reply, Claire twisted Jinx's head to affix it behind her right ear. "This will monitor your activity levels. But you need to record what you eat and keep me updated."

Jinx clucked. "Fat chance."

"Then just tell me over the comm. I'll make notes." Claire narrowed a glare. "I'm serious. You eat a grub-bar, tell me. You drink one of your shukar-loaded kæffees, I need to know. This is the only way I can isolate how much energy a blink utilizes. That is, assuming your weight fluctuation is simply a matter of burning extra fuel when you make a jump. Whatever the case, we need to start boosting your calorie intake to compensate."

"Sure, sure. Whatever you say." Jinx turned to Laris, who'd moved in tight to her side. "Let's go find some trouble for Claire to geek out on, besides my waistline."

CHAPTER SEVEN

"Don't touch the controls." Jinx swatted Laris's hand away as she reached for a knob on the panel.

Feigning shock, Laris examined her hand before laying it in her lap. "When did you learn to fly one of these?"

Jinx gave a shady shrug while keeping a watchful eye on the landscape. The late afternoon sun had begun to cool, but the desert remained searing hot. A glimmering haze blanketed the sands as heat was released. It lifted off in waves that seemed to wrinkle the air.

"I know that look," Laris said. "What did you do?"

"Nothing. I just, ya know, stole a craft to bust off the New World station." At Laris's look, she added, "Hey! It was for noble reasons. I was saving you."

"So, you went hurtling through deep space, in a ship you'd never operated before, and just figured it out all alone?"

"Naw. Booger tagged along."

Laris cocked her head to the side, allowing it to rest on Jinx's shoulder for one brief moment. The tiny two-seater suddenly felt smaller.

Shifting in her seat, Laris scanned the barren landscape, searching in every direction. "I knew it had been wiped out, but there's literally nothing here."

"Unless you count sand and rubble," Jinx said. "It's still pretty cool, but it's definitely different from the images projected in the Takal's office. Of the hundreds they had in rotation, none looked like this."

Laris's eyes flickered with amusement. "How many times a day did you get in trouble and end up there?"

"That's not the point of this particular story," Jinx said. "But if you must know, twice a week was my minimum."

Laris raised a single brow in a look that conveyed judgment or marvel or disbelief. Jinx wasn't sure which.

"Well, a handful of times were on purpose," Jinx said, a tad defensively.

"Why?"

"Does it really matter?"

"No," Laris said. "I'm just curious."

Jinx shrugged. "I had virtual games and some other crap smuggled in. Had to meet the delivery mules there at very specific times."

Laris raised her brow higher. "You broke rules just to get carted off to the Takals?"

"Well, yeah, mostly. Plus, I was bored."

Laris shook her head.

"And," Jinx muttered, "I was trying to check on you before my Galactic Release."

Laris beamed. "Really?"

"Yeah," Jinx replied, mindlessly tugging at her earlobe. "It seemed weird that I was the only one rejected from the VR program. I wanted answers, and I needed to know you were safe."

Laris smiled. "I guess you really are a noble troublemaker."

Jinx straightened her posture. "Yes. Well . . . sometimes. Fortunately for us, I am. It led me to Jacob." With a smirk, she added, "Who do you think my supplier was?"

"Meeting him was—"

Jinx held up her hand. "Do not say 'destiny.'"

"Fine. How about fate?"

"Same thing."

"Kismet?"

"I have an aversion to them all. If situations in life are fated, I may as well hang around and wait for everything to unfold around me." Jinx captured Laris's gaze reflected in the windshield. "When it comes to you, that's not something I'm willing to do. Saving you from

Bayne's amplifier and making our way here was the result of action, not destiny."

"Destiny does not have a single road." Laris's eyes shifted as though she'd smiled, but her lips didn't move. "Back to the Takals and the visions of Earth projected on their walls."

"I always looked forward to seeing it," Jinx said, happy to switch topics. "Sometimes, it was a rainforest, then the next day it was a snow-covered mountain."

"You mean the aftermath of an atomic war wasn't in the rotation?"

"Shocking. Right?" Jinx chuckled. "Don't get me wrong, when I'm battling Tarxis in a virtual reality, this is exactly the dismal landscape I want. But I'd prefer my planet of origin to not be a wasteland."

"I wouldn't give up on her just yet," Laris said. "Dismal or not, I'm selfishly happy you're here."

"This should bother me more than it does." Jinx offered a lopsided grin, then paused to regard Laris. "Epic battles or not, I'd rather have you safely tucked away than responsible for saving OI."

"I'm not responsible for saving organic life, just restoring balance."

"So, you, alone, are supposed to fix this?"

"I'm not alone. The Attendants are very powerful. All of you. I'm just, I guess, like a doorway for something to move through."

Jinx's nostrils flared. "You're more than a freaking doorway."

Laris pressed her palms to her chest as though paying respect to the words that followed. "There's a saying: one who aligns with the vibration of love emits the power of the universe." She lowered her hands and stared out over the vast emptiness. "I'm supposed to align with that energy and anchor it into our reality. I think," she added with a bemused grin.

Jinx shook her head and stared out across the arid landscape. "I'm pretty sure whatever I'm emitting isn't the power of the universe."

Laris locked eyes with Jinx in the reflection ahead. "You're the most beautiful being I've ever known. You just haven't seen it for yourself." Shifting her gaze down, her tone withered. "But this, what I'm here to do . . . it feels like I'll disappear."

Jinx started to speak but stopped short. Whatever Laris needed to do was probably more than Jinx could understand. Pushing her to explain it seemed like a bad idea. Besides, something in her gut told her she didn't want to know. If it was hard for Laris to accept, she knew it would be twice as awful for her.

"Hey!" Jinx nudged Laris. "Disappearing is my thing. I'm the only one in this prophecy allowed to have that particular power."

Laris flashed a sly grin. "I'm feeling greedy. I want the power to teleport!"

"I don't think so." Jinx lifted one of Laris's gangly arms and allowed it to drop with a thud. "You don't have enough meat on your bones to burn the extra calories."

"Fine. You'll just have to cart me around when I have the urge to go somewhere."

"I'm your Protector, not your intergalactic chauffeur."

"And you're the best Protector in the universe."

"I'm motivated."

Laris blushed and shifted her gaze. Her head jutted in a double-take. "Hey, look!" She pointed towards a dark patch in the distance. "I think there's something green down there." It was the first spot to break up the otherwise endless stretch of tan.

A look flashed between them.

"Claire and Jacob are gonna go ballistic." As Jinx maneuvered the craft to close the distance, an oasis took shape. She engaged the ship's comm. "You guys picking up the camera feed?"

Jacob's voice filled the cockpit. "This moment is legendary."

Claire's words landed like a stifled squeal. "Get as close as you can but move slowly. I wanna scoop up samples of *everything* living within that glorious ecosystem!"

Thick greenery hugged the Earth, stretching out forty feet to form a lush circle around pooling water. Jinx carefully dipped down, barely disturbing the air.

"That's low enough," Claire said. "Hover there while I collect samples."

The soft click and hum of gears pulled Jinx's attention up with a nervous shot while throwing a shielding arm over Laris. She let her guard drop as she peered through the roof of the clear quartz cockpit. Thin tentacles emerged from Claire's contraption, snaking downwards to forage for specimens.

"How about a little warning next time?" Jinx grumbled.

"Sorry," Claire whispered back. "I forgot to..."

All words fell away as a swarm of viridescent insects burst out to fill the sky, flashing luminous green against a darkening backdrop. Laris's muted reflection blended with the scene beyond the windshield, fusing her likeness with the single spot of life in an otherwise desolate landscape.

This is what I imagined Earth would be, Jinx thought as she watched the delicate fluttering. They seemed so fragile, as though a strong gust of wind would do them in. Yet here they were, practically ruling the world, and reminding her that OI encompassed far more than her fellow two-legged beings. *They definitely deserve protecting.* This tiny oasis and everything thriving there was as close to the brink as the rest of organic intelligence.

A breathless stretch later, the winged dynasty descended, disappearing back into their kingdom.

Jinx exchanged an enchanted glance with Laris.

"Wow. That was . . ."

"Yeah. It was." Laris beamed.

"I think we've disturbed them enough," Jinx said as she lifted the ship. The sound of spindly legs retracting back into their docking station followed."Claire, you got what you need?"

"She's practically foaming at the mouth," Jacob replied.

"Great, 'cause we're headed back."

"Better make it fast," Jacob said. "Pretty sure Hadu isn't someone you want to keep waiting."

"Crap. I lost track of time." The sun had dipped low enough to perch on the horizon. Darkness hadn't set in, but the hint of stars peppered the sky. Jinx flipped on the rear monitor as she gunned the engine and watched the hopeful glow of the oasis pale with distance.

A chance glance later and she'd have missed the flash, like sunlight hitting metal.

"Jacob, you got a minute to double-check something?" Jinx spoke with a labored calm, careful not to disturb Laris's numinous vibe.

"Sure. I'm just setting up my lab in one of the empty quarters. Claire doesn't like to share her toys, and neither do I."

"Shocker," Jinx replied. "Did you record a visual scan of the oasis as I pulled away?"

"Of course. The camera is still running. Why?" Jacob asked.

Jinx clamped down on the angst ballooning in her belly. "I thought I saw something reflective flash by."

"I didn't pick up on anything technological," Jacob said. "Maybe it was water vapor."

"I don't like 'maybe.'" Jinx resisted the urge to clutch her temples in a nervous grip. "Can we try and get confirmation?"

"No problem. I'll check the footage and ask Claire to review the data on organic life that's coming in. Maybe it'll give us a clue."

"Thanks," Jinx replied while keeping an eye on the rear view. "We'll be back in a few minutes. Can you make sure the hangar security is set up to quarantine the commuter? I don't want any uninvited guests making it onto the ship."

CHAPTER EIGHT

"You're late." Hadu's voice exited the opening door before Jinx could rehearse her excuse.

"Barely," Jinx shot back. Of course, Hadu had been waiting and watching. Begrudgingly, Jinx stepped into the room. "I'd be more than happy to give up hunting for threats just so I could be on time."

"This is not an either/or situation." Hadu sat behind her desk, regarding Jinx. "Besides, I know good and well there are few things you'd rather do than dance with danger."

"True." Jinx scanned the room as she stepped in, searching for a place to sit. "Wasn't there an armchair here?" she asked, motioning towards the vacant spot in front of Hadu's desk.

"It won't be necessary," Hadu said.

"Uh. Okay." Jinx bent to a crouch, prepared to sit on the floor.

"Please, remain standing."

Jinx pushed back up. An uneasiness rumbled her insides. "It's a standing thing. Great."

"No," Hadu said flatly. "Until you understand the power of your word, there is little point in these sessions."

Jinx pinched her brow so tight her entire face puckered. "I was barely late. It's not as though I was standing around wasting time."

Hadu stared back silently.

Jinx threw her hands up in exasperation. "I'm sorry."

"You needn't apologize to me. I'm not inclined to take the actions of another personally." Hadu entwined her fingers as she rested her hands atop her desk. "You do yourself a great disservice when you do not follow through on your word."

"Actually, I feel pretty at peace about running late, today." Jinx widened her stance. It did little to strengthen her resolve. The nerves firing warning shots in her gut insisted she was entering perilous territory. Her stubbornness was doomed to backfire in the presence of Hadu.

"It is in the seemingly small acts that the foundation for greatness is built," Hadu said. "When you come to realize that your word *is* the power that shapes worlds, then you will offer it more thoughtfully."

"I promise, I won't be late again."

"One's word is more than a promise. It is a declaration. It is an intention that guides your actions." Hadu pushed away from her desk and out of her chair. Slowly, she moved across the room towards Jinx as if to punctuate her words. "You must be able to trust that if you say it is so, then so it shall be. Do not take this casually. This understanding will push you to achieve what reason, excuse, and inconvenience will undermine." Hadu paused by Jinx's side, towering over her as she placed a hand on her shoulder. "Honor your word, and mountains will move."

Jinx opened her mouth to speak but realized she had nothing to say.

Hadu gently guided Jinx towards the door. Without a word, she opened it and ushered Jinx out.

Jinx stood slack-jawed, watching as the door slid shut. A stunned moment later, she turned heel and headed towards the ship's deck, knowing she'd find it empty. Perfect for brooding in peace.

CHAPTER NINE

"Wow, you've been busy," Jinx said as she stepped into Jacob's makeshift lab.

"You could say that," Jacob replied, looking up from some complicated contraption he was assembling. "You finally pulled yourself away from the security cameras. What inspired that act of bravery?"

"Food," Jinx replied. "Who knew staring at screens all night could work up an appetite?" She held up a container. "In case you haven't stopped to eat, I brought breakfast. Don't ask me what it is, though. It's shaped like something but tastes like nothing." Crossing the room, she moved through neatly curated piles of supplies, one of which had captured DeeDee's undivided attention. The kid was practically a blur as she examined each item like they were puzzle pieces.

"Done!" DeeDee declared, whirling around and smiling expectantly.

"Nice work," Jacob said. "Wanna send me the inventory list and then start putting things away?" DeeDee shrugged, implying she had nothing better to do. "Claire and I split up the supplies. There was a surprising amount, but I still have a pretty long wish list. I don't even have the right tools to take apart the rest of Bayne's amplifier." Jacob pushed to his feet, admiring his creation. "What do ya think?"

Jinx circled Jacob, eyeballing his latest project without the slightest clue, its glory lost on her. "I give up. I don't know what *that* is or *this*," she said, presenting the to-go container before setting it on the nearest invention-free surface.

"Fuel. Thanks!" Jacob lifted the lid on his breakfast, puckered his face, then sighed. "Someone needs to teach you how to use the meal processor. This is, well, sad." Picking up the fork, he waved it towards his contraption. "I present . . . *the vault.*" Jacob eyed his invention lovingly. "It's sort of a Faraday cage but effective on high *and* low frequencies. I can use it to test ways to protect us against a broad range. With the electromagnetic radiation ramping up in the universe, extra protection wouldn't hurt. And since we have easy access to quartz crystal, I might even whip up some orgonite pucks and put them around the perimeter. That should help neutralize the EMFs until Laris has a chance to balance it." He offered a hopeful grin before moving towards another creation in the works. "I'm building this to capture any rogue nanobots that might have survived Earth's near-annihilation. If they're active, I could reverse-engineer them. You never know what might come in handy. Maybe I'll create my own nano-army."

"Cool." Jinx grinned, imagining Jacob leading a swarm of intelligent pests. "But I hope you plan on insulating them too. Hadu will have a few words to say if you're adding to the crap we're trying to balance out."

Jacob cocked his head and wrinkled his brow. "Duh."

"Just double-checking," Jinx said, instinctively lifting a hand to the EMF protection tag on the back of her arm. "Dare I ask how long your supply list is?"

"It's shorter than Claire's," Jacob shot back.

Jinx hopped up to sit on the desk. "Fine. I'll figure out how to get everything back from the supply station."

"It's called a chair," Jacob said, pointing to one of four arranged around the room. "Have you ever used one?"

Sliding off the desk, Jinx opted for circling the room like a moving target. "Any ideas on how to stretch the ship's shield to include the pyramids? I'd really like a buffer around the ship as wide as possible."

Jacob took a cautious bite of his meal. With a nod of approval, he took a second before answering. "Are you still worried about that flash you saw yesterday?"

"Among other things." Jinx moved through the room, distracting herself with its contents, and paused briefly to watch DeeDee in action. The runt gave her a buzz-off look, sending Jinx on her way.

"Well, Claire's working on it," Jacob said, "but without anchors, the shield will only hold for a brief time."

"What's your idea of 'brief?'" Jinx asked. "Long enough to blink to the supply station and back?" Whether that was even possible was another story.

"We'll have a few hours with no issue. Worst case scenario, the shield doesn't hold and only the ship is protected. Maybe we can have a quick drink at the bar," Jacob said, waggling his brows. "Ya know, pretend we have normal lives with a moment of chill time in the real world."

"Can we hold off on the 'chill time' for now?"

"I don't think ten minutes to be human is too much to eke out," Jacob said. "I'm not good at being confined."

Jinx stopped in her tracks. "I'm dealing with the same conditions you are."

"Oh please," Jacob grumbled. "You were in confinement for two years. This is freedom for you."

"No. It's not. But I'm not pushing against it, either." Jinx moved to Jacob's side, placing a hand on his arm. "I can relate. And I promise I'll get you the time you need to chill. But I don't want to take off and leave this place unguarded a minute longer than we need to."

"I know." Jacob sighed. "Sorry. I'm just getting edgy. That's all. But you and I are gonna kick back with some tunes and litmorian, even if it's just on this ship. If you don't take time to be human, this life is gonna eat you up."

"Fine. You can teach me the art of chill'n." Jinx raised her hand in an oath. "I promise."

Jacob snorted. "That might be harder than saving OI."

"Probably." Jinx smirked. "How much more time do you and Claire need to get your list together?"

"Should be done sometime tomorrow." Jacob lifted his fork for another bite, then decided against it, setting the plate down apathetically. "Have you decided where to drop in from the blink?"

"No. Any ideas?"

"How about my old lab? I can grab some stuff. I wiped everything too dangerous to leave behind, but some of the basic tools and equipment should be salvageable. Well, assuming it didn't get picked clean or destroyed."

Fat chance, Jinx thought. The last time they'd seen the place, a group of hired guns was mounting an attack at the door. "Maybe." She ran a hand along her skull, thinking back to her narrow escape with all the pieces of her brain intact. "Assuming it was Sartillias's militia who crashed your lab, I doubt he's there waiting for us to come back."

"He was pretty motivated to swipe your pineal gland," Jacob said. "At the price he was selling Euphoria tabs, I'm not surprised. But I agree. I seriously doubt he'd post his thugs at my door just to snag one more gland to process."

"He wouldn't have sent in a militia for just me," Jinx said. "Ultimately, he was on the hunt for something or someone else. I was just a breadcrumb."

"You think he was tracking down Laris?" Jacob asked.

"I'm betting, yes," Jinx said. "I think he knows about the prophecy. The way his goons were talking after they nabbed me definitely led me to believe it."

"Maybe he doesn't want the pineal," Jacob said. "Maybe an extraordinarily-functioning gland is how he'd know if he'd found The One, aka Laris."

"Anyone motivated to come looking for Laris is likely after the same thing he is," Jinx said. "Maybe we should try and figure out Sartillias's endgame."

"True. Laris's power to produce a healing frequency might be vulnerable to tampering." Jacob paused to make a slight adjustment to the lineup of tools on his desk.

Jinx stifled a laugh at the minor tweak. "Thanks for fixing that. It was driving me crazy."

"Order on the outside keeps focus on the inside," Jacob said, tapping his skull.

"Whatever you say," Jinx said as she slid into pacing mode. "For now, let's assume that anyone who's hunting down The One is prowling the universe right now and not stationed outside your old lab. If that's the case, is it safe to blink to your door? Can I scope out the situation without attracting attention?"

"Theoretically, yes. The corridor is always pretty quiet. That's why I picked it."

"I suppose that's good enough." Jinx shrugged. "There's no perfect choice."

Jacob raised a finger. "Hold on." Engaging his com, he spoke. "What's up, Claire-bear?" His expression turned to a smirk. "You're so agro." A silent moment stretched. "Fine. What's up, *Claire* minus the bear." Another moment passed. "Perfect. You're a star." Jacob brought his attention back to Jinx. "Claire said we're good to go, but I'll need to shut down and then re-engage the shield to wrap it around the pyramids. For some reason, it won't recalibrate."

Jinx went wide-eyed. "Seriously?"

"Only be down for a second." Jacob tried to sound nonchalant. "Right now, it's our only option."

"I don't like the odds." Jinx knew trouble lived in security gaps, no matter how fleeting. She had waited and watched for opportunities just like this to bypass alarm systems. "Pull up the camera feed outside the ship. I wanna check the perimeter again before we shut it down."

"You've been glued to the security feed for over twelve hours," Jacob said. "Do you really think something has changed in the ten minutes it took you to deliver breakfast or whatever that food-like substance is?"

"Let's hope not."

"OK. Just to ease your mind, one last look." One of two screens mounted on the far wall came to life, offering an aerial view of their surroundings. They zoomed in on every potential hiding place within range, nothing stood out. "What do you think?"

"Uh. Still nervous. But like you said, we don't really have a choice. Hadu needs access to the pyramids, and I want the security field pushed out further." Jinx stared at the screen, hoping it would give a comforting sign. It didn't offer an opinion one way or another. Drawing in an audible breath, she conceded. "Let's go for it."

"Hey Claire, did you catch that?" Jacob asked. "Just let us know when you're ready, and I'll shut down the system."

Jinx fixed her attention to the screen. "Just keep the aerial view stationary."

Jacob gave a thumbs-up. "We go in three . . . two . . . one."

Jinx noticed Jacob's wristband flash red, alerting him that security was down. At least his monitoring system worked, not that she really doubted it.

"Claire, I'm bringing the system back up." Jacob's tone shifted to a controlled alarm. "What do you mean?"

Jinx locked onto the monitor. *Do not take your eyes off this screen,* she warned herself, barely resisting the urge to look towards Jacob.

"I don't see a problem in the system. Try again," Jacob said. The silent moment stretched uncomfortably long. "You got it? Great." Jacob released a heavy sigh, placing a hand on Jinx's shoulder. "The security is up. We have the pyramids covered, but right now it's only a one-way protection."

Jinx pinched the bridge of her nose. "Meaning what?"

"The ship's security was either set up or re-engineered to keep threats out, but it wasn't designed to keep someone from leaving," Jacob replied. "It'll take a little retooling to correct that. But at least for the moment, no one outside the field can get in."

Jinx's insides stiffened. "Not ready to celebrate just yet." Who knew what Bayne had done to the ship or if it was his handiwork at all? Maybe the New World station had designed all their levels that way. Didn't matter why. The fact remained: it was a problem. Jinx didn't budge from the monitor.

"Want me to check the —"

"Something is inside the security field; they're racing towards the ship!" Without thinking, Jinx dropped down, slamming her fist to the ground.

Blink.

Jacob's words trailed behind a moment too late. "You need an S.I.S. suit! The area hasn't been stabilized. The air has too much . . ."

***

A high-pitched buzz crackled like static. Jinx braced herself for the end of the blink as her body took shape; her skin tingled as blood sped to body parts. She hadn't expected the heat of the sand to sear her skin. It was shockingly hot. She sucked in a breath. The air tasted sour. *Crap. Carbon dioxide.* That wasn't the only issue. There were bound to be airborne hazards that could attach themselves or infect her system.

"Make a quarantine space for me. Quick. I'll blink back with this fool, once I nab 'em."

Jinx scanned the landscape, barely catching sight of the invader. Cloaked in white, they blended in with the blazing desert. She fixed her sight and slammed her fist.

Blink.

They were faster than Jinx had calculated — more than twenty feet outside her grasp.

Blink.

The second attempt bombed too. *Time to do things the old-fashioned way.* Jinx took off on foot.

"You better make it quick," Jacob's voice bellowed. "There's not enough oxygen in the air to be out there too long."

"Yeah. I figured that one out." As Jinx raced around the perimeter of the ship, her heart pounded uncomfortably, fighting to get enough oxygen. This guy was fast, and she was struggling to close the distance. If she lost them, they'd likely find a way onto the ship. With no way to contain them within the security field, they could cause some damage before getting away.

"Claire has quarantine units on hangar two set up," Jacob's voice blasted through.

"You need to blink back *now*," Claire interrupted. "It's not healthy to be out there."

Jinx didn't answer. Talking required oxygen she couldn't afford. *This might be the most idiotic thing you've ever done*, she told herself. There were plenty to choose from, so it was hard to say. But losing sight of the threat wasn't an option. There had to be countless spots to tuck away until the timing was right, especially now that the pyramids were within the shield.

"Something is attempting to override the security on hangar one." Jacob sounded calm. Clearly, the attempt was hardly more than a nuisance. "I'm disabling their attempts, but heads up."

Exactly why I want a buffer, Jinx grumbled to herself. *No one should reach the ship. Ever.* Taking a few more strides, she came to an abrupt halt. Hangar one was in the opposite direction. She was chasing a diversion. "Seal off hangar one from the rest of the ship. If someone tries to board, let them."

"What?" Claire yelped.

"Send DeeDee to wait. And make sure they think they have control of the system, then trap them in the hangar," Jinx said.

"You should have just started with this plan," Jacob said.

"Oh, I'm sorry, I didn't map this out in the zero time I had." Jinx dropped to her knee, gasping for breath. "Wouldn't have worked, anyway. They wanted us distracted." A wave of nausea hit. She choked it back, unsuccessfully, and retched. *Gross.* She wiped her mouth, then dragged her hand along the scorching sand, creating a warm, gritty paste between her fingers.

"Seriously, Jinx, you need to get back."

Jinx couldn't tell whose voice it was as she slumped to the ground, fighting the overwhelming desire to close her eyes . . . for just a second. "I have a plan," she muttered as she allowed her cheek to drop to the sand, ignoring the blistering heat roasting her skin.

"Your plan sucks."

If someone was watching the scene from a distance, possibly giving direction, they'd see Jinx go down. At least that's what she was counting on.

"You haven't heard my plan," Jinx tried to say between small sips of air. A dizzying fog swallowed her senses, taking her under.

"What are you doing, dummy?"

Jinx laughed. *Dummy. Way to kick me when I'm down.*

"You won't last long out there."

Laris? Jinx dreamily questioned. *We had a deal, get out of my head.*

"I've kept my end of the deal. You know I'd never enter your mind uninvited. But you've left me no choice. You're being reckless. Now, blink back onto the ship!"

Jinx ran her hand along the sand as the urge to giggle took over.

"Do it now! Unless you prefer that I come out there and save you. I think we both know how that would turn out."

The thought of Laris—or anyone, for that matter—leaving the ship to save her was sobering. "A few more minutes." With two, maybe more, infiltrators circling the ship, she planned to snag at least one.

Crumpled on the sand, Jinx remained as motionless as possible, which wasn't a challenge in her oxygen-depleted state. Landing face-plant inches from her recycled meal, however, was difficult to stomach. But bearable. Helping herself to mere snatches of air, she waited for a signal from Jacob — a message that someone had boarded the ship or signs the assailant she'd been chasing was near.

"He's back, forty feet behind you." Jacob was a whisper in her ear. "But the ship is still silent. No one has boarded the hangar." The sound of muted conversation replaced Jacob's voice for a moment before he spoke again. "Your breathing should ease up a little. Claire engaged the UV transmitter, so it's converting the CO2 to oxygen inside of the shield."

Jinx's weak heartbeat kissed the ground with slow, struggling thumps. *Thank you, Claire.*

The hushed moment shifted when Jacob whispered again. "I don't like this. Blink back and let's figure out a new plan."

Jinx didn't respond. The sound of a cautious step nearing stilled her breath. It was accompanied by a dark presence that could cast a midnight shadow.

"She's down. Yes, I'm sure. The idiot isn't wearing an S.I.S. This infiltration should be a cakewalk."

It took everything not to lunge for his foot and blink. If Jinx missed, he'd just escape and wait for another opportunity to infiltrate.

The invader turned and began running towards hangar one. "I'll be on board in a minute. No. We don't need another backup. This will be wrapped up quickly."

Jinx didn't move until they disappeared into the sand-color abyss. "Jacob, did you catch all of that?"

"Yes," Jacob said. "That guy is annoyingly cocky."

"True. But they're probably highly trained. Once they're on board, let me know so I can get back. If I make a move now, we'll miss our chance to trap them. Someone must be keeping watch."

"How's the air?" Jacob asked. "You holding up?"

"I'll be fine. I'm just ready to contain these guys. Is DeeDee in place?"

"Yeah. She's playing hopscotch in the hangar," Jacob replied. "Well, that and testing some calculations for me."

"What?"

"She's running some numbers through —"

"No," Jinx said. "Not that. What the drek is hopscotch?"

"Oh. That. It's some Earth game. She's been gobbling up a bunch of random data stored in the satellites still floating around the atmosphere."

Jinx felt the sand shift under her bodyweight. The desire to remain there, motionless, blanketed under the oppressive heat, was weirdly tempting — that is, until the oxygen level rose. Now, every breath sharpened her thoughts. Her cells buzzed, reminding her she was alive and built for the fight. Well, that and the blistering pain emanating from her cheek.

"Get ready to roll," Jacob said. "The hangar is officially open."

"Make sure DeeDee knows to hang back in the shadows until both are on board. She is to contain them, not annihilate."

"Roger that."

Jinx closed her eyes while the line went silent, trying to steady her resolve. Her heart hammered, fueled by fight and fear. She was willingly allowing threats on board in hopes of getting an edge. Every choice, every decision had too much weight to bear comfortably.

"Here come our guests," Jacob said. "Closing the hangar in three . . . two . . . one."

Blink.

CHAPTER TEN

Jinx launched into motion as she resurfaced from the blink and raced across the hangar, attempting to look sturdier than she truly was. The carbon dioxide coursing through her system heated her skin to an itchy flush while nausea threatened to expel any last remnants of breakfast.

Pushing past the stabbing pain in her chest and the flaming flesh on her face, she scanned her surroundings to size up the situation. If DeeDee didn't have the intruders cornered, she'd like to avoid being an easy target.

Her dash came to an abrupt halt.

"Hi, Jinx!" DeeDee beamed over her shoulder from across the room, diverting her attention momentarily from the two assailants she kept cornered.

"Stay focused, Booger," Jinx yelled as she took off at a breakneck pace, resisting the urge to buckle over in pain. Turning your back on a Starltonian was never a good idea. Even at a distance, she made out enough features to recognize the species and knew what they'd do next. Their massive horns pinched back as if perpetually craving a fight. Their thick-ribbed skin, which always inflated before an attack, was visible from across the room. She'd only battled the species in virtual worlds but had come face-to-face with them on the supply station. It was enough to know that underestimating them never turned out well.

In the split-second lapse, the Starltonians attempted to maneuver around DeeDee, who, in a rare miscalculation, barely had time to deliver a sloppy roundhouse kick. It was forceful enough to send them tumbling back against the wall, but the inelegance didn't sit well with DeeDee. Her features narrowed as she locked attention on her captives.

Jinx caught the shift in DeeDee's demeanor. *No. No. No. We need them alive.* The thought hammered as Jinx made a running slide to her side. "Nice job, Booger." Jinx bit back the urgency as she delivered the words. Making note of the female assailant's blushing eye, she added, in as chipper a tone as she could muster, "You do that?"

DeeDee didn't seem to register the question. The tension left Jinx wondering if she'd need to clear out if her young warrior didn't snap out of it.

"That's gonna bruise up nicely." Thumbing towards DeeDee, Jinx warned, "Watch out. This one's got a brutal right hook. But I suppose you know that already."

The infiltrators offered little in the way of reaction, seemingly unconcerned with the situation, which didn't surprise Jinx. But the fact that Jacob hadn't picked up on their presence was noteworthy. It meant only one thing: they were unaugmented. Made sense. If you were gonna make a career out of sneaking past security, probably a good idea to not cyborg yourself.

"I'd love to move you two to quarantine without a freaking problem." Jinx felt them sizing her up. "Normally, I'd welcome a quick battle, but we need to move on to the interrogation portion of your visit." Swinging her arm, she motioned for them to step forward. "So, if you wouldn't mind, head to one of the two doors over there. Both are equipped to scan you and clear out the crap we'd rather not have on board."

"Yeah. We know what quarantine is," the female said.

"How 'bout trespassing?" Jinx replied.

The female offered a heated hand gesture. The male remained impressively calm.

Jinx laughed, sending a curious glance towards the male. "What happened? Your normal partner bail on this cakewalk of an assignment? Now you're stuck with her?" When neither responded, Jinx twirled her hand. "Come on. Come on. Let's just get this over with. I walk. You follow." Placing a guiding hand on DeeDee, she gently shifted her attention, effectively breaking the murderous spell. "You take the rear."

Sensing they shared the same irksome traits, Jinx took a step forward, knowing the female wouldn't be able to contain herself. Giving it a fraction of a second, she dropped to the ground, feeling the weight of the female topple over in a failed attack. Jinx considered simply grabbing her and blinking to quarantine, but dragging her in a stranglehold would make a more profound point.

"Booger, please escort our other guest," Jinx called out over her shoulder. Multiple footsteps followed.

By the time Jinx made it across the hangar, she wished she'd simply blinked to the quarantine cell. The Starltonian had, of course, struggled the entire way, which was exhausting. Plus, Jinx was feeling rank after the near-overdose of CO2 and oddly hungry. But the pleasure of shoving the intruder into the cell and locking the door made up for the nuisance.

Pivoting on her heel, Jinx watched DeeDee march alongside the male Starltonian, which would have been comical if not for the gravity of the situation. The adolescent enforcer barely reached his abdomen. He towered over DeeDee with composed power. Jinx studied him as he casually strolled along and wondered why he'd not put up a fight. Moving her attention up, they locked eyes. He smirked, holding her gaze for nearly a moment too long.

Something's not right. I'm missing something. Jinx jerked her attention away and quickly scanned the entire scene. Something so small it was nearly imperceptible zipped high above. It'd easily go unnoticed except for the light glinting off its surface.

"Jacob! Are the vents sealed?" Her question went moot as she watched the thing make its way towards the nearest slats.

"Of course," Jacob called back.

"Double-check!" Jinx raced across the hangar, towards the air vent, and scaled the wall. With a failed swat, the tiny, metal-winged creature disappeared into the vent. Jinx dropped to the ground. "Booger, knock him out and throw him in quarantine."

The sound of one heavy body crashing to the ground disappeared in her wake.

Blink.

***

The edges of the world remained fuzzy like a fading dream.

"Come on. Come on. Come on," Jinx yelled as her body took form with Laris a few feet away. Even blurry, it was clear she was watching something beyond Jinx's view. The familiar feel of becoming solid was coupled with pangs of dread. Jinx threw up her hands, casting a protective bubble around Laris. It snapped into place a second too late.

Laris swatted the side of her neck, sending something to the floor with a barely audible *tink.*

"Wait!" Jacob skidded into view, lunging for the metal pest before Jinx's foot came crashing down. "We might need it," he said, between panting breaths. In one swift motion, he'd sealed it in a container.

Jinx barely regained her balance in time to catch her footing, pivoting awkwardly to avoid crushing Jacob's hand. "That thing just bit Laris."

"I know. I saw it enter the vent."

"I thought you said the vents were sealed," Jinx barked as she reached for Laris.

"They were . . . and still are." Jacob held up the transparent container. "This little guy can increase its vibration to such a high rate it's able to move through solids." Jacob eyed the diminutive metal beast buzzing systematically around the canister. "It can't break out of this, though. I've lined it with —"

Jinx raised a halting hand. "I'm sure it's impressive, but not the right time to geek out," she said, brushing Laris's hair from her neck with no idea what to look for. "We need to get you to Claire."

"I'm fine," Laris said, waving it off.

Jinx pulled Laris towards the door. "You don't know that." Turning to Jacob, she asked, "What is that thing?"

Jacob cradled the box, eyeballing his new prize. "I'll let you know when I figure it out."

"Don't you have enough toys?" Jinx said as they moved into the corridor.

"Hey, this is either sophisticated technology or some archaic, albeit clever, leftover. I'll need to study it. If it did something to Laris . . ." Jacob let the thought dangle. "And no, I never have enough toys." He turned the clear box in his hands, watching the metal creature's futile attempts to escape.

"Where's Claire?" Jinx asked.

"Hangar two. You know, the place you were supposed to quarantine *before* entering the rest of the ship."

"Crap." Jinx leapt back from Laris and Jacob before realizing it was too late to bother.

"She's there, waiting." Jacob grinned. "And not too happy about it."

CHAPTER ELEVEN

Jinx paced the ten-foot quarantine chamber with a cuticle clamped between her teeth. Normally, she'd feverishly gnaw the flesh, but nothing was left except tender exposed skin from her last nervous feast. The best she could do now was suck her thumb. She hoped it wouldn't become some embarrassing new habit. Peering through the clear, soundproof wall, she watched Claire run a series of tests on Laris.

"So . . ."

Claire didn't look up from the data rolling across the screen. "Stop worrying. You're gonna wear a groove in the floor."

"You know what? When you're certain Laris is fine, I'll stop pacing."

Laris sat quietly watching Jinx as Claire removed the sensors from her skin. A wisp of a softly set smile hinted at something Jinx couldn't quite decipher. Amusement. Endearment. Serenity. Probably a shade of them all.

"None of the tests I ran found anything in Laris's system. If she develops symptoms, I'll run more." Claire paused. Glancing up from her screen, she gave Jinx a pointed look. "You're lucky I found only one potentially dangerous bacterium in *your* body."

Jinx stopped pacing, but her foot took up the slack and tapped at a hectic rate. "Yeah. That's me. Lucky."

"I've created an antibiotic that should knock it out immediately." Claire clicked a few keys and hit enter. A machine kicked to life, filling small vials with a blue liquid. A flash later, it went silent, lighting up to cast a lustrous green light. Claire removed one of the vials and inserted it into a roamer that instantly rolled away. "That'll take care of any pests that went airborne when you bounced through the dang ship." Claire inserted a second vial into a small metal cylinder and pressed its tip to Laris's shoulder. *Click*. Then her own. *Click*. Walking to the quarantine, she warned, "Get ready to be misted."

"Oh, come on," Jinx said, throwing up her hands. "Can't I just have the inoculation?"

"You're getting both. I don't wanna take any chances." Claire entered a command into the unit's control panel. A fine, damp mist hissed as it rained down on Jinx, who looked sour about the soggy situation. A moment later, the door to the quarantine opened. Claire tossed her the metal cylinder. "Here. Inoculate yourself. I've gotta go administer it to the rest of the ship."

"Sorry." Jinx slumped and lifted the inoculation pen to her arm. *Click.*

"Please. This is child's play," Claire said. "Give me a real challenge next time."

Jinx followed Claire towards Laris. "You're a twisted genius."

"You're both good to go." Claire held a hand to Laris's back as she eased to her feet. "Just find me if you start to feel anything other than, well, normal."

"I'm fine," Laris said, stretching her arms skyward as if rousing from nothing more than a midday nap. "Honestly. I think it just startled me when it landed on my neck."

Claire headed for the door. Laris trotted along with no urgency in her steps. Jinx kept by her side, watching like a hawk.

Just beyond the opening door, Jacob stood wearing an elaborate filtration mask. No doubt a contraption of his own making.

Claire tossed him a cylinder as she peeled off down the hall. "I told you that mask isn't protecting you. You were already exposed and the filter isn't —"

"I know. I know. But it doesn't hurt either." Jacob brought the cylinder to his shoulder before peeling off the mask. Taking a moment, he checked his hair. His hands moved adeptly, looking as though each strand had an assigned position.

"Hair number two hundred and five is misaligned," Jinx teased as she pushed past.

Laris trotted behind. "No. It was number two hundred and seven."

"You too, Laris?" Jacob said, moving swiftly to their side. "Fair warning, I do tease back."

"I hope so," Laris said, giving him a nudge. "I can take it."

"I believe it," Jacob said.

Jinx lifted a hand to her cheek, feeling for signs of blistered skin. As usual, Claire was a master at patching her up. Nudging Jacob's arm, she asked, "You coming along to question our party crashers?"

"Mm-hm," Jacob replied, moving with determined steps towards hangar one.

"Talk?" Laris asked, sounding dubious.

Jinx paused to glance over her shoulder. "Hey, I'm capable of restraining my impulses."

Jacob choked back a laugh. "Right. Why do you think I'm tagging along?"

Jinx raised a brow. "I'm controlling the impulse I'm having right now, for instance."

"Nobody likes a bully," Jacob teased.

"Hey, they knew what they signed up for when they chose careers as mercenaries."

"Great. It's settled." Laris picked up the hem of her dress and scurried down the hall. "We're just talking to them."

Turning to Jacob, Jinx spoke low. "Double-check that she can't enter the hangar. She thinks if she beats us there, she'll have an advantage." Raising her voice, Jinx called after Laris, "You aren't coming in there with us. I want distance between you and these fools."

Laris turned to flash an impossibly cheerful smile and kept running. "Well, you should have thought about that before letting them on board."

"I was trying to get an edge," Jinx mumbled.

"Claire is just as bad," Jacob said. "Seriously, the most stubborn person I've ever met." A smile claimed his face as if it were permanently linked to the thought of Claire.

"It might be a tie," Jinx replied. "What did you find out about our guests?"

"Nothing. They aren't talking. I listened in on their comms, but it's been silent. Whoever they came with either left or is waiting in the wings."

"Great. Let's hope our chat reveals something more useful." Jinx watched Laris skip through the corridor. It was clear she was enjoying herself. She made the sensation of being in a body look to be a new and delightful experience.

"Has she always been this way?" Jacob asked.

"You mean like a big kid or inexplicably carefree regardless of the situation?"

"Aren't those two the same?"

"I suppose," Jinx said. "And yeah, she has. She's always been tapped into something else. Sometimes, I wonder if life looks different through her eyes. Is she even seeing and hearing the same things I am?" She sighed. "The universe chose well, that's for sure."

Jacob nudged Jinx and looked her dead in the eyes. "Yeah, the universe did."

Jinx swallowed hard. "Back at'cha, genius."

Jacob looked down and smiled as they approached the hangar door. "What's next?"

"You tell me," Jinx replied. "I mean, we can't head out for supplies if the ship isn't safe."

Jacob shrugged. "Without those supplies, I can't build what we need to fortify this place."

"What about Bayne?" Laris chimed in.

Jinx narrowed her eyes and crossed her arms over her chest. "Bayne?"

"What about him?" Jacob asked while nervously fidgeting with something on his sleeve.

"Well, remember, he said he'd ensured that this ship was safe and nothing would get to the Attendants and me."

"Yeah, well, he had that amplifier heavily guarded." Jacob turned away.

Jinx studied him for a moment, thinking back to the day Jacob had mentally entered Bayne's security system to dismantle whatever insanity he'd put in place. Somehow, he had battled through a virtual boobytrap, an augmented reality nightmare, and shut down the amplifier. Whatever he had experienced left him shook, but he'd conquered it. Jacob had a quiet steel running through his veins. "Can you find out if he has any hidden security systems on board we can leverage?"

Jacob's eyes went wide. "You mean, like go talk to Bayne?"

"Yes," Jinx groaned.

"Now?"

"No, I need you near. As you two have pointed out, I'm not great at managing my impulses."

"You won't need to use violence," Laris said. "I can be very persuasive."

"Laris." Jinx ran a hand along her scalp, barely stifling the tantrum she desperately wanted to throw.

"I don't think you're gonna win this one," Jacob said, consoling Jinx with a pat on the back. "You may as well let her join us. Besides, next to you is probably the safest place for her to be."

"I told her the same thing!" Laris practically sang.

Jinx looked away. "That's debatable."

"Give yourself a break," Jacob said. "Heroes don't —"

"Yeah, yeah," Jinx said, swatting the air. "Heroes don't happen overnight." Releasing a burst of air, she wedged herself between Laris and the door while entering the security code. "Fine. I don't have the energy to battle you two, and we're wasting time."

Laris flashed a look of victory as the door opened. Jinx threw out her arm preventing her from dashing in. DeeDee took notice from across the hangar, momentarily pausing to grin and wave exuberantly.

Promptly, she returned her attention to the floor. A complex series of squares and numbers graffitied its surface.

Jinx cocked her head towards Jacob as they stepped in. "Hopscotch?"

Jacob shrugged. "Well, her version anyway."

Lowering her arm, Jinx allowed Laris to run free. She followed behind with measured steps, careful to navigate around DeeDee's masterpiece. There were shockingly few bare spots remaining. "Hey Booger, I may need you to join us."

"But I'm busy," DeeDee said, kicking the air with marked annoyance.

"If you see a fight break out, just get over here," Jinx said, shaking her head with exasperation. "And you two, hang back." Looking at Laris, she added, "Especially you. Please let me do the talking."

Jinx looked towards the chambers. The glass walls were shaded to pitch black. Cracking her knuckles, she moved towards them, entering a code as she stepped up. Slowly, the darkened walls lightened. Jinx allowed her nerves to ease as if synchronized with each lifting shade. As she tilted her head side to side, her spine released a series of cracks. Taking a few steps back, her heart picked up pace as both interiors came into clear view.

The female Starltonian stood captive in the right-side chamber with her arms crossed tightly, staring unblinkingly at Jinx. She delivered a few choice words that didn't make it through the soundproof walls. The single piece of furniture, a chair, was toppled on its side in the corner and badly warped, likely from hammering into the wall . . . repeatedly. The male sat in the left chamber, using the chair like a civilized mercenary, with his hands casually propped behind his horned head.

Jinx paced in front, sizing each one up, hoping to get a glimpse of something useful besides the fact that their hulking size was cringeworthy — not the type most would want to piss off. If it hadn't been for her newly acquired powers and measurable increase in strength, Jinx would admittedly feel far less optimistic.

Shielding his mouth, Jacob said, "Good luck with these two. Their race isn't known for being chatty."

"Shocker," Jinx replied over her shoulder. "I'm giving them audio, so just keep that in mind before speaking." After adjusting the sound, she moved towards the female, hoping her bad temper would be easier to manipulate than her partner's controlled exterior. "Looks like you've already done some redecorating," Jinx said, jutting a chin towards the chair. "Don't get too comfortable. You won't be staying with us long."

The female smirked.

Jinx took that to mean they hadn't been abandoned here or at least that wasn't part of the plan. There was always the slim chance they actually lived on Earth or a neighboring planet and were simply protecting their turf but unlikely. Turning to Jacob, she asked, "What's the most inhospitable place on Earth?"

After a brief pause, he replied, "Looks like an area called Antarctica is pretty extreme. Gets to almost one hundred degrees below zero."

"Hope you don't mind the cold." Jinx mocked a shiver and watched the female's expression twitch, barely. "Just kidding. I actually don't care what you mind. What I do care about, however, is finding out why you're here."

The female's nostrils flared.

Jinx braced herself for what she knew was coming next, determined not to flinch as the Starltonian's fist crashed against the chamber wall. "If you damage our chambers, we're gonna have to dock your pay." Tapping a finger to her chin, she added, "Oh wait, that probably won't work. I'm guessing you won't get paid for this job."

The female laughed. "What makes you say that?"

"You failed," Jinx replied flatly.

"No." The male chimed in. "We completed the mission."

Jinx turned her attention towards the male and fixed her gaze. A long, silent moment passed without breath. She felt the female's smug expression glued in place as if aching for Jinx to turn and receive it. The male, however, kept his eyes forward — fixed on some unchallenging spot in the distance. The three seemed caught in a showdown, of sorts.

"Nice to have a face for the target," the female said and turned a smug looked towards Laris.

"What are you talking about?" Jinx asked, keeping her tone as even as possible, certain she was being goaded into revealing Laris's identity.

The female ignored Jinx and locked eyes on Laris. "How are you feeling, precious?"

Laris moved to Jinx's side and whispered. "I'm fine. I promise."

Jinx shook her head and whispered back. "You clearly don't understand how this works."

"Thanks for satisfying my curiosity." The female's smile barely parted her thin lips.

Jinx grumbled under her breath. *I knew I shouldn't have let Laris in here.*

As insufferable as the Starltonian was, she confirmed one thing: they were sent here to target Laris, which meant the ship had been tracked from Redshift 7. Jinx clenched her fists so tightly they numbed.

Laris leaned in and gently whispered. "Breathe. Just breathe. Don't allow them to disturb your mind."

The warmth of her breath drifted across Jinx's neck. The blood rushed from her unfurling fists to the spot of flesh behind her ear.

"You may want to find a new mission." The female forced a laugh and thumbed towards Laris. "I'm assuming it matters if she's, hm, incapacitated."

Before restraint set in, Jinx dropped to the ground and slammed her fist into the floor. A flash later she was behind the female, pinning her in a headlock. "Jacob, can you get me the coordinates for the crappiest spot in Antarctica and a single S.I.S. suit?" Putting her mouth to the female's ear, she added, "The suit is just for kicks. The thought of you struggling to put it on in below-freezing weather makes me smile. I'm betting the cold chews up your flesh first."

Laris placed a hand on the glass. "This isn't you."

"I live for this," Jinx shot back.

"No. You don't."

"Honestly, this is way more generous than I'd like to be given the situation," Jinx said. "And they can't stay here. It's dangerous. And they aren't gonna give anything up. They're just gonna piss me off."

"Please let me try something first," Laris pleaded.

Jinx struggled to contain the thrashing mercenary. "I'm not letting you in here."

"Come back out," Laris said softly. "Just a chance is all I ask."

The moment stretched as Jinx and Laris locked eyes. "Fine," Jinx growled and tightened her hold. The Starltonian dropped to the ground with a rumble. Motionless. An instant later, Jinx was on the other side of the glass.

Laris's expression sunk.

"Don't worry, she'll be annoying us again in about five minutes," Jinx groused. "What?" she added impatiently, noticing the male watching her with stupefied curiosity. An unasked question distorted his expression. *Oh yeah. Crap.* It dawned on her. Blinking in front of them wasn't ideal. *Whatever*, she thought. *At this point, it doesn't matter.* Turning back towards Laris, Jinx added, "See. I can control my impulses."

Laris's eyes softened to a smile before she closed her lids. Laying her hands on the glass, she slowly walked around the chamber while speaking in hushed tones too delicate to decipher.

The mercenary fixed his gaze forward as though the moment were only a temporary inconvenience in his day.

Jinx felt Jacob move to her side. "What's Laris doing?"

"Your guess is as good as mine," Jinx replied, watching Laris move with weightless steps, blindingly guiding herself along with one hand while the other picked at invisible pieces in the air.

The mercenary's expression morphed, slowly, until his brow rippled in a tight pinch. His eyes jutted right to left as if reviewing information. Confusion flashed. His jaw locked. He pulled from the moment long enough to look towards Jinx and Jacob. "What is —"

"Shhh," Laris whispered, pulling his attention back in.

Moments later, he closed his eyes and lifted a hand to shield his face.

Laris lowered her hands. Her expression seemed to float as she glided towards the second chamber, where the female remained crumpled on the floor. Jinx took a step back to allow the sleepwalking mystic to move through.

"What did you do?" The male's voice was a bewildered whisper.

"Until one has the opportunity to experience the highest expression of themselves and choose, we should tread lightly as to not stunt their evolution." The steadiness of Laris's voice was infused with something vast. Ineffable. It was Laris, but . . . more. "Judgment serves no master. For whom you put in darkness calls you to the darkness. It is the law of co-resonance."

The male looked up, searching Jinx and Jacob for an answer, his features swaying between sadness and serenity.

Jinx shrugged. "Don't ask me. I'm just the muscle. How about something easier to answer: why are you here?"

The question jostled the male from a dreamy state, though he kept a dazed focus on Laris as she moved around his partner's chamber. "We don't ask. We just take jobs. But it must be important to whoever hired us." He glanced back at Jinx, giving weight to his next words. "We're *very* expensive."

"And you have no idea who hired you?" Jacob chimed in.

The male took a deep breath. "We don't know who requested the job, but it's someone with a lot of power. Very few know how to place an order with us," he said, puffing out his chest with practiced bravado, then instantly sunk back into himself. "We only accept contracts that are handed down through layers of people. It protects us and them."

"What did you bring on board?" Jinx narrowed her eyes, uncertain if the techno bug was their delivery or a creature that had made its way onto the ship.

The male stood, turned his chair, and returned to his seat, ending the interrogation.

"Not helpful." Jinx bristled, barely containing herself. The female began to lift from her induced nap. She was bound to be less willing than her partner. Jinx wasn't in the mood. Entering a command, the walls paled to darkness once again. "What do you think?"

Jacob stroked his chin while eyeing the darkened chambers. "Well, there are probably a lot of troublesome species that would want to track us down." With a shrug, he added, "But I just can't imagine this obscure prophecy we're enmeshed in is common knowledge. At least not yet."

Jinx raised her brows. "That brings us back to the one pain in the butt who likely knows about Laris."

Jacob nodded. "Yeah, Sartillias. I'd place bets on that guy. He's got the resources."

"No way he or anyone else is sending an expensive team of mercenaries this far just for pineal glands to cook up illicit party drugs."

"No doubt," Jacob said, mindlessly thrumming the flesh of his chin while staring off in thought. "Whoever it was could have sent in an army to infiltrate this place. Why send only two mercenaries? It's a pointless mission."

"Maybe they just wanted eyes inside of our security field, or maybe they wanted to know how we'd handle intruders. That's what I'd do: study my enemies' strategy and look for vulnerabilities and blind spots. Maybe even distract us with this nonsense" — Jinx motioned towards the chambers — "to deliver something more dangerous aboard."

"Yeah, the bot," Jacob said. "I haven't seen anything like it before, an inorganic creature emitting an organic signature."

"Any way to know who created it or what it does?"

"We're working on it," Jacob said, rocking on his heels. "Maybe we should take a break and check in with Claire."

"Fine. I've got a session with Hadu anyway," Jinx said with an eye roll. "Besides, there's nothing else to do here. I don't think these guys know much more than we do." She turned to catch DeeDee launching into a series of twisting flips across her newly constructed hopscotch sprawl. It had evolved into an acrobatic phenomenon. "You're telling me that this was a game that human kids created?"

"No way. This is far more complicated. But if I could flip, I'd play. Looks cool."

"Hey, Booger," Jinx called out. "Keep an eye on these two."

"But watching them is boring," DeeDee replied before launching into another series of leaps and flips.

"You can keep building your impossible game, just watch them too."

DeeDee shot a hopeful look. "Can they play with me?"

Jinx choked. "Absolutely not. They are not to be released."

"I'll stay." The earthly tone of Laris's voice had returned. She moved towards Jinx, allowing one hand to drag along the chamber.

"I'll go check on Claire's progress." Jacob pivoted and swiftly exited, calling over his shoulder, "I'll keep you posted."

Jinx barely acknowledged Jacob with a raise of her hand. Her eyes remained fixed on Laris. "You know I'm not leaving you here with these two."

"First of all, I can help shift their energy. Secondly, you're not —"

Jinx locked her jaw as a muffled growl escaped. Gripping Laris's hand, she dropped to the ground. "I'm not battling with you."

Blink.

CHAPTER TWELVE

Jinx practically skidded up to Hadu's door. No way she was going to be late. She could have blinked, but running was the only thing that had any hope of burning off her agitation. Transporting Laris without her consent went about as well as she had anticipated. After delivering Laris to her quarters, Jinx had swiftly fled. The look on her face promised the wisdom of retreat.

Jinx gathered her courage before announcing her arrival. Her finger hovered over the call button as she took a few breaths. After yesterday's debacle, she wasn't entirely certain the so-called lessons were still on. Pulling a no-show, however, was out of the question. Pressing past her doubt, she hit the call key. "I'm here."

The words barely left her lips before the door slid open. Hadu stood across the room, her back to the door. Jinx remained in place, scanning the area, looking for a signal, a sign, any indication of what to do next. Empty shelves broke up the otherwise barren walls. Thankfully, the oversized armchair had been returned. Every ache in Jinx's body eased in the hope of flopping down.

"Please, come in. Take a seat." Hadu didn't bother turning around, seemingly lost in the shelves, as though seeing something Jinx could not.

"Thank you," Jinx said with a level of gratitude rarely reserved for sitting. She crossed the room and collapsed into the cushions. A silent moment stretched long enough for Jinx to close her eyes. Lack of sleep and the day's events had finally caught up.

"What was your biggest challenge today?" Hadu's question jarred Jinx from the slumber that had descended unannounced.

Jinx groggily replied, opening her eyes to a slit, "What?"

Hadu turned to face Jinx. "It would serve you well to sleep, but preferably not during class."

"I heard the question," Jinx said. "I just don't understand what you're asking."

With graceful steps, Hadu moved towards her desk, adjusting her robe as she glided into her seat. "It's a simple question. What was your biggest challenge today?"

Jinx squirmed in her seat. "I've been interrogated enough times by the Takals to know questions like yours are never what they seem. It's always some sort of riddle." *Or something equally annoying.*

"Call it what you will," Hadu said casually. "An answer is still required. And unlike you, I'm fully rested and prepared to remain here as long as it takes."

Jinx moaned, allowing her head to drop back in exasperation. The cushioned back of the chair cradled her skull. She sunk into its plushness while staring at the ceiling, allowing her thoughts to drift through the sorted events.

"The glorious day started with a tasteless breakfast, which oddly had flavor when I threw it up while chasing mercenaries through the desert. I nearly passed out from CO2 poisoning while my face cooked on the scorching sand. Had to drag a Starltonian to a quarantine chamber, which wasn't nearly as fun as I'd hoped. Somehow, I allowed a techno-bug to make it onto the ship and into Laris's quarters, where it most likely bit her. I pissed off Claire after carrying viruses through the ship. And Laris is ticked off because, well, I'm just doing my job. Oh, and as you pointed out, I need sleep." Jinx lifted her head to face Hadu. "I dunno. The crappy breakfast was pretty challenging. I'll go with that."

Hadu didn't skip a beat. "Which part, the eating or expelling of your meal?"

Jinx studied Hadu, wondering if she'd actually cracked a joke or if this was her covert way of lulling her into a dialogue. As expected, the woman's placid demeanor didn't offer a clue. "The second part, of which I had no control over."

"I see," Hadu said, leaning back in her chair. "By the sounds of it, there was very little you felt in control of today."

Jinx shrugged. "I suppose."

"And were you hoping to be in control of life rather than shape your response to it?"

"See?" Jinx said, pointing an accusatory finger at Hadu. "This is exactly what I'm talking about. You're gonna pull me into some New World riddle and call it a lesson."

Hadu's expression lifted to something akin to amusement. "You are quite resistant to examining the nature of your mind."

"So I've been told," Jinx muttered, recalling her endless sessions with the Takals. "I'm an action kinda girl. What's wrong with that?"

"It's not a matter of rightness or wrongness," Hadu said. "But when one does not understand the origin of their own thoughts and beliefs, action taken is simply a reaction to life and circumstance. This is not a position of power but a servant to your mind."

Jinx shrugged. "Whatever. I get results."

Hadu leaned forward, resting her elbows on her desk. Bringing her palms together in a steeple, she tapped her chin, silently studying Jinx. "Life is not experienced in the results of one's efforts."

Jinx's face morphed into a state of repulsion. "Please tell me that being happy is *not* the goal of your lessons. 'Cause, I have to be honest, I don't really give a rip about that."

"Don't be silly." Hadu waved the idea away with a flick of the wrist. "If I were to delve into lessons of that nature, it would be to guide you to a state of neutrality. Your emotional state is but an indication of the contents of your mind. That is for you to unpack."

"I'll add it to my to-do list."

"You'd be wise to do so," Hadu said without a hint of humor. "Whatever you find there is a product of your own making. And I dare say, it has served you well. But as you evolve in your role as the Protector, you will undoubtedly outgrow beliefs and thoughts you planted long ago. Leaving them in place will only undermine you."

Jinx let out an exasperated breath, wishing for an end to the torture. "How exactly did asking me about my crummy day lead to this?"

"As I mentioned before, the landscape of your mind is yours to traverse. But in my commitment to assist you in developing habits and tools that will serve you, I will share one observation. You should perform inquiries of this nature on your own."

"Sounds like we're finally getting to the fun stuff." Jinx dropped her head back and rolled her eyes.

"Did you truly experience today's events as challenges or, as I suspect, failures?"

Jinx cringed at the mention of failures. It struck a nerve so sharp it stole her breath. "What difference does it make?" she snapped, as though beating back a demon attempting to claw its way into her awareness.

"In the pursuit of great endeavors comes significant challenges because it requires venturing into the unfamiliar. Those who traverse the path towards greatness with the wisdom of worthiness embrace these challenges as opportunities to grow." Hadu paused long enough to capture Jinx's gaze. "However, those who move forward uncertain of their own merit experience these same challenges as failures and evidence of their unworthiness."

Jinx turned from Hadu, feeling exposed beneath her stare. With nothing to shift her focus towards, she clung to an empty spot on the wall, hoping the void would quiet the rumblings beneath her skin.

"Becoming the Protector requires shedding all the ways you keep yourself small, for they are all illusions. They have only the power you grant them." Hadu stood and moved across the room, coming to a stop between Jinx and the oblivion she stared off into. "Do not feast on fear, Protector. Take solace. We are all confronted by the confines of who and what we have known ourselves to be as we step into an edgeless version of ourselves." Hadu lowered a hand to Jinx's head in a moment of unexpected tenderness. "You shall rise to meet your true nature. Of this, I am quite certain."

CHAPTER THIRTEEN

Jinx stood at the foot of the Sphinx, watching the sun warm the horizon while sipping her third shukar-soaked kæffee of the morning. She'd hammered down the first two in lieu of breakfast — a meal choice that was bound to set off Claire — before taking her third cup on the road. Turning in every direction, she scanned the edge of the security field, searching for threats that might be lurking while ignoring the ones taking refuge in her own head.

"How's the air?" Jacob's sleepy voice poured through the comm.

"Great, but I can still smell pockets of high carbon levels inside the pyramids."

"Don't worry," Jacob replied mid-yawn. "The rovers are putting ultraviolet pods everywhere. It'll shift the CO2 to oxygen pretty quickly."

"Great." Jinx guzzled a few warm sips. "Hey, can we set up movement sensors around the pyramids, near the entrances? If anyone or anything is hiding in here, I want to make sure we can detect them."

"Already done," Jacob replied. "I'm testing them right now." A moment passed. "So, um, how pissed is Laris?"

Jinx sighed, shifting her gaze towards the Sphinx's weather-worn face. "She doesn't get pissed. She gets quiet."

"Oh," Jacob replied. "Well, that's not so bad."

Jinx flashed a woeful glance at the Sphinx as if commiserating. "It's brutal. I'd rather have her yell or something. She uses silence like swords. I end up inflicting my own torture."

The sound of Jacob's shuffling feet was followed by the woosh of an opening door. "Kæffee delivery!" he announced chirpily. Evidently, he was speaking to someone other than Jinx. "Did you apologize?"

"Who, me?" Jinx asked.

"Yeah, sorry. Multitasking," Jacob replied. "I'm bringing Claire some fuel."

"I don't have time to negotiate everything," Jinx snapped back. "We have a lot to do. It's my job to keep Laris safe. Not happy."

"You might wanna rethink that strategy," Claire dropped into the conversation. "She's not a child. She's the savior of organic life."

Jinx leaned against the side of the Sphinx and took another sip. "You two need to stop ganging up. I've already got Hadu scrambling my mind."

"Alright, but —" Claire began.

"Can we just focus on testing the security field?" Jinx held up a device the size of her palm and pointed it towards the desert. A holographic field lit up an electric-blue patch filling ten square feet. As she moved the device, a new area lit up. "How far are we protected right now?"

"Uh, hold on a second. I'll show you the entire shield." There was a pause before an electric-blue dome buzzed to life, casting a soft hue on everything under its protection. "We've got a twenty-five-hundred-foot radius within the field, protected and oxygenated."

Jinx looked up, searching the electronic ceiling. For a moment, she lost herself in the drifting clouds far beyond. Bringing her attention down to earth, to the edge where the sand of the plateau met the pulsing blue wall, she scanned the vast stretches of unsecured desert. "Nothing will make it into this protected zone, right?"

"Uh, well, I mean, I don't know about *anything*," Jacob said. "But anything I can imagine."

"That's triggering every alarm in my head."

Blink.

Jacob lurched, barely stabilizing the kæffee in his hand as Jinx materialized by his side. "Seriously?" He gave Jinx a pinched expression. "You've got to warn me."

"This is exactly why everyone on this ship is going into combat training." Turning to Claire, who was sipping her kæffee, Jinx added, "After the supply run, training begins. I need everyone alert and able to at least try and defend themselves."

"I'm good," Jacob said. "I'm building a nanobot army."

Jinx stifled a laugh. In truth, she wanted to see his techno militia. It sounded badass. But the nerdiness of it still gave her the fits. "An army can't save you from a sneak attack. You need to train."

"I'll be your sparring partner," Claire said nonchalantly.

Jinx couldn't see Jacob's face but knew he was blushing. The training was going to be virtual sparring with a likeness of the universe's less-appealing creatures, but she figured she'd let Jacob glow in the idea of wrestling with Claire. She swept the image from her thoughts, feeling like she'd walked through some intimate moment of theirs.

"Great, I'll start setting —" Jinx stopped short and reached for a surface to stabilize. Her head swam in a wave of heat. Panic bubbled then rushed from her belly to her chest. "Oh, crap."

Jacob reached out. "What's wrong?"

"I knew your crappy diet was going to catch up with you," Claire snapped with tempered alarm. "You can't keep blinking everywhere without —"

"It's not that," Jinx abruptly cut the conversation. "Laris is in trouble!"

Blink.

***

As Jinx completed her blink, she looked across the circle of Attendants sitting in meditation. At the center, Laris rocked back and forth, struggling to self-soothe. Hadu moved around the circle, quietly watching.

Jinx didn't bother with questions but lifted her hands and prepared to cast a shield. She'd seen Laris in this state before. It seemed the disharmony of the universe had once again come to Laris for relief.

"Wait." Hadu raised her hand. "Do not disrupt this process."

"What are you talking about?" Jinx's words raced off her tongue like a whip. "She's suffering. It's my job to prevent this."

"No." Hadu raised a finger. "She must learn to negotiate whatever energy comes towards her without your help."

Jinx couldn't see the invisible forces, but she could imagine. She'd seen a version of this same scene play out while Laris was trapped in the station's VR. Dark, malicious tendrils of energy, formed by the suffering of others, had swarmed to Laris as though she were a beacon of hope. She absorbed every bit of it.

"No way! I can't just sit here and do nothing. She's in pain." Jinx forced the sum of her power to the palm of her hands and cast a barely visible shield around Laris.

Hadu didn't pull her sight from Laris as she spoke. "Would you prefer her to be weak without you?"

"Of course not!"

Hadu looked up, the intensity of her gaze pulling Jinx's attention to her. "Then lower your shield. She must master this on her own. She is powerful. You must trust that."

Jinx regarded Laris settled beneath the protective bubble, bearing the weight of the world without complaint. *Yes. She's more than powerful enough. But am I?* So much of Jinx's identity felt wrapped up in Laris that protecting her was practically self-preservation. At that moment, she felt the smallness of her desire. *Laris wouldn't want this. I can't protect her from every pain. I can only try and get her the time she needs to fulfill her destiny.* Slowly, Jinx lowered her hands, allowing the shield to drop. Without the barrier, it was as though the energy increased its rage, sending Laris into a momentary spasm.

Hadu watched as Jinx stepped back from the circle. "Well done."

Jinx let the comment drift away. It wasn't a moment to celebrate. It sat like a void in her chest. Crossing her arms tightly over her belly, Jinx tilted back to lean against the wall while Laris's shudders slowly softened.

Hadu moved around the circle, snapping her fingers at seemingly random moments. Whatever she was controlling or responding to, Jinx hadn't a clue. *Why am I the Protector? I can't see what they see. I've never even wanted to.* Her thoughts drifted to silence. It wasn't the serenity of stillness, but the loneliness of a spectator. The moment delivered the unsettling memory of yesterday's so-called class. *Hadu was right.* Moments like this felt like failures.

The low droning of a tuning fork brought Jinx back from the vacuum of her mind. Hadu was brandishing it like an eight-inch sword, sending its baritone hum out in waves to swaddle the room like soothing coos. "Becoming our highest expression requires stripping away the illusions that hold us back." Hadu paused as she passed between Jinx and the circle of Attendants. She didn't look towards Jinx, but the words met their mark all the same.

Jinx pushed off the wall, shaking away the tension of the spotlight. Jutting her chin towards Laris, she asked, "Where is this energy coming from? No one even lives on the planets in this solar system."

Hadu slid the tuning fork back into its holster, buried beneath the folds of her robe. "It's likely old energy lingering on Earth and the growing galactic unease." She spoke casually, nearly disarming the power of the words. "It will always seek out the harmony it finds with Laris, and she will always welcome it."

"Basically, there's no end to this? She'll just always be a freaking juju vacuum soaking up all the crappy stuff in the universe?"

"She's not soaking it up," Hadu replied. "She's transmuting it. There's a difference."

"Then why is it causing her pain?" Jinx rubbed her temples and cringed. They felt tender from days of clenching.

"She hasn't mastered her power, but she will." Hadu crossed the room to take a seat. The tail of her robe coiled perfectly to the side as if on its own accord. "There is a subtlety in the nature of suffering. It requires wisdom to discern where her assistance is required from moments it should be allowed to play out, to recognize which is in the benefit of a soul's expansion. At the moment, it's difficult for her to sense suffering without becoming lost in it."

Sounds miserable. I'd rather crack skulls, Jinx thought. *In fact, I'd rather crack my own skull.* She stepped softly around the circle of Attendants towards Hadu. "Why does she even have Attendants if we can't help?" Jinx felt the need to whisper, a concern Hadu didn't share. Most likely, Laris and her Attendants were on some other realm and well out of earshot. "'Cause clearly these ten aren't absorbing any of this. And according to you, I'm not supposed to use my powers to shield her."

"There will be times when you must use your shield. This isn't one of those occasions." Hadu folded her hands in her lap, settling into a regal repose. "Nor is it the job of these ten to absorb disturbed energy."

"Then what is their job?"

Hadu raised a brow or at least the spot of flesh where one normally grows. "Simple answer?"

Jinx snorted. "Please."

"She's an opening that universal energy pours through to balance qi." Hadu motioned towards the Attendants. "They absorb the excess positive, healing energy that flows through her when it's more than she can contain."

Jinx stared blankly. "I'll probably regret asking, but can you explain it in a way that sounds less mystical?"

"You are an electric field, a giant electric field that holds your atoms together," Hadu said. "Whether you call it qi, aura, prana, ka, or a bioelectromagnetic field, it's all the same. Laris is able to allow an energy of pure potential to flow through and restabilize the field necessary for organic life to exist." She paused. "Would you like an in-depth explanation of how scalar waves and zero-point energy are involved?"

Jinx coughed up a laugh. "Absolutely not, though I have a feeling Jacob will nerd out on it at some point while I'm standing within earshot."

When the group finally began to stir, Jinx kicked off the wall where she'd been leaning. Laris's mouth didn't move, but her face lit up, revealing a hint of the smile bubbling beneath. Silently, she bowed her head to her Attendants. Together, they stood as though a single hand had lifted them.

Hadu stood and moved towards the door. “I look forward to seeing you—*on time*—for your next session.”

“On time? That’s a lot to ask, seeing as how I was gonna ditch.”

“Indeed,” Hadu said as she flowed out the door, disappearing into the corridor with Attendants in tow.

“So . . .” Laris said, setting the stage with a smile.

Jinx braced herself. Whatever followed the flashing of dimples was bound to test her patience. “You’re talking to me again?”

“You transported me through time and space without my permission,” Laris replied calmly. “I needed time to regain my balance.”

“I stand by my actions,” Jinx said flatly.

The silence stretched as they eyed one another.

“Glad we had this little chat,” Jinx said and turned to leave. “I’ve got things to do.”

“Can I go explore the pyramid?” Laris asked swiftly, her composure loosening.

“No one is leaving this ship for now, not until I return from the supply station.”

“I can’t live life moving through it cautiously.” Laris fidgeted, seeming edgy in her own skin. “I can’t expect you to be with me every step I take. That’s not living. That’s prison.” She threw up her arms with an agitation Jinx had never seen before.

“Please, Laris. Please just wait a few more hours till I return. That’s all I ask. There is so much we don’t know yet. So many variables I can’t possibly prepare for. But the ship is safe.” Jinx spoke with some hesitation. Nothing is one hundred percent safe, but she needed to believe it was.

“But I need to feel strong and capable, not weak and dependent on you.” Laris twitched erratically then reached for Jinx. “Something isn’t right. I don’t feel right.”

Jinx contemplated throwing Laris over her shoulder and running to Claire when Jacob’s voice sprang from her comm. “Hey, I found something on that nano-insect. You’re gonna wanna see this.”

"Gotta swing by Claire's lab first." Without thinking, Jinx reached for Laris then pulled back, pausing long enough to offer her hand.

Laris smiled and took it.

Blink.

CHAPTER FOURTEEN

"Finally," Jacob said as Jinx walked through the door.

"Don't blame me. Claire had a million questions when I dropped off Laris." Jinx stepped up beside Jacob. "What's your big news?"

"I scanned our friend over there"— Jacob motioned towards the nano-insect — "and created a holographic replica." A tiny 3-D image of the creature appeared and floated between them. Jacob zoomed-in, enlarging it to the size of a human head. "Now we can really see what's going on with this little guy." Piece by piece, he disassembled the holographic version into countless bits. "I took this thing apart at least six times last night. Then, *finally,* this morning I found this," he said, pointing to a flat, hexagonal-shaped piece. "The actual size of this is smaller than a grain of sand." Jacob shook his head with a look of awe. "Fortunately, I can enlarge the image, 'cause otherwise I would never have noticed *this.*" He pointed at a series of circles: a small round sphere situated between two larger ovals, each framed in a triangle that met at their tips. A horizontal line ran through the center. It was a signature he and Jinx knew well.

Jinx threw a hand on Jacob's shoulder. "Sartillias. I knew it."

"He likes to send out his calling card. Not sure why he made this one so difficult to find." Jacob spun the holographic piece around, highlighting the markings. "Here's where it gets interesting. I've seen Sartillias's logo before. It's imprinted on every tab of Euphoria he produces. But it never occurred to me." He shook his head and pointed at the image. "That's the symbol for torsion fields. With Claire and me looking into ways to leverage the pyramids, these fields have been on our radar, so it was easier to put the two together."

"I have no idea what a torsion field is, but what could that possibly have to do with Laris?"

Jacob shrugged. "I don't know, but the torsion field is the nature of a scalar wave, and—"

"What?" Jinx cut Jacob off. "You and Hadu must be conspiring, 'cause she just mentioned scalar waves."

Jacob raised a brow. "Really? What did she say?"

Jinx cocked her head. "You give me way too much credit." With a shrug, she added, "I don't know, but it had something to do with how Laris's powers work . . . balancing qi or something."

"Interesting," Jacob said while tapping his chin. "The frequency of the scalar wave is determined by the frequency used to create them — harmful or healing."

Jinx's brows shot up. "Uh, 'harmful' as in weaponized?"

"Yup. But I don't know if weaponizing Laris is what Sartillias is up to," Jacob said. "We've just been looking at ways to magnify her energy, but who knows how he would leverage Laris's frequency? The torsion field is linked with topics of time and organizing particles into matter. For all I know, it could provide access to time travel or alternate dimensional realities or even create new realities."

"What a relief." Jinx offered a lopsided grin. "Nothing to be concerned with, then?"

"Nothing at all."

Jinx moved around the translucent images, inspecting each one before returning her focus to the tagged piece. "Besides the fact that he steals pineal glands to produce club drugs, what do you know about Sartillias?"

"Honestly, not much. Most of the talk that went around the supply station was probably rumor. I'm guessing only a few have ever met him, and I doubt they lived to tell the tales." Jacob fiddled with a few of the other holographic parts. "He's from a very small race that lives in the shadows doing unethical and illegal crap."

"What do you mean, 'small?'" Jinx asked. "Like, he's tiny?"

"No. I mean, they're few in number, relatively speaking," Jacob said. "I have no idea how big they are, but they're tough. I mean, supposedly, their race throws out their offspring when they're infants and only keeps the ones that can survive on their own."

"That explains a lot," Jinx said, turning as Laris walked in. "How'd it go with Claire? Are you feeling better?"

Laris smiled as she approached, lifting her hand to trace the length of Jinx's arm. "I'm feeling great," she purred.

"Did Claire give you one of her concoctions?" Jinx asked laughingly. Claire was known to *experiment*.

"I wish," Laris said with a laugh that was uncomfortably off.

Jacob and Jinx exchanged a baffled glance.

"Hey, uh, Claire," Jacob called over his comm. "I need your input on something. Can you come to my lab and bring some juice?" Pause. "Yes, *that* juice." Pause. "No. I'll explain when you get here." Pause. "Fast would be better."

Jinx pinched her brow and muttered, "What aren't you telling me?"

Jacob held up a finger, cautioning Jinx to wait a moment . . . silently.

"What's up?" Claire practically skidded in. "You got more info off that nanobot?"

Jacob jutted his head toward Laris, who was slinking around the lab.

Claire furrowed her brow, then instant clarity washed over. "What the drek? No way. She was fine a few minutes ago," she whispered. "You were right." Casually, Claire approached Laris, concealing a small, silver device. "How are you feeling? A little warm? A little scattered?"

Laris turned with narrowed eyes. "Actually, I've never felt better." Looking down at Claire's hand, she chuckled. "Good luck." Laris flipped her wrist and the room rattled. A look of delight claimed her face. "Well, isn't that a handy trick?" she said, regarding her palms.

Jinx lifted her hands cautiously. "Laris, you aren't yourself right now. You need to listen to me."

Laris moved towards Jinx with prowling steps. "I could hear all of your thoughts. If I wanted to. Yours too," she added, smirking at Claire.

Turning towards Jacob, she popped out her bottom lip to a pout. "But not yours. Clever, aren't you?"

Jinx shot Jacob a look. "Dude?"

Jacob shrugged. "I built an invisible barrier to block anyone who tries to infiltrate my mind."

"Thanks for sharing," Jinx mumbled, signaling to Jacob to keep the conversation going as she edged her way towards Laris, cornering her like some feral creature.

"It doesn't work that way," Jacob said, airily. "It's just part of my power."

"Whatever," Jinx grumbled, taking another step. "You should still share."

"Give me a break," Jacob moaned. "You can blink, cast shields, and kick ass."

"Sadly, none of those are making a bit of difference," Jinx said, taking a few swift steps to reach for Laris.

Laris jumped back with a hardened expression. Lifting her hands, she wiggled her fingers and smirked. "Wonder how much damage I can do. I mean, with universal negative energy at my disposal, I should be able to wreak some spectacular havoc." Taking a deep breath, she said, "Let's have a little fun!"

"Whoever you are, you're not Laris." Jinx raised her hands, feeling the energy pulse between her palms. She'd only ever conjured the power to protect Laris, but now she hoped it would save her from herself. "I'm giving you one chance to put your hands down."

"You're giving *me* a chance?" Laris studied Jinx. "How generous."

Whatever or whoever had a hold of Laris was annoying. If it was Sartillias and his stupid nanobug, well, he was officially more irritating than Bayne had ever been.

"The only thing I dislike more than being toyed with is someone messing with Laris." Jinx pulled back her hands and flung a field around Laris.

Laris twerked her hands in response but didn't pierce the shield. The energy she cast clamored to break free. Again and again, Laris fired at the invisible cage until the energy rose to a roar.

Jinx's stomach turned to bile as the dark energy escaped the barrier to seep into her system like sludge. *How the drek is Laris transmuting this?* A swell of unruly emotions surfaced. They didn't feel like her own, but still, they clouded her mind, pulling her along on the wave of misery Laris was hurling at her.

"You can't hold me forever," Laris hissed, slamming another torrent against the shield.

"Stop!" Jinx forced every ounce she could conjure to reinforce the shield, repulsed at the idea of soaking up what Laris was firing at her. It ricocheted and barreled back into Laris.

Laris stumbled back, wickedly delighted as everything in the room wobbled, sending equipment bouncing across desktops until it crashed onto the floor.

Jacob dove, barely catching a crystalline box. "This is gonna wreck my equipment. We can't afford to lose anything." Looking to Jinx, he snapped, "End this!"

Laris exploded in venom-drenched laughter. "I'll end it." Lunging forward, she threw her arms around Jinx and pressed into her lips.

The kiss was forceful and frenzied. Sadly, the chaotic lip-mash was Jinx's first. Her upbringing on the New World station hadn't been a hotbed of hormonal activity. Quite the opposite. Even still, she could imagine what one would be like, and this most certainly was not it. Rather than pull away, Jinx pulled Laris in tight, keeping lips fixed, then dropped to the ground. Giving a quick, get-ready glance to Claire . . .

Blink.

Instantly, they were next to Claire, who didn't hesitate to bring the tranquilizer down to Laris's neck.

Jinx saw the clarity of Laris's gaze return and felt the soft caress of her lips linger. Moments later, her body went limp. Jinx held tight, cradling Laris tenderly in a protective embrace as her head slipped away.

Claire released a sigh, muttering under her breath. "That was kinda hot."

Jacob flashed her a wide-eyed look.

"I mean, you know, apart from the whole devilish destroyer thing," Claire added.

Jinx scooped Laris up and stood. "Please tell me you can fix this."

Jacob released a burst of relief that jostled his lips loudly. Carefully setting down a handful of tools he'd spared from a deadly plummet to the ground, he shook his head. "I can't make that promise. I think that the nano-insect injected a DNA-based nanobot into her system. Either it's interfering with her cognitive abilities or"— Jacob hesitated and cringed — "it's giving someone else access to her thoughts."

"What do you mean, 'access?'" Jinx roared. "Like, reading her thoughts or controlling them?"

"Both."

Jinx pulled Laris in tighter. "Can't you mentally control it? I mean, it's a machine."

"I've been trying"—Jacob threw up his arms—"but it's blocking my attempts. It might take some time."

Claire raced to the door. "Get to my lab. We need to put her into a deep freeze, now! If she has self-replicating nanites or nanobots, they'll use the iron in her blood to reproduce and take over her system."

Jinx dropped her head, feeling the warmth of Laris's cheek on her flesh. "Fight whatever is in there," she whispered. "I can't bear to lose you, and the universe can't afford to."

CHAPTER FIFTEEN

Jinx felt Jacob's eyes on her as they trailed behind Hadu and Claire. "Stop watching me. I can handle this."

"Last time I checked, even mentioning Bayne's name sends you into volcanic mode. Talking to him is bound to turn atomic. I just want to make sure you don't explode. The world needs you." While attempting to suppress a smile, Jacob added, "I mean, eventually you'll do something besides pass out from CO2 poisoning or make out with demonic Laris."

Jinx strangled a laugh, grateful she could count on Jacob to diffuse the tension. "How about I get us stuck in oblivion during the blink to the supply station? We could add that to your list."

"Not funny. You don't play fair," Jacob muttered to himself. "Seriously, I'm over here trying to lift your spirits and you're threatening eternal fragmentation."

Jinx looked up, placing a hand on his shoulder. "You're right. We'll get there in one piece — not a single, meticulously groomed hair out of place. Promise."

"That's an acceptable answer," Jacob said. "And you better inhale a gluttonous amount of calories before we leave. It's a big jump. You're blinking us both across multiple galaxies."

Jinx pulled a fistful of grub-bars from her pocket. "Got lunch handled."

"Actually," Claire interrupted, "I don't think the distance is a factor. I've been crunching the numbers, and it looks like the issue is mass. Unless she's hauling someone or something else with her, she burns an extra ounce every fourteen jumps, no matter how much distance she's covered. Essentially, the weight of her cargo is the biggest factor. I'll know for sure after the supply run. That should provide all the data I need."

Jinx was starting to feel more like a lab rat than a legend-in-the-making. "You can both stop worrying," she said, pulling a half-eaten protein bar from the pocket of her hoodie. Shoving it into her mouth, she didn't bother to swallow before continuing. "I got it covered."

Claire released a sigh of frustration. "All of these blinks you take every day add up. Plus, you hardly sleep on top of working out."

"Fine," Jinx grumbled. "Just tell me how much extra I need to eat."

Claire gave her a sideways glance. "I did. Yesterday. Remember?"

Jinx shrugged. "Been busy, dude. You know, passing out and kissing demons. I suppose our little chat escaped my memory."

Hadu casually glanced over her shoulder as if taking note but said nothing.

"I should scan Jinx's brain before the supply run," Claire said, seemingly to herself or possibly Hadu. Either way, she didn't bother looking up from the data scrolling across a hand-held device. "She needs a routine analysis at the very least."

"I'm right behind you, in case you forgot," Jinx groused.

"Your presence is quite impossible to miss," Hadu replied with a dose of levity that cut the edge.

Claire snorted but kept her attention glued to her device.

"Great," Jinx said, shoveling in another mouthful. "Happy to hear I haven't lost my touch."

Jacob watched Jinx closely. "You really don't remember your chat yesterday?"

"No," Jinx scoffed. "Maybe I'm not losing weight. I'm just losing my mind."

Claire paused her steps, jerking up from her data. "Or your memories."

Jinx shook her head and sped up to push past Hadu and Claire. "That's ridiculous. Thoughts don't weigh anything."

"All of life is merely energy," Hadu said as Jinx bristled by. "This includes thoughts. And they most certainly have substance."

"Great," Jinx groaned, feeling certain the elusive nature of reality and the mind would be a new fun topic during her sessions with Hadu. *Whatever. If my memories disappear, I'd never know. It'd be like the moments never happened. Wait. Crap. What about things I need to remember to help protect Laris?* Shaking her head, Jinx shoved the fear down. "Do *not* start rattling off in my ear," she said as Jacob shuffled up to her side. "I honestly can't wrap my head around anything else right now. I feel like I'm gonna snap."

"I won't. I get it," Jacob said. "Let's just focus on Bayne."

"Great," Jinx said, annoyed that Bayne had become a more appealing topic. "Are we clear on what we want to talk to him about?"

"Yep. Claire is adding to the list right now, in case we need supplies we haven't considered."

Jinx gave a thumbs-up, coming to a stop beside one in a long stretch of identical doors. "Besides asking about additional security and possible solutions for Laris's nanobot, what else are we hoping to achieve?"

"We have some questions about his amplifier," Jacob replied. "I think we might be able to use it to leverage energy that runs beneath the pyramids in addition to increasing the distance that Laris's frequency can travel." He shrugged. "Those are just a few ideas."

Jinx pulled her hand from the door's security panel and ran it along her skull. "Did we talk about that? I mean, should I remember that this was on the list?"

"Well..." Jacob's words were drowned out by Hadu rattling through Jinx's mind.

"Your insecurity is your greatest undoing. Consider that your mind is shifting as you step into your power, rather than a sign of unworthiness. You are the Protector for a reason, not a mistake. Nothing aligned to that purpose is at risk. Embrace that truth and set forth from there."

Hadu's voice drifted away as Jacob trickled in. ". . .but it's not a big —"

"Never mind." Jinx waved the conversation away. "Let's just get this party rolling."

As the door swung open, Jinx braced herself, expecting to see an annoyingly smug Bayne glaring at her from across the room. Instead, the man who'd attempted to end her life and hijack Laris didn't even acknowledge their presence. He was meditating. Despite the fact that he'd grown up on the New World space station where meditation was more important than breathing, it still came as a surprise.

They all stood silently for what felt like an uncomfortable stretch of time before Jacob elbowed Jinx and mouthed, "What's up?"

Jinx returned his silent question with an eye roll and a head wag, mouthing back, "Rules." Disbanded space station or not, the guidelines were still observed. Topping the list: do not disturb a denizen in meditation. It was one of the few rules Jinx felt compelled to follow.

"Please refrain from bringing electronics into this space." Bayne opened his eyes, casting an accusatory glance at Claire.

Claire seemed unphased as she flashed the underside of her handheld device. "Got an EM guard on everything."

"I can still feel the disruption in my field."

"Don't worry." Jacob tapped his skull. "I'll take notes."

Claire shrugged, opened the door, and set the device outside.

Bayne stood slowly. He'd ditched his stuffy suit for the customary white gown that most denizens wore. Its softness did little to mellow his edges. "To what do I owe this" — he paused to sigh — "pleasure." Looking blankly at Jinx, he added, "Shall I assume your role as Protector is more than you are able to fill?"

Jinx felt her face flush as her heartbeat ramped up. *Jacob was right, I might turn atomic.* The anger she felt towards Bayne was a blaze not easily tamed.

Hadu stepped forward before Jinx could fire back a few choice words. "The Protector is stepping into her role quite adeptly. But, as you know, there is much at stake and many known and unknown threats to negotiate."

Bayne nodded silently.

"In light of the magnitude of the situation and the dangerous road ahead, we would appreciate any insight and thoughts you might have regarding a few immediate concerns."

Bayne seemed to mull over the request as he regarded Jacob. "I always wondered who the twelfth Attendant was." He shook his head. "It seems I hadn't bothered to consider that someone other than a New World denizen would be part of the prophecy." With a wave of his hand, he added, "Arrogance was always a limitation."

Jinx was taken aback by his casual admittance of his own shortcomings. Her face must have revealed it.

Bayne smirked, likely his version of a smile. "Maybe if you'd stop being afraid of your weaknesses, you'd recognize them for what they are."

"Oh really?" Jinx said, widening her stance. "And what's that?"

"Opportunities," Bayne said, brushing out a wrinkle in his robe. "A known weakness is far less powerful than one we refuse to acknowledge."

Jinx wanted to clobber him. "Interesting. That insight didn't stop you from following through on a pretty arrogant plan."

"That, my dear, was a very sound plan. The universe would be shielded from harmful electromagnetic energy and high-frequency bands, and the rebalancing between OI and IOI would be well on its way. And you wouldn't be facing the issues that have brought you to my doorstep." Bayne stood silent and still as if daring someone to challenge his words. "Now, shall we get on with discussing solutions, or shall we continue battling wills?"

Claire piped in, "I vote for solutions."

Jinx moved to plant her hands on her hips but slid them into her pockets as restraint. Her breathing eased in response. "We've got a few issues, but the most urgent is Laris. She has a nanobot in her system."

Claire cautiously added, "We think —"

Bayne raised a hand, pausing further explanation. The room went silent while he chewed on the news flash. "I'm assuming you put her in a deep freeze." His tone suggested he wasn't looking for confirmation. Turning to Jacob, he asked, "What are your thoughts on removing it?"

"Well, Claire and I —"

"I'm perfectly aware of Claire's intelligence and ability to solve quite complex problems," Bayne said. "I don't, however, know how your mind works. So, please, let's shelve the chivalry for a moment."

Jinx had never seen Jacob harden until now. His ever-present charm disappeared beneath an unyieldingly flat expression. "I'm not here to be assessed. I know what I'm capable of. And without Claire, I'd be half as effective, at best. It's not chivalry. It's simply the truth."

Bayne only nodded, as if Jacob had revealed some crucial piece of information.

"The soundest solution" — Jacob motioned to Claire, who was looking uncustomarily enchanted after the compliment — "*we* have come up with involves confusing the nanobot, causing it to evacuate Laris's system. Nanoparticles interact with light when under the influence of an electric field, so we should be able to create an environment to manipulate the bot."

"Even if we can't remove it," Claire interjected, "we should be able to interfere with its antenna so that it can't be controlled by an outside source."

Bayne clasped his hands behind his back, firming his already crisp posture. "What makes you think the bot is being controlled?"

Jinx fidgeted with the interior seam of her pocket. The need to gnaw her cuticle or launch into a frenetic round of pacing was reaching a fevered pitch. "Laris is behaving strangely."

Bayne's dull expression dimmed a degree. "And by 'strange,' do you mean aggressive?"

"Among other things, yes," Jinx replied, matching Bayne's gaze.

Bayne's expression softened, his voice absent of ridicule. "I warned you that she'd be vulnerable to her dark side."

"This isn't her dark side," Jinx argued. "She's not herself."

"As much as you'd love to believe that Laris is immune to the laws of the universe and the duality of all that exists, that simply isn't the case.

Nothing exists without its opposite present. What we each express is a matter of choice. This nanobot, most likely, can only trigger something that is there to begin with."

"Fine," Jinx said. "For the sake of argument, let's say that this bot is unleashing something in Laris. By removing it or interfering with its communication, she should be able to regain control. Right?"

Bayne steepled his hands, allowing the tips to rest on his chin. "Possibly. Or she may decide she enjoys certain aspects that would interfere with her stepping into her role as the One."

Bayne didn't say it, but everyone was probably thinking it. This is why he tried to put Laris and her Attendants in a never-ending sleep, hooked up to an amplifier, safely tucked away from threats.

"Well then, that's *her* choice to make," Jinx said. "Not ours."

"Indeed. Unfortunately, the survival of OI is at the mercy of her whim."

CHAPTER SIXTEEN

"Make sure you both come straight to my lab the minute you return from the supply station," Claire said as she carefully removed sensors from Jacob's head.

"Hadu already called dibs," Jinx replied while ripping off the devices attached to her skull. She unceremoniously heaped them next to Jacob before hopping off the examination table. "She expects our sessions to start on time, despite the fact that I'm blinking across galaxies and have absolutely no way to control the timing of this little mission. Though, honestly, I'm not sure what's worse, your probing and prodding or hers."

"I'll sort it out with Hadu," Claire said as she scooped up Jinx's piles of discarded tabs, placing them on a tray next to Jacob's. "It's essential that I run tests on you both as soon as possible."

"Fine." Jinx fixed her attention on the cryo-tank that held Laris in deep freeze. The glass was misted over, but she watched, waiting for movement.

Jacob hopped off the examination table to stand next to Jinx. Speaking low, in practically a whisper, he eased Jinx from the tank. "Hey, Claire knows even more about nanobots than I do. Seriously, Laris couldn't be in better hands."

"I know, I know." Jinx reluctantly stepped away from the tank. "I just don't like leaving this place unprotected."

"I understand," Jacob said as they moved across the lab towards Claire. "But we need supplies. I mean, we have a lot to work with here, but there are a few things we have to have in order to stabilize our shield and loads of other stuff we need for our future."

"And, if worse comes to worst, I hate to say it, but Bayne is here," Claire said. "I'll leverage him if I need to."

Jinx bit back her protest and nodded. She knew Claire didn't share her impulsive nature. A move like that would be well thought through.

Turning to Jacob, Claire asked, "You got the list?"

Jacob tapped his head. "All right here."

Claire made a face. "Seriously? What if you both experience memory loss with the blink?" She held out a notebook. "Here. I wrote *everything* down."

Jacob took the notebook, opened it to a random page, and read. "Dear diary, today I —"

Claire shook her head, chuckled, and handed him a pen. "Here's an archaic writing utensil, just in case I forgot something." Pushing them towards the door, she added, "Go. Save the day. I've got work to do."

Jinx moved through the door, stepping out into the hallway. "Let's go. It's time to blink between galaxies."

Jacob moved quickly to her side as they headed down the silent corridor. "Please reconsider the bar as our first drop point. I'm one hundred percent certain I'll want a cocktail after this. Hopefully in celebration. If not, then to numb the pain of being disfigured during this insanity."

"Seriously, that's the most public and populated place on the supply station. I'm not blinking there," Jinx said. "We need to avoid announcing our arrival."

"I'm joking. Kind of." Jacob flipped through Claire's notebook as they wound through the corridor. "Too bad we can't just blink to one of the commuter pods."

"I thought about that," Jinx said, "but landing there is bound to set off alarms. And you won't be able to disengage them fast enough."

Jacob nodded as they approached his door. "True."

Jinx leaned against the wall while Jacob unarmed his security. After a series of beeps, the door slid open. "It's settled. We'll blink to your old lab first. You can start gathering what you need while I round up your two freaking cases of litmorian."

"No way, I wanna go with," Jacob said. "I might not have a chance to see Pallas again."

"Who?"

"Pallas. You know . . . the bartender who served you right before a winged Draco rearranged your face."

"Oh. Yeah. Her." Jinx felt nervously flushed at the thought of seeing Pallas again. The bartender had made a pass. Well, as far as Jinx could tell based on her painfully limited experience. *The world is falling apart and I'm nervous to see some alien chick. It's official, I'm ridiculous.* "Fine. I'll help you scavenge what's left at your lab and track down whatever else you need. Then, we can go *quickly* to the bar. Together."

"Great." Jacob gave a thumbs-up looking around his make-shift lab. "Oh, there it is." Walking across the room he reached for his wristband. "We'll need this."

Jinx eyed the band. "For what?"

"I'm gonna need access to my money for the supplies."

"What if someone is tracking your accounts?" Jinx asked, "If there's activity, they'll know where we are."

"Please. You think I have accounts linked to my own name? I dealt in illegal technology. Nothing is trackable." Jacob wiggled the wristband in the air. "All I do is punch in code 09990 and my system pulls from multiple alias accounts and scrambles the purchase location."

Jinx watched Jacob flip through Claire's notebook as he moved through his lab. "What are you doing?"

"Just checking for anything I may have forgotten to add to the list."

Jinx put her hands on her hips. "You're stalling."

Jacob didn't look up as he set the notebook and the wristband on the desk. "No. Just. I mean. It's important to double-check." There was a stifled wobble in his voice. "Let's avoid making the blink twice."

Jinx knew she couldn't comprehend the magnitude of a blink across this distance. She didn't ask the specifics that clearly Jacob had calculated. In her mind, knowing the potential risk wouldn't prevent the inevitable. They needed supplies. It was an unavoidable risk. "You got any geek friends on the supply station that you trust enough to help us with supplies?"

"No way. They all have agendas." Jacob scoffed, then paused, tapping his forefinger to his lips. "Well, maybe one. Remember the IOI that, um" — he cleared his throat — "came to my lab on the supply station."

Jinx refrained from displaying her disapproval. Jacob had been sending this IOI into the New World's VR through an illegal layer he'd built. The IOI wasn't just touring the VR and watching the denizens from some invisible layer like it was a sideshow. She was merging with one of them — learning what it was like to be human. Emotions. Moods. Thoughts. All of it, supposedly. Jinx pushed the thought of the now-defunct VR from her mind. Who knew what was happening to the thousands of denizens stuck there? Hadu was right, she couldn't afford to worry about that situation. Hopefully, the fact that they couldn't get out also meant that others, like uninvited guests, couldn't get in.

"Yeah. I remember your side-hustle as a VR tour guide."

Jacob looked up. "That was a serious exploration. IOI doesn't value OI because they don't understand us. Most of them don't want to. To them, organic life is incapable of evolving fast enough. But Lumi is part of a group that wants to protect OI. So, you know, her group is, in a way, trying to achieve the same thing we are. Or at least they were before the VR crashed." Jacob rifled through a drawer, pointing to the contents. "See. This is why I'm double-checking. I need more trepothium."

Jinx reached for the notebook and pen. "Alright. I'll add it." She scribbled her best guess at the spelling knowing it had no chance of being accurate. She shrugged, then added a few notes of her own — namely the wristband password and IOI's name — before tossing the pen. "Is that it?"

"Yeah." Jacob scanned the room in a final sweep. "I think so."

Jinx reached for the wristband and shoved it into the pocket of her hoodie, along with the notebook. "Great," she said and dropped to the ground.

Jacob whipped around. His eyes shot wide as he leapt towards her. "No!"

"Sorry, genius. We can't afford to lose you." Jinx slammed her fist into the ground. The world disappeared beyond the now-familiar, high-pitched buzz.

Blink.

***

Most blinks were quick, covering short distances, leaving no time to contemplate the reality-bending jaunt. This was different.

It began like all others: a flash of extreme brightness followed by an explosion that fractured the shapeless view into pinpoints of lights. Jinx didn't bother looking for her body amid the nothingness that had swallowed her. She knew by now there wouldn't be one. While she couldn't wrap her mind around the idea that she was currently held together by thought alone, she clung to the concept all the same.

For the moment, only her thoughts and the points of light piercing the dark void seemed to exist. If time passed here, wherever here was, there was no sign of it. Apart from counting the thoughts bubbling up, Jinx had no sense of time or space. She *was* keeping track, however. And according to count, too many thoughts had crossed her awareness while nothing around her changed. *Ohhhh crap. Crap. Crap.* Barely pulling herself off the proverbial edge, she steered her thoughts towards something less terminal. *No. Don't freak out. Do. Not. Freak. Out. You aren't stuck.* Jinx grasped for anything less anxiety-inducing but couldn't get past the question of what the heck was happening. *What did Jacob say about blinking?* He had tried to explain it, telling her that when the molecular structure vibrates at incredibly high speeds it ceases to be solid. Once that happened, it could "travel" anywhere by thought alone. Jinx had, as usual, zoned out during the majority of his tutorial. Luckily, a snippet had managed to stick with her. *My thoughts! Focus on where I'm going. Where am I going?* Focusing felt like casually grasping at clouds as though nothing particularly urgent was unfolding. *Somebody needed something. Oh yeah, the supply station. Jacob needs litmorian. Wait, that can't be right. Am I blinking across the galaxy for litmorian?* Jinx lazily reached for another thought, but nothing surfaced. *Okay, I must be going to the supply station for litmorian.*

As if the universe was simply waiting for Jinx to follow a thought, make a choice, decide a destination, the pinpoints of light responded. They pulsed, then stretched to form lines that twisted and turned until the nothingness resembled a bright maze or motherboard. As her surroundings shifted, memories of the supply station trickled in, building on one another slowly. Each thought appeared like a projection. The lights rearranged themselves to form a snapshot of a memory then dissolved, making way for the next recollection.

The thought of litmorian led to the memory of the bar, then her search for Jacob, then her brawl with a winged Draco. And then a memory of the bartender, Pallas, popped up. Unlike the other memories, Pallas didn't come and go. She lingered. Her features sharpened: piercing green eyes that were a sharp contrast to her skin — a metallic grey, like burnished steel. She didn't have scales but looked as though she should.

As the image floated through Jinx's awareness, all else stood still. Everything appeared to have stalled, giving that single impression the spotlight. Jinx pushed the memory away, but Pallas didn't disappear. She moved beyond a doorway. The door remained open as a second door appeared, followed by another and another until the lights morphed into an endless corridor of doors.

What just happened?

"You are not your thoughts. You are not your memories. You are not your body. Simply choose." The words did not feel her own, and yet they felt...familiar.

Jinx wanted to laugh, but without a body, it just wasn't the same. *Pretty sure that's all there is. If I'm not thoughts, memories, or body, what the drek am I?*

No answer came. Only silence.

Hello.

Still, only silence.

Choose? Jinx stared down the long corridor of doors. There were too many to count. The end was nowhere in sight. *Fine.*

Suddenly, doorway after doorway came rushing forward, revealing what existed beyond: worlds filled with familiar faces, each scene slightly different than the one before. Only one triggered a response. Jinx moved swiftly through it.

CHAPTER SEVENTEEN

Life was slow to solidify. While Jinx's surroundings remained a blurry buzz, and the pinpoints of light gathered to shape reality, her heart hammered uncomfortably. The details of her journey through the void drifted away like a fading dream. She didn't attempt to fix it to her memory or make sense of it. She couldn't. The specifics of her life and this mission rushed to the surface of her awareness, pushing aside all else but dealing with the world she was about to drop into. *I don't care where I land, just let it be somewhere and in one piece.* As long as she arrived with her body intact, she'd fight, run, or blink if trouble was waiting to greet her. Worst case, she'd cause a scene, which wouldn't be the first.

Sounds of chatter and clanking surfaced, making ripples across the fluid shapes still forming. High-pitched laughter woke Jinx's flesh, sending adrenaline-infused goosebumps across her skin. Sweat and booze drenched the sticky air now clinging to every inhale.

A pileup of swaying bodies to her left was coming into focus while a bar top spanned out of view to her right. Jinx wanted to kiss the drunken floor almost as much as she wanted to clunk Jacob for planting the idea of the bar in her brain. There couldn't be a more public place to materialize out of thin air. At least it was dark. *Diversion. I'll need a distraction.*

A high-pitched buzz rattled her eardrums as the world locked in place. Jinx braced herself, feeling the gripping weight of her body — a sensation she always reveled in — while her chest rattled to keep her thrumming heart caged. A blast of cool air rushed past on the wings of laughter. The clink of cocktails and bodies brushing by marked the moment she'd fully arrived.

Jinx quickly shifted from her crouched position to kneel on all fours, knocking into an innocent few. Ice-cold liquid splashed against her neck and continued down her back until seeping into her shirt. *Great. This was my last cleanish shirt.* Flicking an ice cube towards the floor, Jinx allowed a moment to pass. *Focus,* she urged herself as she pushed to her feet. *It's showtime.* Bodies brushed past clumsily, knocking her off her footing towards the two unhappy faces waiting to greet her. One of them jiggled an empty glass accompanied by a far-too inebriated expression.

"Sorry. Guess I need to watch where I'm going," Jinx said, while casually scanning the packed bar for witnesses. Fortunately, most were facing the bar, attempting to get a drink. But a few who'd been pushing past paused to rubberneck the collision.

The drunken pair eyed her for a moment before stumbling past to disappear into the crowd. Jinx cocked her head towards a remaining spectator — a delicate-looking, furball of a species propped up on the nearest bar stool. Based on their elfin height, Jinx wondered how they managed to finagle a seat without getting trampled on. "There's nothing to see here," Jinx said, flicking the back of her shirt in a futile attempt to dry it out.

"Siz bir soniza oldink bu erda edingiz," the puny puffball said in a surprising alto tone.

Jinx smacked a palm to her head. "Translator," she grumbled. "I forgot to bring a language translator."

The furball flashed a dumbfounded look, as though it was more likely to leave home without your own head. "Iltimoz, qurilma. Va pushti ichimlik," they said to the nearest bartender.

The bartender offered a sideways glance, giving Jinx a quick once-over. "Nijeh râlk miphken," he chuckled before searching the bar for some difficult-to-locate item. The furball joined in on the laugh.

Jinx took note with indifference. She may not understand the languages passing between them, but she'd experienced the reaction to "her kind" during her previous white-knuckle race through the supply station. New World humans were deemed the wing nuts of the galaxy, and possibly the vast territory beyond, due to their reclusive nature, limitations on technology, and all-around monasticism. The white robes didn't help. Nor their aversion to digital currency. Jinx had ditched the customary uniform the moment she could voice an opinion — along with a few other customs she didn't care for. Even still, she'd stick out. The New World created an aura not easily overlooked but quickly mistaken for naivete.

"Hjirg iz iph," the bartender said, tossing a small container over pickled patrons, nearly clunking Jinx in the head. "Yn denph eazen," he said, motioning for Jinx to open the box and place the buds in her ears.

"No duh," Jinx muttered, then waved a half-hearted "thank you" and pivoted, prepared to quickly make her way through the crowd and out the door.

"I said, you weren't here a second ago," the fur ball announced in a pitch that blanketed the surrounding bar babble.

Jinx turned and forced an unconvincing laugh. "How many of those have you had, buddy?"

Furball watched Jinx unblinkingly. "I can drink these all night long and still be certain of what I saw." Taking a sip from a flamboyantly fuchsia concoction, they added coolly, "And I saw you appear out of nowhere."

Jinx regarded the creature for a moment, deciding to keep it jovial. Pressing through the bodies, she squeezed up to the bar. Thumbing towards her new pest, she yelled, "Can I get two of these hallucination cocktails?"

"How about you wait your turn?" Luminous green eyes looked up from the bar well, pinched with impatience as they locked onto Jinx, then morphed into something deviously-playfully. Exchanging a few quick words with another bartender, she made her way over. "You here to make another scene?"

Another? What is she talking about? Jinx looked around, then pointed to herself. "Me?"

"Uh. Yeah." The bartender chuckled. "You're the only one I've ever seen attempt to take down a winged Draco."

Crap. She knows me. Why don't I remember her? Jinx shrugged. "I suppose. If I'm in the mood."

"You don't want one of those," the bartender said, thumbing towards furball's pink beverage. "Takes a professional drinker to handle that kind of firepower." She winked. Setting two glasses down, she filled them with green liquid that burped gold. "Didn't think I'd see you back here after torpedoing your body into that Draco." Sliding one of the burping liquids across the bar, she locked eyes on Jinx and added, "But I'm happy to be wrong about that."

A familiar warming sensation swept across Jinx's face. She quickly broke away from the bartender's gaze and eyed the glass. "I'll pass. Not really into grog."

"You just pester bartenders for fun?" The bartender smirked and kicked back her self-served shot. Licking her lips, she added, "Well, I suppose litmorian is an acquired taste."

Jinx eyed the glass. *Looks foul.* Sliding it towards the furball, she said, "It's all yours." They eyed the beverage dubiously before declining the gesture, opting to focus solely on a vivacious creature who'd slid up to the bar. Based on the difference in height, it seemed an impossible match. Jinx returned her attention to the shot and slid it back towards the bartender. "Thanks anyway, but I gotta head out."

"My shift is almost over," the bartender said. "Why don't you hang for a bit? I'll join you after I clock out."

"Can't. I've got some things to take care of," Jinx blurted far too abruptly and pushed away from the bar, then paused. "Actually, can I get a couple of cases of litmorian to go?"

"Thought you didn't like grog," the bartender said. Lifting her wrist, she spoke into the device strapped there. "Deliver two cases to—" She looked towards Jinx expectantly.

Where am I going? Jinx stared back blankly. Blinking to a familiar location or person was doable. She just needed to bring the person or place to mind. But Jinx didn't know the actual address of Jacob's lab.

She'd only been there once, which was of little use since she was carried there unconscious by her pintsized savior, DeeDee.

The bartender raised an eyebrow. "These going to your unit?"

"Not mine. A friend's." Jinx waved it off. "Never mind. I don't know Jacob's address."

The bartender chuckled. "Jacob?" She shook her head. "I think I know who you're talking about. Describe him."

Uh, he thinks everything needs to be put in a specific place and always has disinfectant around. Jinx inwardly smiled, happy to know that if memories were drifting away, Jacob wasn't among the missing. "He's a medium-built, dark-skinned human with impeccable appearance and a super-geek brain." Looking through the crowd, all of whom had been augmented in some way with technology, she added, "And he's not augmented." That was a rarity no matter what species you were. To Jinx's knowledge, only the denizens of the New World refrained from adding cybernetics to their body, and apparently the unfortunate inhabitants of Kushta couldn't afford to. Reaching up, she mindlessly felt for the EMF shield on her neck. Even that wasn't a permanent addition but a necessary one.

The bartender offered a curious glance. "You and Jacob are *friends*?"

He makes me laugh. Keeps me focused. Has my back. And I'd do just about anything to keep him safe, Jinx considered. "Yeah, we're friends. But the way you say it makes me want to say no." Jinx pushed away from the bar. Sliding her hand into her hoodie's pocket, she gripped the notebook and wristband. "Look, don't worry about it. He can sort out the litmorian himself."

The bartender spoke into the wristband while eyeing Jinx for confirmation. "Deliver that litmorian to unit fifty-nine-twenty, wing xerus."

"Sounds right." Jinx shrugged, attempting to seem nonchalant while promptly committing the address to memory. Chances were, she'd have to get there the old-fashioned way . . . on two feet. Finding an audience-free spot to blink was unlikely.

The bartender rounded up a handful of empty glasses from the bar, setting them out of view. "I'm pretty sure our Jacobs are the same.

Either way, mine keeps a tab running for litmorian deliveries. Although, a few cases is a big order even for him. Worst case, he sends it back." Sliding a small, clear card towards Jinx, she added, "Hit me up if you're having a party. 'Cause, it sure sounds like one is shaping up."

Reluctantly, Jinx reached for the card. Without bothering to inspect it, she slid it into her pocket. "Thanks." Looking around for a potential blink-worthy spot, she asked, "Where's the head?"

The bartender pointed to the back of the bar. There was a line. A long line. "Good luck. Public bathrooms are at a premium around here."

Great. Getting inside Jacob's lab unnoticed was going to be a hassle. Clutching the contents of her pocket, Jinx turned to go, offering a lazy over-the-shoulder wave. Scanning the crowd, she searched for the least congested route to the exit. There were none. The scene conjured clear memories of her previous trip here and catapulting her body into a winged Draco to avoid being nabbed. Subsequently being hauled off in an unconscious state, followed by a failed attempt to carve a tiny gland out of her brain, had been Sartillias's way of welcoming her to the supply station. *Fun times.*

Weaving across the humid dance floor, Jinx made her way through the silent disco, careful to avoid the perspiring herd of gyrating bodies — many of whom looked to be partaking in Sartillias's illegal dadah, Euphoria. Jinx pressed through and towards the faintly lit exit, which stood like a beacon on the other side of the heated pileup. Oddly, the moment didn't conjure her usual desire to GetDown3000.

As she squeezed around the last body standing between her and the exit, Jinx gave a final glance over her shoulder to see the first bartender waving insistently in her direction. Opting to ignore him, she reached for the door and pushed. A high-pitch tone pierced the bar chatter filtering through the translator still nestled near her eardrums. She practically boxed her own ears in an attempt to yank out the buds. Before she could hurl them across the room, an impressively large paw attached to an equally hefty bouncer interrupted the pitch. Silently, they motioned for Jinx to hand over the goods and be on her way.

***

The bar felt cool in comparison to the sticky heat beyond its door, no doubt generated by the flurry of foot traffic bustling past. Thick, pungent layers of spices, wafting around countless dining hubs, were carried along on the breeze of passersby. Stepping into the crowd, Jinx allowed herself to be swept up in the throngs of bodies and corralled past a long lineup of food handlers accosting pedestrians with trays of samples, urging them to make a purchase. Not bothering to feign interest in what they were peddling, Jinx shamelessly snatched bite-sized morsels off every tray within reach. Most were unremarkable, a few were noteworthy, and a couple required mental stamina to swallow. Foul-tasting or not, she needed the fuel.

Leaving a few dozen agitated-looking sample peddlers in her wake, Jinx made her way to the nearest guest services screen. It stood solitary among the sea of holographic advertising billboards vying for the attention of thousands of visitors and residents shuffling through.

"Map," Jinx said as she stepped up to the kiosk.

The screen turned iridescent blue. An eager voice replied, accompanied by white lines forming wave patterns that rolled in sync with the speech. "Welcome to Kepslar 10. We have over ten thousand quadrants to support unique habitat requirements, each with five hundred levels for optimal work and leisure. To better assist you, may I have more information?"

The whiz of a taxi flying overhead pulled Jinx's attention up. She watched it rise and quickly disappear as it headed for a level far out of view. "Can I see a map of wing xerus?"

The blue screen saver was replaced by a map that looked like a donut. The center was an empty circle indicating the space reserved for taxis to move between levels. The ring, however, was filled with hundreds of lines indicating hallways and corridors. Jinx touched the screen. Instantly, the spot zoomed into view.

"May I assist you in finding a unit?"

"Nope," Jinx replied, not wanting to announce her destination. Who knew if Jacob's unit was being monitored? If it was, they'd have a few cases of litmorian to sign for. Moving her finger across the screen, she located unit fifty-nine-twenty and headed for the nearest mode of free transportation.

A few creatures of various sizes stood in line waiting for the next shuttle. It seemed impossible that one cylinder could accommodate the ten-foot passenger slouching in the queue as easily as the six-inch commuter currently taking a seat. But Jinx watched as the plump giant ahead of her tucked in all ten legs and arms to slide into the very same seat that had just carted a minikin away. One by one, each rider stepped into a clear tube, took a seat, and buckled up before being whisked away.

"Wing xerus," Jinx said as she strapped in. In a silent shot, the tube took off, turning the vibrant scene around her into a distant blur.

CHAPTER EIGHTEEN

"Please prepare yourself for a turn," the tube announced before shifting from vertical to horizontal. The details of Jinx's surroundings remained obscured as she darted through the quadrant. "We will arrive at wing xerus in sixty seconds. Please make sure none of your belongings have shifted loose during the trip." The tube came to a soft stop, returning to a vertical position before opening the door. "Enjoy the rest of your day."

Enjoy? Jinx thought as she exited the tube. *I'd settle for making it home in one piece.* Making note of the security cameras, she moved through an otherwise empty corridor. There were no shops. No tourists. Nothing but a wide, unremarkable hall. The silent emptiness was a welcome relief. The hustling traffic, flashing advertisements, and pushy purveyors crammed into the main floor left her senses popping on overload. In the absence of the clamoring, Jinx noticed her tension, as if her angst could disrupt the quiet around her.

Sliding her hands into her pockets, she moved along inconspicuously, pausing every forty feet to scan down the numbered hallways until hanging a left at fifty-nine hundred. It was indistinguishable from the others, nondescript doors leading to each unit.

Walking close to each door, she listened for activity. It seemed odd that absolutely nothing was happening here. But Jacob had picked the spot because it was remote and easy to remain under the radar. *Maybe all geeks running illegal activity set up shop here and just kept to themselves.*

As Jinx neared the lab, a neighboring door slid open then quickly shut, but not before she got a peek. A nervous-looking, two-foot, iridescent pink species scuttled out of view while cradling a box within two of their six tentacles. The room they dashed back into was covered in wall-to-wall geek-dom. It seemed to imply that Jacob hadn't been the only intellectual on the wing.

Kind of short for a Suxar, Jinx considered. She'd only seen a few on the supply station, and they were all over six feet tall. Pulling her hood tightly forward, she made her way to Jacob's now-defunct lab. She hadn't expected the litmorian to be there waiting. But there it was, two cases stacked by his door. "Payment Required," flashed in red on a thin, electronic receipt. Jinx attempted to lift one of the cases, it didn't budge. Until the debt was settled, they'd remain anchored to the floor.

The door's security keypad was equally vigilant. A locked cover was in place, preventing access. Unlikely that this was an extra measure the bar took to ensure payment. Someone was trying to prevent entry. Maybe the station's security had the unit sealed up after the mini-war that was waged here days ago, presumably on Sartillias's orders. Possibly this was his handiwork too.

Simply waltzing through the door was officially off the list. On the bright side, if it was locked from the outside, chances were no one was inside. If they were, they clearly weren't accepting litmorian deliveries. Blinking was the only option. The place was certainly empty enough, practically devoid of life except for the jittery Suxar. But vanishing into thin air would grab the attention of anyone monitoring the hall's security cameras. Jinx intended on keeping her skills on the downlow. It gave her the advantage of surprise, should she run into any issues, a probability she'd come to expect.

Jinx ran through every option for getting inside the lab, ranging from ludicrous to complicated. Chances were it was trashed, but there was bound to be something salvageable. More importantly, she needed information on how to track down Lumi, the IOI Jacob had been working with. Someone had to help round up supplies.

The barely noticeable sound of a door sliding open filled the otherwise eerily silent corridor. The swooshing of tentacled-feet followed. Jinx pivoted to trail behind. Maybe the neighbor could be useful; they had enough technology to assume so. The Suxar clumsily picked up the pace, trembling as they glanced back. Jinx paused. Raising her hands, she attempted to gesture that she wasn't a threat. The Suxar went wide-eyed, releasing a high-pitched, sonic squeal.

The deafening sound was practically paralyzing, not to mention attention-grabbing. *Crap. So much for staying under the radar.* On impulse, Jinx cast a shield around the Suxar, which did little to calm the creature, but unexpectedly provided a sound barrier trapping the high frequency. "I'm not trying to hurt you."

The Suxar didn't take Jinx on her word and dashed back towards their unit, frantically tapping in a security code. Jinx watched, committing the numeric sequence to memory but didn't make a move until the creature was safely back inside. Swallowing hard as the door slid shut, Jinx attempted to tame the jumble of nerves firing off in her gut, threatening to eject the buffet of samples she'd inhaled. There were a few morsels she'd prefer not tasting again. *That was extreme*, she muttered to herself, making her way back down the hallway while shaking off the episode. *Maybe it's a young Suxar.* It seemed odd since the species was very protective of their young and not prone to leaving their offspring alone. Regardless, something was making them painfully nervous and desperate to leave. Jinx had disrupted them twice. Hopefully, it wouldn't be long until they attempted again. This time, she wouldn't impede their efforts. Blinking from the Suxar's unit was currently the best option, which wasn't saying much.

Leaning against the litmorian delivery, Jinx watched and waited. She'd give them a few minutes to scram. Otherwise, she was going in. The Suxar would just have to freak out for a minute until she blinked. Safer to allow a skittish creature to witness her blink than have it captured on a security cam. Besides, the Suxar didn't look like a threat. Certainly didn't act like one. And if they told anyone they saw someone disappear, no one would likely believe them apart from the drink swilling furball at the bar. The supply run was already taking too long to get something accomplished. Being cautious was becoming an annoying luxury.

The distant sound of a transport tube welcoming its passenger to wing xerus echoed through the empty halls. *Drek.* Someone arriving was not an encouraging development. The desire to pace was barely controllable as the arrival's footsteps grew louder. *Of course,* Jinx groaned, hearing them make their way down the hall. The Suxar's nervousness had amped up her own.

Keeping her head down, Jinx fussed with the cases of litmorian as if they vouched for her being here. The footsteps stopped and a door slid open then promptly closed, temporarily quelling the fear of confrontation. Moments later, it slid open again accompanied by the Suxar's gut-wrenching squeal. "Quiet down before I give you something to scream about."

Jinx's anxiety was instantly replaced with the need to protect, barely managing her impulse to burst in with fists raised. Quickly, she scanned the delivery receipt with Jacob's wristband. It flashed, "Please enter authorization code." Flipping open the notebook, she double-checked and punched in 09990. "Thank you for your business. Please enjoy."

You know what, if I make it back in one piece, I just might. Lifting the boxes, she moved with calm, stealth precision down the hall. The Suxar silently squirmed as they were dragged out the door by a beast of a creature. They were hardly taller than Jinx but built like a barrel with arms that reached the ground. A single horn curled off their forehead. The tip looked like it had been sanded to a lethally sharp point. And if that wasn't enough, they'd embellished it with spikes.

In all of her virtual games, she'd never battled this creature before but knew of them. They were on a shortlist of species that shared her language. The similarities ended there. The hermaphroditic species had evolved to exclude crossbreeding. While their bloodline had remained pure, as intended, the evolutionary turn had spawned an indifference for other lifeforms. Jinx fought the urge to smile in anticipation as she picked up her pace. "Hey! Do you guys know where your neighbor is? I've got an order to deliver."

Speaking to some unseen ear listening in on a comms system, the brute said, "Send another Gula for clean up." The bully paused to turn around, giving Jinx an unimpressed once-over. "Never mind. Forget the backup. I've got a free hand."

I love being grossly underestimated. Jinx picked up her pace as the door to the Suxar's unit began to close, barely sliding her body in its path and triggering a sensor. The door stopped and reopened. "Not here to cause trouble," Jinx said, hopping through the doorway, leaving the annoyed-looking Gula in the hall. "Just gonna drop this delivery in your unit and be on my way."

As hoped, the Gula followed, dragging the Suxar behind.

Jinx slowly set down the litmorian, stalling for time, waiting for the door to close. "If you plan on kicking my butt, you might need both hands."

The Gula didn't agree. Instead, they grinned, exposing teeth too brown to be healthy while lifting the Suxar like a floppy club. Jinx considered blowing out her own eardrums as the pitiful creature blared its deafening cry. The Gula, on the other hand, seemed delighted by the sound.

Taking a step forward, the Gula swung the Suxar, bringing the creature down like a hammer towards Jinx as she pivoted slightly out of range. The fiend lost their footing in the unexpected misfire, stumbling a few steps forward before turning back for a second shot. Shifting her weight, Jinx thrust her foot squarely into their gut. The force sent the goon sailing across the room and into the wall. Rattling their head, they stood, momentarily considering the Suxar still clutched in their nubby fingers before flinging it across the room.

Jinx watched the Suxar helplessly flail, unsuccessfully reaching for something to grab hold of before landing with a thud and hobbling out of view. "I'll try not to enjoy kicking your butt."

The Gula snarled as it rushed towards Jinx with its sharpened horn aimed and oversized arms hammering the ground. Matching pace, Jinx ran a few steps before torpedoing her body over the Gula, landing, and ramming the beast from the backside. The impact did little to budge the beast who'd braced themselves for the hit.

I do not have time for this, Jinx considered as she pitched her body off the ground, grabbing the Gula tight while they attempted to buck her off, thrashing the room in the process. Sliding her arm around their thick neck, Jinx squeezed as they swung their fists backward and into her face. *Crack.* Her nose crunched, sending mind-splitting pain throughout her body and the familiar river of blood down her chin.

As the Gula gave a few final, futile squirms, Jinx took to the satisfying task of counting the number of times her nose had been broken. *Too many to count*, she decided. None as gratifying as this, to be sure. The others had always been from plowing into an invisible containment shield during her routine shenanigans on the New World space station. She sported its unnatural banana curve like a badge of honor.

Jinx released the Gula, allowing them to crumble into an inelegant, unconscious heap. "What to do with you?" she considered, while simultaneously removing their comm and scanning for something absorbent to plug her gushing nose. Grunting as pain exploded, Jinx regarded the river forming down the front of her shirt and pants. *Great. If I find Jacob's friend, I'm sure the massacre I'm sporting won't set off any alarms.* The supply run was shaping up nicely.

Jinx wasn't gentle as she bound the thug's arms and legs before hauling the heap of flesh across the room. "What are you made of, solid rock?" She nearly blew out her nasal dam while cramming the beast into the closet.

Scanning the room and broken contents now littering the floor, Jinx called out. "Hey, sorry about the damage. But it's safe . . . for now." The Suxar wasn't in any hurry to rush out, though likely watching from some dark corner. Jinx took it as an invitation to snoop. The place was packed full of brainy tools and technology, none of which she had a clue about. But chances were pretty good that Jacob and Claire could make use of it. *Maybe I should just take as much as I can and hope for the best.* The Suxar would have to abandon it all. They couldn't stay here. Chances were, they hadn't planned on it anyway.

"Hey, you can come out of hiding." Jinx threw a tarp on the ground and began stacking random items on it. Fingers crossed that anything placed on the tarp would make it through a blink. "I'm not gonna hurt you, but you better leave while you can." Her warning failed to coax the Suxar out. "I'm just gonna borrow a few things." Jinx pulled the small notebook from her back pocket and opened it to a random page. "Feel free to help me if you know what" — Jinx attempted to pronounce a few items on the list — "sp-li-ton-ium 020, exme-tha-lium."

Not bothering to examine anything before adding it to the pile, Jinx grabbed a box-shaped device. It was the same one the Suxar had been clutching when they attempted to leave the first time.

The moment her hand touched the cube, the Suxar came hobbling out, screeching like they were on fire. Jinx immediately jerked back as the Suxar wrapped two of six tentacles around the object and backed away. Its sonic cries were reduced to a whimper.

"It's okay. It's okay," Jinx said, easing away. "I don't want the box."

The Suxar plopped down on the ground cradling the box as if their life depended on it.

"I don't think anyone is out there," Jinx said, putting her scavenging on pause. "You can make a run for it."

The Suxar looked up. Defeat pulled at the features on their face. "Mitutu," they whispered. The single word landed like a verdict.

Mitutu? Well, we don't speak the same language. Shocker. Jinx watched the creature, wondering if they were equipped with a language translator, as she returned to the task of collecting supplies. "We don't wanna leave any of this for that idiot," she said, thumbing towards the closet. "Right?" Moving cautiously towards the back of the room, she headed towards a door. "Anything useful in here?"

The Suxar leapt up and scrambled as far away as possible.

Jinx paused. Her stomach sank as the Suxar watched her in terror. Every fiber of her being begged her not to open the door. Nothing good could be beyond it, but the necessity to secure the area won out. Opening the door a crack, she peeked in. She didn't need to go further. The smell was enough to confirm that the two bodies had been there a while. She closed the door, holding back the lump bobbing at the top of her throat. She wondered if other bodies were scattered throughout this wing, other tenants that didn't vacate quick enough for whoever wanted this place cleared out. Maybe they foolishly put up a fight. *Why are we saving OI,* Jinx thought, *if this is what we do?*

Collecting herself, Jinx turned back towards the Suxar. "I'll make you a deal, you help me gather supplies and I'll get you someplace safe. Wherever you want to go." The Suxar just watched without response. "Can you understand me?" The Suxar was, most likely, wearing a translator. Unfortunately, Jinx wasn't. The Suxar continued to watch with an unflinchingly blank expression as Jinx opened the notebook back up. "Do you have any bi-edif-olium?"

The Suxar quietly studied Jinx for an exaggerated moment, then guardedly moved across the room dragging the box along. With a free tentacle, they pointed to a row of metallic-looking bottles.

"Now we are getting somewhere." Jinx continued to read items off the list as the Suxar pointed them out or shook their head, no. "Let's hope you know what you're pointing at," Jinx said, adding additional random things to the pile.

Jinx read off the final item before dragging the cases of litmorian over. The Suxar regarded the cases curiously then waddled to a shelf, grabbed a bag, and added it to the pile. "Zuru," the Suxar said with a pained smile.

Jinx pointed at the bag, "Zuru."

The Suxar nodded. "Zuru."

"Great." Jinx moved around the pile, making sure nothing was hanging off the edges. "I don't know what that is, but you're talking. Maybe I'll get a name out of you."

The creature sized Jinx up for a moment before answering. "Nammu."

Jinx turned. "What?"

The Suxar pointed a tiny tentacle towards themselves. "Nammu."

"Cool." Thumbing towards herself, she made her own introduction. "Jinx."

Nammu repeated the name . . . or tried to. It sounded more like a high-pitched horn. Jinx choked down a laugh, thankful for the fleeting comedy. Her thoughts drifted to the grim scene beyond the door. How had this little creature managed to push forward? She shook the thought loose, filing it away for later. If she came face-to-face with the one responsible for this, she'd go rabid.

"You did good, Nammu. It isn't everything on the list, so we need to hunt down a few more things." Jinx flipped through the notebook. At least ten things were missing. Hopefully, things they could find in Jacob's lab, but whether they were trashed or not was another topic. "We need to go next door, and I don't want you to be scared. So, I'm gonna do it first."

Nammu returned Jinx's gaze, oblivious to what she was talking about.

"Don't have time to ease you into this." Jinx slammed her fist into the ground, wondering if there was an easier way to blink. It was the first time she was considering ways *not* to pummel something.

Blink.

The moment the trip was complete, Jinx leapt to her feet and sped across the room. If someone was there, she didn't intend on being an easy mark. Fortunately, the sprint was short-lived. Luckily, the place was empty, and the technology that filled the shelves remained undisturbed. The control panels sat lifeless, their light snuffed out days ago before she and Jacob fled the place. The militia who'd raided the apartment hadn't busted through the security wall. That didn't mean they hadn't tried. And if they'd gone a different route and infiltrated in a less destructive way, there were no signs. The lab looked perfectly preserved like a crime scene. Dead and abandoned. Jinx imagined the place would feel forlorn without Jacob, no matter what.

An even grimmer scene sat on the other side of the security wall. Cameras kept eyes on the space. It was a wreck. The bodies DeeDee had worked over were gone, but evidence of the battle was everywhere. For the moment, the place was barren. With any luck, it would remain that way for a while longer, a hope Jinx held loosely.

CHAPTER NINETEEN

Persuading Nammu to blink amounted to trickery and nabbing.

Not my proudest moment, Jinx thought as she carelessly chucked the treasured possession — the mystery box — into the air. But it had to be done. Nammu had gone into hiding. Whether the impulse to tuck themselves out of sight was in response to Jinx blinking out of the room or at the moment she magically reappeared was anyone's guess.

"I need your help," Jinx said as she tossed the box back and forth between her hands as though preparing for a pitch. "And you need mine." Slinging the box in the air, she spun in a tight circle in time to catch it on the descent. "If I lob your little cube enough times, eventually, I'll miss, and it will go crashing to the floor." Jinx moved through the room, peeking around corners and under tables. "You can't stay here, and you probably can't sneak out on your own. But if you come and help me for a few minutes, I can take you anywhere you want to go."

Either Nammu was less concerned about the box than Jinx had assumed or they didn't believe she would destroy it. She didn't want to, but she would. There wasn't time for democracy or cajoling. "Well, friend. I guess you leave me no choice. I'm tossing your box in the air. If you want it, you better move fast. I won't catch it."

Jinx held the box out as she counted down. "You better start moving in five . . . four . . . three . . . two . . . one." True to her word, she heaved the cube up and stepped back, watching as it reached ceiling height and began the downward plunge. Jinx scanned the room before casting her gaze towards the floor, watching the spot where Nammu's prized possession would soon shatter into countless pieces.

Down, down, down it went while Jinx resisted every urge to save the box and simply be on her way. *That's a shame,* she thought as it reached the ground. Her insides recoiled in expectation, but a crash didn't follow. The cube only tumbled away. *That little sneak*, Jinx thought with lighthearted admiration, then dove for the box and the tentacle that was reaching to snare it first.

Blink.

The ride was nearly instant, hardly enough time to monitor her passenger's transition in and out of formlessness. But Jinx kept a close eye as the world reformed, bringing the creature back into focus.

Nammu stood stunned as the details of Jacob's abandoned lab came into view. A long, silent stretch passed, long enough for Jinx to wonder whether the Suxar had entered a fright-induced stupor. "Are you —"

Before Jinx could utter her next word, Nammu wrapped a tentacle around her arm and shimmied buoyantly. Evidently, the unexpected ride was worth the thrill.

"Business first." Jinx pulled out the notebook. "We have to locate these items. The faster the better." Rattling off a few, Jinx set the Suxar into motion, scouring the lab for the remaining supplies while collecting anything that looked useful or portable.

Throwing open every drawer, Jinx didn't bother to inspect the neatly placed contents before unceremoniously scooping them and tossing the items onto the growing pile. Feeling Nammu's eyes on her, she paused the scavenging. "What is it?" The question was pointless. She wouldn't understand . . . or so she thought.

"Mitutu," Nammu said, pointing through an open door.

That is officially my least favorite word. Jinx was pretty sure, after seeing the grisly scene next door, that mitutu wasn't something to celebrate. Oddly, Nammu didn't look alarmed.

Jinx crossed the room, expecting to see the two clear pods Jacob used for his unsanctioned and totally illegal tours through her station's VR. What she hadn't expected was that one of them had a passenger. Lumi was in a seated slump, her face squashed against the pod's clear wall.

Jinx rushed in. The IOI remained motionless as if powered down. Questions sprung in rapid-fire. Namely, *how the drek did she get in here?* There was no way she had come through the front door after the security panel was locked. Jinx looked for air vents. *No.* Those were bolted from the inside. Likely a security measure Jacob had put in place.

Jinx reached in, lifting Lumi's lifeless arm. *Bingo.* The device needed to roam through Jacob's virtual layer was strapped to her wrist. Jinx left it in place. The IOI had snuck into the lab, at some point, somehow, and entered the New World VR without Jacob — or at least attempted to.

With the VR in lockdown, if Lumi had succeeded in getting in, she didn't make it back out. Hopefully, that wasn't the case and she'd simply run out of juice. Jinx dashed out, squeezing past Nammu who stood transfixed at the doorway. Returning with a portable charging station, Jinx made the connection and offered an unverified prognosis. "Everything is alright. *Not* mitutu. Just . . . sleeping." Guiding Nammu away from the doorway, Jinx skimmed through the notebook, leaving Lumi to recharge. Hopefully. "Know where we can pick up some more supplies?" Nammu lifted two tentacles in what Jinx assumed was a shrug. "Well, let's hope Lumi wakes up in time to help. Otherwise, I'm headed home with what I got."

Jinx circled the lab, tossing anything remotely interesting onto the pile while intermittently checking on Lumi's progress. She hoped a few more minutes would deliver results. Blinking back to Kepslar 10 for missing supplies was something she dearly hoped to avoid. "I'm gonna haul over the other supplies from next door," Jinx said, dropping to the ground. "Wait here while I" — Nammu lunged for Jinx — "or you can tag along."

***

They didn't waste any time gathering the pile of supplies and blinking back to Jacob's lab. The Gula was coherent and enraged, ramming their head into the closet door in an attempt to escape. Massive welts rearranged the surface. From the looks of the battered door, it wouldn't take too much longer. Jinx considered knocking them out again, but there was no point in adding risk to the situation by engaging the thug. There was always a chance for a misstep. Besides, someone was bound to come looking for them soon. Time was tightening; Jinx needed to bolt.

She didn't bother to verify if everything had made it through the blink from Nammu's. Jinx just dumped the two piles of plunder together. It looked unchanged. Nammu appeared as keen as the first blink. *Good enough.* Moving around the married piles, Jinx imagined Jacob cringing at her lack of care in heaping the supplies haphazardly. He'd keep it to himself, she decided, figuring if everything, *or anything*, made it through a blink across the universe he'd be elated.

Adding Lumi to the pile of supplies felt weird, though Jinx had put a bit more care into placing the IOI than the items she'd poached. The recharge hadn't done squat, and simply leaving her here, powered down and helpless, was unthinkable. Since plugging something in was the extent of Jinx's technological smarts, figuring out what was wrong was officially a Jacob problem.

"Where do you want to go?" Jinx asked, feeling Nammu's eyes trail her every step as she secured the technology treasure for takeoff.

"Itti za e," Nammu muttered.

"Any chance you can translate that into my language?" Jinx replied while testing the sturdiness of the mound with her foot.

Nammu pointed a tentacle towards Jinx. "Itti za e."

How is it that Jacob has this much technology but not a single translator? Squatting eye-to-eye with Nammu, Jinx held out her hand. "We're gonna have to find a way to get to the main floor unnoticed and use one of the station's translators."

Nammu spoke more insistently. "Itti za e."

As Jinx squatted there, wiggling her fingers for Nammu to grab hold, a muffled argument erupted on the other side of the wall. Time had officially run out. Someone was entering. "Come on," Jinx said. "Hope you like Earth."

As Jinx reached for Nammu, the voices raised. Something was off. The cadence of their words sounded more like protest. Maybe someone ended up in the wrong place at the wrong time. Jinx looked towards the security feed, but all it captured was the studded-horned Gula hulking in the open doorway, reaching for someone just out of view.

"Azụ azụ ị na-asọ oyi!" The churlish voice sounded vaguely familiar. Based on Nammu's scandalous expression, the words that had been flung in agitation were blush-worthy.

Pulling the bartender's calling card from her pocket, Jinx flipped it around and read the name inscribed. *Pallas*. Apart from that, the clear, mark-less object left her clueless. "How do you use this?" she asked, waving it at Nammu, who answered with a blank expression. Shoving the card back in her pocket, Jinx rushed to the wall. She couldn't hear every word, but the rise and fall of their tone were telling. Maybe it was just a squabble amongst deviants. Or . . . maybe someone innocent was in trouble.

Shaking her head, Jinx dragged the cargo into the pod room. Nammu followed, watching as Jinx sealed them in. "Stay here with the supplies. I'll be right back."

Nammu went wide-eyed as Jinx brought her fist down for a blink. The awareness of something attaching itself to her leg accompanied the familiar sensation of dematerializing.

Blink.

The jump deposited Jinx in a stationary travel tube, wedged tightly along with a six-legged hitchhiker strapped to her leg. Not the detour she was hoping for. Their arrival triggered the tube's host. "Occupants exceed the allowed number. Please exit and request a two-passenger tube."

Jinx peered out of the clear tube, searching the empty hall before exiting. "How many minutes to the main floor?"

"The ride is exactly two minutes and ten seconds," the helpful transit system replied.

"Great." Jinx hopped out, peeling Nammu from her leg, and quickly set the squirming creature in the one-seater. "Listen to me. Just take this tube to the main floor and then right back."

Nammu rebelled with tiny tentacles flailing. "Na!"

"I'll be right here in exactly four minutes and twenty seconds. Waiting for you. I promise." Jinx hit the door closed and watched the tube race off, carrying an utterly terrified passenger. Turning, she sprinted down the hall feeling every muscle in her body heat up in preparation but hoping no one worth saving was there. Her gut assured her that wasn't the case.

As Jinx rounded the corner, there was evidence to back up her gut's prediction. The bartender, Pallas, was mouthing off as she struggled against the Gula pulling her along. "Amaghị m ihe ị na-ekwu, onye nzuzu."

The Gula didn't loosen the grip. "Tell it to my boss."

"Oh, hey, there you are," Jinx yelled as she slowed to a trot and casually moved down the hall.

Based on Pallas's seething glare, she was certain Jinx was the reason for the current predicament. It was a reasonable assumption. Jinx's bloody, bruised face, and red-splattered ensemble made it a challenge to argue otherwise. The Gula practically sparkled, clearly keen to have another shot at pulverizing her. Shoving the bartender into the wall, the Gula released a howl. The sound of multiple feet moving briskly down the corridor was an answer to the call.

"Ihe a bu wzit." Pallas growled and pushed herself off the floor to stomp down the hall towards the travel tubes. Locking eyes with Jinx she practically hissed. "I should have known better. You're a real wzit."

"Thanks for attempting to tell me off in my own language," Jinx said, picking up her pace as the Gula headed full speed towards her, followed by two more in their wake.

"Let me put it in language even you can understand," Pallas said, as Jinx raced by. "Do me a favor and destroy my calling card."

Jinx didn't bother to respond. Making a mental time check, she quickly plotted out her first move. *Around three minutes left. That should be more than enough to wrap this up.* The sooner, the better. The last thing she needed was a dragged-out battle involving a growing gang of rogues and a tiny, six-legged creature caught in the crosshairs.

Let's do this, Jinx thought as she kicked off the wall and catapulted her body into the first Gula, sling-shotting him backward to tumble into his backup.

The first of the three rowdies sprang to their feet with surprising agility, leaping over their pack to rush forwards in swift but lumbering steps. As the beast barreled a meaty fist towards her, Jinx dropped to spin on the heel of one foot while slicing through his steps with the other leg extended.

Impressively, the Gula only stumbled, but couldn't catch his balance before Jinx had sprinted past to cannon into the other two. A precisely placed round-house kick to the neck took one down for the count. Unfortunately, the uppercut she reserved for the second thug managed to plow into his studded horn with spectacular speed, eliciting an explosion of pain that began on Jinx's fist but rapidly spread throughout her body. It burned so profoundly that she was certain her flesh was on fire.

The single silver lining was the sight of the Gula clawing their head in confusion as their horn snapped off and careened down the corridor. Luckily, they felt compelled to go after it.

With crap-hand cradled, Jinx turned her attention in time to dodge the first Gula mid-swing.

"You and your friend are marked." The Gula laughed brutally and sailed by, pivoting as they took another swing. "You're not making it out of here. Got eyes everywhere."

"Not everywhere," Jinx said, plunging her shredded fist into their gut, launching them into the air. Her hand erupted in mind-shattering pain as the brute fell to the ground. *You have two hands, idiot. Why use the injured one? Why?* In truth, it didn't matter. Everything hurt. Gula venom raced through her body, wreaking havoc.

Swoosh. The sound of a tube arriving barely rose above the alarms firing in Jinx's brain, assuring her that pain totally sucked and should be avoided. More importantly, time was up.

Blink.

Jinx barely refrained from yelling as the tube opened. "Hop on." A more-than-willing Suxar latched on. "We gotta go." Gathering any missing supplies had officially been bumped off the list. The new priority, get home and end the friggin pain.

The sound of feet stomping down the hall, followed by the more distant sound of multiple feet running, yanked Jinx's attention around.

"How the drek did you get ahead of me?" Pallas shot Jinx an accusatory glance as she approached the travel tube. "Hapụzie," she said, shaking her head as she attempted to push past. "You're trouble. You know that?"

"Yeah, I've been told." Jinx looked beyond Pallas as two fresh Gulas appeared from one of the hallways off the main corridor. Grabbing hold of Pallas's arm, she dropped to the ground. "You're about to like me a whole lot less."

Blink.

CHAPTER TWENTY

It had taken only a second to blink to the supplies stashed in Jacob's lab but quite a bit longer to corral Pallas and blink back to Earth. Taking an unwilling passenger through the fabric of the universe wasn't Jinx's preference. There were no guarantees the jump would go off without a hitch. But leaving Pallas at the supply station wasn't an option. It wouldn't have ended well for her.

While Pallas protested loudly, Nammu squealed as they dematerialized. Jinx focused on the Suxar's enthusiasm as the world drifted away, dissolving until the vast, unknowable layers of the universe swallowed them. Everything recognizable disappeared, replaced by glowing pricks of light piercing the blackness, waiting to be shaped into the next destination.

It was a far-less complicated journey home, the details of which evaporated as swiftly as they had the first go-round. As the blink completed, Jinx kissed the cool metal of the hangar floor. The blessed moment shifted as a foot throttled her waist, temporarily replacing the fiery pain emanating from her shredded hand.

"Who the wzit do you think you are?" Pallas pushed to her feet, stumbling to catch her balance.

A second voice blasted over a speaker somewhere in the hangar. "You're an idiot!" It was Jacob. "I can't believe you just took off without —" There was a long pause. "Is that . . . is that Pallas?"

"How do you know me?" Pallas yelled, spinning around in search of the surveillance camera and intercom as if it would hold some clue.

"What is this place?" Something fierce was reshaping her face, some exotic mix of reptile and wolf.

Jinx released an audible sigh as she awkwardly pushed to her feet. With Nammu clinging tight, it was an inelegant struggle. "It'd be great if you guys could just run a quick quarantine scan and get in here." Gesturing to the supplies and passengers, she added, "I kinda got my hands full."

Nammu cautiously unhitched from Jinx, looking around without moving out of reach.

"Hey," Jacob called out to someone near him, "did you put a Suxar on the supply list?"

The sound of something crashing to the floor was followed by running footsteps echoing through the speaker. "What?" Claire's voice lit up the space with unbridled enthusiasm. "No way. I would have put way more on the list if I knew we could add a Suxar."

"Guys —" Jinx interrupted, lifting her throbbing hand to present it.

"Is that Lumi?" Jacob's voice was a jumble of excitement, confusion, and concern.

"Seriously! Guys, can you —"

"Hold tight. I'm running a scan right now." Claire reclaimed composure. "You look like drek."

"Thanks," Jinx said. "I put effort into this look."

"Looks like you had help," Claire said.

"Funny. Can we speed this up?" Jinx watched as Pallas's frustration and fear distorted her features into something that promised an eruption of epic proportions.

"Jacob's on his way down."

"Jacob?" Pallas snarled. "He's part of this kidnapping?"

"It wasn't a ki —" Jinx threw up her arms, instantly regretting the unnecessary motion. Her hand felt like it detonated, stealing her breath. Heat blazed through her body. Sweat shifted from a light mist to quickly forming beads that rained down her face to pool around her eyes and mouth.

"Taking me against my will to...wherever this is" — Pallas waved her hand around; the tension made her muscles and bones disturbingly pronounced — "is called kidnapping." Racing towards the hangar door, she unsuccessfully attempted to open it. "And however you managed to magically transport me is . . . I don't even know. What did you do, drug me?"

Jinx watched as Pallas devolved into manic, feral mode. "I couldn't leave you at that station. It was dangerous."

Pallas whipped around. "You don't get to make those decisions for me. I'm a full-grown Urbarramah. Who exactly do you think you are?"

Jinx looked down, thumping awkwardly at the floor with the toe of her shoe, and muttered. "Supposedly, the Protector."

Pallas's jaw twitched. "I don't need your protection. I'm a bartender."

Jinx rolled her eyes and scoffed. "A bartender? Well then . . . in that case . . ."

"I'm bred to handle hooligans."

"You didn't look like you were capable when the Gula was dragging you down the corridor. Honestly, I —"

Claire's voice piped through. "Hate to bust up the romantic moment, but I'm about to mist you guys. You're carrying some low-risk bacteria, but otherwise, you're safe. Looks like we can skip the quarantine cells."

The hiss of air being forced was followed by a slightly peppery aroma. A minute later, the door to the hangar opened. Jacob was on the other side, prepared to rush in. He stopped short. Pallas was up in his grill, lifting a steely finger to his face. "I want to go home. Now."

Jacob raised his palms, passing a look between Jinx and Pallas. "Can we back up a second?"

"You can't keep me here, Jacob!" Pallas moved swiftly away, sniffing the hangar on the hunt for another exit. Her wolf-like features dominated her reptilian traits as if laying dormant until threatened.

"I don't know why Jinx brought you," Jacob said. "I can only guess it wasn't safe to leave you there."

"That about sums it up," Jinx said as she walked towards Jacob. Nammu followed tightly, clutching their prized possession, the box. Slapping Jacob on the shoulder, she nodded towards the impressive pile of supplies. "A few things are missing, but I added some random stuff too."

"Don't worry." Jacob's voice had the lofty quality of a brain lifting from slumber. "We'll figure it out." He stood transfixed on Pallas and to a lesser degree, the pile of appropriated supplies.

"She gonna be alright?" Jinx said softly, nodding towards Pallas with a furrowed brow.

"Yeah. I mean, I hope so." Jacob bobbed his head side to side, avoiding a definitive answer. "Her species isn't good with captivity."

"Join the club."

"It's a little more than that." Concern claimed Jacob's face. "It was, uh, part of their conditioning to be locked up in very, very tight spaces."

"Remind me again why we are saving OI?"

"That's a question for Laris. But I do know I'd be super-bummed if something happened to you." Jacob placed a hand on her shoulder. "Maybe just try and focus on the people you care about and trust that that's all you need to wrap your head around."

Jinx held Jacob's gaze a flash longer than comfortable, ending the moment by fussing with the nasal dams still lodged in place.

Jacob offered a lopsided grin. "Happy you made it home in one piece."

Jinx raised a brow and chuckled. "Well, for the most part."

"How about not doing that again?" Jacob rolled the tension from his shoulders.

"Can't make any promises." Stepping into the hall, Jinx called over her shoulder. "I'll just leave you two to catch up."

"Great. Should be fun." Jacob watched Pallas as she combed the area methodically. "You're going to Claire's lab first, right?"

Jinx jerked around, flashing wide, hopeful eyes.

Jacob sank a little. "Ah. No. Sorry. Laris is still in cryo. It's just, you know, the tests."

Jinx slumped. "I need food, a shower, a minute to snap my nose back in place, and something to kill this pain. Can't the tests wait?"

"No. If you eat, it'll throw off the tests. I'll be there in a few with snacks. Besides, I'm sure Claire can whip up some concoction that'll leave you numb. Just hang there for a bit. I want to hear what went down at the station." Jacob eyeballed her shirt and mock-gagged. "And I'll bring you a fresh shirt, assuming you own one that's massacre-free."

"Forget the shirt. I'm dying everything red."

"With your own blood?" Jacob said. "There's probably an easier way."

"Since when do I do things the easy way?" Jinx replied, glancing over Jacob's shoulder. Pallas was racing across the hangar towards them, clearly ready for a fight. "Later." Jinx pivoted, swiftly putting distance between herself and the heated reunion.

CHAPTER TWENTY-ONE

"Welcome back," Claire chirped as Jinx eased Nammu through the door. Wiggling a syringe, she added, "You get in a tussle with a Gula?"

"A few, actually. How'd you know?" Jinx offered her shoulder for Claire to administer the dose of relief. A cool rush spread down her arm within seconds. Everything in her body eased.

"I recognize the signs," Claire said. "I heard their horns deliver a gnarly pain. Surprised you're still standing."

"Well, I'm sure whoever those thugs answer to isn't too happy I made it in and out relatively unscathed." Jinx eyed her hand, amazed it had been the epicenter of such agonizing discomfort.

"How'd ya cross paths with the likes of them?" Claire said as she took to cleaning the wounds on Jinx's knuckles. "They tend to stick to the underbelly of life."

Jinx drew in a short breath as Claire examined the cuts that hadn't yet numbed. "They were patrolling the corridor outside of Jacob's old lab. I'm pretty sure they had cleared out everyone living off that hall. Maybe the whole wing. If Sartillias wasn't responsible for barricading the area and sealing up Jacob's unit, then somebody equally cut-throat has taken an interest."

"What makes you say that?" Claire asked.

Jinx subtly motioned towards Nammu. "I'll tell you later."

Claire nodded and dropped to one knee, getting eye level with Nammu. "Shumsu?"

Nammu pinched in tighter to Jinx and cocked their head to the side. After studying Claire for a moment, they replied hesitantly. "Nammu."

"Of course, you speak Suxar," Jinx said, shaking her head. Her vision trailed sluggishly behind as loopiness set in.

"Fluently? No way." Claire laughed as though that was ludicrous. "But their language is similar to Sumerian. We've been looking into Earth's ancient languages just in case we run across any relics that survived, like stone tablets. So, I memorized a few words. Not nearly as much as Jacob." Pointing towards the mysterious box Nammu was still clutching, she asked, "Narum?"

Nammu's expression lifted for a flash then sunk with an unspoken recognition, prompting them to pull the box in tighter.

"I think it's a music box," Claire said, answering the question Jinx had plastered on her face. "I'm not a hundred percent sure. The Sumerian term for a female singer was the closest thing I could think of." Pushing to her feet, Claire added, "It's customary for those devices to project holograms of parents singing lullabies. Some even store grandparents and further back." She paused for a moment, staring off into space until clarity washed over. Smiling gently, she asked, "Bubussunu?"

Nammu nodded with newfound eagerness.

Engaging her comm, Claire spoke. "Hey, after you weigh the cargo Jinx brought back, can you grab a bunch of those grub-bars? Our guest is hungry." With a chuckle, she added, "By all means, finish your argument first. No rush." Claire moved towards the examination table, motioning for Jinx to follow. "Come on. I have a bunch of fun things to hook you up to." Waggling her brows, she presented a plethora of neatly arranged sensors. "And a feast fit for a troublemaker," she added, holding up a bag of fluid.

Jinx eyed the liquid. "Perfect. Who needs to chew their food when they can just absorb it?" Hopping up on the examination table with Nammu in tow, Jinx turned her attention to the fastidious display of sensors laid out on a tray. "Didn't realize you and Jacob shared a fondness for organizing."

Claire lifted one of the sensors, peeling back a tab to expose a sticky side. "I don't. This is Jacob's handy work." Pressing the sensor to the back of Jinx's skull, she added, "He went on a cleaning spree while you were gone. Pretty sure it's what he does when he gets nervous."

Jinx flashed her mangled cuticles and nails chewed past their bed. "Got my own coping skills."

"Me too," Claire said. Placing a few more sensors around Jinx's head, she added, "I understand why you left Jacob behind. And just for the record, I think you made the right call, but he was pretty upset. Well, worried is more like it."

"As long as he and his brain are safe, I don't care what he organizes or how much he worries." Jinx scanned the lab, settling on Laris's cryo-tank.

"Don't worry," Claire said, following her line of sight. "We'll fix her." Claire punched a few commands into a tablet. The screen instantly displayed a long column of numbers, each one increasing or decreasing. "Did you experience anything that felt like you lost a memory, like something you should remember but didn't?"

"Well, Jacob's buddy Pallas seemed to remember me, but I don't recall meeting her."

"Hm. Anything else?" Claire asked while affixing another sensor.

"Honestly, not really. But it's hard to tell for sure."

"What about the blink, anything unusual about it?"

Jinx looked down at Nammu, nuzzled into her side. "You mean besides transporting myself and others across the universe?"

Claire chuckled. "Yeah, besides that."

"Whatever I did recall from the blink just drifted away moments after it completed." Jinx ran a finger along the ridge of her nose, assessing the damage.

"Want me to snap that back in place for you?"

"Naw, I got it," Jinx replied. "I've done it enough times. Besides, that concoction of yours numbed my world."

The sound of the door sliding open was followed by a cheerful entrance. "I've come bearing gifts," Jacob called out, entering the room with an armload of grub-bars. "And I sent you the info on the supplies."

Claire offered a thumbs-up and continued scrolling through the data feed.

Jacob saddled up next to Jinx. "Looks like you hauled nearly a thousand pounds. Impressive."

"Only if I get paid by the pound." Jinx attempted to smile but cut it short as a thin stream of drool escaped.

"Well, your brain scan looks normal," Claire announced.

"Are you sure?" Jacob smirked, watching Jinx attempt to wipe the slobber from her chin.

"Yes. Her brain is fine." Claire nudged Jacob and handed Jinx a tissue. "But if you're losing memories, then something shifts during a blink."

Jinx brushed it off. "I'm not really that concerned about forgetting who Pallas is."

"Chalk it up to a multiverse," Jacob suggested. "Infinite versions of the same reality, all differing to varying degrees. Maybe you're just dropping back into a version of reality that is only off by a fraction — hardly enough to see a difference."

"What?" Jinx went wide-eyed. "That sounds like something I should be worried about."

"Ignore him," Claire said, shaking her head. "Don't worry. I'm keeping an eye on everything."

Jinx looked at Jacob and Claire, then turned back towards Laris's tank, certain that at least a few in her world were too deeply embedded in her soul to ever disappear. Everything else was noise.

"Were you able to confirm your theory on her weight loss?" Jacob asked, waving a grub-bar in the air as if to ask permission to hand it over.

"The data is still incomplete. I need the details of her trip first. There are too many outstanding variables, like the number of times she blinked. What she carried. What she ate, if anything."

"My clothes still fit. And despite the drooling, I'm fine." Jinx snatched the grub-bar from Jacob's hand and handed it to Nammu, who struggled to free it from its wrapper. "You and Booger should get along just fine," she said, taking the bar with barely time to open it before tiny tentacles snatched it back. "Chew."

Claire seemed prepared to push her point further when three fully loaded hover-carts arrived and floated through an opening door. She squealed and rushed towards them.

"Don't get too excited, some of these supplies are mine." Jacob trailed close behind.

"You done with the tests?" Jinx asked. Miraculously the intravenous fluid had curbed her hunger, but her desire to chomp on something solid lingered.

"Except for a few details regarding your trip, I have the data I need," Claire answered. "And I could use a second set of eyes evaluating it."

"My eyes are all yours," Jacob said with a sly grin.

Jinx stifled a groan, taking one of the grub-bars from the pile. "You manage to calm Pallas down?"

"Not quite, but I got her set up with a room, some food, and litmorian. Who knows? Maybe she'll like it here," Jacob replied, offering a wink.

Jinx rolled her eyes. "I'm not playing hostess. If she likes it here, it won't be on my account. I assure you."

"Hey, you never know," Jacob said. "Eventually, we'll save OI, and you'll have some non-lethal time on your hands. You might enjoy having someone else to kick it with."

"No. I won't," Jinx insisted while reaching up to remove the sensors in the hopes of escaping the conversation.

Her efforts were swiftly thwarted as Claire dashed back to smack her hand away. "Don't touch." Carefully removing a few of the sensors, she laid them back on the tray. "Maybe you'll decide to share your heart with someone other than Laris."

Jinx dropped her head into her hands, momentarily forgetting about her jacked-up nose. A dull pain, minimized only by the grace of Claire's concoction, pounded across her skull, reawakening her usual irritation. Her words growled out. "Seriously? First of all, I'm pretty sure Pallas is only interested in painfully reshaping my body. Second, I don't have time or interest in anything other than keeping everyone safe. That's not changing."

Jacob abandoned the cargo to cross the room and lay a hand on her shoulder. "That's not a balanced life, even for a superhero."

Jinx jostled her hand as if swatting the thought away. "What about the supplies? Do you have what you need to fix Laris?"

"I haven't had time to go through everything yet," Jacob replied.

Jinx pulled out the notebook. "Well, here's your list. If it's not crossed off, I didn't get it. And I'm only assuming that the other stuff is right. I was depending on guidance from..." Jinx thumbed towards Nammu, who had inhaled the grub-bar and was prying a second one from Jinx's hand.

Jacob took the notebook and quickly skimmed the list. Turning to Claire, he said, "Looks like we'll need an alternative for hydro-gel." Flipping through a few more pages, he added, "And also xeomepher."

Claire pushed a tablet towards Jacob. "Here. Switch." She wiggled her free hand as a request for the notebook. Thumbing through the pages, she said, "Looks like we have what we need to try and remove Laris's nanobot."

"But we don't have one of the chips needed to anchor the ship's security field around the pyramids." Jacob looked towards Jinx. "We'll just keep resetting it until we figure something out."

Jinx wanted to slump with the news, but she was barely staying upright as it was. "How long does it hold without the anchors?"

"So far, the security field lasts a couple of hours then it starts to break up," Jacob said. "The other option is to just secure the ship for now, but Hadu won't be happy about that. She wants access to the pyramids."

"Yeah, well, I just want a security buffer around the ship. How long does it take to reset? Like, how long are we vulnerable?"

"Same as last time, less than fifteen seconds."

"Let's keep resetting it for now." Jinx sighed. "I'll return to the supply station if I have to."

Momentarily abandoning the data-filled tablet, Jacob scooched in next to Jinx. "You wanna talk about what happened on the supply run?"

"Nothing out of the ordinary. Rammed my fist into a Gula's venom-fueled horn and took a few blows to the face." Jinx gestured to her blood-shot nose, perfectly coordinated with the rings forming around her eyes. All had turned a few glorious shades of black, blue, and red. "Then saved a Suxar, found an IOI in your lab, and pissed off a bartender. You know, the usual."

Jacob chuckled. "Wow. Sounds like a blast. Sorry I missed all the fun."

"IOI?" Claire asked, looking towards the supplies.

"I asked DeeDee to take Lumi to my lab and try and reboot her," Jacob replied.

Claire raised a brow. "Why is she powered down?"

"I'm not sure that she is," Jinx said. "I tried to recharge her, but nothing happened. It looks like she may have been trying to enter the now-bunk VR without you. I don't know what happened, but she was slumped in one of the cryos with a sensor still attached."

Jacob shook his head. "She might be stuck in the VR with the denizens."

"Why wouldn't she be able to get out of the VR?" Claire asked. "She's IOI. They aren't confined."

Jacob leaned back, propping an elbow on the examination table, as though he were chatting it up at a cocktail party. "She was merging with a few of the denizens to better understand human nature, more specifically our potential."

Claire gave an inquisitive look. "You mean, to see if we are worth saving?"

"Honestly, before Jinx showed up on my doorstep, I didn't realize that organic life was so close to the brink of extinction. I knew some IOI aren't fond of us, and most species are augmented to such an extreme they're practically inorganic. But I didn't realize EMFs and frequency bands were rising to a rate we couldn't shield ourselves from. I'm guessing Lumi knew and was gathering proof that organic life had critical value before it was too late." Jacob pushed upright, gently squeezing

Jinx on the knee before moving back towards the mound of newly acquired supplies. "Thanks for not leaving her behind."

"Welcome," Jinx said, reaching up to rip off the remaining sensors while Claire had her back turned.

"Go ahead," Claire said as if her vision was three-sixty.

"Great!" Jinx hopped off the table before the verdict was turned, then reached back to steady herself. Her brain felt like it sloshed in a pool of spotty nirvana. "Now, can we just focus on fixing Laris?"

"Why don't you fill us in on your other passengers and the details of your trip," Claire said, sliding in beside Nammu still perched on the table, licking the grub-bar wrapper clean of crumbs.

Jinx gave a quick rundown, minus a few gory details, while Claire cozied up to Nammu, and Jacob picked through the supplies.

"And Nammu helped you gather all of this?" Claire asked, eyeing the tentacled creature adoringly.

"Yup. Couldn't have done it without them," Jinx said, discreetly edging away from her little assistant, leaving the bonding to Claire. Crossing the room, she circled the cryo-tank, unnerved to see Laris in this position again — all-too reminiscent of Bayne's contraption. This time, however, the fault fell on her, at least in Jinx's mind. Allowing anyone access to the ship, no matter how secure it seemed, was reckless. Unfortunately, being careful, cautious, and patient didn't come naturally, and learning these new traits promised to be a painful crash course.

"We've got what we need to get started on Laris," Jacob said. "Why don't you go get some rest."

"What's the point? Hadu will hunt me down." Jinx grabbed a fresh grub-bar from the pile and walked towards the door. "Later. Off to my next round of torment."

"Good luck," Jacob said.

"Thanks. Pretty sure I'll need it."

CHAPTER TWENTY-TWO

"Please, take a seat." Hadu motioned towards the armchair as Jinx entered the room.

Jinx flopped down sideways. Slinging her legs over the arm, she sunk into her seat far more casually than she'd ever consider if not for the painkiller turning her brain to mush. "What exactly are we covering today?"

"I'm not sure yet," Hadu said while gracefully taking a seat across from Jinx. "It depends on what issues arise."

"You're making it up as you go?" *Sounds like a flawless approach to training.*

"Yes. And no."

Jinx raised a brow. The New World station had always managed to conjure more questions than answers. True to form, these classes were shaping up to be equally riddle-some. She lifted a hand to the bridge of her nose. A mild throbbing was surfacing through the numbed haze. Most likely, the pain in her hand would soon follow. Jinx mentally braced herself for the discomfort she'd need to endure. Admittedly, she preferred it over the opiate fog. "I'm guessing you have some sort of agenda for today."

"I do," Hadu said, "but you'll need to clear your mind first."

"I'm clear." Jinx swiveled around, plopping her legs in front. "Lay some wisdom on me."

Hadu sat silently watching Jinx as if waiting for the pain of her injuries to sharpen her senses. "Your trip to the supply station was successful, I presume?"

"I made it back. I'm pretty stoked about that." Jinx moved her hands behind her head, prepared to kick her feet up on the table between them, then caught herself before garnering a lethal look from Hadu.

"Indeed," Hadu said. "That outcome is fortunate for us all."

"Was that a compliment?"

"You needn't trouble your mind with concerns of compliment or criticism," Hadu replied. "All action will undoubtedly be the recipient of both."

"Well, that takes the pressure off," Jinx said while shifting in her seat. Her skin was beginning to heat as the Gula venom overpowered the painkiller.

"Pressure does not exist outside of your own mind."

Jinx gave a thumbs-up, hoping her silence would bring a swift end to class. Beads of sweat were forming on her forehead, a precursor to unsavory sensations.

Hadu smoothed the fabric of her gown, though no wrinkles existed. "Claire informed me of your jumps. It appears you landed in a few spots you hadn't intended."

Thanks, Claire, Jinx grumbled silently to herself.

Hadu folded her hands delicately onto her lap. "It is her job to keep me informed."

"Stop listening in on my thoughts," Jinx said, wrapping her arms around her midsection like a protective cocoon.

"These details aid in your training," Hadu said softly. "If your blinks are not taking you where you intend, it is a result of an unfocused mind."

"I'm more interested in keeping you out of my head."

"It is, indeed, important to learn to shield your mind," Hadu said. "But to achieve this, you must learn to silence it first."

"Seriously? I can barely keep it together." Jinx cradled her hand, feeling the agitation of pain and interrogation churn. "There are so many issues running through my head right now. I can't even begin to silence the madness. And please don't tell me I shouldn't have skipped meditation classes on the ship."

"The only way you will succeed as the Protector is to understand stillness as masterfully as you do action. The world will continue to speed up around you. You will not have control over what lands on your doorstep or when. If you can not combine action with stillness of mind, you will be at the mercy of luck to deliver only what you are capable of handling."

"Fine," Jinx said. "How do you suggest I achieve this?"

Hadu set a white candle, now stubby from frequent use, down on the table between them. A waterfall of hardened wax formed ridges that ran down the sides. "I was a very poor student of meditation," she said, striking a match and carefully lowering it to the wick. "Stillness did not come easily, but I've had hundreds of years to hone the skill. Even still, I often need to lure my mind."

Jinx studied Hadu as she watched the flame dance. The power of her presence had always entered a room well before she stepped in, as though her beingness were too large to be contained within the confines of her flesh. It was impossible to imagine she'd ever struggled with herself or life in general. Jinx assumed she had always bent it to her will. "Great. You've got it all mapped out. Saves me the effort."

Hadu looked up. "I am not here to give you answers. That is a job for no one. I'm here to help you cultivate tools." With that, she stood and walked towards the door, tossing words over her shoulder. "Simply watch the flame as if nothing else exists." The light in the room faded as the door opened. "I'll return when I hear less chatter in your mind or when the sun rises. Whichever comes first."

Jinx whipped around. "Are you serious? The world is about to collapse, and you want —" The door slid shut. Jinx stared at it, slack-jawed. Popping up from the chair, she charged the door. *I don't have time for this.*

"Return to the candle." Hadu's voice blasted through her mind. Well, it wasn't her voice, but it was her words.

"Get out of my head, you prehistoric witch." Jinx punched in a security code that should have worked. It didn't. *Great. Just great.*

"Return to the candle."

"This is not helpful," Jinx yelled through the door.

"Return to the candle."

"Why don't you try and make me?" Jinx shook her head, embarrassed at her lack of originality. *Seriously. That's the best I got? What am I, five?*

"Return to the candle." The words arrived with a patient promise that resistance was futile. "If you can not quiet your mind, you will never secure it. Now, return to the candle."

"Fine. Be that way. I'll just blink out of here." Jinx squatted. Pulling back her fist, she prepared to hammer it into the ground. A high-pitched buzz erupted in her head, threatening to burst her eardrums. It instantly immobilized her, bringing her to her knees. A moment later, silence.

"Return to the candle."

"You're insane."

Jinx clamped her ears, waiting for a retort. None came. Pulling back her fist once again, ready to plunge it into the floor, she stopped. *What the heck did she do to me?* If Hadu could immobilize her, what's to stop someone else? *I'm not prepared for this.* Fear rushed in as if waiting for an invitation. The full force of it was as crippling as Hadu's high-pitch brain melt. But the pain was jagged. Her heart raced erratically. All the fears and concerns she sloppily crammed to keep moving forward spilled out with nothing to dam them. Jinx wanted to puddle on the floor with them, too tired to fight them or the venom-induced pain heating her flesh.

"Return to the candle."

Jinx's thoughts drifted beyond the pain and frustration. She barely recognized she was standing and moving across the darkened room towards the single flickering light. That tiny flame had more fight than she could conjure. Falling into the chair wasn't defeat, but it wasn't victory either. It was a numbing absence of anything else. Staring at this flame was quite literally all she could muster.

At first, she stared past it. It existed somewhere in the periphery of her view. Her mind was in some state of paralysis, the kind that happens when fear and upset overwhelm you to the point of short-circuiting your system, like a creature frozen in shock. It's a type of silence, but not the sort Hadu was pushing for. Not the type that comes in peace.

Slowly her focus shifted to the flame as her mind reached for something to anchor it. The light shimmied, reacting to subtle shifts in the air that Jinx couldn't detect. Taking her first deep breath, she felt it shudder on the exhale. Each breath that followed smoothed a bit more as she watched the flame and its erratic dance. There was nothing else to do, nothing she could do, but be here, watching this flame. There was nothing to fight, figure out, fix, or f'up. The moment washed over her. And she allowed it to.

Jinx wasn't certain how much time had passed when the door opened, but something in her soul was soothed — maybe for the first time, ever.

CHAPTER TWENTY-THREE

"Seriously. No more kæffee for you. Your pacing is not helping my concentration," Claire said, without bothering to turn from the data she was entering. "Go eat breakfast."

Holding up a grub-bar, Jinx started to speak. "I've got brea —"

"A real meal. One that doesn't come in a wrapper."

"Later," Jinx said, plopping down in the chair next to Laris's gurney. Her legs immediately rattled, unwilling to chill. Then every limb went rigid. "I just saw her eyes twitch!"

"Perfect," Claire said calmly. "I'm going to slowly increase the thiophene and ease her awake." A few moments passed in heavy silence. "So far, so good. I'm not seeing any activity that would suggest the nanobot is still active. Looks like we've successfully confused or disabled it." Moving to another screen, Claire called out, "Hey Jacob, can I get your eyes on something?"

Jinx leapt to her feet. "What's going on? What's wrong?"

"Nothing," Claire said. "It's just that Laris's iron levels are really low."

Jacob abandoned his task of sorting through supplies and joined Claire. "Did you check it against her iron levels going into the cryotank?"

"I didn't measure it when I put her in deep freeze. It was such a rush," Claire said, shaking her head, seemingly at herself. "But normal iron levels should be right around forty percent."

"Wow. That's a big drop," Jacob said. "Even if she was anemic, that's significant."

"She's not anemic." Claire brought a hand to her chin as she deciphered the data. Her tongue clicked, keeping pace with each passing second. "I know this idea may sound extreme, but what if" — Jacob locked eyes with Claire, their voices blending in a unified theory — "self-replicating nanobots fed off Laris's iron."

Claire shrugged. "Yes, but I'm only detecting one nanobot in her system." Quickly, she raised a hand of caution before anyone could flip out. "It's disabled."

Jinx clasped her skull. "Can we back up for a second? Are you telling me that there are, possibly, more versions of what infected Laris running around the ship?"

"Not possible," Jacob said. "I've scanned the ship. Nothing is here that isn't accounted for. And besides, if there was, I would have trapped it in *the vault*."

Claire cocked her head, offering a look of amusement. "You're gonna annunciate dramatically every time you talk about the frequency cages you built?"

"Uh, of course," Jacob replied. "I have a few of *the vaults* positioned throughout the ship. We're covered."

Jinx crossed her arms impatiently, mostly in growing agitation with herself. "What aren't you telling me? Is there a bigger problem I should know about?"

"Well, it's *possible* that the nanobots replicated and exited the ship." Jacob spoke as if each word was carefully curated. "I've left the ship a few times for a bunch of reasons. So, there were ample opportunities for something to exit."

Jinx resumed her pacing, unable to keep her body in a state of stillness . . . ever. A significant reason meditation and its supposed perks were lost on her. "Let's say there *are* more nanobots birthed from Laris's blood — gross, by the way — and they *did* exit the ship. Could they still be within the security field?"

"No," Jacob said without hesitation. "I've set up a few cages around the perimeter and even outside the field to collect any airborne technology still running around since the mass destruction. And I've caught a few cool but archaic bots." He widened his stance. "The vault, I mean, *the vault* works."

Jinx looked as though daggers would launch from her eye sockets. "Just spit it out already. What's the friggin problem?"

Claire moved around the gurney, methodically checking Laris's nails and eyes, comparing whatever her observations were to the data on the monitor. "Her low iron levels would suggest, in this hypothetical situation, that the original nanobot replicated utilizing the iron in her blood and then went somewhere in search of more iron while carrying her DNA."

Jinx offered an impatient wave to get on with the bad news.

"If that happened," Jacob began, "there's either a swarm of bots that are continuing to multiply, or they were engineered to locate mass quantities of iron and morph into, well, versions of Laris."

Jinx brows shot to the ceiling. "What?"

Jacob waved his hands. "That doesn't mean they have powers. And most likely wouldn't. I don't think so, at least."

"Sleeping beauty should be rousing any minute now," Claire said. "I've got most of her vitals stabilized."

As if on cue, Laris stirred.

"Can we just shelve this conversation for the moment," Jinx whispered. "I really don't want to add this to her plate of crap to worry about."

"Whaz go'n on?" Laris croaked out the inebriated words while casting a wobbly gaze between the three.

"You had an, um, episode," Jinx said, fidgeting nervously with her nails. "How are you feeling?"

Laris attempted to push up to her elbows only to abandon the effort and roll to her side. "Ep'sode?" Reaching out, she stilled Jinx's nervous hand-fidgeting with a touch. "Why don'you tell what real happ'n?"

"What's the last thing you remember?" Claire asked.

"Iz'a blur. I confused sometimes." Laris closed her eyes. "Sorry."

"You're doing great," Jinx said and stroked Laris's head. "How are you feeling now?"

"Tired." Laris curled into herself, snuggling into the blanket. "Iz'a okay. Just power increasing."

"You're probably right," Jinx said, tucking the blanket tightly. "Get some sleep." Looking to Jacob, Jinx nodded towards the door. "Let's double-check the ship."

***

"I know it doesn't look like much," Jacob said, pointing to a small, metal-mesh box in the corridor. "But it would capture any nanobots moving through here. I put the 3-D printer to work and pumped out dozens of these for the inside and outside of the ship." Jacob flashed his wristband. "If any had captured a bot, I'd get a signal. So far, none of the cages inside the ship have gone off. We're clear."

"And the ones outside," Jinx asked as they stepped onto the deck of the ship.

Jacob moved towards the windshield, surveying his handiwork scattered among the pyramids. "The ones outside the security field snared some archaic little bots. Perfect for reengineering, but nothing else."

Jinx stepped to Jacob's side to follow his line of sight. "If nanobots did self-replicate, they made it off the ship and outside the security field before you set up the traps?"

"This is all speculation. But yeah, that's possible. The field was down for fifteen seconds or less every few hours."

"Alright," Jinx said with a tired laugh, wearily considering the ramifications of one impulsive act to protect everyone. "I don't know what to do with that information, but I'm sure it'll come back to bite us in the butt. For now, I'll have to shelve the possibility of countless Laris replicas running around. Let's focus on anchoring the security field." Patting Jacob on the shoulder, she added, "I can head back to the supply station and get whatever else you need." She hoped the answer was, no. The thought of blinking that far and into a dodgy situation was unsettling, to say the least. Even for a thrill-seeker.

"I've been racking my brain on how to get around using coils to anchor the security field," Jacob said.

Jinx's thoughts drifted into the shadow the Great Pyramid cast across the sand. It seemed to dominate the desert and her mood. "Yeah. Sorry about not getting everything,"

Jacob nudged Jinx's arm. "Are you kidding me? I can't believe you managed to get nearly everything. It probably worked out better that I wasn't there. You got loads of random stuff I hadn't thought of but can use for other problems. Plus, it forced me to take a close look at the pyramids."

"You mean when you weren't reorganizing Claire's lab?" Jinx offered a lopsided grin, thankful for the win.

"Yes. Between housekeeping tasks, I took a deep sample from the pyramid wall." Jacob pressed a hand on the windshield while peering out over the plateau. "Looks like whoever built these was pretty advanced. Some serious engineering went into the construction. They aren't just stone either. There's dolomite, granite, and copper within the walls. They were built to conduct some sort of energy, including piezoelectricity."

"You realize all of that means absolutely nothing to me," Jinx said laughingly. "All I need to know is, will they help with anchoring the security field?"

"Won't need them for that, but we will need them for other stuff," Jacob said. "Originally, at least according to records, they were covered in limestone."

Jinx pretended to nod off.

"Fine," Jacob said, shaking his head. "I'll spare you the details of why that's important. But we can leverage these structures for a lot of things."

"Great. Thanks for showing my brain a little mercy. I'm afraid to ask, but what's your plan for the security field?" Jinx cocked her head. "I beg of you, the simple version."

Jacob pointed to a tall, lean, four-sided pillar in the distance. "For now, I think I may be able to use that obelisk as a receiver to attract and anchor the security field from the ship. I'll need to cap it with something like a granite crystal to conduct the signals. There's plenty of that around here. Our rover brought back images of another pyramid northwest of here. It contains twenty huge granite boxes that weigh at least one hundred tons each. I think they were energy capacitors."

"You mean, batteries?" Jinx clarified.

"Exactly. They're perfect for storing energy. The solid granite means there's no interruption in the magnetic field."

"What does this have to do with the security field?"

"Well, a few are cracked, so I can't use them as batteries because the fracture will interrupt the magnetic field. But I can laser cut them to cap the obelisks. I've located six of these pillars in decent condition. I'll be able to stretch the security field out farther than just these pyramids. I'll be able to get it a few miles out."

Jinx grabbed Jacob's head, tilting it down to kiss the top of his skull. "This is why your brain should be protected. What made you think of that?"

Jacob stuttered his words while reeling from the shock. "Uh, I was really just thinking about our original idea of using the pyramids to broadcast Laris's energy out to the ionosphere, and if I could loop the energy that the Earth naturally emits through them. It would be like a power grid. The more I look at the way they're built, the more certain I am that they were designed to do something like that. If they were generating currents, whoever built them probably needed a way to direct the currents, that is if the energy was supposed to be used locally and not just shot out into space." Jacob shrugged. "The obelisks stood out like an antenna."

Jinx allowed Jacob's words to wash over her, not attempting to understand but basking in the results of his mind-play. She was more certain than ever that leaving him behind on the supply run was a smart move — maybe her first. She hoped it would not be her last.

"I'm not inventing anything here." Jacob turned from the view to cross the room, making his way to a cabinet. "I'm just using what someone else built. Who built these and why is a different mystery altogether.

It sure as heck wasn't a primitive race using hand picks and a wheel barrel." Lifting a bottle from the well-stocked shelf, Jacob popped the top. "Thanks for this, by the way." Pouring two glasses of litmorian, he offered one to Jinx.

Jinx puckered her face. "I've tasted it once. Well, sort of, but enough to know I don't like it. It's almost as rank as loustar liver."

"Nothing is as gnarly as loustar liver." Jacob tossed back his shot and sipped the second while waving Jinx to follow. "Fine. I've got something you might be interested in." Walking over to the control panel, he punched a few keys. "I tapped into some satellites that have been drifting in Earth's atmosphere for over five hundred years. I pulled out a ton of data. Most of it is ridiculous but entertaining. Among the garbage, I found something you might like."

A few more clicks of the keyboard and sound filled the room.

Jinx pinched her brows straining to decipher the noise. "What is that?"

Jacob leaned against the control panel and took another sip. "Music."

"Really?" Jinx closed her eyes, listening for something familiar. A smile lifted the corner of her mouth. "Yeah, I suppose it is."

Jacob smiled as though this moment, this discovery, was his greatest feat yet. "Here's another one," he said as the song switched.

Jinx's eyes lit up. "Dang. I like that. Can you reprogram Get-Down3000 with a new set?"

"You know it," Jacob replied. "I'll make it number two on my list of priorities."

"Please tell me that the security field is number one."

"Of course. I'm getting the schematics for cutting the granite together now."

The sound of a sliding door brought pause to the conversation, then a halt as DeeDee strolled in carrying a large contraption, presumably a Jacob invention, over her head. She moved as if she and the freight were exempt from gravity. The rumble that followed her clumsy delivery revealed otherwise.

Jacob dashed over to his creation, inspecting it carefully for damage. He'd miraculously managed to stifle objections. No point anyway; it'd fall on deaf ears. DeeDee was already halfway out the door.

"Hey Booger, hold up," Jinx called out over the music.

DeeDee paused, skating airily backward a few feet before pivoting around in one fluid motion in tandem with the beat, then launched into a series of jerky arm and shoulder pumps timed to the music.

Jinx gaped. "What was that?"

DeeDee sighed. "I didn't mean to drop it. I forgot it was heavy."

"No, I mean, what did you just do?"

Lighting up proudly, DeeDee replied. "Moonwalk and Harlem Shake."

Jacob looked up from his examination. "You stopped her to ask about dance moves?"

"No. But I *will* be looping back around to that later. Clearly, there's loads of stuff I actually care about stored on the satellites you've been hacking."

"Duly noted," Jacob replied.

"What I wanted to know is how heavy are the granite pieces?" Jinx asked. "The ones you need for the obelisks."

"Each one will weigh close to nine hundred pounds," Jacob replied.

"How 'bout DeeDee and I head out to get them? She can cut them on the spot, and I'll blink them to their locations."

Jacob pushed to his feet, brushing off nonexistent dirt. "I don't know. We should double-check with Claire. That's six thousand pounds in total plus your body weight and DeeDee's. That'll take an extra —"

"Stop. Seriously. I've got the whole burning extra fuel issue handled. I may not be a math wiz, but that entire project will only burn a half pound of weight." Jinx turned her body three-sixty, as though presenting irrefutable evidence. "Do I look like I'm in danger of wasting away?"

"Fine. But if Claire blows a fuse . . ." Jacob let the visual dangle.

"Great. It's settled. Send the info to DeeDee," Jinx said. "I'll also need an aerial view of all the locations. I need to see where I'm blinking."

Jacob returned to the control panel, engaging the monitor to pull up a map. Six spots were tagged with a luminous green dot. "Here's the first target." Zooming in on each of the locations, he added, "The dimensions of each one are a little different, so make sure the right cap is delivered to the correct location. Gently."

"I think I've proven my stellar courier skills," Jinx said, brushing knuckles to shoulder proudly. If nothing else, her original career path had been validated. She'd make one heck of a mule.

"Your partner could use a brush-up," Jacob said, glancing over his shoulder towards DeeDee, who looked indifferent to the accusation. Chances were she was breaking into satellites and downloading dance tutorials, among other things. "Just leave the caps at the base of each obelisk. I'll send a drone to lift and secure to the top."

"Hey Booger, you up for a project?"

DeeDee returned from her cyber-romp and shrugged.

"You can show me these new dance moves of yours," Jinx added, which elicited a smile and an enthusiastic shimmy.

"Grab an S.I.S.," Jacob called out as Jinx reached the door. "All but one of the obelisks are outside the security field, so the carbon levels will be way too high." The music shifted past a few songs, though Jacob hadn't touched a thing, at least not manually. "I'm gonna get cracking on this," he said as he lowered the amplifier from the ceiling and turned up the tunes. "The Great Pyramid is about to get an upgrade."

CHAPTER TWENTY-FOUR

Jinx circled the last of the six obelisks she and DeeDee had retrofitted. "So? Are these hunks of stone working or not?" Pulling the bottom edge of her tank top to her face, she attempted to wipe the sweat from her forehead. It did little more than drag salt crystals across her flesh. The late afternoon sun showed no signs of letting up, as if intent on sucking the moisture out of life.

"It's a go!" Jacob's voice practically bounced. "Honestly, I'm kinda shocked it worked."

"Happy to hear I didn't waste away in the sun all day for no reason," Jinx said.

"How's it all look from out there?" Jacob asked.

"Looks pro." Jinx lifted a hand to shade her eyes as she scanned the deeply etched markings covering the pillar. The clarity of the symbols had long since worn away except in spots. The few that managed to survive time, weather, and war were a faint whisper of what was once there. The new addition, a finely buffed cap carved from black granite, blazed bright — a sharp contrast to the dull-grey pillar beneath it.

Jinx shifted her attention to the surrounding desert. The other obelisks stood too far apart to be seen from any single location, but all were now connected by an invisible barrier buzzing between them. "How many miles does the security field stretch?" Jinx asked, looking towards the top of the sixty-foot-high monument.

"We've got about a thirty-mile radius that stretches six hundred feet high," Jacob replied.

Turning three-sixty, Jinx scanned her surroundings. It was littered with crumbled fragments that now looked natural as opposed to remains of something man-made. The relic graveyard served as a testament to the durability of the pyramids and Sphinx still standing among the rubble.

"And the field looks stable?" Jinx asked, leaping from stone to stone towards a large slab near the foot of the Great Pyramid.

"So far," Jacob replied. "I'm testing it thoroughly."

"Can you set up something to run tests every hour?"

"Good idea," Jacob said, though Jinx figured he'd already thought of that.

Jinx paused her leaps from boulder to boulder, crouching down to inspect a darkened pocket between the stones. "Let's double-check every inch inside the field. We need to make sure there aren't any threats hiding in the shadows."

"Roger that. I'll deploy the rovers. You know where to find me if you think of anything else."

The comm went silent as Jinx ran her hand along the surface of the stone slab. The spot was shielded from the elements, preserving a piece of the story once inscribed there. Whatever the narrative was, all that remained was the image of a bearded man with wings who was pointing a large pine-cone-shaped object at someone or something that had faded away. Jinx had no idea what to make of it, but it struck as odd that he was wearing a wristband that looked eerily similar to the ones Jacob had used during his unsanctioned romps through the New World VR.

Something in the air shifted. Jinx fought the urge to whip around. It wasn't a threat. Those didn't generally arrive on a lavender-infused breeze.

"Even our ancestors knew the pineal gland was important," Laris said, stepping to Jinx's side.

"That's your takeaway, looking at a man carrying a purse and a pinecone?" Jinx chuckled.

Laris squatted to get a closer look. "The pinecone represents the pineal gland, I suppose because the shape is similar." Running her finger along the image, she said, "I've seen faded images like this one etched into many of the stones. Our ancestors must have known of its connection to spiritual awakening."

"Or they just really like pinecones," Jinx said with smirk.

"Oh, come on." Laris snickered, playfully shoved Jinx. "Seriously, what do you think it means?"

Jinx shrugged. "Haven't given it that much thought." She wasn't sure why she didn't mention the wristband. Maybe it implied this reality was a virtual world too. If so, it came with questions Jinx didn't want the answers to. Life was complicated enough.

Laris stood, slipping her hand into Jinx's as if to assure her there was nothing to fear. Jinx didn't pull back, but stepped away from the image, bringing Laris along.

Hopping to the top of a stone, Jinx steadied Laris while she gathered the hem of her dress to follow. "Did you commune with the pyramids today?" Jinx flashed a wry grin.

"You make fun, but yes." Laris smiled though her gaze seemed miles away.

Jinx placed a hand beneath Laris's chin, tilting her head upwards. "What's up? Are you feeling okay?" Searching her eyes, she added, "I should get you to Claire."

Laris placed a hand over Jinx's. "No. I'm fine. I promise."

"Your poker face is terrible, Laris. Or maybe I just know you too well."

"It's nothing. It's just that . . ." Laris dropped her eyes as her voice faltered. "The idea used to inspire me."

"Are you referring to the whole saving organic life gig you got going on?" Jinx teased, testing the severity of the situation. Laris seemed too lost in thought to respond. "It's okay to feel uncertain or afraid. I'm scared of screwing up every second. Well, actually, I do screw up . . . a lot." Cradling Laris's face, she added, "Whatever choices you make, they'll be the right ones because it's *you* making the choice. Your heart's too big to ever falter."

Laris slumped as her shoulders curled in like pinned wings. "Once I reach my full power, it will envelop me." Her whispered words whirled like ghosts uncaged. "I'll melt into the vast boundlessness of the universe."

"I don't understand." Jinx bit back her usual snarky response, like *dumb it down for me*. This hit something too deep to lighten with deflective remarks. Laris was struggling with what she was being called to become. Jinx understood, well, sort of. She had only wanted to save Laris, but now it seemed all organic life depended on her not screwing up. That was a tall order, especially when OI continued to do things not worthy of saving. Jinx didn't mind being selfish, but she knew Laris did.

Laris searched Jinx's eyes and pulled away. "Maybe Bayne was right," she said, hopping off the stone and towards the pyramid. "The only way to protect OI is to make it impossible for anyone or thing to interfere with the process."

Jinx remained perched on the stone, watching Laris weave through the rubble. "I don't think his machine could have protected you from outside forces."

"Maybe those aren't the most dangerous," Laris replied over her shoulder.

Leaping down, Jinx skipped from rock to rock, testing her balance with the most precarious spots to land on. "Then what is?" she asked, teetering on a narrow edge.

"I'm questioning myself in ways I never have."

"You're allowed to be human." Jinx shifted to balance on one toe. "I constantly question myself and whether I'm qualified to be your Protector. Honestly, I'm shocked the universe couldn't come up with a better candidate."

"But you *want* to be the Protector, right?"

Jinx hopped down. "Yes. Of course. My desire to protect you never wavers." Reaching out, she paused then pulled back to walk quietly by Laris's side. *Is she questioning her ability or her desire?* The idea seemed an impossibility. If anyone could step into the role of the One, it was

Laris. Jinx had never been convinced that saving lifeforms hell-bent on screwing things up in profoundly self-serving ways was worth the effort. But it had always mattered to Laris. And that was enough.

"When my shift happens, I'm not sure I'll even exist in this physical form." Laris's words hovered weightless as though they hadn't taken root. "I may become something formless like sunlight."

Jinx's gut sank. "Are you just giving me the heads-up so I won't be shocked if you suddenly disappear?" *No amount of warning would keep that from being a total bummer,* she thought. *I'd rather remain blissfully unaware. Now, I'm just going to wonder when you'll evaporate.*

"I'm supposed to..." Laris struggled to find the right words while sifting through thoughts. She seemed to wrestle with herself, trying to work it out in her head while grappling with the reality of the situation. "I mean, the energy that rebalances our field is supposed to move through me. I'm simply the point, a doorway, through which it arrives." The gravity of the words sounded as though they pulled life from Laris as they rolled off her tongue.

Jinx studied Laris's weighted expression, worn down with confusion. *Is this just now sinking in?* Laris had spoken the same words, conveyed the same message, multiple times. But always with an air of tranquility. In all fairness, the prophecy and their part in it had only surfaced days ago. Hardly long enough to wrap your head around it.

"That doesn't mean you'll disappear." Jinx took her hand as they walked, assuring herself as much as consoling Laris. "It's okay to be afraid."

"I'm not afraid." Laris turned, locking eyes with Jinx. Taking a deep breath, she wiped away tears that tipped over the edge then offered a meek smile. "I suppose I'll be more evolved when the time comes."

Jinx wanted to say, *f' the universe. Nothing can or should ask someone to be so selfless.* But she didn't. It wasn't what Laris needed or wanted to hear. She'd trained her whole life for this, even though it was unknowingly. They all had. But easing the pain of others came naturally to Laris. It's who she was. Maybe the nanobot triggered thoughts and emotions she could normally sort out.

"Heroes don't happen overnight," Jinx said, offering the words Jacob had once delivered when she needed them most.

Laris laughed in response, but it was off, as though a reaction to some private joke. Her gaze rested somewhere in the distance.

Jinx jerked to attention. "What's going on? Are you alright?"

Laris shook her head, bringing herself back into the moment. Her soft, gentle expression returned. "I think so. I mean, I flashed hot for a moment."

"We need to get you back to Claire," Jinx said, cautiously tugging Laris's hand to guide her. "I think the nanobot might still be active."

Laris slipped her hand from Jinx's grip and turned towards the ship. "No. I don't think it is."

Jinx followed, allowing a few steps between them. "Where are you going?"

"To speak with Bayne."

"Please don't." Jinx gently reached for Laris's arm. "He's not concerned with you, your life, your well-being. He only has one answer to the problem of saving OI."

Laris laid her hand over Jinx's. "Yes, I know."

Please give me a chance to fix this, to keep you safe. Jinx choked back the words. If Laris chose to follow some half-baked plan that Bayne cooked up, it wouldn't likely be better than his first. But if that's what Laris chose, then Jinx knew she shouldn't stand in the way, shouldn't make this more difficult, even if the world felt unstable beneath her feet.

"Fine," was all Jinx could manage to muster. Laris slumped. Jinx mentally slapped herself. "No matter what you choose, I have your back."

Laris smiled gently, repeating words Jinx had delivered in a moment so similar it now seemed timeless. "You'll bloody the stars —"

Jinx pulled Laris into her, cradling her in an embrace. "Gladly."

Laris remained curled in the armor of Jinx's caress for a few deep breaths before unfurling. With a touch of her cheek, she turned to go, leaving the lavender breeze behind.

Jinx fell into a hypnotic moment, watching the length of Laris's gown ripple softly beneath hushed wind until she'd finally moved from view.

The serene moment ended abruptly. *Crap. Training.* The sun was dipping behind the Sphinx, making it officially Hadu-O'clock. Jinx slogged across the sand, dragging the toe of her shoe into the terrain. The heat continued to rise from the Earth, but the air brushing against her skin was cooling with the setting sun. Pausing at an entrance to the ship, she watched the sun disappear, making room for the stars. Soon they'd own the sky, offering promises of something peaceful and uncomplicated.

CHAPTER TWENTY-FIVE

"Welcome. Please make yourself comfortable," Hadu said, motioning towards Jinx's usual armchair while lowering herself into the one opposite.

Jinx plopped unceremoniously into her chair, nearly whacking her knee on the squat table that sat between them. "What brand of torment do you have for me today?"

Sliding her hand into the pocket of her robe, Hadu pulled out a small, dark, rectangular object and laid it on the table.

Eyeing the device, Jinx asked, "No candles today?"

"Were you hoping to spend the session quieting your mind?"

"Nope. I'm good." Tapping her skull, Jinx added, "I've got it on lockdown."

"Distracting your mind and quieting your mind are very different pursuits."

Jinx shrugged. "As long as I'm moving forward, what difference does it make?"

"If your mind is disturbed, whether consciously or unconsciously, it disrupts your frequency." Hadu sat back, with arms perched on the sides of the chair as though it were a throne. "Need I remind you that we are vibrating particles. The nature of those particles is another topic altogether. But for the sake of today's lesson, I'd like you to keep this in mind. You are a vibration."

Jinx gave a thumbs-up. "Got it." In truth, she didn't 'have it'. She'd never been able to wrap her head around it, despite being introduced to the topic many, many times while growing up on the New World station. Apart from knowing it was intrinsically linked to her ability to blink, both topics remained a mystery.

Hadu raised a brow. "If you had put a fraction of the effort into your studies as you did smuggling contraband items onto the New World station, you'd truly know what I speak of."

"I don't think so," Jinx said. "But maybe if class had been a little less mind-numbing, I would have paid attention." She stretched, feeling the tightness in her muscles burn from a long day of hauling rock. It was a sensation she always reveled in. "Besides, how is any of this supposed to help me in protecting Laris?"

"Taking responsibility for managing one's frequency is an obligation. We are all constantly merging with the energies of others. When two or more energies come together for a period of time, a new frequency is created. This trinity is the very fabric of our reality, seen and unseen." Hadu sat a little higher in her seat. "Your duty as a fellow being does not begin and end with your role as Protector."

"Fair enough," Jinx said, careful to bite back any flippant remarks. They had a habit of popping out without warning. "Not really sure what kinda vibe I'm supposed to be putting out. And honestly, if something is going on, like a threat, I'm not gonna take a moment to check myself."

Hadu's patience showed no signs of waning. "I'm not suggesting you control a normal response to danger. I'm inviting you to become familiar with your natural state of equanimity."

"I'm pretty familiar already," Jinx said. "And it's wound a little tighter than yours."

"I am certain you have experienced moments that feel like gentle rolls rippling in a pond," Hadu said. "This is your natural state. All else are fleeting feelings you linger in far too long. When you cultivate this level of stillness on a regular basis, you will swiftly know when it is disrupted, whether by your own thoughts or interference from another."

Jinx thought of Laris and the constant flow of energies bombarding her experience. If for no other reason than helping her, Jinx decided this was worth attempting to understand. "Let's say I get a handle on this. How am I supposed to use it?"

Hadu softly nodded, as if sensing a break in Jinx's position. "Mastering your equilibrium puts you in a position to either block or transmute frequencies that would otherwise dominate your experience and, hence, impact your instinct, mental clarity, and ability to take action with calm resolve."

Jinx leaned forward, taking a closer look at the gizmo on the table. "This little device of yours is supposed to keep my frequency in balance?"

"No," Hadu said, flashing her palm as though halting the idea. "Bringing your frequency into balance and maintaining it is your job. This is simply a training tool to assist you in learning how to detect when your energetic field is in balance and when it is not."

"Sounds like something Jacob would dream up." Jinx reached for the device, then paused. "Uh, should I pick it up?"

Hadu nodded. "Indeed."

Jinx lifted the gadget and twirled it in her hand. It was small enough to fit in her palm. Apart from a wristband, the shiny, black instrument had no discernible characteristics. "Let me guess, I'm supposed to wear it?"

Hadu gave a silent nod.

Jinx attempted to fasten it to her wrist, but the band was too long to strap tight.

"Allow me." Hadu pushed to her feet and moved to Jinx's side. "Wear it high on the arm," she said as she slid the device up Jinx's forearm to rest in the crease below her shoulder. "Wearing it close to the heart will ensure that it recognizes your frequency and can make calculations without interference."

Twisting her head, Jinx searched the device, looking for lights or some sort of indicator alerting her it was on and diligently gathering intel before spitting out data. "How does this thing work exactly?"

"Once it becomes familiar with your frequency, it will send pulses that mimic the rate of oscillation in your electromagnetic field."

"So . . . I'll feel it thrumming my arm?"

"Exactly," Hadu said. "You will quickly begin to distinguish between chaotic pulses and calm rolling waves." Hadu patted Jinx's arm and moved towards the door, signaling class had come to a close.

"Wait, you mean we're done?" Jinx remained in her seat, uncertain if she was reading the situation right.

"The intention of these sessions is to simply introduce you to tools and concepts, not hold you captive," Hadu said. "And the only way to leverage new ideas and unfamiliar tools is to take them into your day."

Jinx stood, ready to bolt out the door. "Fine by me."

"I would suggest spending a bit of time meditating, allowing the device to mirror the effects that a tranquil state has on your frequency."

"You know I'm not going to do that," Jinx replied. "But I'm happy to go test the effects of dinner and sleeping."

"There are many ways to lose yourself in a blissful state." Hadu held out a candle, silently instructing Jinx to take it. "As you are well aware, the effects of the flame are quite pronounced. Take this as an alternative to your usual methods for clearing your mind." Hadu gently guided Jinx out the door. "I believe you call it GetDown3000," she said, flashing a hint of a smile as the door closed between them.

CHAPTER TWENTY-SIX

Despite being painfully tired after a day of manual labor in scorching temperatures, Jinx tossed beneath the sheets. The device strapped to her forearm sent pulses as frenzied as her sleepless squirm. Rolling on her side, Jinx stared at the lifeless candle sitting on her bedside table. For a brief moment, she considered lighting it, then pushed the idea away.

Unable to convince her body that three hours of sleep wasn't enough, Jinx kicked off the covers. Glaring at the ceiling, she pleaded with her mind for a moment of peace. *The security field is stable*, she assured herself. But uncertainty wound her insides into a permanent knot. *Jacob sent out a few re-engineered bots to scan the area.* Her body ignored the assurance, amping up her anxiety levels until she caved in.

Thrusting herself out of bed, Jinx shuffled into the bathroom and flipped on the faucet, exchanging an annoyed glance with her reflection. The exhaustion was taking its toll. Even without the discolored flesh spanning out from her previously broken nose, her eyes would have revealed her weariness.

Just secure the area, then you can catch up on sleep, she promised, splashing her face with lukewarm water. Blindly, she reached for the towel which wasn't there. She had abandoned it on the floor near her bed after a ten-second shower and wardrobe change the day before. *Whatever.* Folding her shirt up, she wiped the moisture while gathering her shoes and hoodie, then headed out the door . . . quietly. The courtesy felt futile. Stillness hung like bated breath. If anyone was sleeping, it wasn't restful.

It was a short walk to the hangar. Jinx had picked quarters closest to one that faced the Great Pyramid. If Jacob was focusing his efforts on charging that thing up, then most likely, that'd be where trouble would brew. Zipping up her hoodie, Jinx braced herself for the cold. She didn't mind. It cleared out her exhaustion-induced fog. Stepping out and into the darkened, cool desert felt as uncertain as her own path. Her surroundings existed as featureless shapes against a barely lit backdrop. The handheld light revealed a few feet, just enough to plan the next couple of steps. It was better than laying in bed awake and worrying.

Jinx cast light towards the Sphinx. The impressive figure's exaggerated slope vaguely resembled the indomitable creature of its past. If it had been intended as a guard, the ravages of time had done little to deter its sense of duty. Even mother nature hadn't been able to relieve it of its post near the foot of the pyramid. It seemed unlikely the five-hundred-foot-tall triangle needed protection. It all but threatened to swallow up the sky. But then again, power came in all sizes.

Finding a few footholds, Jinx scaled the Sphinx and looked out over the night-soaked sands, waiting for her instinct to kick in. If something lurked, it wasn't giving up clues. Sliding down the nape of the neck, Jinx hit the ground and made her way south, weaving through a cluster of deteriorated stone structures and past two more pyramids nearly as daunting as their neighbor. The remains of more rock structures created a border, beyond which sat seemingly barren stretches of sand. Jinx turned back to look out over the stone oasis. Jacob's bots were undoubtedly scouring every inch of it, inside and out, zipping through the vast tunnels and chambers hidden within. Jinx turned and set her attention towards the unknown that lay beyond.

For the first mile, she moved at a fast clip past piles of rubble, evidence that something had once existed in the wasteland. There was no way she'd cover a thirty-mile radius on foot, not quickly at least. But for now, moving solitary along the foreign terrain triggered something familiar and comforting. Virtual combat with real and imagined species over exotic and harsh landscapes had kept her company in those years alone while priming warrior instincts for her then-future self.

After a few more miles, Jinx slowed to a stop, enjoying the clarifying rush of endorphins released from the run. There was nothing but more of the same in every direction. And so far, no word from the ship. Jacob would have alerted her over the comm if something had been found. Exploring the area on foot would have to wait for another day. With time, she planned to learn every nook and cranny of her new domain. *May as well check the anchors*, Jinx decided.

Blink.

Jinx unfolded from her squat to gaze eighty feet up towards the top of the obelisk. Pointing a field detector towards the sky, the grid that protected them lit up overhead. Bringing the device down, she confirmed the field reached the ground about twenty feet out.

"Hey." Jacob's voice whispered through the comm. "I see you're up. The security system has been popping off, tracking you."

Jinx smiled. The sound of his voice reminded her she wasn't alone, a sensation that unwittingly blanketed her during quiet moments. "Yup. I'm out checking our security. Happy to hear it's tracking movement."

"We've got bots for that, you know. You're allowed to clock out."

"Says the genius who's awake in the middle of the night."

"I do my best thinking in the dark," Jacob said. "What's your excuse?"

"Sleep is for chumps," Jinx replied.

Jacob laughed. "How's it look out there?"

"So far, pretty quiet. The anchor to the west seems to be holding up. I haven't checked on the other ones yet." Jinx moved along the edge of the field, losing thought in the seam where the security and sand met. "Anyone else up?"

"Probably. I think everyone is too wired to rest, except maybe Nammu."

"Why? Is Claire still in mother-mode?" Jinx asked while mindlessly moving the detector along the security field, lighting up its otherwise invisible neon grid.

"She's full tilt," Jacob replied.

Good, Jinx thought. If anyone deserved the attention, it was Nammu. "It shouldn't take me long to finish the rounds."

"Great. Swing by my lab when you're done."

Jinx stiffened. "Why? Is something wrong?"

"No." Based on Jacob's tone, his expression likely included an eye roll. "It's called hanging out with friends. I'll teach you."

"Perfect. More life lessons," Jinx muttered as she scanned the security grid overhead. Its neon lines barely outshined the dense canopy of stars stretching out beyond.

"I promise, mine will be way more fun than Hadu's."

"Way to set the bar low," Jinx replied.

"Gotta create my curriculum according to your current level. Thus far, you've shown no natural ability in the areas of play, party, and doing nothing."

Jinx shut off the detector and shoved it back into her pocket. "I'll be sure to let Hadu know she can leave those topics off her long list."

"Pa-leeze," Jacob scoffed. "She's not qualified to teach the art of hanging."

"I'll be sure to share your thoughts with her."

As hoped, Jacob took the bait. "Not funny!"

"Sure it is," Jinx said, dropping to the ground. "I'll see ya soon." The comm went silent bringing her back to the stillness around her. *Hang out?* It sounded way too normal. But then again, the madness was bound to ease up . . . occasionally. Right? Maybe carving out a few moments wasn't such a bad idea. Jinx brought her fist down swiftly, inspired by something other than the fight.

By the time Jinx reached the final obelisk, her thoughts had shifted from the task at hand to GetDown3000. If Jacob had loaded up the program with new tunes, her itinerary for the day would consist of one thing: mastering the dance moves DeeDee had discovered. Hanging out might be shifted to a priority for once.

Like the checkpoints before, the security field was intact. Nothing even mildly alarming to note. Jinx shut off the detector. Anticipation bubbled up, lifting the corners of her mouth. Looking east, she could make out a hint of her new home. It wasn't yet dawn, but the sky was beginning to lighten a shade, promising the sun was only a few hours away. The pyramids broke up the horizon like mountain peaks in the distance, waiting to usher in the sun, just as they always had. For now, they communed with the stars like a promise to anchor them in place.

It couldn't be more than nine miles, Jinx decided. She'd knock that out in under an hour running at full throttle. As eager as she was to get back, blinking wasn't going to keep her in shape. Powers alone were not enough to make up for crappy stamina. Pulling out her flashlight, she scanned the area and took off.

A mile in, she almost wished there was an obstacle or two to soar over, a hurdle to clear. There was nothing but flat, packed sand. Occasionally, she swung the light towards the security line. She couldn't see it, but chances were it was pretty close. The land beyond was peppered with rock formations, most of which looked severely weathered but faintly man-made. Some were free-standing stones, while others looked to be an entrance to something long forgotten.

With a few miles to go, Jinx had her rhythm. Nearly everything had drifted from her thoughts but the feeling of her body. A smile crept up as she pulled in deep breaths and looked around, taking in her new home. Just as swiftly, her breath caught. Movement outside the security field sent alarm prickling across her skin. The contrast was painfully jarring. Instantly, she stopped, dropped, and killed her flashlight. Something beyond the border stirred. It was brief, but she'd seen it catch the breeze — fabric billowing in the air. It disappeared through a cluster of decaying pillars. Beyond the columns stood a massive archway stretching twenty feet high.

So much for hanging out. "Jacob," Jinx whispered into the comm.

He responded instantly. "You heading back?"

"No. I think I saw something beyond security."

"Like what?"

"I'm not sure," Jinx replied. "But I'm gonna go check it out."

"OK. Looks like you're on the southern border a few miles away from camp."

"Yeah," Jinx confirmed. "Whatever I saw, is about three hundred yards out."

"Got it," Jacob replied. "I'll send backup."

"Hopefully it won't be necessary, but I'm always happy to see DeeDee in action." Jinx engaged her S.I.S. then blinked beyond the security field.

CHAPTER TWENTY-SEVEN

Unfolding from her blink, Jinx pressed herself against the outermost pillar. Peering around the edge, she looked towards the archway. Whatever she'd seen had disappeared, possibly through the opening.

Blink.

Jinx skulked towards the building, stopping a few feet from the entrance. Slowly, she sidestepped, keeping her back pressed against the rock wall until she reached its edge. *Seriously? How tall were my ancestors?* she thought, craning her neck to view the top of the crumbled arch. The height seemed overkill. Peering into the pitch-dark building, only silence greeted her. Kneeling down, she ran her hand along the sand until finding a loose stone fat enough to fill her palm. Pulling back, she pitched the rock through the archway with sufficient force to do some damage should it meet a target. A split second later, she heard a flat smack, not the thud of stone hitting sand or the dull drone of rock meeting rock.

Jinx groaned. Entering blindly gave whatever was inside the advantage. Glancing towards the distant pyramids, she looked for signs of her adolescent backup ripping across the desert. Nothing. *I've faced worse. I've got skills. May as well use them. I can always blink out if things get hectic.*

Before caution could protest, she flipped on the flashlight and ran in, prepared to start swinging. Within a few steps, Jinx skidded to a halt. Laris stood staring flatly, tossing the errant stone between her hands, preparing for a pitch.

"Laris?" The shell was hers or seemed so anyway. But whatever was behind her expression looked like a bitter aftertaste. The moodiness of it distorted her face. "How about we go pay Claire a visit?" Jinx took a tentative step forward.

Laris smirked, pulled back, and hurled the stone.

Even if Jinx hadn't moved, it wouldn't have hit her. Not with any real force anyway. "Well, at least you still lack coordination," Jinx muttered. The awkwardness of the toss buoyed her hope.

"Nothing I can't fix with a few minor tweaks." A low, deep voice rumbled from the darkness, sounding as though the world would crumble beneath it.

A moment later, the surroundings lit up. Behind Laris stood eleven duplicates. *Crap.* "Hey, genius," Jinx called out to Jacob. "Got confirmation on the Laris clone theory you were tossing around."

"Are you serious?"

"Yup. Not the sweet version either." Jinx scanned the room for the light source. A blur illuminated the far corner, a shape coming into focus one pixel at a time. If it was true to size, the creature was massive. The twenty-foot-high archway now seemed reasonable, though unnecessary for a hologram — which this was. Hologram or not, the figure was daunting.

Jacob was firing questions, all of which Jinx tuned out. She didn't silence her comm, however. The familiar chattering was unexpectedly fortifying. Besides, she didn't want to send Jacob into a nervous cleaning spree by shutting down communication.

"Ladies," the creature said as he stood to present his full height. "Let's find out which of you, if any, are worthy to survive."

"I assume you're *not* talking to me," Jinx said, watching the Laris army stand at attention. "Because *lady* would be a bit of a stretch." Jinx took a few steps to the side, testing their response, and readying her body for action. None of the Laris crew moved. "I mean, maybe if I learned to use a napkin once in a while . . ." Jinx studied the holographic creature. It had to be Sartillias. Or his projection anyway. His stature left no doubt as to why he would have survived his brutal youth.

Sartillias smiled sardonically, exposing two sets of teeth. Turning to the side, he moved with unexpected grace across an absent stage, with one arm casually resting on his back while the other was free to punctuate his every word. His webbed fingers came to sharp points, mirroring the shape of his elongated head. His noseless face created an uninterrupted slope, resulting in a massive, sharpened bullet-shaped head attached to a long, thick neck and broad, chiseled shoulders. His tail, nearly as wide as his body, floated behind, waiting for an order to crack its whip.

"The question is, do I release them all at once or one at a time." Sartillias paused, tapping a thorned finger to his chin. "Truth is, I don't expect any of them to survive." Turning, he locked eyes with Jinx. "I'm more interested in testing your willingness to kill what you love?"

He may as well have clenched her insides and ripped the contents out. Jinx pushed back the bile and forced a smirk. "What's wrong? You still bitter about being tossed out as a pup?"

"We don't suffer for our weak," Sartillias replied. "The question is, will you?" Silence stood between them for a moment. "I'm bored. Let's have fun, shall we? Ladies" — Sartillias raised his hands, his tail followed then swung down with a crack — "attack."

The stone-throwing Laris charged forward; the others followed. Jinx quickly pivoted out of reach. It was hard to take them seriously, but then again, she doubted Sartillias would waste his time. There had to be a catch. Leaping next to the hulking hologram, Jinx nearly stumbled as he swung. Dodging it was pointless. It was hardly more than a light show, but reflexes were hard to control when a mountain of muscle was coming at you.

Sartillias laughed. Cruelty oozed over everything. "Hm. I was hoping for more of a challenge than you're capable of."

Jinx ignored him as she searched for the source of the hologram. Something was allowing him to project his image to Earth while he stood somewhere watching the events unfold like a production for his amusement.

The Laris crew raced forward. One dove for her legs, but Jinx gently shook them off. Replicas or not, she had no intention of hurting them. But remaining in the tight space would end up in an annoying round of dodge Laris. With a final glance, Jinx abandoned her search. Leaping over the bumbling army of twelve, she made her way out the door.

"Jacob, are you still with me?"

"Of course!" Jacob sounded frantic. "What's happening?"

"Too ridiculous to rehash right now." Jinx moved towards the edge of the security field. "You got any ideas on how to disable the Laris army? Can you hack their systems and shut them down?"

"I already tried that the minute you told me they were there. Did you listen to anything I said?"

"No dude, I was busy sizing up a twenty-foot-tall, pain-in-my-butt hologram."

"You might need to, um, take them out of commission," Jacob said.

"I'm not hurting Laris or anything that was formed from her DNA."

"They aren't Laris," Jacob said. "I mean, the bots used some of the iron in her blood, but most of it came from some other sources."

"I don't care what was used. Part of it came from Laris."

"Well, I don't push for violence, IOI, OI, or otherwise," Jacob said with a sigh. "But I don't have any way to shut them down or reprogram them. At least not yet. They might evolve quickly and cause a lot of trouble. Especially if Sartillias is controlling them."

Jinx paused to evaluate the Laris squad as they exited the building. "I know, I know. They're a security risk."

"DeeDee should be there any minute," Jacob said. "She'll handle it, but I may not be able to reboot them afterward."

"Other options, please?"

"Listen to me, they aren't Laris." A hint of panic colored Jacob's plea. "You have got to get that through your head."

"Well, they fight like her." Jinx watched one tear across the sand, only to trip on the edge of their gown and land a spectacular faceplant. The closest behind tumbled in her wake. The rest managed to negotiate the pileup. Behind them, Sartillias came strolling out to watch his creations wage clumsy warfare. Jinx could faintly make out a small device floating above his hologram. It moved with his every step, delivering his image with accuracy while he remained at some unknown location. "You enjoying the show?" Jinx shook her head, watching the replicas untangle themselves. "Seriously, is this the best you got?"

"Careful." Sartillias crooned his warning while lifting his gaze to something beyond Jinx. A subtle smile parted his lips as if waiting in anticipation — the taste of it shaping his face.

Jinx followed his attention, at first with relief, towards a figure racing across the sand. A mini-tornado kicked in their wake. *DeeDee.* "Fine," Jinx whispered to Jacob. "I'll let Booger handle the replicas, but send her a message to not annihilate them, if possible."

"I can't make any..."

Jacob's voice drifted into the background as the Jinx locked onto the shape moving in the distance. Her hope swiftly plunged. A white gown whipped in a wind of its own making. *Great. Just great. Laris is delivering herself to Sartillias.* Jinx dropped, ready to blink Laris to safety. She'd leave the army to DeeDee, who hopefully was near. Bringing down her fist she froze as a dull tip ripped through the flesh of her back before twisting. Excruciating pain promptly followed the shock. Tumbling to one side, Jinx struggled to grip the object twirling through her insides. Her attacker pressed close, locking her chin to Jinx's shoulder. *It's not Laris. It's not Laris. It's not Laris.* Jinx repeated as she pried herself free and pushed the replica away. The mantra fell flat as she faced her attacker. Laris or not, the moment had venom.

Applause came from behind. "What they lack in grace, they make up for in ingenuity. There's hope for them yet."

The replicas moved to pile in. Clumsy hands labored to grab hold, clinging tight while Jinx plunged her fist to the ground. The blink ended across the security field moments before a war cry boomed. The real Laris raged in the distance as light exploded around her, pouring from her core in a red furry that rolled in fiery waves towards the replicas, toward Sartillias, towards the security field. "Laris, no!" Maybe it would damage the field. Maybe it wouldn't.

Jinx raised her field to block it and braced herself to take the hit. It slammed her into the security field with spine-twisting force, flinging the replicas free. They landed in a heap as Jinx struggled to push to her feet. The impact continued to send debilitating waves erupting along her bones.

The replicas on the other side charged the security field, sending sparks flying as they met it. Jumping back, they turned towards Sartillias for direction. He looked unimpressed. "Back to the drawing board." With the dismissive wave of his hand, Sartillias sent his creations to the ground in an electrified spasm until stillness set in.

Normally, Jinx would balk at his theatrics. Sartillias likely pushed some unseen button to decommission his replicas. The gesture was just his godly flare. But the sight of Laris dying in such a graphic and heartless way gave shape to her greatest fear. Suffocating grief crashed through the mental dam that contained it. She disappeared for a flash behind the emotion, lost in the abyss. Then an inescapable cold as endless as deep space cracked from her core, waking her with merciless lucidity. Jinx found herself locked in an unforgiving glance with Sartillias. At that moment, she knew intimately what was behind his eyes and wondered how closely she walked that seductive edge.

Tearing herself from his gaze, Jinx turned back towards Laris. She was speeding across the sand in an almost inhuman way, with hands raised like loaded guns.

"You need to stop," Jinx yelled. Lifting her hands, she cast a field around Laris, cringing as the effort tugged at the object still buried in her back. The pulses of energy Laris fired crashed against the barrier that formed a bubble around her.

"Crap." Jinx watched, horrified, as the caged energy returned to Laris with an angry force, stopping her in her tracks before disappearing beneath her flesh.

Laris locked eyes on Sartillias; something dark took her over. Racing faster, she covered the distance. Jinx made a hobbled dash to intersect. Grabbing her, she held tight as Laris thrashed, clawing to get to Sartillias. "Let me go."

"Ahhh, there's my lovely." Sartillias moved towards the security field. "You're tapping into your true power, your best virtue." Licking his lips, he added, "Savor your darkness."

"If I embrace it, it will only be to flatten your world should you lay a finger on Jinx.."

"Whatever it takes to free you from your shackles."

Jinx bound Laris in a painful embrace, feeling the muscle in her back tear as the foreign object rearranged itself. Her words flowed in a strained whisper. "Don't give in to him, Laris. It's not you. It's not what's in your heart."

"Maybe it is." Laris growled as she struggled to break free.

Jinx glanced over her shoulder, locking eyes with Sartillias. "You realize OI won't survive if you destroy Laris."

"How very unimaginative of you." Sartillias scoffed. "In their current state, OI is a burden. At their best they're little more than a nuisance — but useful, nonetheless."

Laris growled, twisting and turning to break free and charge Sartillias in a futile fit of rage.

Jinx dropped down, pulling Laris with her. "He's just using our bond to make you vulnerable." Squeezing Laris's hand, she pleaded, "Please, let me be your strength, not your undoing."

Laris went still as if the words reached some quiet corner of her mind. Quickly, Jinx raised her fist before the opportunity passed. Bringing it down, Sartillias's words echoed beyond the blink.

"Keep the tempest safe. I'll come for her soon."

CHAPTER TWENTY-EIGHT

Laris circled the gurney, watching Claire repair the gaping hole in Jinx's back. "Do not put me in deep freeze."

"You're a hazard to yourself right now," Jinx said, moving to sit up. 'I don't even know how to protect you when you're working against me."

"And *you're* working against me," Claire grumbled, pushing Jinx back down, shaking her head as she ran an ultraviolet light over the wound, stimulating its rapid healing. "Can you just sit still for another few minutes?"

Jinx dropped her face flat to the gurney, muffling a gnarl. "Even without your episodes, I'm barely able to protect you."

"I have to master these thoughts and emotions," Laris said, kneeling to eye level with Jinx. "It's part of the process, I suppose."

"But they aren't yours to master, Laris."

"Well, at least some are mine," Laris said, gently running a hand along Jinx's cheek. "Others are thoughts and emotions that rush towards me from out in the universe, but they trigger something within me. Either way, I must learn to transmute them. I can't do that if I'm unconscious." Her whisper was a plea.

Jinx held Laris's gaze, searching her face for proof. "How can you be certain it isn't Sartillias's nanobot?"

Laris nodded towards Claire and Jacob. "Just ask them. The nanobot is inactive." Tilting her forehead to touch Jinx's, she spoke with calm resolve. "No matter what else I am, it doesn't change that I'm human with thoughts and emotions that can work in my favor or to my detriment."

"Laris, you've never acted in anger before the nanobot," Jinx said, shaking her head rebelliously. "You can't expect me to believe that you suddenly have a violent temper."

Laris pulled back and stood. "Just because I've never acted out of anger doesn't mean I haven't had angry thoughts. If there is something in my system, it's only exploiting emotions I already have."

"I saw something dark come over you."

"It was fear. You were in danger," Laris said.

"No," Jinx said. "I wasn't."

Laris folded her arms over her chest. The gentle expression slipped away. "Well, I thought you were."

"It's not your job to protect me." Jinx pushed up, forcing Claire backward. The pain only added to her mounting frustration. "It's your destiny to save everyone else. Which, by the way, I have some opinions on."

Laris laughed. "Yes, I know all about your opinions."

Claire stepped between them. "Can you try and not undo all the work I just did to heal your back. It could use a few more rounds with the laser, but clearly, that isn't in the cards. Just try to go slow and careful while your body adjusts to the new tissue."

"Oh. Sure. No problem." Jinx hopped off the gurney, eying her bloody, torn shirt before slipping it back on. "I'll just ask the universe to put danger on hold while I heal."

"That'd be great," Claire said, mockingly chipper. "Since you have a direct line with the forces that be, I have a few other requests I'd like to submit."

Jinx rolled her eyes and moved towards Laris. "Are you sure you won't give the masterminds just one more chance to confirm that it isn't something in your system? Just, ya know, yank it out."

"If I master my response to these thoughts and emotions, nothing can reign over me. It's part of my path." Laris dropped her arms, her expression softened in response. Slipping her hand into Jinx's, she added, "That is, in truth, part of everyone's path."

Jinx stood flustered for a moment. The unknowable, the ineffable, swam in the air around Laris, offering glimpses beyond the veil. Jinx started to speak, but her words bumbled as she reached for them. Thankfully, the clumsy moment was interrupted.

DeeDee burst into the lab, strolling through, dragging two Laris replicas unceremoniously behind by their feet. The journey across the desert had taken a toll. The replicas were battered. DeeDee on the other hand looked like her usual bright-eyed self, clearly anticipating acknowledgment for a job well done.

Jinx leapt to the door to pick up the replicas, brushing them off while situating their clothes. "Booger!"

DeeDee opened her mouth, undoubtedly to protest, but quickly shifted her attention to Nammu who appeared out of nowhere, carrying two ice cream sandwiches. Scampering up excitedly, they handed one to DeeDee and pulled her out the door.

Jinx flashed Jacob a look. "What did I miss?" she asked, carrying the replicas to a civilized resting place.

"Supposedly, they had an epic game of hopscotch going when DeeDee was called for duty," Jacob replied.

"It's over-the-top," Claire laughed. "Nammu has been chomping at the bit to finish it."

Jinx's brows lifted. "Hold up. Let me guess, DeeDee didn't leave immediately. That's why it took her so long to get there last night?"

Jacob shrugged. "We could tweak her databrain to make sure she stays focused, but . . ." No one finished the thought, a silent agreement passed between them. DeeDee deserved free will as much as anyone.

"It shouldn't have escalated," Jinx said. "That's on me. Besides, DeeDee would have been there if I was on the brink. That much I know for sure."

"So . . . what do you want to do with your doppelgangers?" Claire smiled as she eyed the Laris-replicas as if she'd already come up with a few nerdy ideas of her own.

"Oh, I hadn't thought about it," Laris said, moving towards them. Gently, she brushed their hair back. "Are they salvageable?"

Jacob moved in to take a look. "Maybe. I'm not picking up on any permanent damage. At least not these two. The others are toast. The only problem is making sure that Sartillias doesn't have access to their mainframe."

"For the sake of argument, if he doesn't have access, what do you want to do?" Claire asked, speaking to Laris. "This is a choice only you should make."

"They should have the chance to choose for themselves," Laris replied, clasping the hand of the closest one. "If they are revived, that is."

"Might want to consider teaching them to fight." Jinx slowly rotated her arm, testing the muscles around the wound. "Which reminds me, everyone here needs to log in hours. I've set up a VR program to train you."

"What about the mercenaries?" Jacob asked.

Jinx offered a puckered expression. "What about them?"

"We could just train with them."

"You're joking, right?"

"Yes. Sort of. I mean, they would come in handy as extra protection to take some of the load off you. Whatever Laris did to them seems to have had an effect."

"The only thing I'm willing to do is dump them far, far outside the security field."

"You might want to give them that option," Claire said as she ran diagnostics on the clones. "Has to be better than the quarantine cell."

"Looks like mothering Nammu has made you extra sympathetic," Jacob said with a grin.

Claire looked up from her task. "Uh, no it hasn't. I want my quarantine cells back. We need those available at all times."

"I'll think about it," Jinx said, watching Laris silently contemplate her look-alikes. "I don't feel comfortable having them on board anyway."

Laris gently laid down the hand she was holding and crossed the room. "I'll be in the Great Pyramid, meditating,"

Jinx started to speak but Laris cut her off. "But . . . I will train in whatever self defense techniques you wish."

"If your meditating doesn't pan out and your alter-self surfaces again, will you reconsider a nerdier approach?" Jinx thumbed towards Claire and Jacob. "These two love a puzzle."

Laris looked over her shoulder as the door opened. "I will handle the situation if it comes up again." With that, she disappeared into the hallway.

"Bayne had something to do with this or Hadu has convinced her that meditating is enough," Jinx said, shifting into pacing mode, making a point to avoid a view of the clones. "How can we speed up Laris's process before things get messy?"

"Well, we've been playing with a few theories on how to leverage the pyramids," Claire said.

Jacob engaged one of Claire's monitors and brought an image of the Great Pyramid to screen. "The biggest issue we're running into is the absence of an external layer. Originally, the pyramids were covered in limestone, which absorbed water, adding pressure to the structure."

Claire chimed in. "We're pretty sure this process was designed to activate the quartz crystals that are in the granite walls. When they're vibrated or stressed it stimulates the flow of electrons."

"What do you mean?" Jinx said. "That tower of rock won't turn on without a layer of limestone."

"It needs some sort of exterior layer." Jacob stroked his chin while presenting their theory. "The limestone probably insulted the pyramid too. There had to be something keeping the electricity contained."

"And that's where we're stuck," Claire said. "It would take a long time to mine enough limestone to replace the outer layer."

Jinx moved to Jacob's side, uncomfortably aware of the tension in her back where the skin and muscle tightened as they healed. The effect spurred an idea. "What about adding a layer of latex that would shrink, ya know, with heat?"

Claire and Jacob shared a glance. "Not a bad idea."

"Seriously?" It was a shot in the dark.

"Hey, we don't have all the answers," Jacob said. "You should hear some of the crappy ideas we were brainstorming."

"Please spare me the list," Jinx said, nudging Jacob's shoulder. "Is that it?"

Claire shrugged. "It's all speculative. We'll have to test whether we can even create scalar waves using Laris's frequency and blast them past the ionosphere. If we can, it'll still take time to entrain enough energy waves in the universe to restore balance."

"Fair enough," Jinx said. "Then no matter what, our biggest issue is still defense. We can't survive by only protecting a thirty-mile radius. We need a security barrier around the entire planet. Can we leverage some of those old satellites you found floating around space?"

"Theoretically, yes." Jacob adjusted the screen, pulling up a celestial map marking the coordinates of each satellite, which was little more than a splattering of dots and numbers. "Not sure how many are operational, but it looks like there are between two and three thousand floating around."

Jinx eyed Jacob. "If they can send signals between them, we can create a security web. Right?"

Jacob nodded.

"Great!" Jinx smacked her palms, rubbing them in expectation of the next step. "What can I do to help?"

"Well . . ." Jacob turned from the screen with a pinched expression. "You can take an obelisk to the moon."

"Fine," Jinx said, slowly lifting her arms to test her mobility. The nerves pricked her flesh in irritation as she stretched her strained muscles.

"Seriously?" Jacob continued to cringe as he watched Jinx struggle to move. "I hate asking you to make a jump when your body is thrashed."

"What? This is nothing. Just a flesh wound." Jinx gave a lopsided grin that barely concealed a grimace. Her body was healing fast, but the pain was taking its time. "I'm not built to sit on the sidelines. If you need something done, and it's in my power, the answer is always, yes." Jinx struggled to bend at the waist, confirming that every range of motion delivered pain. "What's with the thingamajiggy you need delivered to the moon?"

"Obelisk," Jacob said, shaking his head. "You know, the thingamajigs you spent all of yesterday retrofitting?"

Jinx offered a thumbs-up, then launched into a rousing session of geriatric-inspired calisthenics.

"Having one on the moon could be used to help direct the frequency from our ionosphere out into space," Jacob replied.

"It may not be necessary," Claire said. "We just don't know how any of this is going to pan out. Just trying to solve potential problems."

"Sounds good. I like options." Jinx crossed the room towards the fridge. "Just get all the info together for me. I'll be back to make the haul."

"It'll be a few days before we're ready," Jacob said.

Claire locked onto Jinx like a target. "During which time, you need to either shovel in more food or swing by here every day so I can hook ya up to a feed bag."

Jinx gave a thumbs-up while rummaging through the food supplies. "I'm on it."

Claire persisted. "I'm serious. The obelisk weighs somewhere between one and two hundred tons. That'll burn a lot of fuel to transport."

Jinx held up a handful of bars before shoving them into her pockets. "See. Fuel."

"Where are you going?" Jacob asked.

"To bury La—" Jinx stopped short. "I'm going to bury the replicas."

Jacob rose from his seat. "Want help?"

Jinx was relieved he didn't suggest salvaging them for parts. They'd had short, unappreciated lives, wiped out like they didn't matter. Maybe it occurred to them as they were casually dismissed with a wave of a hand. Maybe it didn't. Either way, it didn't sit well. "No. You've got enough on your plate."

"I get it," Jacob said. "It's unnerving. I'm still rattled that Lumi is out of commission."

"No luck rebooting her?"

"No. And honestly, I can't devote time to her right now." Jacob kicked at the floor. "That weighs on me."

"You'll figure it out. You always do," Jinx said, grabbing an ice cream sandwich before heading towards the door.

Jacob raised a brow. "Wow, you've expanded your menu to include something other than grub-bars."

"Nope." Jinx waved the frozen treat. "I wanna take this to Booger on the way out."

Claire snorted. "Better take two. Nammu has a heart-melting pout."

"Naw," Jinx replied as she opened the door. "I'd rather watch Booger struggle with sharing. Bound to be comical. I could use the relief."

Stepping into the hall, she unwrapped one of the bars and eyed it unenthusiastically, vowing to herself to hit the kitchen for a real meal, soon. Claire's threat of force-feeding was inspiration enough to clear a plate or two of chow.

"You call yourself the Protector?" An annoying voice called out from behind. "How exactly are you gonna save the world if anyone can sneak up on you?"

Jinx didn't pause to turn around or bother swallowing the mammoth mouthful of food before speaking. "I heard you. I was ignoring you."

Pallas quickened her steps to pull up next to Jinx.

Jinx kept her eyes forward, wishing she'd grabbed a beverage to wash down the chalky paste called food. "Did you need something or are you just waiting for a chance to kick me in the gut?"

"As much as I enjoyed that moment, I'm not here to incite a battle."

"Not in the mood for riddles," Jinx said. "Just spit out whatever you're here to say so I can get on with the rest of my fun-filled day."

Pallas kept her sight forward while moving alongside Jinx. "No one should bury their dead alone."

"Not *my* dead." Jinx didn't bother asking how Pallas knew. Likely, she was a stealthy eavesdropper. It's what she'd do if the roles were reversed. Pallas seemed the sort.

"Close enough," Pallas replied. "Besides, yours or not, it's not something you want to do alone. Trust me."

Jinx now understood why Pallas and Jacob were friends. Some version of kindness lurked below her volatile exterior. "You need an S.I.S. if you're tagging along," Jinx said as she opened the door to hangar one and pointed towards a cabinet. "Grab two."

"Let's be clear," Pallas said. "I'm not prone to take orders, especially from you."

Jinx shook her head. "Hope you're good with silence, 'cause that's the only way we're gonna work well together."

"I'm a bar tender," Pallas said with a laugh. "Of course I don't like silence."

Opening the cabinet door, Jinx pulled out two devices and chucked one to Pallas.

"I don't need this," Pallas said and tossed it back. "I'm augmented, like the majority of civilization. Remember?" She tapped her head. "The little chip I have planted in my skull can perform way more functions than that outdated device."

Jinx shrugged, clamped the device to the bridge of her nostrils, and headed for the exit. It was the best she'd been able to round up during her white knuckle race through the supply station. Top of the line S.I.S. devices could translate languages, connect to the galactic web, convert air in even the most inhospitable environments, and countless other essential and mundane tasks.

Pallas followed Jinx across the hangar. "So, where the drek is the rest of your cult? I thought the New World station had thousands of denizens."

"Not a cult," Jinx said flatly as she opened the hatch to the hangar. The heat of the late morning sun greeted her with the heft of a stone wall. Ignoring Pallas's question, she took off, hoping footsteps wouldn't follow.

Keeping pace, Pallas ran by her side. "You didn't answer my question. Where are your people?"

"Your guess is a s good as mine," Jinx replied.

"Are you just naturally evasive or am I getting special treatment since I'm a guest?" Pallas took a few deep breaths as they raced across the plateau. "I know Jacob isn't part of your quirky gang of peaceniks," she said. "I'm guessing Hadu is. She seems the type. But what about Claire? I mean, she seems kinda normal."

Jinx came to an abrupt halt. A silent moment stretched as she locked eyes with Pallas. "I'm gonna need to respectfully ask you to please not try so hard to piss me off. It's been a very long week, and I really need this run to clear out my head. Please don't ruin it for me."

"You know what, you dragged me here, against my will," Pallas barked. "I actually liked my life. The least you can do is try and make me feel welcome. I haven't asked any deeply prying questions. And believe me, I have more than a few." Pallas kicked the sand. "This isn't my fight. Whatever your little group of weirdos is up to has nothing to do with me, but I'm trying to make the bset of it."

Jinx took a deep breath trying to still her temper. The mood monitor strapped to her arm sent racing and erratic pulses across her flesh, mirroring her frustration. She took another breath.

"You're right. You didn't ask to be here. For that I'm sorry," Jinx said, and she meant it. The pulses slowed in response. Jinx turned and moved into a slow jog, motioning for Pallas to follow. "Our station, over five hundred identical levels like the ship we're on, split apart in an effort to conceal which one was carrying Laris. I don't know where everyone is. They're all over the cosmos right now."

"What's so special about Laris?"

Where to begin, Jinx thought. "Didn't Jacob fill you in on anything?"

"Yes. But I want to hear it from you," Pallas said. "It's called, getting to know someone. You should try it. It's what normal OI do."

"Well, there's the problem," Jinx said. "I'm not normal."

"Pretend," Pallas said with a chuckle.

"Honestly, there's not much more I can tell you," Jinx said. "OI is in danger of extinction. But according to some obscure prophecy, Laris has the power to prevent it. Sartillias is coming for her with plans to use her power for who knows what. And we're trying to stop that from happening."

"Fair enough," Pallas said. "But you don't seem like the type who would stick their neck out to save all of OI."

"It's not a choice I would have made on my own."

"Yes, you would have," Pallas laughed. "Laris."

"What's that supposed to mean?"

Pallas shrugged. "Just, Laris."

Great. Just what I need. Someone else to analyze me. Jinx shook her head. "I'll make you a deal. We run in silence until we get where we are going, and I'll have a so-called normal conversation."

"Deal," Pallas said and picked up the pace, summoning her wolf-like features to emerge. Her mouth and nose swelled to a subtle snout that softened the severe quality of her pewter-green flesh.

"Please don't make me regret it," Jinx yelled as she followed. "Otherwise, I'll have to dig an extra grave."

"Others have tried and failed," Pallas yelled back. "But good luck."

Maybe this won't be so bad, Jinx considered, watching the sun glint off Pallas's leathery hide.

CHAPTER TWENTY-NINE

I really need to switch to black, Jinx decided as she moved along the pristine corridor. Her formerly white tights and tank were a dismal shade of dust after the unnerving task of burying the Laris clones. Luckily, roaming the territory within the security field, looking for threats, had burned away the funerary angst, but sadly, not the grimy evidence. Filth was low on the list of occupational hazards, but surprisingly annoying.

Jinx paused to brush loose debris off her hip. *Crap.* A darker streak appeared beneath the path of her exceptionally grubby hand. Reaching for the door, she regarded her blackened palm, contemplating a quick shower before tackling the next irksome task. Class.

"I assure you, taking a shower is not worth arriving late." Hadu's voice exited the opening door. "You have barely beat the clock as it is."

Jinx stiffened. The pulses streaming off her monitor, however, exploded like fireworks across her flesh. She wanted to hurl the arm band down the corridor. Begrudgingly, she left the annoying contraption in place and stepped into the room. "I'd be more than happy to give up crawling on my belly through narrow, underground passages in your precious pyramids to hunt for threats in the dark, just so I could be on time."

Hadu regarded Jinx with subdued humor. "I know good and well there are few things you'd rather do than exactly that."

"Fine," Jinx huffed. "But I can't keep coming here every day. That's insane." Plopping down in her usual chair, she moved to rest her dingy hands on the upholstered arms, then pulled back, tucking them safely under her armpits.

Hadu breezed across the room, pulling a pack of wipes from somewhere beneath the endless folds of her robe. Handing them to Jinx, she turned to stroll around the room, the long tail of her stark white kimono following dutifully behind. "When you understand the value of consciously evolving, you will make a point of getting here without a fuss."

Jinx pulled a wad of wipes from the container and began sanitizing her hands. The contrast between the now cleanish palms and sullied forearms was comical. There weren't enough wipes on the ship to tackle the entire disaster zone. Nothing short of a high-pressured shower would do the trick. "I can barely get through one of your lectures," she grumbled, stuffing the muddied wipes back into the empty container. "Battling Sartillias is bound to be less excruciating."

Hadu didn't bother turning from the tour of her room, pausing only to inspect random artifacts she'd purposefully placed. "You will either experience the value of these concepts during their successful application or reach for them when you fail. The choice is yours." After adjusting a small golden statue ever-so-slightly, she headed towards her desk. "But all roads lead to evolution. One is simply more agreeable than the other."

Jinx fought the urge to sprawl out in the oversized chair. Its plushness wasn't helping to stave off her overwhelming fatigue. "Pep talks aren't your strength, I've noticed."

Hadu took a seat, gracefully placing her entwined hands on her desk. "I highly doubt you'd find much motivation in such things."

"True," Jinx said, shifting impatiently in her seat. "Any chance we can make this a short session." Jinx reached for an important-sounding excuse. "I have a massive stone-stick-thingy to transport to the moon."

Hadu's expression glazed over as if dipping into an unseen realm. Stillness hung for a moment, then broke. "Jacob and Claire are not yet ready for you. Though, I feel certain you are aware of this fact. Regardless, the sooner we get started, the faster we can send you on your way."

Jinx sunk further into the chair. Resistance was futile. Hadu had a gravitational pull, like a black hole where even light couldn't escape.

Looking around, Jinx took note of some changes. "Someone's been busy decorating."

The walls and surfaces were carefully curated with pieces Hadu had undoubtedly collected over her hundreds of years. It wasn't cluttered by any stretch, but it was a far cry from the minimalist approach of the station. Surely, everything in the room held intrinsic value or purpose. Hadu didn't seem the type to cling.

"While I appreciate the value that adorning a room may provide, beauty is not my intent."

"Me either," Jinx said unabashedly. "Speaking of your motive, what's the torture for today: more candles, annoying gadgets, riddles, chanting, tuning forks, or just a sharp stick in the eye?"

"If a sharp stick in the eye is your preferred method for cultivating satori, then I have plenty to choose from." Hadu opened a finely polished wooden box to reveal a half dozen sharpened sticks.

Jinx doubted their intended use was eye skewering, but she wasn't placing bets. "I find it hard to believe that my state of mind is really worth all this effort." Jinx pushed up from her seat, in part due to her untamable restlessness. But mostly, she wanted to see Hadu's collection up close.

"You are no good to Laris if your mind is vulnerable," Hadu said calmly. "Sartillias will know your every move."

Jinx leaned forward, eyeing a tiny silver egg covered in intricate markings. "He can't read minds."

"Probably not. But if he has access to Laris, he will have access to you."

"Speaking of Laris, are you planting idiotic seeds in her head." Jinx reached out to touch the egg, then pulled back. Bringing a muddied hand to anything in the room felt irreverent, even for her. "She's determined to use meditation to control whatever is messing with her mind."

"Control over one's own mental body is essential. Without it, failure is imminent."

"It's pushing her over the edge," Jinx said, pulling away from the egg to casually explore Hadu's other treasures. "I think Claire and Jacob need to try and remove whatever is triggering these emotions and thoughts."

"I suppose you'd have your own challenging thoughts and emotions surgically removed if you could," Hadu said.

Jinx turned her attention from the exotic exhibition. "Is that a real procedure? If so, sign me up. My emotions trip me up every time. Feel free to take them away. I'd be a much better Protector without them."

"You would not *be* the Protector without your emotions," Hadu replied. "Power isn't in the absence of thoughts and emotion. It is in the mastery of them. They hold potent energy that when directed wisely can shift the fabric of reality for better or worse."

Jinx groaned and returned her attention to the knickknacks, thingamabobs, and whatsits scattered around the room. "Do I have to stare at a candle again today?" she asked, glancing back at the egg with curiosity.

"No. I'm here to introduce you to new ideas and tools, not babysit while you practice." Hadu motioned towards the wall, her wide sleeve billowing behind in an absent breeze. "Now, if you'd be so kind as to bring over the egg, we can get started."

"Seriously?" Jinx asked, presenting her still-filthy hands, suddenly feeling like DeeDee on a particularly messy day.

Hadu waved the gesture away. "Please, no object is so precious as all of that. What I hold dear can not be tarnished." Motioning an arm around the room and all that it held, she added, "These are simply talismans to help point the way."

Point the way to what? Jinx thought but resisted asking. After eighteen years with the likes of Hadu and the rest of the New World denizens, she knew the answer would be wrapped in an enigma. She spared herself the annoyance. She had enough unanswered questions to puzzle over.

Lifting the oval object from its resting place hardly took two fingers, but Jinx felt compelled to cup it gently in the palm of her hand. "Out of everything in your room, why this?"

"You selected it. Not I," Hadu replied.

Jinx smiled inwardly. *Kinda cool.* "You mean whatever I seem interested in determines what you teach?"

Hadu smiled thinly but remained silent.

Sitting down, Jinx set her hands on her thighs allowing the egg to rest in her palms. "What now?"

"Can you enter this egg?" Hadu asked.

"What, you mean like blink inside of it?"

"Yes."

Jinx scoffed. "No. Of course not."

"Do you know what is inside of the egg?"

Jinx eyed the small oval for a moment, contemplating the weight of it in her hand. "More silver, I suppose."

"Maybe," Hadu replied. "But you can not know for sure."

"Yes, I can. I'd take it to Jacob or Claire and have them scan it."

"What if the interior is lined with beryllium?"

"I don't know what that is, but I'm guessing you can't scan through it." Jinx looked at the object. "Great. I'll just fill my skull with beryllium, and we'll be all set."

"Don't worry. We'll work on shifting the contents of your head in the future. For now, let's focus on shielding your mind from external influences." Hadu stood and crossed the space between them. Reaching down, she tapped a bony knuckle on the egg. "You need to build an impenetrable shield."

Jinx cocked her head. "Are you serious? That's not realistic. Besides, I can't fight that way."

Hadu sighed and shook her head. "Not a physical shield."

"Oh," Jinx said. "Well, why don't I just cast an energy barrier around my head?"

"And then what? Hold that in place," Hadu said. "I presume you need your hands for other things."

Jinx allowed her head to flop back to rest on the chair, feeling too tired to think straight. "Then how?" she asked wearily.

Hadu moved to stare down at Jinx, blocking her view of the ceiling with her massive head. "Mentally," she replied, gently touching her finger to Jinx's forehead before stepping out of view. "Each day you must imagine a bubble, as solid as the egg you are holding, wrapped around your entire body."

"My whole body?" Jinx asked, scanning the ceiling for a distraction. "I thought we were just dealing with my head."

"Thoughts and emotions move through your entire auric field. By building this shield each day, you protect your space, your thoughts, and your emotions from external influences." Hadu remained a towering presence at Jinx's side. "If you would devote a few moments a day to managing your energetic field, you would know quite quickly when someone or something is entering without your invitation."

Jinx lifted her arm, presenting the monitor strapped in place. "According to your latest gift, I have no control over my so-called energetic field. Which, by the way, is kind of annoying to be reminded of constantly."

"You may opt to transform it or argue for your limitation," Hadu said. "The choice is always yours."

With a groan, Jinx abandoned the ceiling, shifting her focus back to Hadu. "Fine. What do I need to do?"

"For now, simply take a few moments out of your morning to imagine a large bubble, as solid as the egg you are holding, wrapped around your entire body."

"Seriously? It's that simple?"

"Were you hoping for something complicated, like staring at a candle?" Hadu teased and moved towards the door. "Feel free to keep the egg as a reminder throughout your days."

Jinx pinched her brow and stood, careful to protect the tiny keepsake in cupped hands. "We're done?"

Hadu nodded as she opened the door. "I have work to do in the pyramid before Sartillias arrives."

"You mean I'm supposed to figure out, on my own, how to create this impenetrable shield?" Jinx asked, following in Hadu's wake.

"All in life begins as a thought, and I'm certain you do not suffer from a lack of imagination."

"I have more faith in my ability to haul a two-hundred-ton chunk of stone through space and time than I do in my ability to master these techniques of yours before that goon arrives," Jinx said, pausing at the open doorway.

"True. But that doesn't mean you are ill-prepared. Your potential isn't measured by this or any battle. You will always evolve. And in that endeavor, you'll discover new limitations to master." Hadu lifted a hand to Jinx's shoulder. "I have faith in you. And I believe you have more faith in yourself than you acknowledge."

With a nudge out, Hadu disappeared behind the closing door.

CHAPTER THIRTY

The past few days had proven to work up a bottomless appetite. After endless hours of scouring the thirty-mile security field and equally taxing Hadu sessions, Jinx was famished. For once, a block of food substance stored in a nondescript wrapper wasn't going to cut it. Besides, she needed to appease Claire and her insistence on upping the caloric intake before blinking to the moon. Luckily, the 3-D food printer was more than obliging. After shoveling down two plates of warm, well-formed nutrients, Jinx launched into her morning routine, making a quick pit stop at the newly appointed combat training lab before heading out to the sands of the plateau.

DeeDee had taken it upon herself to train Nammu, though, from the looks of it, the six-legged warrior was better suited for charming someone to death. Pallas and Claire were both deeply entrenched in their own VR battles. As expected, Pallas's wolverine had surfaced. Jinx watched and wondered what her beast looked like in full-blown action. *Undoubtedly lethal,* she decided. And Claire was holding her own against the virtual threat she'd opted to fight. Jinx made a mental note to peek at the recording. As usual, Jacob was nowhere in sight.

Dipping out of the lab before her army in training took notice, she headed back down the hall. "Where are you?" Jinx called out over the comm. "At this rate, even Nammu will be able to take you down."

"Good morning to you too," Jacob shot back. "I'm headed for hanger three."

Blink.

Jinx appeared at the entrance to the hangar as Jacob approached. "Where ya going?"

Jacob stumbled, instinctively reaching for his heart. "Seriously?" Taking a second to collect himself, he added, "You scared the drek out of me."

"*This* is why you need to train."

"I'll leave the fighting to Nammu." Jacob reached around Jinx and entered a code. The hangar door slid open.

"If Hadu can insist I train in some mystical crap every day, then you can set aside thirty minutes to at least learn a few defense techniques."

Jacob slid past, waving passively in his wake. "I know. I know."

Jinx shuffled up to his side. "Go with Claire. You can scrimmage."

Jacob perked up but kept his sight forward. "She didn't tell me she started training. Hm, just like her to try and get an edge. OK. It's officially moved to priority number one." Tossing Jinx a piece of thin, rubbery material, he added, "First, I need to test how this responds to the elements."

Jinx wiggled the small square piece in the air. "Nice! Is this our new pyramid cover?"

"Yeah," Jacob chirped. "I combined your idea of a material that shrinks in the heat with an ability to absorb water."

Jinx held up the tiny sheet. "Might need more than this. Have you seen how big the pyramid is? You'll need at least twice this much."

Jacob eyeballed it. "Really? You think so? I don't know. According to my calculations, this should do the trick."

"You might wanna double-check your math."

Jacob smiled and snagged the rubbery sample. "I want to leave it out in the elements overnight. I need to confirm it won't have reactions I haven't accounted for before we start pumping this stuff out and applying it to the pyramid. I don't want to make a big mess and waste resources."

The smell of sand baking in the late morning sun, drenched the air, rising in thick wafts to greet them as they stepped out and onto the plateau. Jinx hadn't missed the edgeless darkness of deep space since arriving on Earth, but she was certain she'd miss the sun. "Any progress on identifying a rock for me to move to the moon?"

"Yup. There's one in some place called Paris."

Jinx raised a brow.

Jacob shrugged. "I'll show you the satellite images. It's not in Egypt, but it was originally from here."

"The sooner the better. I'm getting way too comfortable with my new routine." Jinx dragged the toe of her shoe along the sand as they walked, feeling the warmth of it seep through to caress her skin. "How are we looking on the satellites?"

"More than half are responding." Jacob shielded his eyes, looking towards the sky as if he'd see them floating overhead. "We can get a pretty good security grid up and running before the end of tomorrow. Hopefully, Sartillias won't arrive first."

Jinx clucked. "Sartillias is probably somewhere on Earth already. I'll just have to deal with him when the time comes."

"Fun times." Jacob nudged Jinx playfully as he came to a stop. "This spot is as good as any." After laying the rubbery sheet on a wide flat stone, he pulled a cylinder from his pocket. "We got a sample of the water running below ground, beneath the pyramid." Jacob poured the water over the material. "The added weight and pressure should trigger a piezoelectric chain reaction, which could" — Jacob raised crossed fingers — "turn this machine on."

Jinx lowered to a squat, watching as the sheet expanded from paper-thin to nearly an inch thick, absorbing the water like a sponge. "Cool. But how do you plan to get the water from below ground to the surface of the pyramid?"

"We're gonna force the water from the river a few miles away to the subterranean chamber below the pyramid."

Jinx brows rose. "Ah. It'll have nowhere to go but up." Anointing Jacob's head with a drop from the water sample, she added, "I declare ye, lord of the geeks."

"We'll see." Jacob offered a lopsided grin and stood up, shading his eyes from the sun's glare as he moved towards the pyramid. "Now, to mount the amplifier."

Jinx pushed to her feet and leapt to the top of the nearest boulder. "You're done altering your masterpiece?"

"Yup. Claire is adjusting a few things, then sending it out."

Jinx leapt to the top of a tilting pillar. "Well, while you bust that out, I'll head to the moon." Screening her eyes, she looked towards the peak of the pyramid, where Jacob's souped-up amplifier would sit. "Hey, hold up." Jinx threw out her arm, bringing Jacob to a pause. "I think I saw something near the opening of the pyramid."

"What? What do you mean, something?" Jacob stammered.

"Dunno. I'm gonna check it out. Wait here."

"What?" Jacob jerked his attention to follow Jinx's line of sight. "You expect me to just sit here like bait?"

"You're right." Dropping to the ground, Jinx grabbed Jacob's hand and punched the earth.

Blink.

The ride ended at the entrance to the pyramid, a deep, wide ledge at the foot of an opening in the stones. Jinx sprang upright, placing Jacob safely at her back.

"I thought we agreed that you can't blink me without a heads up," Jacob whispered coarsely.

Jinx shrugged in response, barely biting back an impish smirk.

Jacob eyed her suspiciously then looked over the edge. "Well, you saved me from the effort of scaling sixty feet of stones. That was gonna be my first workout, ever."

"Don't worry, I'll let you climb the other four-hundred feet to the top without my assistance."

"Ha. I'm not mounting the amplifier in place," Jacob ribbed. "I've got someone else in mind for that task."

Jinx stifled a laugh. Ironic. Her role as Protector was shaping up to be more of a delivery mule. The courier industry, legal or otherwise, had been her career path of choice before the prophecy redirected it. Slowly, she moved towards the entrance. "Just stay close."

"I can take care of myself," Jacob insisted.

With training, sure, Jinx thought. Jacob looked surprisingly fit for someone who never broke a sweat. But he lacked the skill that only comes with practice. The merit of repetition was a concept Hadu took great pleasure pointing out to Jinx. "I'm sure you can. But I'd rather risk my body than your brain."

"Then why exactly am I up here creeping around with you, trying to get the jump on a possible threat?"

"Consider it inspiration for combat training."

Jacob's expression soured. "This is all a sham?"

"I didn't say that."

"Fine," Jacob said, leaning back against a single, stone block — one of the few million multi-ton rocks that made up the pyramid. It jutted out from the wall to tower over him by nearly a foot. And yet, he didn't seem dwarfed in its shadow. "If I'm injured in battle, somebody better put me back together exactly in the way mother nature intended."

"I'll get you to Claire. She'll nurse you back to health."

Jacob opened his mouth to protest, but the spark in his eyes revealed otherwise.

Jinx pulled him along with her, towards the wall, silently instructing him to keep his back pressed against it. Sidestepping, they made their way to the opening between ten-foot-high stones. Thrusting an arm out, she pressed herself and Jacob tighter. *Shh*, she motioned.

The hushed moment stretched long enough for Jacob to fidget. Jinx remained motionless, feeling for vibrations against the stone and listening for sounds from the interior. Something was moving around. Jinx gently swatted Jacob's shoulder, grabbing his focus. She held up five fingers. Then four. Then three. Then two. Then one as someone stepped out of the pyramid. Jinx remained motionless, gesturing for Jacob to do the same until their target caught sight of them.

Laris's eyes went wide. Then perplexed, followed by a smile. "You've been working with Hadu. I couldn't even sense you."

"We could have killed you five times before you hit the ground," Jinx declared, shifting her attention between Laris and Jacob. "See! This is exactly why you need to train. You never know what's lurking around every corner."

Laris laughed. "It's usually you."

Jacob moved away from the wall. "Don't feel bad, she does the same thing to me, often."

Jinx stepped next to Laris while Jacob moved towards the entrance, disappearing through the mouth of the pyramid. "You haven't logged in a single hour."

"Versions of me have." Laris pinched her mouth in an effort not to smile.

"Your twins can't learn to fight for you."

"My battles can't be fought with a swift kick, no matter how masterful." Laris widened her eyes innocently.

"You gave your word to learn to fight. I'm not gonna let you charm your way out of a promise." Jinx narrowed a glare, watching for the darkness that crept in without warning.

Laris held her gaze without challenge as she spoke. "You always search my eyes as if uncertain who will greet you. I promise, it will always be me, even if you don't like what you see." Laris took a seat on the sun-soaked stones, patting the ground beside her.

Jinx held Laris's gaze as she followed. "How's it going? Any sign of your better half?"

"She's always lurking beneath the surface." Laris made a sloppily ghoulish face, holding it until Jinx cracked a smile. "Enough about me, how are your classes with Hadu going?"

Jinx looked towards the Sphinx sitting as determined as always. It was less than a half-mile away, but the mound of stone had fixed its every curve into her memory. "Honestly, I don't hate it. But I don't feel any different."

"Well, you are different. Honestly, I've always been able to sense you. Today, I couldn't. Besides, it's only been" — Laris waved her hand overhead in a sweeping arch while biting back laughter — "fourteen passes of the sun."

Jinx titled back to rest on her palms. "I've missed this."

"What? My knack for comedy?"

"First of all, comedy is a stretch," Jinx said. "But yeah. The world feels right when I see you happy."

Laris squeezed tightly to Jinx, dropping her head on her shoulder. "I'd meditate all day for ten minutes of this, with you."

"Please." Jinx rolled her eyes. "You'd meditate all day anyway."

Laris laughed. "True."

Jinx sat silent in the uncomplicated moment. They seemed few and far between lately. "What do you think of this place?"

"Earth?"

"Yeah. And this triangle you hang out with all day."

"I like the idea of being on our planet of origin. I wish we could see more of it — I mean besides the satellite images." Laris paused, gliding her hand along the pyramid. "You know, even after all that the planet has been through, you can still feel its heartbeat in these stones. I've spent so many hours here, I can feel an endless, gentle thrumming."

"Are you sure it's not just Jacob's bots exploring every corner?"

"Well, that too. But mostly, I feel like —" Laris paused to give Jinx a look. "I know you're gonna roll your eyes, but I feel like I'm connecting with the pyramid."

Jinx shrugged. "It's not stranger than anything else going on."

Jacob poked his head out from the entrance. "Hey, it might get a little disruptive out here. Sorry in advance."

"You 'bout to mount Bayne's amplifier to the top of the pyramid?" Jinx pushed to her feet, offering Laris her hand.

"First of all, I've tricked that thing out," Jacob said. "It may have been Bayne's a few weeks ago, but now it's a uber-augmented, mega-awesome Jacob-nator." Jacob strolled past them, hopping down the gigantic stone blocks at top speed. "And yes! I'm about to install it."

"Dude, how much kæffee have you had?" Jinx called out after him, her voice filling the plateau.

"I had a full night's sleep. I'm ready to make some magic!"

Jinx and Laris slowly made their way in Jacob's wake. They watched as he bounded down the pyramid towards Claire, who was exiting the ship with the amplifier in tow. "Danger won't inspire fitness, but geekery will," Jinx remarked, watching Jacob tear full speed across the sand. The sound of Jacob and Claire jabbering excitedly as they hauled the amplifier towards the pyramid brought the monochromatic plane to life.

Jinx and Laris hopped down from the final block as the bots negotiated the first step up, preparing to haul the amplifier to the top.

"You finally found a replacement for me?" Jinx asked.

Jacob didn't peel his attention from the bots. "No way. You're still my number one delivery hero, carrying packages to the ends of the universe."

"Speaking of, are you ready to haul an obelisk to the moon?" Claire asked, waggling her brows. "If so, I've got a bag of liquid food with your name on it."

"Is that really necessary?" Jinx gruffed.

"It weighs a hundred and forty-three tons," Claire pointed out. "If I don't pump you full of calories, you'll be eight pounds lighter when you return."

"I might just stay on the moon. I get the feeling those feeding sessions are going to be an annoying part of my homecoming?"

"Careful," Claire warned, pulling Jinx along. "I might just force feed you every day. Can't have you evaporating into oblivion."

Jinx chuckled as Claire struggled to drag her in tow. "I'm sure you would survive without me."

"Maybe," Jacob teased. His voice faded with distance. "But I'd have a hard time building something without your mind-blowing delivery skills."

"I'm next level!" Jinx yelled over her shoulder.

CHAPTER THIRTY-ONE

Jinx flopped onto her bed, grateful she'd opted to blink back to her quarters after delivering the obelisk to the moon. She wasn't ready to be swept up in Claire's tests and Jacob's questions. Closing her eyes, she took a few slow breaths, trying to recapture the sense of peace she'd felt on the moon. She'd stood by the towering pillar after setting it in place, captivated by a profound hush that wrapped itself around her. It seemed the chaos of the universe could not penetrate the absolute blackness of its sky. Until this moment, Jinx hadn't missed the darkness of deep space after feeling the glow of the sun on her skin. But the cool quiet of this barren moon claimed a piece of her heart. Tranquility lived in its stillness. She'd only lingered for a few fleeting minutes, but it was enough to make a mark.

Rolling over, Jinx stared at the ceiling, mindlessly lifting a hand to touch the frequency monitor strapped to her forearm. The gentle, rolling vibration it had briefly played felt like the heartbeat of the moon. But now, the thrumming on her flesh felt unsteady as she struggled to reclaim serenity.

"You back?" Jacob's voice pierced the quiet, jostling her nerves with its unexpected arrival.

"Yup," Jinx replied.

"Good." Jacob's voice slowed with a deep exhale. "The security in the ship pinged."

"Yeah. Sorry. I should have come to you first." Jinx allowed her focus to dwell in the emptiness of the ceiling until her monitor slowed its roll. "I just needed a minute before heading to Hadu."

"Don't worry about it," Jacob said. "I figured it was you. Our security would have set off all sorts of alarms if something else was going on. So, did everything go according to plan?"

Jinx pushed herself upright and hopped off the bed. "Yes sir. Your hunk of stone is officially on the moon."

"Good work, hero," Jacob said.

"When are you gonna test it out?"

"It'll be a few days," Jacob said. "We've still got some things to do in prep."

"Thanks for sparing me the details," Jinx said with a laugh.

"Hey, I'm learning," Jacob shot back. "Don't forget to check in with Claire. You know she'll have a fit if you don't."

"I'd rather face her wrath than Hadu's," Jinx said as she moved across her room.

"You heading there now?"

"Yup."

"What do you think?" Jacob asked. "Are Hadu's sessions, uh, helping?"

Jinx engaged the door's control panel, allowing a moment to consider Jacob's question as it slid open. "Honestly, sometimes it just feels like she's turned up the volume on all the crap I'd gotten good at ignoring," Jinx said as she stepped into the corridor and headed for Hadu.

***

Jinx moved with mindful steps across the room and took a seat in her usual spot across from Hadu without clunking her knee into the table or collapsing gracelessly. She felt the weight of Hadu's stare, certain her mentor had made particular note of her tempered movements.

The two sat in silence. At first, Jinx allowed the moments to stretch, even welcoming the quiet, until her habitual need for action took over.

"Am I leading today's class?" Jinx asked while fidgeting in her seat.

"It is always you who leads the class," Hadu said. Cocking her head to the side, she studied Jinx and the space around her. "This new level of stillness suits you."

"It won't last," Jinx said.

Hadu folded her hands in her lap. "Whether it does or does not is entirely up to you."

"Well, if I move to the moon, I should be good to go."

"You can remove yourself from all of life, but the rumblings beneath your skin shall accompany you."

"No," Jinx said. "I'm pretty sure that some alone time on a dark, empty planet would do the trick."

"What did you experience on the moon that shaped this belief?"

"Silence," Jinx said, without skipping a beat.

"Please," Hadu said, with a roll of her wrist, implying that Jinx should elaborate.

Jinx stretched, lifting her arms skyward. Entwining her fingers, she lowered her hands to cradle the back of her head. Releasing a deep sigh, she searched for the feeling, uncertain of how to describe it. "I don't know. Life was just quiet. *I* was quiet." Jinx closed her eyes, suddenly emotional at the thought of it. "For a brief moment, there was nothing I had to do. Nothing I had to be." She allowed her hands to slide down and settle on her shoulders as her head dropped forward without struggle. "I just '*was*.'"

Hadu permitted a long pause to punctuate Jinx's words with silence.

"I've never felt that way," Jinx said, looking up, expecting Hadu to comment. She didn't. "Whatever. I can't explain it."

"On the contrary," Hadu said. "I'm pleased to see that you're allowing the chatter of the mind to disappear. It is from this still place within you, that your true nature arises."

"Great," Jinx said. "All I have to do is make regular visits to the moon."

"There is no place and no one that can conjure calm or conflict within you," Hadu said. "This state of mind you experienced was by your own doing. As is its absence."

"I didn't do anything," Jinx said. "In fact, I've barely practiced anything you've talked about. Seriously. Apart from wearing this stupid arm alarm" — Jinx tugged on the monitor's band cinched to her forearm— "I've done practically nothing."

"While it may be true that you have put only minimal effort into cultivating the tools I have introduced, you've listened, nonetheless," Hadu said. "And that is as adequate a place to begin as any. New ideas, once contemplated, go to work on unpinning the mental structures we've put in place."

"Good to know. 'Cause I have no plans to take up meditating."

"Simply continue exploring the concepts we cover," Hadu said. Her voice showed no sense of urgency. "The mind from which you make today's choices will drift away, giving room for reason far beyond your current understanding."

Hadu rose from her seat. Jinx watched as she crossed the room. "Is that it?" she asked. "No mental tricks you want to share?"

"You ask that often," Hadu said warmly. "It seems as though you'd prefer I draw sessions out longer than necessary?"

"Well, no," Jinx said, hopping out of her chair to follow. "I'm sure Claire will be thrilled to get her hands on me sooner than later."

Hadu put out a hand, blocking Jinx from stepping out the door. "You needn't worry, Protector. I'm simply here, by your side, reminding you of that which you already know." Placing a hand on Jinx's shoulder, she added. "Your heart will guide you, just as it always has."

"Well then, my heart appreciates the pep talk," Jinx said.

Hadu smiled softly and ushered Jinx out the door. "There are no words the heart can hear. Only the desire to listen from there."

CHAPTER THIRTY-TWO

Jinx shielded her eyes from the light reflecting off the slick, white exterior of the pyramids, watching as bots covered the last few feet of the smallest of the stone giants. The three now glowed, coated in a rubbery concoction. "These things are starting to taste less terrible," she said while chomping an oversized bite of her grub-bar.

Jacob turned his attention from the amplifier perched atop the largest pyramid to brush errant crumbs off his shirt. "Talking and chewing should not happen simultaneously," he said with a furrowed brow. "Do you ever eat anything else?"

"Occasionally I choke down a plate of whatever the 3-D printer is spitting out." Jinx held up the bar as if presenting evidence. "This is more efficient. Besides, it has everything I need: nutrients, calories, some sort of other healthy crap I'm supposed to have." Jinx nodded towards the amplifier, its metal surface competing with the pyramids for the most blinding glare. "How's the testing going?"

"Promising." Jacob presented the screen of his handheld device. It was lit with colorful graphs. "We've been tracking everything that could possibly change."

"And you're sure the pyramids turn on like machines?" Jinx asked, shoving down the final bite of her bar before wiping her hands on her persistently filthy pants. "I mean, it's just kinda hard to believe that those stone giants do anything but sit there."

"I'm counting on more than that," Jacob said. "We're hoping they'll 'turn on' *and* vibrate to match the frequency that Laris emits."

"I thought you were just using the big pyramid," Jinx said. "What are the two smaller ones supposed to do?"

Jacob lifted an eyebrow to a sharp peak. "What are you up to?"

Jinx expression went blank. "What do mean?"

"You put a lot of effort into avoiding my explanations," Jacob said, giving Jinx a once over. "Your interest is suspect."

Jinx shrugged. "No agenda. Promise. Just curious."

"Well, it was Claire's idea." Jacob's eyes sparkled. "I can't take credit."

"Do I need to remind you that I have a very short attention span?"

"Fine," Jacob said with a sigh. "The three pyramids will hopefully work together like a generator. The big boy over there is the capacitor. It acts like a big battery, which we will be able to use for a lot of things." Jacob nodded towards the two small pyramids. "Those will act as transformers. If they can match the frequency that Laris emits, they can cancel each other out." Jacob waggled his brows. "Then it's game time. We'll be able to produce the scalar waves we need. And even better, Laris won't need to sit there producing it."

Jinx's jaw dropped. "What?"

Jacob bit back a smile. "I was gonna surprise you."

"I'm tempted to get really excited," Jinx said. "But I have a feeling there's a catch."

"It's all theoretical at this point," Jacob said. "And even if it works, it's still susceptible to failure or interruptions in the field it produces. Laris would still need to be around for rebooting or recalibrating it."

"You mean, I should contain my excitement?"

"For the moment," Jacob said.

Jinx threw an arm around Jacob's shoulder. "I'll try." Casting her attention towards the sky, Jinx asked, "Is it picking up a signal?"

"Is 'what' picking up a signal?" Jacob asked. "Working on lots of 'its' these days."

"The stone-stick-thingy you had me haul to the moon four hadu-dazed ago."

Jacob shook his head. "Does Hadu know you've taken liberties with her good name?"

Jinx shrugged. "I can't help it if her brain-addling sessions have become my way of tracking time."

"If only there were celestial bodies we could use for marking time," Jacob said, "like a big ball of fire that appeared each day."

"Eh. Whatever. You have your methods and I have mine." Jinx watched the horizon, where the moon was making its exit, allowing the sun to take over. "So? Is the moon's obelisk working or not?"

Jacob followed her gaze. "Not sure yet. Can't test it until we move our security field out to the satellites." A weighted silence sat between them. Jacob shifted the quiet with slowly delivered words. "Which . . . is good to go . . . by the way."

"I know." Jinx released a dread-soaked sigh, bringing her attention back to Earth to focus on the Great Pyramid. Laris was barely noticeable at this distance, but the folds of her gown kicked in the breeze as she sat meditating at the entrance. "I'm mentally preparing." Staring beyond, across the endless stretch of desert, she imagined a soulless force raging towards them. "If Sartillias is on Earth, which I'd bet he is and not alone, then moving security out there" — Jinx gestured towards the heavens — "will leave us vulnerable to threats already here."

"Yeah, but —"

"I know. I know. We need to keep any other threats from making it to the planet."

"If it makes you feel more at ease, none of the feed I'm getting shows any activity. The satellites are scanning every inch of the Earth and the sky. Nothing cloaked or otherwise is showing up. There's a lot of eyes up there working nonstop."

Jinx laid a hand on Jacob's shoulder. "I wish that made me feel better, but it just reminds me that Sartillias is trained for war. He's hiding somewhere we don't have eyes, just waiting for the perfect time. I can feel it." Jinx looked towards one of two smaller pyramids, where Hadu stood watching over the Attendants. Her presence towered like an indomitable force shielding her flock. "I wanted to wait until the pyramid was running and everyone had some defense training."

Jacob followed her line of sight. "They're stronger than you give them credit for. I mean, chances are, they can do something besides meditate."

"Special powers or not, they're still vulnerable," Jinx said. "But I can't force them to train, and I don't think we can afford to wait much longer. This planet needs to be off-limits."

"If I was able to keep our security field up while adding one at satellite level, I would." Jacob dropped his head as if failure or fatigue or both weighed him down. "I just don't have what I need to build a secondary security system. We have to use the ship's."

Jinx nudged Jacob's arm. "You must be kidding. Thanks to your brain, we've lasted this long." Throwing an arm around his shoulder, she added, "I'm just trying to keep up."

Jacob cracked a smile. "Yeah, well, maybe if you'd eat a real meal, you'd have the stamina."

"No way. I like portable food."

Jacob returned his attention to his device and the shifting graphs lighting up its screen. "I'm nearly done running tests on the amplifier. In a few minutes, Claire and I will try charging up the pyramid. If that looks good, there's only one thing left to do, shifting security out to the satellites."

"I'll be ready." Jinx committed before fear got a foothold.

"Finally," a voice squawked from behind. Pallas cracked her knuckles as she stepped up beside Jacob, peering around him at Jinx. "I'm bored with training."

"Then you need to up your level," Jinx said, not pulling her eyes from Laris's direction.

Pallas clucked. "You gotta be kidding me. I've ruined Tarxis twice." Nudging Jacob in the ribs, she chuckled. "Haven't seen you back in training since your scrimmage with Claire."

"I tend to avoid humiliating situations, but thanks for the reminder."

Pallas smiled with a wink. "What are friends for?"

Jacob held up a finger of silence, as four bots peeled away from the pyramid and headed for the ship. Engaging his comm, he spoke in a barely contained squeal. "Ready for some fun?" Claire's high-pitched response escaped the privacy of Jacob's earbuds. After a moment of silence that followed, he added, "Yup! All we have to do is unblock the underground passage to the river and see if our new layer absorbs and holds the water." Another stretch of silence passed. "I wouldn't dream of starting without you. Hurry."

"Good luck," Jinx said as she took off towards the pyramid. "I'm gonna get closer if you're about to take your testing up a notch."

Covering the half-mile stretch in a winded sprint, Jinx nearly slid into the base of the pyramid. The mammoth structure radiated heat as the sun bounced off the glistening exterior. Reaching out, she pressed her palm to the thick, latex-esque skin, snatching it back from the burn. A slight indentation remained for a moment, held in the spongy coating. Jinx squinted as she looked up towards the entrance where Laris sat in stillness. There were no longer footholds to scale to the landing or, for that matter, descend.

"How exactly did you plan on getting down?" Jinx yelled.

Laris peered over the edge and smirked.

Blink.

"I have better things to do than taxi you around," Jinx said, leaning against the entrance.

"Are you sure?" Laris glanced over her shoulder. "I read the prophecy manual. It clearly states that the Protector should provide transportation to the One, at all times."

"Hm, really? I suppose I should have a look at this manual. I don't like neglecting my duty."

"I'll lend you my copy."

"How generous."

"How's it going down there?" Laris asked, nodding towards Claire and Jacob, who were gesturing wildly as they pointed to the top of the pyramid and sky above.

"We're about to find out," Jinx replied as she offered a thumbs-up to Jacob after he pantomimed, get ready.

Laris closed her eyes, adjusting her posture. Her body slid into position with fluidity, implying lotus was its natural shape.

"Do you mind if I stay?" Jinx asked softly. "I mean, will it be a distraction?"

Laris opened her eyes to a slit and admired Jinx tenderly. "You're never a distraction."

Jinx's belly erupted in a flutter. She wondered if Laris would ever lose the power to send her reeling. She hoped the answer was, no.

As Laris drifted into meditation, Jinx looked towards the Attendants still gathered below, catching Hadu's gaze with a startle. *How long has she been watching me?* It was too far to see Hadu's expression, which rarely shifted. But she bowed her head and took a seat — joining the Attendants. Lifting a padded wand, Hadu ran it along the edge of a golden bowl. The hum softly rose to meet Jinx. For the first time, she felt the sanctity of the moment more profoundly than the war racing through her veins.

"Here we go." Jacob's voice ground Jinx back into the moment. "Five . . . four . . . three . . . two . . . one."

The air hung still with only the endless hum of Hadu's tuning bowl swimming through the silent plateau. Jacob and Claire remained fixated on the peak of the pyramid, waiting for the amplifier to show signs of life. Jinx forced a breath through a tightening chest as she volleyed her attention between them and Laris. If Jacob and Claire's plan worked, and the pyramids emitted the same frequency that Laris harnessed, the amplifier would help send the scalar waves through the cosmos to balance the bioelectromagnetic field. Jinx mentally crossed her fingers, waiting for signs of success.

"Here we go." Jacob's words were followed by a low rumble, like a massive, ancient beast clumsily pushing itself up to stand on shaky legs.

Jinx peered over the platform, watching the pyramid's rubbery, white sheath begin to swell and tighten as it filled with water flowing up from some unseen source. Below, Claire studied data scrolling across a screen, measurements of whatever the pyramids were producing. Jacob hadn't taken his eyes off the amplifier. Suddenly, Claire jerked attention up from her screen, observing the two smaller pyramids intensely. Jinx stiffened, watching their anticipation.

With a jolt, the large pyramid came to life followed by a whoosh of serene melody, like the pulse of a million singing bowls. Its resonance flowed through Jinx's flesh and into her core, blending until there was hardly a sense of where her body began or ended. Laris hadn't moved, except for the rhythmic rise and fall of her breath. Had Laris created this energy with her Attendants so often, that its presence whirling through the pyramids was barely noticeable to her?

A sense of floating euphoria filled Jinx as she regarded her surroundings. Nothing felt urgent. Her attempts at meditating had never produced this. Her thoughts briefly drifted to Sartillias and the club drug he'd produced from the pineal glands he'd filched from unsuspecting New World denizens. Had this been the effect they produced? No wonder there was such a big market for it.

A high-pitched note pierced the rapturous bubble. Claire, Jacob, and Pallas shot their sight skywards, shielding their eyes to follow something's path. Jinx looked up in time to catch a thread of light blast through the atmosphere. Nearly simultaneously, the light around Laris shifted, barely catching Jinx's peripheral view. She snapped her attention back as Laris flashed to a translucent state then returned to something solid. *Was it a play of light? It must have been.* Nothing else had appeared luminescent. Jinx sat with unblinking focus, afraid Laris would disappear.

"That's a wrap." Jacob's words flowed through the comm as the melody of the pyramids died down. "We're heading back to the lab to go over the test results. You coming?"

"Later," Jinx whispered, keeping her attention on Laris.

"Roger that," Jacob replied. The sounds of an ecstatic Claire filtered through the background.

"Stop goggling." Laris snickered and slowly opened her eyes.

"That's not a word, and if it is, it's not what I'm doing."

Laris slowly untangled her limbs to stretch and plop backward to lay on the stone beneath her. "I knew she was alive."

"She?"

"The pyramid."

"You're assigning gender to rocks now?"

"Absolutely." Laris stared off into the clouds above. Deep contentment shaped her expression. "So, what's new?"

Jinx bit back a laugh. "Not much. Same old boring stuff. Different day."

Laris patted the stone slab beside her. "Cloud watch with me."

Jinx scanned the plateau before laying back. Her internal disquiet had returned full force with the silencing of the pyramids. The monitor strapped to her arm echoed the same. Jinx ignored both. "How was your nap?"

"See, now that's why you never mastered meditation. You confused it with napping. They are very different." Laris took hold of Jinx's hand and squeezed. Jinx didn't pull away.

"Well, it always put me to sleep," Jinx said. "To be honest, if I had known the effects, maybe I would have tried a little harder. Doubtful. But maybe."

"What was it like when the pyramids woke up?"

"You couldn't feel it?"

Laris shrugged. "I don't know what's going on around me when I'm in deep meditation."

"It was" — Jinx fished for the right word — "I guess, blissful. Is that what you're putting out to the world?"

"It's not me." Laris was quick to waive off glory. "I just allow the energy to flow unhindered from, well, wherever it comes from."

"It's more than that, Laris. I wish you had the slightest idea of how special you are." Jinx felt Laris's grip tighten around her fingers, the heat between their palms swirling.

"I love you too," Laris said as casually as observing the weather.

Jinx allowed the words to remain unchallenged until a tranquil silence settled between them. "I think *that* one looks like Nammu," Jinx said, pointing towards a tentacled cloud.

Laris pointed at another formation. "What about that one?"

***

The sky shifted a few shades darker before Jinx stirred. Pushing herself swiftly to her feet, she surveyed the stillness of the desert. The Attendants and Hadu had long since departed. The world, at that moment, seemed to belong to her and Laris. But reality nudged. "I'm gonna go check in with Jacob before heading to Hadu. Do you want a lift?"

Laris remained reclined, searching the pre-dusk sky. "No. You go ahead. I'm gonna stay here a while longer."

"Just let me know when you're ready, I'll come get you." Jinx squatted, preparing to exit. "Try and stay out of trouble."

"But you love trouble."

"Only if its name is Laris."

Blink.

CHAPTER THIRTY-THREE

Jinx hovered over Jacob and Claire, watching data scroll across a screen like she'd have the slightest inkling what any of it meant. "So, um, did you guys pick up on anything unusual during the test?"

"Besides three towering stone beasts roaring to life?" Claire spoke breathlessly, revealing the adrenaline rush of the day hadn't worn off.

"Why? Did you notice something abnormal?" Jacob asked.

Jinx hesitated, sensing Jacob's watchful eye. "It's probably nothing."

Jacob cocked his head full tilt. "The sooner you tell me, the quicker we can look for a solution."

"I don't know. It was probably just a play of light. A lot was going on."

Jacob rolled his hand, gesturing to spit it out.

"Fine," Jinx said. "Laris turned translucent. I think."

Claire remained fixed on her data. "That makes sense," she said matter of factly. "She's raising her vibration to levels beyond what our brain can perceive."

"Oh. Well, that clears that up." Jinx ran her hands along her scalp.

"You OK?" Jacob held Jinx in a studied gaze.

"No. I'm not. The thought of Laris disappearing is a bit disturbing."

Jacob eased Jinx away from the screen. "Listen. Everything in our universe vibrates, but at different rates. What we see is not all that is there. In fact, we see very little of what exists. We can only see electromagnetic energy that has a wavelength of three hundred and ninety to seven hundred and fifty nanometers. Laris is just speeding up the vibration of particles that make up her physical form."

Jinx slumped, pinning her head in a vice-like grip. "And this geekified fact is supposed to make me feel better, how?"

"I'm trying to put it in perspective for you," Jacob said. "Just because she flashes in and out, doesn't mean she isn't there. You just wouldn't see her in those moments."

"That does very little to ease my concern." Jinx plopped down in a chair.

"Or she's moving between dimensions, which all exist in the same space, but vibrate at different rates," Claire said, turning from the screen. "Similar to when you blink."

Jinx stared, expressionless, at Claire. Then Jacob. "Thanks for frying my final brain cell. I think I'll go eat something besides a grub-bar and attempt to jumpstart my gray matter. Maybe it'll make sense then. Though doubtful." Jinx moved towards the door.

"We may be able to anchor Laris even when her vibration speeds up," Jacob offered.

"Now that makes me feel better. But Laris wouldn't want us tinkering around." Jinx turned with a half-shrug. "I'll ask her, anyway."

"Fair enough," Jacob said. "Oh, and hey, um . . . we're looking good on moving the security out to the satellites. So, you know . . ."

Jinx spoke over her shoulder as the door eased open. "Tomorrow. I'll be ready tomorrow. Tonight, I think we all could use a break."

"What have you done with the real Jinx?" Claire asked. "You must be an imposter. The real Jinx never takes a break."

The door slid fully open, where Hadu stood calmly waiting. "Come. Your session is about to begin," she said and turned. "You'll have plenty of time to eat afterwards."

"I need a day off, you heartless sorceress!" Jinx kicked the air as Hadu disappeared down the hall. The exchange left her feeling like DeeDee in a barely controlled tantrum. Pulling a grub-bar from her pocket, she peeled back the wrapper and choked down a bite. "I'll come find you when Hadu is done torturing me."

"You finally ready to learn the art of chill time?"

"Maybe." Jinx paused at the door. "I don't know what tomorrow has in store, but just in case it turns hectic, I'd like today to end on a high note. Together. All of us."

***

Jinx flopped into the chair, uncertain as to why she was so exhausted. She'd spent the better part of the day cloud-watching with Laris, not scouring the area for threats or crawling through tight passageways in the pyramid or training for battle. Though she'd felt on edge for the majority of it.

Hadu sat silently watching as though spectating the action beneath Jinx's flesh. "It is your fear of tomorrow that drains you."

"Get out of my head."

"That was merely a deduction. An observation." Hadu relaxed her posture, leaning back in her seat. "I've tested your mental shield. You've done well, though it's far from impenetrable."

Jinx felt for the egg-shaped talisman in her pocket. Hadu had been right. It had helped her focus on shielding her thoughts. "Glad to hear I might be ready for Sartillias in one way or another."

"You'll never prepare for every possibility. They are infinite."

"Well, that's inspiring. Way to rally the forces." Jinx twisted her neck until her spine cracked. "You realize that tomorrow we are making ourselves vulnerable to our biggest threat."

"You're giving all of your energy to imagining potential failures of tomorrow." Hadu pushed to her feet, the swoosh of her robe following in her wake as she strolled around the room.

"At the moment, my very empty stomach is taking the majority of my focus." Jinx's stomach released a thundering grumble, confirming the claim.

"Then we should make this session particularly brief." Hadu ran her hand along a shelf of precisely placed amulets, totems, and charms. Her spindly fingers communed with each piece she touched. "That is unless you'd prefer to sit here contemplating life and reality with me until the sun rises."

Jinx's face pinched sourly. "That would be a *hard* no. I have absolutely no interest in an all-nighter, contemplating life."

"Then we shall keep our discussion brief." Hadu reached across the shelf, adjusting a blue, crystalline trinket ever so slightly. "Why keep your mind trapped in tomorrow when life is happening in this moment?"

"Uh, Sartillias. He may very likely swoop in and cause a lot of very big problems. So, you know, that's sort of triggering a few alarms." Jinx launched her hands into the air, allowing them to fall to the arms of the chair with a thud. "I kind of need to be prepared. It's my only friggin responsibility."

"Strategizing and worrying are two very different mental pursuits. Only one has the potential to deliver favorable results."

"Hey, I've been strategizing and planning and preparing." Jinx groused, crossing her arms tightly across her chest. "But the situation is nerve-racking. I worry about screwing this up."

"Understood. But know that you can not direct your mind to both simultaneously," Hadu said. "An unfocused mind will leave you exhausted and ultimately ineffective, scattering your energy between concerns of past moments and fears of future possibilities." Hadu shifted her attention to a new row of ornate objects. "Infinite energy, the power of all that is, can only be harnessed in the present moment."

"Fine." Jinx practically growled. Her hunger had worn away the ability to stifle frustration, which was flimsy at best. "What exactly should I do instead?"

"Become the master of your mind," Hadu said. "Be present in the moment with the awareness that where your mind goes, your world will follow. When you drift, come back, then align with the energy that shapes worlds. I assure you, Sartillias will be doing the same, quite intentionally, in fact. The laws of the universe are unbiased in how they are applied." Hadu moved across the room. "Once you embrace the simplicity of this truth, you have the advantage."

"Oh great! I was hoping for some good news," Jinx said with feigned enthusiasm. "And why, exactly, is that?"

"You have sided with the more potent of two forces." Hadu silently watched Jinx as though waiting for a response.

Jinx fidgeted under Hadu's gaze, knowing the silence would drag on until she coughed up a guess. Grumbling under her breath, she looked down, shaking her head. "I'm just watching out for my friends the best I can. That's all."

"You are doing more than that," Hadu said. "We exist in a dualistic reality where one may align with negative forces, as Sartillias has done. But the power of this energy is limited. Its field is disruptive and disconnected. Or one can align with the positive, as you are attempting to do, where energy is unified and expansive, creating exponentially more power than that which is directed towards it."

"Great. We're good. He's bad. Got it." Jinx didn't want to pick it apart. Her hunger pangs were relentless.

"It is neither good nor bad. It is the fabric of life," Hadu said. "Understanding its nature will aid you in leveraging the power present in each moment."

"Honestly, it's not likely I'll be able to turn off my thoughts and just be in the moment," Jinx said. "There are too many things we're supposed to be focused on."

"I'm not suggesting you drift through life without thought. But you must be mindful of where your thoughts are leading you. Do not blindly follow," Hadu said. "They will pull you from the present moment far more often than necessary."

Ushering Jinx up and towards the opening door, Hadu brought her palms to meet. "Now, go. Eat. Then be present with your friends and practice the art of, I believe you call it 'chill'. That will fuel your efforts far more effectively than fretting for tomorrow."

Jinx lifted slowly from her chair. *You're right,* she wanted to say but couldn't get the words out. Her insides had been swimming in untamed emotions all day. Clearing her head seemed an impossible task, making her wish for the quiet of the moon. Sliding past Hadu, Jinx smiled softly, feeling grateful there was someone to keep her in check. Yet annoyed all the same.

"See ya tomorrow," Jinx said as she stepped into the corridor.

Hadu's attention followed like a reassuring hand until the door slid shut. Moving down the hall, Jinx forced her mind to focus on the next unnerving task, one she'd kept to herself. Learning the art of chill would just have to wait a few minutes longer.

CHAPTER THIRTY-FOUR

Jinx pushed through the cafeteria door after shoveling down enough chow to satisfy her relentless hunger for days and put a halt to Claire's force-feeding. It didn't, however, alleviate the dread currently gaining momentum. Despite her chat with Hadu, her heart pounded as she wound through the crisp, white corridor, bringing to question the rationale of her plan. *I have to cover all the bases*, Jinx assured herself as she paused at one in a long line of identical doors. Engaging the unit's comm, she announced her arrival. "Got a minute?"

True to form, the occupant offered a thin response. "Indeed."

Jinx paused, allowing her hand to hover before entering the security code. As the door slid open, the placid expression that welcomed her arrival seemed neither validated nor vexed.

"Please, do make yourself comfortable," Bayne offered as he motioned towards a chair.

"I prefer to pace," Jinx replied as she entered the room allowing the door to close behind her. "Besides, I'd like to make this visit as brief as possible."

"Very well," Bayne replied as he took a seat. "The floor is yours both literally and figuratively."

"I'll cut to the chase," Jinx said. "I need your help. Possibly."

Bayne allowed his hands to settle softly in his lap, studying her quietly for an excruciating moment. "Go on."

"I know you're aware that we're moving the security shield out to the satellites tomorrow."

"Among other things," Bayne added.

"Yeah, well. I'm less concerned about the pyramids and the Jacobnator." Off Bayne's look of bewilderment, she clarified. "It's his new name for your amplifier."

"I'm quite aware of his expanding lexicon."

Jinx inwardly smiled at the notion of Jacob shooting off memos regarding his renaming of most things he put a hand to. "Once we move the security field, we're vulnerable to anything that's already on Earth," Jinx said as she set to wearing a groove in the ground while laying out the various scenarios that could potentially unfold the next day. Bayne, to his credit, listened attentively without interruption.

"There's only one situation I can't foreseeably control," Jinx said, bringing the long list of conceivable threats to a close.

Bayne silently nodded, acknowledging this last bit was the reason for the visit.

"If for any reason I need to blink everyone, along with the ship, to safety, I need you to step up."

"I see," Bayne said. "And have you considered the destination?"

"Mars. The moon. Does it really matter? They can take the ship anywhere from there."

Bayne untangled his fingers to lift a hand from his lap. "Why enlist my help?" Apparently, his question required gestures for punctuation.

"If things get hectic, everyone will be too dazed to think straight. Everyone but you and Hadu, that is. And assuming Claire's calculations are correct, there won't be anything left of me after the blink. That'll only make things worse." Jinx ran a barely steady hand along her scalp. "I'm banking on the idea that the ship and everyone in it would make it through the blink, even if I didn't."

"Energy is the language of the universe, and its nature is balance. If your calculations are correct, then the energy you possess beneath your flesh is enough to complete the blink — a trip requiring no more and no less as tinder." Bayne studied Jinx for a solemn moment. "And you will dissolve into the vast unknowable."

"Thanks for keeping it light." Jinx released a heavy sigh, mostly in relief that the conversation was coming to a close. "Don't get too excited, though. We're just talking about the worst-case scenario."

"I'll try and contain my enthusiasm," Bayne replied as he pushed to his feet. "Your decision to speak with me implies you are a far more provident Protector than I gave you credit for. If you do not live to see the closing of another day, take great pride in your willingness to set aside ego for the greater good."

"Greater good? That's a stretch," Jinx replied. "I'm not a hero." Moving towards the door, she added, "Just help my friends, should it come to that."

"Let's hope it doesn't," Bayne replied in a tone absent of all pretenses.

The sincerity took Jinx by surprise. Peering over her shoulder, she nodded a silent thanks and slipped away.

Shaking out her limbs, Jinx blazed through the hall, attempting to burn off her angst. It would take more than one of Jacob's chill sessions to calm the clamor of nerves torching her insides.

She headed their way, nonetheless.

CHAPTER THIRTY-FIVE

Jinx allowed herself an extraordinarily long shower to soothe the nerves that kicked. The thought of moving the security field out to the satellites sent bursts of anxiety that had a bite. She tried to follow Hadu's counsel to be in the moment. But simply taking a shower, rather than imagining Sartillias descending upon them, seemed an impossible feat. It wasn't waging war or her own safety that disquieted her mind, it was the feeling of powerlessness to protect everyone. *If thought is shaping my day, I'm toast. We're all toast.*

Stepping out of the shower, Jinx wiped the steam off the mirror and stared at her reflection, determined to burn away the doubt nesting there. *You can do this. You're strong. You're fast. And you know how to fight. You can do this. You're the Protector for a reason.* Jinx repeated her mantra over and over and over until her core yearned for the fight. She hoped her battle cry wasn't summoning Sartillias, that her words didn't have the power to weave the future. But if they did, she planned on being primed.

Picking up the cleanest-looking shirt and pants off the floor, she gave them the standard sniff test before slipping them on and shifting into ready-mode. Searching her room, which had remained remarkably bare except for the growing piles of clean and dirty laundry, Jinx reached for the metallic egg. She moved to slip it into her pocket but butted up against something. Pulling it out, she flipped the object around in her hand, wondering why she had saved Pallas's calling card. It had been in her pocket since the supply station run. Jinx was about to toss it, then paused. Something about it conjured a sense of normality in the midst of all of this. Opening a drawer, she tossed it in. Ordinary as it was, it seemed a talisman of sorts, a reminder that life held more than the fight, should she ever choose to allow it.

***

Lighthearted chatter wafted from the kitchen, accompanying Jinx as she shuffled through the hall. Silently pushing through the door, she offered a brisk nod to Claire, Jacob, and Pallas, then beelined it for the kæffee. It was nice to hear the bonding of last night spilling over into today. She didn't want it to stop. But she didn't want to join in, either. Fortunately, everyone knew to give her a wide berth until after she'd sucked down her first cup.

While filling the largest cup to the brim, she shoved something resembling a pastry into her mouth, grabbed a second for the road, and jetted back out and off the ship to commune with the wide-open desert.

The morning sun warmed Jinx's usual spot at the foot of the Sphinx. The comfort of it made it an easy moment to lose herself — sipping her kæffee as she scanned the surroundings. It was the same as every day before: Laris and the Attendants gathered to meditate at the foot of the smallest pyramid while Hadu circled them with a singing bowl in hand.

"Mornin' sunshine. Have you finished your kæffee yet?" Jacob's voice sang.

Jinx grunted in response.

"I'll take that as a 'no.' How 'bout I give ya thirty minutes, then join ya with a refill."

"Make it five," Jinx replied, feeling lifted at the notion of her second cup being delivered. With replenishments on the way, she shifted from leisurely sips to ravenous gulps. Her pulse picked up as she searched the sky, wondering if trouble would descend upon them or kick up a sandstorm while raging across the desert. Taking a deep breath, Jinx attempted to steer her mind to the moment, feeling the sun wrap her in a wave of heat as it cleared the horizon. A few breaths later, the monitor on her arm slowed its pace. It was far from a tranquil roll, but the change didn't escape notice.

The sound of Jacob's gleeful whistling was a welcome reminder to focus on the moment. "Is it safe to approach?" he asked between chirps.

"Only if one of those cups is for me."

"Hey, I promised you a refill, and I'm a man of my word." Jacob plopped down beside Jinx and handed her a cup.

"My hero," Jinx said, taking a sip of the steaming beverage. "I need the fuel after last night's epic round of chill."

Jacob rolled his eyes so hard they nearly squealed. "You must lack something in your DNA needed for learning that particular skill."

"What!" Jinx responded, shooting for a tone of sincere indignation but missing the mark. "I came *and* ruled GetDown3000."

"Yes. And then you promptly left after delivering the beatdown." Jacob took a sip, eyeing Jinx over the cup's lip. "That's not chilling."

Jinx lazily waived the accusation away. "You're just sore 'cause my dance moves are untouchable."

"Whatever." Jacob reached into his pocket to pull out a handful of grub-bars. "Here. If the day gets crazy, fast, I don't want you passing out from lack of sustenance. I want to see all of your best combat techniques, not a faceplant."

Jinx's expression curled into a lopsided smirk. "You don't seem the least bit concerned."

"Can't afford to. My brain dulls when I'm stressed." Jacob nudged Jinx with his shoulder. "What happened to the blind optimism you had when we first met?"

"It's at the bottom of this cup," Jinx said, raising the kæffee to her lips.

"What's the plan?" Pallas yelled impatiently from a distance.

Jinx turned to see a group of unlikely crusaders exiting the ship. Pallas led the way with prowling steps. Jinx inwardly smiled at the cunning nature lurking beneath the elegance of a huntress. DeeDee was steps behind, beaming her usual uncomplicated smile revealing nothing of the lethal weapon she could instantly morph into. Nammu trotted along, watching DeeDee with sibling-esque devotion, armed only with indomitable innocence and a blood-curdling, sonic cry.

"Your militia has arrived," Jacob announced as Claire and the Laris clones appeared, following in the wake of the approaching ensemble.

"I guess it's time to open the gates." Jinx swilled back a few gulps of kæffee, watching Claire blindly step along, trusting her feet while keeping her gaze locked on a handheld device. The clones, however, scanned their surroundings with robotic swiftness. "What's our timing?"

"Claire and I can shift the security to the satellites as soon as you're ready," Jacob replied.

"Short and concise," Jinx said. "You finally figured out how to hold my attention."

"Oh, there will be plenty of geekery, but I'll spare you as much as I can."

"What about the pyramids?" Jinx asked as Pallas and the entourage trickled in around them.

"We'll power them up at the same time we shift security to the satellites," Jacob replied. "It shouldn't interfere with the setup."

Claire looked up from her device as she stepped beside Jacob — adding input as though she had been present the whole time. "If it does, we'll hold off until it's stabilized."

"Are we splitting up to cover more ground?" Pallas's tone was a barely restrained restlessness. She seemed to exist in a cage of her own making.

Jinx furrowed her brow, intimately familiar with the power of clinging shadows to haunt the mind. "You need to burn off whatever is kicking your insides."

Pallas puffed up. "What's that supposed to mean?"

"You're looking for a fight. That's not what this is about. All of you, listen up." Jinx paused, looking at the group until she was certain their attention was on her. "No one is to go beyond this site. If Sartillias or anyone or anything else surfaces, we stand our ground. Our best chance of surviving an attack, protecting Laris, and getting those mountains of rock to blast to life is if we work together." Jinx looked towards the pyramids, watching Laris stand in the distance, unwinding from meditation and leisurely stretching as though she hadn't a care in the world. Jinx shifted attention to DeeDee. "Booger, you need to stick by Claire and Jacob. Flatten anything that comes at them."

"No."

"No?" Jinx stared blankly. "Booger, I'm not gonna argue this point with you."

"But I'm supposed to protect you!"

"We can protect ourselves," Claire said flatly.

"No. You can't," Jinx said. "Not against threats showing up with Sartillias or any other thugs with training."

Jacob and Claire flashed knowing smiles between themselves.

"What?" Jinx barked.

Jacob lifted his palms, clearly for show, miming a raising of the dead from the depths below. Within seconds, a swarm of airborne bots collected overhead. "Most of these are dated technologies still lingering on the planet. After we started engaging the satellites, they gravitated around the outer perimeter of the security field one after the other."

"We haven't had time to re-engineer them to do anything particularly wicked," Claire added. "But they can move at a nice clip and cause a fair amount of damage on impact."

"It's not enough." Jinx placed a hand on Jacob's shoulder and looked towards Claire. "If anything happens to you two, we're in real trouble."

Jacob began, "But —"

Jinx raised a hand, silencing any pushback. "I trust you two in all the decisions you make, please trust me when it comes to strategy. I've thought about this and little else. I've played every scenario out in my head. We will very likely be facing a formidable threat when we shift the security, with little odds in our favor. If something happens to either of you, chances are I'll be faced with a few crappy options that undoubtedly involve being on the run to protect Laris and enlisting Bayne's help." Jinx turned back towards DeeDee. "Keep me safe by keeping them safe."

DeeDee pressed her arms defiantly across her chest.

Jinx shook her head in exasperation and stood to go. "When you guys are ready to hear me out, let me know. In the meantime, get everyone's comm set up on the same line. Please."

"May we join you?" the clones asked in unison. "Assuming you are now going to Laris's side."

"Suit yourselves." Jinx darted off on foot across the plateau, quickly shifting from jog to sprint, hoping the motion would clear her head. She didn't bother looking back. The sound of swift steps working to keep pace was not far behind. The clones had physically advanced well beyond their donor. Human Laris had yet to display anything remotely athletic.

Jinx's heart was hammering by the time she reached the Great Pyramid. Coming to a sliding halt at Laris's side, she asked, "Need a lift?"

"Happy to see you're taking *all* of your Protector duties seriously."

"I promise to protect and taxi you at all times, forevermore."

Laris wound her arm around Jinx's and turned to watch her clones move at a swift and graceful clip. "A few more weeks and they might keep up."

"Well, DeeDee can keep up with me. And she's a clone. In fact, she surpasses me in a lot of things." Jinx studied Laris for a flash. "They do have a will of their own, you know."

Laris smiled. The curve of her lips was subtle, but its presence could eclipse the sun. "I should hope so."

"Just don't forget that Sartillias had a hand in their creation. Who knows what sort of influence that could have on their response to, well, everything?"

"No one here is immune to the laws of existence — OI or IOI beings alike."

Jinx rolled her eyes. "You know how I feel about riddles."

"It's not a riddle. You're just calling it that to avoid contemplation."

"That's because you and Hadu are determined to wear me out with conversations that are as productive as chasing my own butt. Which, by the way, I'd rather do." Locking eyes with Laris, she added, "All I care about is making sure the rest of the day is free from drama."

Laris slid her hand into Jinx's, entwining their fingers in a reassuring embrace. Neither one paused their steps as the clones moved to walk by their side, studying Laris while mimicking her expression, attempting to capture the nature of it.

"Speaking of the rest of the day, I'd like to borrow your clones," Jinx said.

Laris scrunched her face. "Borrow? They don't belong to me any more than DeeDee belongs to you."

"First of all, it was an expression." Jinx eyed the clones. Neither looked the slightest bit put off by her choice of words. "Second, Booger is not a clone of me. And based on the fact that your clones have mastered martial arts in a matter of days, I'm beginning to wonder what you even share in common."

Laris shrugged. "Nice hair."

Jinx choked back a laugh.

The clones eyed one another, more specifically their hair. "Yes. We agree. The hair is very . . . nice."

"You two have names yet?" Jinx asked as they reached the foot of the Great Pyramid.

"If you prefer to acknowledge us separately, I will respond to 1111.01."

"And I will respond to 1111.02," the second clone replied. "It's the most logical. We have utilized Laris's original birth number, 1111. And added —"

"You're more than a number," Laris said. "And certainly more than a version of me."

The clones stared vacantly for a flash. Jinx knew the look. It was the same expression that often claimed Jacob's face when he was crunching data and mind surfing the vast edgelessness of technology. "Dream up something later," Jinx said abruptly. "I want you two safeguarding the Attendants today. How do you feel about fighting Sartillias if he gets near them?"

"Feelings do not constrain us. We are quite capable of fighting if that is the most logical action to take."

"Great. They are officially yours to protect. At all costs."

Blink.

"I thought we agreed that you can't just blink me somewhere without asking." Laris looked uncharacteristically sour as she pulled her hand from Jinx's grip and looked over the edge. Her clones were now a sixty-foot drop away. They briefly looked up the side of the pyramid. After spotting Laris, they turned and walked towards the Attendants still gathered with Hadu at the foot of the adjacent pyramid.

"We don't have time to waste brainstorming names. Jacob and Claire are down there waiting to shift security out to the satellites. I need to piece together something that resembles a security team. And you need to, well, save the world." Jinx cringed as she nipped at the raw flesh capping her fingertips.

Laris gently guided Jinx's hand from their torture chamber. "Unless you plan on growing new ones, you might want to find a better way to manage your stress."

"I'm working on it."

Jinx took a deep breath and reached a hand to her monitor, feeling it pulsate erratically in her palm. *Be in the moment.* The thought held little weight until she made note of everyone below. Claire and Jacob had their heads together in animated discussion, no doubt reviewing every step and imaginable issue associated with moving the security field. Pallas was running sprints, hopefully in an attempt to burn off her thirst for blood. DeeDee had miraculously stayed within twenty feet of Jacob and Claire, watching them while simultaneously playing some watered-down version of hopscotch with Nammu, both hopping between rudimentary squares etched in the sand. The clones stood stoically guarding their new wards, the Attendants. And lastly, Hadu — an ineffable being who seemed as lethal with a blow as she was potent in prayer — moved gracefully around the circle of Attendants waiting in lotus. Jinx allowed the moment to sink in. Even with all its uncertainty, it soothed a beast that felt greater than the threat of Sartillias. Fear's power to isolate evaporated in the recognition of her tribe. Jinx wasn't one person standing alone. She was a piece of the tapestry they all made up, collectively. This moment was peaceful. Fortifying. Jinx turned to Laris. Her eyes were wide but not searching, promising that only good things await. That all is good, no matter the packaging.

"Shall we dance with the unknown?" Laris smiled as the words slipped from her lips.

Without pulling her gaze from Laris, Jinx spoke into her comm. "Jacob, how are we looking?"

"Ready to rock, whenever you are." Jacob cleared his throat. "And, uh, sorry about earlier. You're right. We need someone watching our back."

"We all do," Jinx replied. "So, do I need to come down there and wrangle Booger?"

"I don't need to be wrangled!" DeeDee's voice boomed in the background while her look of reproach spanned the distance between them. Gone were the days of eager, childlike reactions. Her recently cultivated independence seemed to blossom and take root with the arrival of Nammu.

Jacob took a few steps away and lowered his voice to a whisper. "Naw. I think we're good. But you have to keep in mind, if she has to choose between saving us or saving you, there is no stopping her. She will always come to your side."

"Let's hope it doesn't come to that," Jinx said, watching Pallas pause her sprints to scale to the top of the Sphinx. "Have you had a chance to set up a group channel?"

"Of course, Jacob replied. "That's not even a real task. You wanna switch over?"

"Yup. But make sure the Attendants and Laris aren't on it. Not sure about Hadu, though. Let's add her and see what happens."

"Here we go." A brief pause followed before Jacob spoke again. "We're officially live."

Jinx took a seat on the ledge, pulling Laris down with her. The entrance to the pyramid towered at their back and the plateau below spanned out to the horizon. Their feet dangled over the edge to rest on the pristine white sheath that now coated the stone goliath's surface. "Can everyone please check in so I know you can hear me?"

"Onboard," Jacob answered enthusiastically.

"Here," Claire said.

"What?" Pallas grumbled.

"Eeeee!" Nammu squealed.

"Can I go get something?" DeeDee asked, a request that unquestionably involved things that melt.

"We are present," the clones announced in unison.

Jinx waited a moment, noting that they were one short. "Did Hadu drop the channel?"

"Looks like it," Jacob replied.

Jinx looked towards the Attendants and Hadu. They were in the midst of a gathering of their own. "First of all, Booger, you can go get 'something' after we're done shifting the security field. I want to make this as quick and painless as possible. If we can all focus for a few minutes. That'd be great."

"Where do you want me?" Pallas blurted from her perch atop the Sphinx.

"Right where you are. You've got a solid view from there. I need you to be our eyes. If you see anything heading our way, immediately announce it over the channel. You need to constantly shift attention from searching the sky to surveying the land."

"Then what?"

"We won't know the next steps until we know what, if anything, we are up against. Do not run off swinging. We need to make sure that everyone else can stay focused on shifting security, charging the pyramids, and raising the frequency, not fending off thugs. It's a tall order, but it's what we're here to do."

"Fine," Pallas said, "but if anything takes a step within a half-mile of this area, I'm taking off towards them."

"The further away you are, the more vulnerable the group is. We need a tight, controlled area. There aren't enough of us to start branching out. So, before you run off to draw blood, just remember that we are weaker without you."

Jinx slid her hand around Laris's, allowing a silent moment to stretch between them. "Are you ready?" Her whisper was for Laris's ears only.

"I was born ready," Laris replied with a wink.

"Now you're stealing my lines?"

Laris shrugged. "I'm allowed. It's in the manual."

A concoction of laughter and fear formed a lump in Jinx's throat. "Whatever I have, consider it yours." Pushing to her feet, she drew a deep breath, steadying her voice like a nervous trigger finger preparing to take aim. "Jacob. Claire. Let's get this party started."

CHAPTER THIRTY-SIX

Each breath became a faint rise and fall as Jinx waited for the security field to be lifted. Scanning the scene below, she searched for signs of trouble while Claire and Jacob monitored the status. She wasn't sure if it had been the Great Pyramid suddenly lurching to life with coughing roars or the warnings raging through the comm that tripped her heart.

Pallas's voice exploded. "Kaÿwzit!"

The update was sadly lacking details, but the urgency of tone and the expletives that followed were enough to grab everyone's attention. The alert was accompanied by a distant tremble that rattled the desert, threatening to disturb the dead.

The plateau took on an eerie silence as everyone on the channel turned to follow Pallas's line of sight, except the clones who didn't flinch or shift their focus from the Attendants. DeeDee paused her game only to *first* take note of Jinx still watching over Laris and *second* towards Jacob and Claire a mere few feet away.

Don't lose you head, Jinx told herself as she watched the distant horizon come to life, animated by dark silhouettes charging across the sand. For now, they were hardly more than obscure shapes, but Jinx knew that soon she'd see the soulless eyes of every face.

"It's like they appeared out of nowhere." Panic coated Jacob's words.

"Exactly," Jinx whispered, careful not to disturb Laris's tranquil state. "Hold your positions, everyone. If it's Sartillias, this could be another one of his projections."

"Or not." Pallas delivered words like bullets. "His species is bred to hide in the shadows."

Jinx lifted a hand towards her teeth, prepared to chew threw bits of cuticle, then changed her mind. Slipping her hand into her pocket, she held tight to the metallic egg nestled there. Slowing her breath, she spoke. "Jacob, Claire, what's our time frame?"

"Hard to tell," Jacob said. "The Great Pyramid is up and running, so we've got all the power we need. But it'll be another minute or two before the amplifier kicks on, which, at the moment, won't make a difference. The smaller pyramids are still silent."

Jinx looked at Laris, seemingly undisturbed by the calamity unfolding around her. "What about the security field?"

"The satellites are slowly kicking on, but the grid isn't in place," Jacob said. "We need a few more minutes."

Jinx shifted her attention to the sky, wondering if additional threats would descend. There were no signs of an aerial attack, but she began mapping out an exit strategy should one unfold. Her heart raced rapidly, producing beats that exploded in her belly. *There's no way to handle it all.* Her monitor matched her angst with thundering rolls. *I'm gonna chuck this friggin thing.* Returning attention to the plateau, she steadied her focus. *Get it together*, she cautioned herself, bringing her thoughts back to the present each time they drifted, which was annoyingly often.

Jinx looked to Jacob and Claire, desperate to ask the status but didn't. Taking their focus away from getting that security grid in place would only slow the process. Lifting her hands, Jinx directed her attention to her palms, summoning every bit of power she contained, ready to use it in any way she could to buy them more time. The energy crackled as she watched the lineup of thugs cover the distance between them.

God, he's a showman, Jinx thought as a surge of adrenaline sent her pulse into rapid-fire. The massive frames of an army of slayers were perched atop grotesque seven-legged creatures resembling skeletal spiders. The battalion of thugs spanned out behind their leader. There was no mistaking the titanic, horned beast, even at a distance. His cape billowed behind as his mechanical steed sped across the plateau, sailing inches above the terrain like some glorious homage to ancient Rome.

Jinx couldn't see Sartillias's face, but she imagined the level of pageantry plastered on his expression.

They're getting too close. Jinx stepped away from Laris as she spoke. "Jacob. Claire. Give us an update."

"Uh, well, we have a throng of..." Claire rattled off a slew of colorful descriptors in the foul-mouth fashion Jinx had come to expect, as high-pitched ringing rained down from overhead. Its sharp edge mellowed within moments to match the same rich tone emanating off Hadu's singing bowl. "Yes!" Claire exclaimed. "The transformers are responding. All three pyramids are officially running."

"The amplifier is up," Jacob announced. "I mean Jacob-nator," he said as the melodic hum challenged the rumble of the ground beneath their feet.

"What about the security grid?" Jinx wanted to yell but bit back.

"Not yet," Jacob replied, unable to sturdy his voice.

"I'm not standing here waiting for death to come take me," Pallas growled through the comm as she slid down the side of the Sphinx and raced towards her demise.

"Hold your ground, Pallas," Jinx said. "We have to get the security grid in place to keep anyone else from making it to the planet. We can find a way to pick off Sartillias's men over time, but we need safety. You have to trust me."

"Why exactly should I trust you?"

"If you leave, you'll die."

"There are worse things than death."

"Maybe. But I'd prefer it if you didn't welcome it."

Pallas howled as her body bucked, eager to shed its skin. "If he gets close enough for me to see the soulless void in his eyes, I'm going in with every ounce of bitterness stored up in my bones and unleashing."

"No," Jinx said. "You'll head to the ship with everyone else so we can take off."

"You're assuming we'll have time!" Pallas practically hissed. "The closer they are, the less likely it is we can fire up the ship and get out of reach."

"I don't plan on letting it come to that," Jinx said. *If time runs short, I'll blink everyone and the ship out of here*, she assured herself.

As Jinx listened to Pallas, Jacob, and Claire fume, a wave of bliss coiled through her, carried on the rolling sound emanating from the pyramids. Jinx turned toward Laris. The sunlight shimmered a little brighter around her as if the rays wished to match the radiance of her spirit. Her stillness seemed eternal. Jinx would do anything to protect the peace that dwelled there.

Keeping her hands readied like loaded guns, Jinx waited for Sartillias or his army to open fire, assuming the vibration pouring through the amplifier didn't sedate them first, a possibility that sounded like a long-shot to her. Despite the feelings of bliss welling up, Jinx doubted it had the power to disarm a band of savage creatures whose momentum had been building for a lifetime — at least, not on a dime.

Hopefully, there were a few show-offs and trigger-happy thugs to provide the power Jinx needed to set her plan into motion. The more ammo heading their way the better. Encasing ammunition and sending it back had certainly stopped Laris in her tracks, quite violently. The same ricochet effect could take out an army. But whether Jinx would survive in the process was another matter.

The sound of gasping yanked Jinx into a terrifyingly lucid moment. No shots had been fired, but Laris erupted into fits as though being pummeled.

The rapture emanating off the pyramids instantly morphed as Laris sprang to her feet. The benevolence of her gaze took on a wicked spark as her lips twisted to a wintry grin.

"Jacob!" Jinx yelled, as the violent shift from bliss to crisis vibrated around them. "Shut down the amplifier!"

"What's happening?" Claire's voice rattled as the ground beneath her feet quaked. "The frequencies are shifting. The waves are totally off."

Jinx swung to face Laris. "She's not transmuting the army's energy. She's absorbing it." Every ounce of ruthlessness swirling around Sartillias and his army was rushing towards Laris, shifting her vibration to something toxic. Jinx's fists ached to fly forward towards Sartillias as waves of fury replaced the bliss emanating from the pyramids. Their bitterness poured through Laris.

"The amplifier isn't responding. I can't shut it down without destroying it," Jacob yelled. "Laris has got to snap out of it long enough for the transformers to lock in the right frequency."

"Easy for you to say," Jinx yelled as she watched Laris's back arch, beckoning the full force of the malevolence to unite with her flesh.

"It's done! The security grid is officially stabilized." Jacob spoke through a clenched jaw. "Should we survive the masquer heading our way, we're golden."

"Everyone on the ship!" Jinx yelled through the comm as she pressed her palms towards the army. "I'm trying to contain this, but you need to go."

"We can't leave the amplifier running," Claire pleaded as Jacob attempted to pull her towards the ship. "It'll just keep sending out the wrong frequency."

"That's it! I'm not waiting any longer." Pallas lunged into motion, arms raised in battle, shifting to the hunter beneath her flesh.

DeeDee stood watching Jinx with unflinching focus as Nammu pressed tighter to her side. Hadu and the Attendants hadn't wavered. They remained in deep meditation as the clones stood watch.

"Laris, you have to shift out of this," Jinx pleaded as she forced every trace of power surging through her system towards Sartillias. "Fight it!" The momentum exploded from her palms, racing forward, taking Pallas to the ground as it pressed past to crash into the army with atomic force. The seven-legged steed and their dragoons should have tumbled backward, taking flight with acrobatic splendor. But they didn't even wobble. "What the drek going on?"

"Let it come to me," Laris hissed as she gripped Jinx's arm. Her body twitched. A war waged beneath her flesh—desire twisting, whirling together in an eternal dance between light and dark.

Jinx dropped to her knees, her hands fighting to maintain their gated position. "No," she whispered hoarsely.

Laris knelt softly by her side. Her eyes cleared to placid pools, now spared from the energy battering Jinx's shield. "You must."

Jinx helplessly watched the scene deteriorate below as her body trembled to remain steadfast. The army was closing in as the roar of Sartillias ripped across the desert. Pallas had pushed to her feet and prepared to race towards death while Jacob implored Claire to head to the ship. Jinx shared a pleading glance with Laris. "It will break you."

"No. It will free me," Laris whispered.

Jinx shook her head. *No way. You're delirious.* She kept the thought to herself, knowing that Sartillias would begin blasting at any moment. The power of it would put an end to this. She hoped.

"You must," Laris whispered, laying a gentle hand on Jinx's cheek.

Jinx sat perfectly still as her heart raced. She wanted to let the world disappear and melt into the moment with Laris, but the threat pounding down on them insisted she not lose herself.

"Release me," Laris said, almost demanding.

Release you from what? Jinx struggled to get a read on Laris, but her thoughts swam drunkenly.

With a gasping breath, Jinx was brought painfully into the moment as shots raged against her shield. The power of their fury sent reverberations along the invisible containment, pummeling her mercilessly. She held her ground, absorbing every impact that bloodlessly ripped along her flesh as she hurled the ammo back towards the front line, but nothing happened. The troop raged forward unimpeded. *Something not right.* Panic erupted. Jinx scanned the plateau below, watching as Jacob took hold of Claire's arm causing her hand-held device to slip from her grip.

"Come on. Leave it." Jacob's plea roared through the comm. The rumble of troops racing across the desert nearly swallowed the sound of his voice.

I've got to get everyone to the ship, Jinx decided as she readied her fist for flight. Turning towards Laris, she reached to take her hand. Laris's lips didn't lift, but a knowing dwelled beneath her gaze as she stepped just out of reach.

The scene shifted to a dreamy cadence as Jinx noticed Sartillias's warriors take aim the second her hands were lowered. The first shot locked on her while a second raced towards Jacob.

"Jacob, drop now!" Jinx yelled as she prepared to pivot.

Nammu released a blood-curdling cry as DeeDee took off in an attempt to outrun Jinx's demise. Springing off the nearest crumbling structure, she launched her tiny frame into the air but failed to intercept the shot. As she regained footing to speed after the racing bullet, Claire spun her body towards Jacob, pushing him clear of the shot meant for him. In an instant, she fell to the ground, writhing as Jacob knelt to her side. Shock quickly dissolved into rage, waking his swarm of drones from their slumber. They swirled around him before racing towards Sartillias.

The shot DeeDee failed to intervene arrived with an illusory slowness as darkness bled, claiming the edges of Jinx's awareness. Her view of Laris faded beyond a small circular scope, twisting like an aperture closing, as her window to the world spiraled shut.

***

Complete darkness set in as Jinx allowed herself to be carried away, ushered weightlessly along, drifting through the silent nothingness. Laris's words, *release me,* seem to follow uninvited. The phrase, the moment, the experience all felt loaded, but Jinx was certain they weren't. *They couldn't be.* She pushed away the desire to pick those final few seconds apart, turning her attention instead to her own predicament. *Maybe I'm passed out or accidentally blinked. Maybe its CO2 poisoning,* she considered. *Or I'm dead,* she added, with far less concern than the idea warranted. None sounded right, but she twirled the possibilities around, nevertheless. As Jinx struggled to make sense of it, vaporous shapes appeared as though formed from smoke. They spun like tops, furiously twisting until merging into a single whirling vortex, pulling her in with strangling force. Hardly a thought could escape the pressure. With a pop, Jinx jerked awake; her body bucked like falling inside a dream. She tried to gasp, but something blocked her air passage. Nearly choking on the tubes, she reached for her throat, then yanked to a halt, restrained by the wires and sensors holding her arm in place.

"She's out!" The words were urgent as footsteps raced around.

"Hurry. Get her unhooked before it pulls her back in." The voice seemed familiar.

Jinx struggled to identify the sounds whirling around. Her thoughts dragged in and out as though caught in an undertow.

"What about the others?" the first voice asked.

The others? Jinx's heart thrashed against her chest with violent beats too rapid to pause between. *Where am I?* Opening her eyes felt like a struggle as she strained to get a view. The walls of her enclosure were tight and misted over from the warmth circulating through the damp pod. Stretching two fingers, she wiped a small clearing, revealing a white room beyond in hazy clarity. It seemed familiar. Jinx tried to recall it clearly while snatches of memories flooded her awareness. The sun blazing down on a battle. Faces distorted from fear. *I must have blinked somewhere?* Jinx attempted to decipher what was going on. *Laris?* Panic set in. *Where are Jacob and Claire? Where is everyone?*

The voices around her morphed into urgent, unintelligible sounds rising and falling in heated bursts as an alarm sounded. Flashing light filled the room, sending vibrant red in pulses across Jinx's pod.

Something is wrong. Jinx growled as the ferocious need to protect took hold. Her body felt as though it were folding in on itself as she resisted the world whizzing in chaos around her. Another alarm sounded as Jinx demanded the darkness to take her back, feeling her heart pound and her bones break as the nameless void callously swallowed her whole. The thought of Laris latched on, accompanying Jinx through the silent nothingness that stretched eternally then burst into a luminescent wave.

The radiance morphed into ripples of air simmering in the desert heat; its blanket of beige shifted as shapes crystalized. Three glowing white peaks rose from the plateau as though pulling the earth to greet her. A cacophony of sounds shattered the silence as the sensation of physicality seeped into her awareness. A buzz was followed by a tremble, then a profoundly suffocating weight as reality clamped down. With a jarring halt, the forces beyond the mist spit Jinx out like a bad taste.

A murky mist concealed the world around her, revealing only a fluttering white silhouette at her side.

"Laris?" Jinx whispered as the shape vanished beyond a shadowy veil.

CHAPTER THIRTY-SEVEN

A stampede of hooves pounding the plateau sent tremors beneath Jinx's feet, ushering her fully into the moment with shocking clarity. She stood, once again, on the platformed entrance to the Great Pyramid as Sartillias raced towards them atop a glistening, mechanical chariot, inviting the full magnificence of his stature to be admired. His broad shoulders and pronounced chest looked inflated even at a distance, elegantly postured and impervious to the ruggedness of the terrain. His army took up the rear as though ordered not to crowd his entrance.

The amplifier still hummed overhead, but the tone had settled into a tranquil roll despite the troop of derelicts racing steadily towards them. Quickly, she looked to either side. Laris wasn't there, but a hint of lavender clung in the air. Confusion and uncertainty tangled in her gut. Scanning the plateau below, Jinx watched as Jacob took hold of Claire's arm, causing her hand-held device to slip from her grip.

"Come on. Leave it." Jacob's plea roared through the comm. The rumble of troops racing across the desert nearly swallowed the sound of his voice.

The scene sent alarm coursing through Jinx's system. *This already happened.* "Jacob, drop and pull Claire with you!"

"What?"

"Unless you want to hold Claire's bloody body, drop to the ground, now!"

"But — "

"Now!"

As Jacob dropped, pulling Claire with him, Jinx pivoted, watching DeeDee lunge towards the speeding bullet and miss. The sting of something grazing her cheek sent a dull pain that quickly turned to a fiery burn. Jinx's adrenalin kicked up, clearing the final remnants of fog that had followed her back from beyond. *Laris.* Jinx scanned her surroundings again, but she was nowhere in site.

A bone-chilling screech pierced the chaos, pulling Jinx's attention down towards the base of the pyramid. Her heart sunk as she watched Nammu hobble tearfully in DeeDee's wake.

"Booger, get Nammu, Jacob, and Claire to the ship."

"But—"

"I'm right behind you. Go!" Jinx dropped to the ground, slamming her fist with more fury than ever to land in the center of Hadu's ring of Attendants. The site of the Laris clones standing around the edge of the gathering conjured a wave of grief. "Get everyone together, now. I'm blinking you to the ship."

With one soft-spoken command from Hadu, the Attendants took hands, creating an unbroken chain.

"You too," Jinx ordered, waving the clones into the pileup.

Blink.

After delivering the group to hangar one, Jinx blinked back to race by DeeDee's side. She was clutching Nammu while herding Jacob and Claire across the sand at top speed. Jacob's nano army had been sent speeding towards Sartillias's forces. It arrived with the impact of metallic ghosts. The splendor of the horned thugs gliding across the sand atop grotesquely elegant creatures remained undisturbed.

"What's happening?" Jacob said, delivering words between breathless strides. "Nothing is wrong with my troop. They should have caused some damage."

"Booger, drop to the ground. Now!" Jinx yelled as she lunged for Jacob and Claire, pulling them down as ammo raced overhead. As DeeDee and Nammu tumbled to her side, Jinx rolled to clutch the pileup of bodies.

Blink.

"Get the ship out of here," Jinx ordered as the group materialized on the cool metal floor of hangar one. Hadu and the Attendants had resumed their meditative position while the sound of artillery peppered the outside of the ship. The clang of metal hitting metal echoed the urgency in Jinx's tone. "Now."

"We've got to lock down the amplifier so the frequency can't be tampered with," Claire said as she pushed to her feet.

"You mean Jacob-nator!"

"Seriously?" Claire snapped. "We can't leave it unguarded for Sartillias or anyone else to leverage."

"It's taken care of," Jacob said. "Besides, I've installed a self-initiating kill switch. If anyone tries to alter the amplifier or transformers in any way, the whole thing will shut down."

"Great. One less thing to worry about," Jinx said, raising her fist in preparation for another blink, dreading the impact with an unforgiving floor. "Jacob, run to the deck and get the ship out of here. Claire, just deal with the viruses or bugs or whatever else you're about to flip out over after we get the ship to safety."

Blink.

Jinx materialized next to Pallas, who seemed oblivious to anything but the fight ahead. She practically foamed at the mouth as she ripped across the desert, kicking up a dust storm in her wake. As Jinx reached to take hold of her arm, Pallas snarled, exposing the lethal fangs hidden behind her now puffy muzzle.

"Why must everyone put up such a friggin fight?" Jinx yelled as she tackled Pallas.

Blink.

Jinx dropped Pallas inside a quarantine cell and swiftly escaped. The sound of Pallas thrashing the walls played in the background as Jinx made her exit.

Blink.

Staying low to the ground, Jinx sandwiched her body between the fiery heat lifting off the sand, the sun hammering down from above, and the bullets racing overhead. She didn't bother wiping the sweat dripping from her brow.

"Everyone is on board," Jinx announced into the comm. "Get the ship out of here." Between the dizzying heat, the constant dodging of ammo whizzing around, and the baffling voyage to who knows where and back, Jinx was losing steam. Claire's nagging about calorie intake rumbled through her brain. *She's right. I need to eat more.* Jinx decided to keep that insight to herself. She wasn't in the mood for an "I told you so."

"I'm on the deck," Jacob replied. He was out of breath. Jinx smiled imagining him running top speed through the corridor.

The levity of the moment, she realized, probably had as much to do with the Laris frequency rolling in powerful waves through the atmosphere as the thought of Jacob doing anything remotely athletic. Fortunately, the scene ahead was enough to fuel her desire to fight, though the site of Sartillias in all his grandeur was borderline comedic. Jinx shook her head, watching his cape whip airily at his back.

The army was covering ground too quickly, faster than Jacob was moving. Putting herself between the army and the ship, Jinx raised her hands, feeling the energy crackle between them, conjuring a shield she knew wouldn't last long against a force this size. With a burst, bullets hammered the shield. The impact reverberated through her bones but failed to derail the front line as the bullets ricochetted back.

"Jacob, why haven't you left?" Jinx yelled as sand spun in furious funnels, pummeling her as she struggled to hold the violent shield in place.

"Sorry. It's taking a minute to reconfigure a few things," Jacob said. Nervousness coated his every word. "I was leveraging some of the ship's systems to bounce our security out to the satellites."

"I can't hold this shield in place much longer." Jinx knew she'd have to blink them out of here soon. That'd be the end for her. *So what?* she thought. *Is this even real? Would I end up nowhere or wake up in a cryo-tank on the New World station and realize this was all part of the zen training program or some hacked version of it? Would Laris be there? Where the drek is she?* All Jinx knew for sure is that she had to protect her friends. Real or not, keeping them safe was non-negotiable.

"We're ready!" Jacob's declaration paused Jinx's internal uproar. "Get on the ship."

"No." Jinx wanted to yell, but it sounded more like a grunt. "I need to find Laris. When I do, I'll blink us out of here. Now go, or we all die."

"So help me, if something happens to you, I'm gonna figure out how to use that pyramid to bring you back to life so I can kill you myself."

"I don't doubt it, genius. Now go!"

The ship released a deep hum then shot off, but Jinx didn't dare turn her attention from the army. She fully expected a barrage of artillery to blaze skyward towards the ship.

Five...four ... Jinx began her count down, giving the ship ample time to clear out. It didn't matter where they went. She'd find them. Locating Laris was another matter altogether.

Three... A wave of relief swelled with the realization she wouldn't need to blink the ship to safety. Disappearing into oblivion was nearly as terrifying as failing to protect her friends.

Two... The mental reprieve was swiftly followed by a sense of loss. *Did Laris transcend? What if she's gone — evaporated like some mystical mist?* The nagging memory of Laris's words bubbled up. *Release me.*

One... You better be here, Laris, Jinx muttered silently and raised her fist, ready to blink to the pyramid. Light streaming through the approaching army brought her to a standstill. *I knew it.* The translucent warriors were nothing more than ghoulish projections riding shotgun alongside a slew of guided ammo launchers. The mechanical artillery kicked up gritty plumes as they rolled across the plateau. The revelation was accompanied by a thunderous roar booming from behind. Jinx turned to see Sartillias in the distance. She wondered if this was his actual flesh and bone or a hologram. He stood arrogantly perched at the opening of the pyramid where Laris had always sat meditating. Where they had laid back and watched clouds together. The Great Pyramid, wrapped in its glistening white sheath, was inseparable from thoughts of Laris. A lump formed in Jinx's throat. Her memories were being trampled on.

Blink.

Jinx leapt to her feet with fists ready for attack. "Is your profit from Euphoria really worth all of this effort?" With a sneer, she added, "Not to mention your utter inhalation."

Sartillias glanced at his hand as though inspecting a recent manicure for flaws. "Do I seem like someone who's greatest aspiration is a drug ring?"

Jinx's forehead furrowed.

"Ah, there's the look I was eagerly anticipating. Vexed. Befuddled. Defeated," Sartillias said. "Thank you for obliging me a closer look. It makes all of this so much more rewarding."

"Defeated? How do you figure?" Jinx moved slowly around Sartillias, fixing him beneath a narrowed glare.

"I suppose I am getting a little ahead of myself."

Find Laris, Jinx told herself. *If she's not here, she's nowhere.* The thought landed like lead in her belly. Dropping to the ground, she prepared to make a swift departure into the depths of the pyramid. "Unless you have a death wish, don't mess with the amplifier. You, along with the rest of OI, sort of need it to survive."

"Now, there you go again. Such narrow vision," Sartillias said, fluffing his cape jauntily. "Why would I want OI to die out? I can't rule over corpses." Tapping a clawed finger to his elongated chin, he added, "Though I do like the sound of that."

"Great. Something to keep me busy," Jinx said as her fist raced towards the stones beneath her. Before her knuckles made contact, a vicious roar ripped from the belly of the pyramid.

Sartillias raised a finger to his ear as a hungry smile parted his lips. "I hear my tempest rousing from her slumber."

Bile rose like acid sludge as Jinx recognized the roars echoing through the pyramid's winding chambers. A moment later they came to a sharp halt. Jinx raised her fist in the ready once again.

"I'd advise against it," Sartillias said sharply. "You won't like where you land — in pieces, no doubt. The underground canals you used to run water beneath the pyramids are terribly cramped. Fortunately, one was just wide enough to transport our little darling."

Jinx turned to face Sartillias. Gravity and grief and shock tugged at every feature of her face.

Sartillias applauded slowly, apparently for himself. "*There* is the look of defeat I mentioned earlier." Licking his lips, he added, "Success tastes so sweet."

Rage rattled every bone in Jinx's body. Her mind went blank as she lunged for Sartillias, prepared to snap his thick neck. She barreled forward only to clasp air. A cruel smile lifted the corner of his mouth as he stepped backward to hop gracefully off the edge and onto his now-hovering, mechanical chariot. He remained floating a few feet away as Jinx regained her balance.

"I suppose this is where we part ways . . . for now," Sartillias said. "But please do try and refine your tactics before we meet again. While I do prefer to keep you breathing as an incentive for, well, you-know-who, I'd prefer our little games to be a bit more stimulating."

"Bite me," Jinx said as Sartillias sped away.

CHAPTER THIRTY-EIGHT

Jinx paced while Claire reviewed a blinding amount of data filling up a four-foot screen. "Well, all your levels look normal. Your organs are fine. Your adrenal gland took a beating, but it's not showing any signs of stress. Except for some dehydration and weight loss," — Claire paused to give Jinx a look of disapproval — "I'm comfortable with how your body held up."

Jacob looked on with hands in pockets and legs splayed. "So, you're just gonna let that gnarly wound on your face scar up?"

"Save your breath," Claire said. "I told her a few more rounds with the laser would fix it."

"It matches her jacked up nose," Pallas said, clearly still fuming from the ordeal.

Ignoring the comment, Jinx raised a hand to her cheek where the bullet grazed her flesh. The wound was closed, but a thick mar would remain. "I need a reminder to play smarter."

Jacob moved to Jinx's side, laying a hand on her shoulder. "We're gonna get Laris back."

"She may not want to come back." Jinx tried to shake off the thought of Laris stepping out of reach in those final moments and the bullet that followed. "We don't even know where Sartillias took her or why he wants her."

"One step at a time," Jacob said.

"I have to get a better handle on how he operates and what his agenda is," Jinx said, trying to control the trembling of her hand as she gnawed the flesh around her thumb.

"Oh, please," Pallas said. "That dodgy kaÿwzit isn't that complicated. His agenda always revolves around power and money."

"And we're certain all of this isn't just about processing Euphoria?" Jacob asked.

"I'm sure," Jinx said. "I don't think he's giving up that side venture, but that's not why he needs Laris. Whatever he's after is bigger than that."

"OK," Jacob said. "Then what do we know about his motives?"

"We know he wants to keep OI alive," Claire said. "Other than the fact that he told you as much, he chose to leave the generator and amplifier running."

"Seriously." Jacob threw up his arms. "Is it so difficult to remember Jacob-nator?"

Claire's smile suggested she enjoyed Jacob's tantrums far too much to comply. "Based on those details, we can assume he's gunning for some bloated, self-appointed position like OI overlord."

"That sounds like a delight," Pallas said.

"I know you don't really feel up for figuring out what happened when you, uh, disappeared and returned to some future moment." Jacob's eyes sparkled as he spoke. "But it might be connected to Sartillias's endgame."

"How exactly does disappearing into some weird reality after taking a bullet fit into that lunatic's plan?" Jinx could hardly breath deeper than shallow sips of air. Folding at the waist, she allowed her arms to dangle and her head to hang as she attempted to gather her emotions or at least push the panic away.

"You somehow saw the future." Claire turned from the data scrolling across her screen to face Jinx. "It's possible that you traveled back in time or possibly landed in an alternate reality."

"An alternate reality?" Pallas rolled her eyes. "Please. No one in their right mind would pick this crummy version of life if they had a choice."

"Well, things could get tricky if quantum mechanics is at play," Jacob said.

"Ahhh," Claire cooed eagerly. "The quantum multiverse creates a new universe when a diversion in events occurs."

"Like getting shot," Jacob said.

"Meaning what?" Jinx felt her patience slipping.

"Meaning, you may have created an alternate reality that has a different outcome or different chain of events."

"Fantastic." Jinx pinched the bridge of her nose.

Pallas broke out in laughter. "The idea of multiple versions of you running around multiple versions of reality trying to save multiple versions of Laris is too comical for words."

Jinx shook her head. "Do you ever give it a rest?"

Pallas shrugged. "If I'm in a good mood."

"Does creating spinoff realities really seem like something Sartillias might want to leverage?" Jacob asked.

"Honestly, no," Jinx said. "I think he's interested in dominating one world."

"Does this mean we're scratching the whole multiverse theory off the list?" Claire asked.

A deep line appeared between Jinx's brows. "What list?"

Claire held up her tablet. "The list of possible explanations for your experience in relation to Sartillias's end game." Claire dragged her finger across her screen as she scrolled through the list. "Some theories factor in Laris's frequency as a key component."

"Did you put, *the pyramid really does raise the dead*, on your list?" The corners of Jinx's eyes crinkled as she watched Jacob light up. "Settle down, genius. I was kidding."

"You're no fun," Jacob said.

Claire nudged Jacob and smiled as she flashed her screen. "It's on the list," she whispered then winked.

"Sartillias knows something we don't," Jinx said. "He set up an elaborate distraction to position himself, unnoticed, in exactly the spot he'd need in order to access Laris, unchallenged." Jinx combed her fingers through her tightly cropped hair. "He must have known I'd disappear at some point."

"I wonder if fear of death triggers a blink or hurls you into the unknow?" Jacob thrummed his fingers to his chin.

Pallas smirked, barely revealing the tip of her fangs. "I'd be happy to help you test that theory."

"I still don't know what those pyramids are capable of," Jacob said. "They're producing some extremely potent scalar waves. And — "

"I know. I know. Torsion field." Talking about the experience, and picking this reality apart, left Jinx uneasy. "But we agreed your quantum blah blah theories were off the table."

"No. Time travel is still on the list," Claire said, holding up her tablet as evidence.

"Well, if time travel is in the cards, feel free leave me at the friggin supply station where you found me," Pallas said, yanking on the sensors attached to her arm.

"Do you mind?" Claire moved swiftly across the room to stop Pallas from mucking up her equipment.

"Time travel does seem like something Sartillias would want to leverage." Jinx launched into a rousing session of geriatric-inspired calisthenics. Her body felt stiff in places she didn't know existed. "But that doesn't explain how I woke up in a cryo-tank for a minute and then left. Time travel only explains returning minutes earlier."

"True," Jacob said. "And you're sure it wasn't a blink — triggered by some variable we haven't accounted for — and you just drifted for a while?"

"Positive," Jinx said. "This was different. I was in Owen's lab. I recognized his voice. He was talking to someone. They were both totally stressed, racing around while alarms went off." Jinx braced her body to twist side to side, feeling her spine crack into alignment. "From what they were saying, it sounded like I was pulling out of a virtual experience. But . . ."

"But what?" Jacob asked

Jinx shrugged.

"You came back for us," Claire said softly.

Jinx gave Pallas a look. "Most of you."

"Feeling is mutual," Pallas grumbled under her breath.

"Do you think Laris was there too and followed you back?" Jacob asked.

"I don't know." Jinx resumed pacing around the room, eager to try anything that felt like action. Standing around chewing on concepts was excruciating. But she knew that heading out, guns blazing, in an effort to track down Sartillias wasn't going to get results. "What's left on this list of yours, Claire?"

"First of all, I didn't author this list alone, so I can't take all the glory." Claire motioned towards Jacob. "We have a handful of far-fetched ideas remaining and one reasonable theory."

"All your ideas sound crazy," Jinx said. "What's the quote-unquote reasonable theory?"

"The Nick Bostrom theory is, so far, our best guess," Jacob said. "According to your experience, we might be in a simulated reality."

Jinx stared blankly for a moment, allowing the idea to sink in. She'd already wondered the same after the experience, so it wasn't a massive shock. But hearing Jacob and Claire come to the same conclusion seemed to shape it in stone.

Jinx moved into pace-mode, full tilt. "If we're in some sort of virtual reality, and Laris is somehow a key to exiting at will — among other things — I can imagine Sartillias wanting that sort of leverage."

"This is still just a theory," Jacob said.

"Yeah. I know," Jinx said.

"But at least we can get to work trying to prove it or rule it out," Claire said.

"If we do prove it, then, we just have to figure out the rules and beat Sartillias at his own game." Jinx mentally crossed her fingers.

"It's more complicated than that," Jacob said.

Jinx slumped. "Show me some mercy. I need something uncomplicated to latch onto. At least for now."

Jacob smiled gently. "OK, hero."

"Good luck with that," Pallas huffed. "Even if this is a virtual reality, who's to say we aren't countless levels in." Shaking her head, she hopped off the examination table. "Why do you guys even care what this reality is? How is that gonna get you any closer to saving Laris or protecting OI?"

Jinx shrugged. "I don't care what this reality is. I just want Laris to be safe. And the more we know about Sartillias's motives, why he needs Laris, and how this reality operates, the better chance we have of succeeding." Jinx locked eyes with Pallas. "Besides, do you really want to live in a reality where that guy is in power?"

"Nope," Pallas said. "Whatever he's got planned is bound to be bleak."

"Well, I'm up for a challenge." Claire's enthusiasm for nerding-out lightened the mood.

"I'm in," Jacob said, settling into a relaxed stance to lean against the desk. "Any excuse to design more toys."

"Great," Jinx said, clapping her hands together. "Start making a list of what we should be watching out for and ways to test this theory." Jinx took a deep breath, feeling her tension ease up.

"Once we get back to Earth, we can test the pyramids," Jacob said. "Maybe they're actually some sort of portal in and out of the simulation."

The sound of the door sliding open brought the discussion to a halt. "You're late." Hadu held an expression that could summon the pharaohs from across the veil.

"Seriously?" A muscle in Jinx's jaw twitched. "We're camped out on the dark side of the moon, trying to figure out how to save Laris, and you expect me to keep track of when the sun passes over the friggin cat."

"Sphinx," Hadu said and disappeared down the hall.

The monitor on Jinx's arm rattled off in frenzied beats as she turned on her heal to follow. "Tomorrow, we officially begin watching this world like hawks, looking for any signs that suggest this reality is a simulation," she called over her shoulder as the door slid shut. Moving through the corridor, Jinx passed Laris's door, pausing for a moment to press her hand gently to its surface. Closing her eyes, she brought her other palm to her heart. A deep, slow breath later she stepped away. *Watch your back, Sartillias, I'm coming for you.*

ABOUT THE AUTHOR

Winn Taylor

Winn is a copywriter by day with a background in Fine Arts and multiple certifications in those oddball, alternative healing modalities you'd only find in California. If she's not reading or writing or creating art, she's clanging a tuning fork while backpacking through some third-world country. And chances are, she can guess your rising sign.

AFTERWORD

Thank you so much for spending your time with Jinx. I hope you stayed up well past your bedtime, happily immersed in her world. We are both eternally grateful. Without you, she doesn't live beyond these pages. If you love Jinx, consider leaving a review on Amazon or GoodReads. It not only inspires me to continue creating but nudges other readers to take a chance on Jinx.

xo

Come Find Us

www.WinnTaylor.com
Instagram: @jinx_chronicles
Twitter: @jinxchronicles

CPSIA information can be obtained
at www.ICGtesting.com
Printed in the USA
LVHW101216270722
724473LV00003B/149

9 798986 053714